SR Condor is an award-winning playw[...] as *RSVP* (about a garden party from he[...] toxic masculinity and hairdressing) and [...] is compelled by a terrible childhood dr[...] debut novel.

The author lives in Whitstable, Kent, with a needy rescue tabby cat.

When not writing, SR Condor is a keen cyclist but is yet to discover a dead body – real or imagined.

Find out more at srcondor.com.

CHRIS ON A BIKE

S R Condor

FYNLEY

Published in 2023 by Fynley Publishing

Text copyright © SR Condor 2023

The right of SR Condor to be identified as the author of this work has been asserted in accordance with the Copyright, Designs and Patents Act 1988 Sections 77 and 78.

All rights reserved. No part of this publication may be reproduced, stored in a retrieval system, or transmitted in any form or by any means, electronic, mechanical, photocopying, recording or otherwise, without prior permission of the copyright holder.

This is a work of fiction. Names, characters, places and incidents are products of the author's imagination or are used fictitiously. Any resemblance to actual events or locales or persons, living or dead, is entirely coincidental.

ISBN 978-1-7393285-0-4 (paperback)
Also available as an ebook

Page design and typesetting by SilverWood Books
www.silverwoodbooks.co.uk

To Deborah – for falling off her bicycle and inspiring this book.

Prologue

We never know when our time is up. When our thoughts are our last.

If we did, we'd prepare. Think profound thoughts about the meaning of life or our place on this planet. As Chris sailed through the air towards the lamppost, she wasn't prepared. Her final thought was: damn, forgot to buy cat-litter.

One

'Sorry to wake you, Christine. Just taking your blood pressure.'

The dark, friendly eyes of Nurse Mary Semenyo gleamed in the twilight of Baxter Ward. Chris felt a familiar squeezing sensation on her arm and then, quickly and efficiently, Nurse Mary was packing away the equipment.

'Looking good. Exactly how we like it. Get back to sleep now and I'll see you after breakfast.' She turned to go and there was the flash of a smile. 'Who's Grayson?'

'Sorry?'

'You were talking in your sleep.'

'Was I?' Chris's rebooting brain started a list entitled 'Embarrassing Things I Might Have Said Under the Effects of Morphine'.

'You were just having a dream. Hope it was a nice one.' And with that, Nurse Mary dissolved into the gloom.

It hadn't been a nice dream. At least Chris didn't think so. It had been more a vague mist of unconnected images that she struggled to put into a coherent story. Something about climbing stairs, running away from something or someone, and always that tune playing, that bloody tune. Her dreams were always vivid but never like the ones you saw in movies, never with a plot line. The drugs only made it worse.

Get back to sleep? No chance of that. Chris may have managed only a couple of hours, but now that she was awake, the chorus of snores, groans, farts, mechanical pings and electronic hums seemed deafening. Her eyes adjusted to the artificial moonlight of bedside monitors, safety lighting and, to her left, the glow from a computer screen at the nurses station. Somewhere distant, a few bays away, an agonised moan rose and fell. If hell existed, thought Chris, then Trauma and Orthopaedics at Kent Coast Hospital was not far off it. She half expected to see Hieronymus Bosch setting up his easel in the corner of the room.

She glanced at the heart-rate monitor by the right-hand side of her bed. It indicated a reassuring sixty-eight beats per minute. 'So I'm still alive then,' she said out loud. 'That's something, I suppose.'

Rather than counting sheep, she tried counting hospital beds. Unsurprisingly, it was a full house. Five men and Chris as the odd one out, a miscast woman in a man's world. Sleep was still elusive. Some soothing ambient music might shut out this horror, if she could only embrace the pain, shuffle over and reach the bedside cabinet. That cabinet held all her worldly possessions, which currently amounted to a water bottle, phone (with earphones generously loaned by Nurse Mary), and a badly scuffed cycle helmet.

Two lip-biting minutes of shuffling and the phone was still tantalisingly out of reach. I could use the call button, ask Nurse Mary to get it for me, thought Chris. But for her to use the button it would have to be an actual case of life and death – and even then she'd find herself apologising profusely for being such a nuisance. Just another six inches… Shit! The leg twinges started again.

She should have asked Mary for a top-up of painkillers. Pre-op had been morphine heaven, but they'd been steadily reducing the dosage ever since. Apparently it was important to determine the patient's pain threshold, and Chris was pretty certain she'd reached that twenty minutes ago.

She wasn't good with pain, never had been. She'd experienced the joy of childbirth just once and then said 'never again'. Much as Chris adored her now geographically distant daughter, Chloe, all the epidurals in the world could not persuade her to repeat the experience. That had started the schism with Simon. He couldn't understand why it wasn't in her nature to breed at will. *Nature?* Try forcing a rugby ball out of your scrotum and see how *natural* that feels. Then Simon started cooing about the miracle of childbirth and that set Chris off. 'If childbirth is a *miracle*, how come there are getting on for eight billion miracles on our bloody planet? Water into wine I get, parting the sea is cool, but tearing my lady-bits in half? You want more kids? Get a womb!'

Of course, Simon didn't get himself a womb; he got himself a new wife. One that shot out kids like one of those bingo hall ping-pong ball machines. And Chris and Simon remained on speaking terms, not just because of their common interest in Chloe's welfare but because they both ended up with the lives they wanted, lives that didn't involve making each other miserable.

That had been nearly thirty years ago. Chris had had a few meaningless relationships since. Hugh from the book club – which was a bad idea as she had to dump him and the book club simultaneously. He'd had to go, though; he was into fantasy cosplay and Dan Brown novels, for Gawd's sake. Then there was Peter from speed-dating. Chris had thought the speed element was supposed to refer to the efficiency of the matchmaking process, not the brevity between entry and ejaculation.

So now she'd reached a personal milestone and was happily looking forward to the Third Age, in which she would rebrand as a Crazy Old Cat-Lady. Well, if you could be a COCL with just one cat, Aitken, a gorgeous grey and white rescue tabby. She used to have three, but Stock had gone to that great litter tray in the sky the previous summer and Waterman had disappeared shortly afterwards. She assumed he'd found pastures new – someone who was prepared to offer him better than economy own-brand supasaver reconstituted meaty chunks in gravy.

Thinking about cats past and present made Chris sad again, and misery was not conducive to sleep. She hoped that Next-Door Nick had remembered to feed Aitken.

The distraction of self-contemplation was enough to bring the phone within Chris's grasp. She sent a quick reminder text to Nick, hoping that he wouldn't mind getting pinged at 3 a.m., and then scrolled through the music selection on her phone. She slipped the earphones in, hit 'play' on Sigur Rós, closed her eyes and waited for dawn.

*

Mr Spatchcock, the consultant, was 'delighted' with her progress, but Chris just couldn't warm to him; it was something about the way he bounced and jingled as he walked on his built-up heels. He was accompanied by two trainees and talked as though Chris was deaf, bewildered or simply not there.

'This is Ms Heron.' He emphasised the 'Ms' with a lisp, as if warning that a militant lesbian feminist had infiltrated his ward. 'She is the lucky recipient of a full hip replacement as a result of a road traffic accident.' Here he paused for comic effect. 'Her bicycle was in a collision with an ice cream van!' Mr Spatchcock roared with laughter and his trainees dutifully followed suit. Hilarious.

'I wasn't in a collision with an ice cream van,' Chris muttered. 'It collided with me.' One of her bugbears was the way road accidents were reported: 'a juggling unicyclist collided with a petrol tanker', like it was a fair fight.

In Chris's case, a Mr Softee ice cream van had clipped her with its wing mirror, sending her careering over the kerb, her flight brought to an abrupt end by a lamppost. The driver paused as if to confirm the damage caused and then sped off. To add insult to actual injury, he activated his chimes as he made his getaway. She lay in a crumpled heap on the pavement accompanied by the sound of 'Greensleeves' – *dah, dah, dah-dah, d'dah, dah, dah-dah*.

When I get out of this place, Chris vowed, I will make it my mission to hunt down Mr Softee and seek vengeance.

Mr Spatchcock was still holding court. 'Fortunately, Ms Heron is very fit for a… um' – he checked his notes – 'sixty-year-old woman. It must be all the cycling, eh?' And he actually gave Chris a jocular nudge.

Chris smiled and nodded because this was the man in control

of her painkillers, a man who had to be indulged at all costs.

'We'll have another look after the weekend and, all being well, you'll be good to be discharged. Before the summer is out you'll be back on your bicycle, but this time' – he paused again for comic effect – 'I'd recommend some stabilisers, eh?'

Painkillers or not, Mr Spatchcock was fortunate to be out of range of a right hook.

Nonetheless, his assessment cheered Chris's mood. She'd almost resigned herself to never getting on a bicycle again, even though it was the best and cheapest therapy she knew. There was something about the combination of fresh air, exercise and motor skills that helped her work through any issues. An hour a day on the bike was worth more than a lifetime on a psychoanalyst's couch.

*

Now that all the medical appointments had been completed, Chris killed an hour by cataloguing the intake of Baxter Ward, partly to check that her close encounter with a lamppost had caused no lasting concussion and partly because she was a sucker for detail.

Bed 1: Mine.

Good: By the window with a view of the helipad and car park.

No helicopters had landed in her two-day residency, but she had great expectations.

Bad: Low down in the pecking order.

Any nurses, doctors, porters or orderlies had to pass beds 3 to 6 before reaching her and so tended to get hijacked by the other inmates.

Bed 2: Ray (opposite). Chirpy Cockney guy, early seventies. Fractured leg, 'dodgy ticker' and undetermined bowel issue. Seems like good egg.

Ray had offered to describe his bowel symptoms in detail, but she had politely declined – sometimes ignorance really was bliss.

Bed 3: Poor Baby. Fiftyish. Broken hip? Pain in arse.

Her nickname for Bed 3's occupant originated from his

countless video calls with his wife, who responded to his every whinge, gripe and moan with 'Oh, you poor baby!' – and not in a sarcastic way either.

Bed 4: Brokeback John. Eighty-plus. Fell off a ladder.

She hadn't actually seen John as he was buried beneath a mountain of sheets, tubes and wires. Above his bed was written 'DNR' in large letters. On her first sleepless night she had tried to guess what this stood for – 'Dangerous! – Never Rouse!' or 'Dhal Not Rice!' She settled on 'Danish National Railways' and happily imagined John as a Scandinavian Casey Jones, the cap-wearing driver of a steam train wending its way through snowy fjords. The following morning, curiosity got the better of her and she googled 'DNR' on her phone to discover it stood for 'Do Not Resuscitate' and that made her very sad.

Bed 5: Scaredy Thomas. Late eighties. Dementia?

Thomas was afraid of the nurses, of the drugs trolley and even of Lovely Lina, who discussed the menu choices for the coming day. Thomas whimpered during the day and sobbed at night. Once or twice, Chris had cried with him, for him. In her darkest moments she wondered whether, if she'd been physically able, she would have crossed the ward and used a pillow to make Thomas scared no more. Perhaps it was her dark thoughts rather than the throbbing in her hip that prevented sleep.

Bed 6: Mr Jelly. Seventies. Multiple injuries.

Mr Jelly's real name was Bob and, like Brokeback John, he'd fallen off a ladder. Chris blamed the demise of those government information films for all the ladder-related injuries. She imagined the hospital as being fit to burst with unfortunates who had flown a kite near an electricity pylon or picked up sparklers without gloves. Bob did have a catchphrase, though. Every time he was asked about the menu selection or whether he'd like a hot drink, he answered 'jell-y' in a singsong Welsh accent. Breakfast, lunch and dinner – 'jell-y' – flavour unspecified.

The stocktake merely reminded Chris that she was trapped.

She felt the strongest urge to phone her daughter, to hear her voice, but she didn't dare rouse her fellow patients. She would video-call her next week, at which point Chloe would see only her mother's top half and so would be none the wiser about the accident. When I've made a fuller recovery, decided Chris, I'll tell her the truth. By which time the drama would have declined in status to an amusing anecdote, not something that would cause Chloe to panic and jump on a plane.

*

At some stage during Chris's third sleepless night, in the early hours of Saturday morning, they came for Brokeback John. A soft-footed posse of nurses and porters wheeled his bed silently out of the ward.

Chris wept and, fumbling for her phone in the darkness, texted: *I love you.*

Chloe replied almost immediately. *What's wrong?*
Nothing's wrong. Just being a loving mum. xx
You're scaring me!
LOL
What's funny?
I'll Zoom you on Wednesday xx. Chris attached the goofiest-looking emoji she could find, hoping that would throw her daughter off the scent.

Two

A weekend on Baxter Ward was the longest weekend ever. Longer than that weekend in Chelmsford when they had formally introduced Simon's parents to baby Chloe. His dad had burnt a slide show of family photos onto a CD and synched it to a loop of 'Suddenly' by Lionel Richie in their honour. They all watched it eight times over a thirty-six-hour period. Chris cracked. On the drive home Simon called her 'petulant' and 'disrespectful'. Chris declared that people had killed with less provocation, and their argument woke baby Chloe in her car seat. Chris still got panic attacks whenever that song popped up on TV or radio.

On the plus side, the vibe on the ward was much more chilled. With no silverback consultants marking their territory, the nurses all seemed more relaxed. Excitement was provided by The Hunt for Nurse Mary's Missing Pen – though four immobile men and one slow-moving woman on crutches hardly constituted a thorough search party. 'It'll turn up, I guess,' said Mary in a sad voice that suggested she knew that she'd never see her burgundy ballpoint again.

Chris's highlight was the arrival of a care package from Next-Door Nick, which comprised a pair of her jeans (tight, so unwearable at this current time), a jokey T-shirt that read 'Trick Cyclist' (that she wouldn't be seen dead in), a family-sized pack of KitKats (that she shared with the rest of the ward) and, most importantly, her laptop (complete with charger). Chris hadn't asked for any underwear, deciding she'd have to make do. Giving Next-Door Nick access to her home to feed Aitken was one thing; giving him free rein to forage through her bedroom drawers would be a step too far. There were knickers in there that weren't fit for public scrutiny.

Physio Melanie rated Chris's progress as 'awesome', making Chris as proud as a seven-year-old being awarded a gold star for her maths homework. She'd made it to the loo and back on crutches and climbed three steps. It was agony, but Chris just smiled thinly and hoped she wouldn't faint or throw up over Melanie's orthopaedic sneakers. Melanie followed the physical tests with questions to judge whether it'd be safe to discharge Chris on Monday as planned. The assessment was more of an interrogation. 'How many stairs do you have? Do you have a stand-alone shower or a bath? How high is your bed?' Chris answered all these with confident lies. After all, who'd ever counted their own stairs or measured the height of their bed?

Melanie's final question was a zinger and caught her off guard.

'You don't live alone, do you, Christine?'

'Why do you ask?'

'It's important that you have someone there for the first forty-eight hours. For your own well-being.'

Ah, shit! Chris had to think fast. 'It's just as well that I have Aitken to look after me.'

'That Aitken?' Melanie nodded at the phone sitting on Chris's lap, the screensaver proudly displaying a photo of her beloved cat eating out of his personalised food bowl.

'Ah yes, not just Aitken, of course. Grayson will be there.'

'And Grayson is...?'

'My significant other.'

Melanie took out a pen. Alas, not a burgundy ballpoint. 'Can I take down a number for Grayson? Just for the record?'

Chris reeled off an eleven-digit number. Not quite at random. It was Chloe's first mobile but with a couple of the numbers transposed. This seemed to satisfy Melanie.

'So, have I passed?' Chris asked tentatively.

'Yep, Mr Spatchcock's approval permitting, of course.'

In a celebratory mood, Chris decided to boot up her laptop and catch up on work emails. Working from home was a massive improvement on office life, but it did mean you were never off duty, and the demands on an intrepid freelance proofreader had never been greater. Luckily, she could be more honest with her clients than with her own daughter, so Chris sent an email to explain that, due to unforeseen circumstances, the check on 'Pagan Rituals and Magical Spirituality in Medieval Sardinia' wouldn't be ready on Monday as scheduled, and she sent another to accept an exciting offer to work on 'The Book of Genesis – a Treatise on Bitcoin Blockchain' with the proviso that they'd need to push the deadline back a week. Chris could, of course, understand the content of neither, but she could spot a misused apostrophe or errant typo a mile off.

She was midway through speed-reading an obtuse academic paper on 'The Safety of Sildenafil Citrate in a Residential Care Environment' when a new arrival was wheeled into the now vacant Bed 4 space. Male and young – well, in his mid-thirties, at a guess. It was difficult to tell as he was swathed in bandages, as if he'd come straight from the set of *The Curse of the Mummy's Tomb*. The extent of his injuries suggested he'd been in a serious road accident, although, according to Baxter Ward odds, he'd probably fallen off a ladder.

Chris welcomed the new arrival with a smile and a cheery wave. But there was a look in his single visible eye, strangely colourless and with a constricted pupil, which told Chris that it would be wise to resume her email trawl and avoid Bed 4 for the rest of the morning. Bed 4 had now been assigned a nickname: Evil Eye.

After lunch, Chris struck up a conversation with Ray in the bed opposite. She noted that Evil Eye was eavesdropping, so she mounted her crutches and shuffled across to the chair beside Bed 2. Ray turned out to be engaging and interesting once you got off the subject of his bowels. He was a cheeky chap who'd spent a lifetime in logistics. 'There's nuffink I couldn't shift!' he said proudly.

'I 'ear you're out tomorrow.'

'Fingers crossed,' said Chris, not wanting to tempt fate.

'Beginning to think I'll never get out of 'ere.'

'Broken leg? You should be out soon enough, Ray.'

'It's not that, it's me 'eart. It's buggered. I'm only seventy; it doesn't seem fair.'

Chris agreed that life wasn't fair in any shape or form.

'If I do get out,' continued Ray, 'I'm straight down The 'Are and 'Ounds to get slaughtered. What about you?'

'Oh, I've got a list. First thing is give Aitken a big snog.'

'Lucky geezer.'

'He is. Then I'll chase up the police, see if they've made any progress on my case.'

Ray harrumphed. 'The filth? You'll be lucky. Couldn't catch the clap in a brothel that lot! What's next on your list?'

'Buy a new bike and catch up with an old friend.'

About an hour before lights out, three consecutive days of veggie curry made their mark on Chris's digestive system and she faced the catwalk down the ward to the loo clad only in a backless gown. Her journey became a crablike sideways shuffle as she edged past the other beds on crutches whilst trying to hold the back of her gown closed. As she inched past Bed 4, Chris heard a groan that sounded like 'Phwoar!', so she stared fixedly down at the lino and accelerated from snail's pace to tortoise. She found it hard to imagine that a sixty-year-old woman with a new titanium hip and an eight-inch scar could arouse anyone's passions, but experience had taught her that men were, indeed, a strange species.

Upon Chris's return to the sanctuary of her bay, her mobile was flashing to indicate a received text. It was from Next-Door Nick and attached was a photo of Aitken snoozing on the sofa.

How's the (im)patient? Aitken's knackered after chasing pigeons – none caught fortunately. When's his mum expected home?

The photo provoked a twang of homesickness and Chris spontaneously kissed her phone. Luckily nobody in the ward seemed to notice. She replied: *Monday hopefully. Send my love to Aitken – thanks for looking after him. X*

The 'X' was automatic. Chris spotted it just after she'd pressed 'send'. Damn. Still, it meant nothing – everyone put an 'X' on their texts, didn't they? She'd even done it to clients and had never lost any business as a result. Still.

Nick's response was rapid. *Need picking up? X*

A Pandora's box of cyber kisses had been opened. Was it too late to slam the lid shut?

Nah, thanks for the offer. I'll just get a cab. No kiss. Definitely no kiss. Get the message, Nick.

Okey-dokey. Offer stands. Night XX

Bugger, the kisses had doubled. Well, Nick was a nice guy. A semi-retired lecturer in his early sixties – single, solvent and eligible. Kind, too. He'd been really supportive when Waterman had gone missing last year. A lot of women would have swiped right, but… no… not her type. Chris turned her phone off and buried her head under the blankets until lights out.

It was as the light faded that it started. *Thump! Thump! Thump!* A metronomic beat in 2/4 time. Chris instantly knew what it was and from where it originated. The evil-eyed occupant of Bed 4 apparently believed that the cover of darkness affected sound as well as vision and was engaged in an enthusiastic bout of onanism. Evidently, his injuries and dressings were not such an insurmountable barrier.

Chris put her fingers in her ears and counted backwards from five hundred, but, evidently, stamina was Evil Eye's possibly only redeeming feature. Surely the glimpse of a proofreader's right buttock could not have inspired this frenzy?

What to do? Press her call button to summon the duty nurse? Chris had heard that nurses had a trick that involved slapping the tip of an erect penis with the back of a teaspoon to dissolve any amorous urges, and Night Nurse Yola looked as though she would be prepared to give any errant member a mighty thwack. From the sound of the frenetic Bed 4 activity, Nurse Yola would need to upgrade to a ladle.

As usual, cowardice won over valour and Chris turned her phone back on, rammed in the earphones and cranked up the volume on *Vespertine* by Bjork. Bizarrely, Bed 4's nocturnal activity provided a complementary back-beat to the music and merciful sleep swiftly followed.

No restful sleep-in for Sunday, though, as, first thing, the porters arrived and wheeled Evil Eye off to a destination unknown. Unlike Brokeback John, he was fully conscious and none too appreciative. His departure was roundly welcomed by the residents of Baxter Ward, who doubtless would have cheered, clapped and stamped their collective feet if the risk of adding to compound fractures hadn't been too great.

The second excitement occurred during breakfast. Chris was idly poking at a Weetabix marooned in a lagoon of semi-skimmed when milky waves started to lap at the biscuity shore. Not unlike the approach of the T-Rex in *Jurassic Park*, this gradually increased in vibration and volume, heralding the arrival of a helicopter on the landing pad outside her bedside window. No patient was unloaded; it just sat there, engine idling. This sparked a lively discussion between beds 2 and 3 about the purpose of this visit and whether its proximity to the recent transfer of Bed 4 was purely coincidental. Chris expressed the hope that the 'copter's purpose was to teach Evil Eye to sky dive without a parachute and this received universal approval.

Such was her distraction that when Chris's phone started to vibrate in harmony with the helicopter, she automatically and unthinkingly answered it. It was Chloe.

'Hi, hope I didn't wake you. How's my lunatic mother this morning?'

'No, no, Chloe, love. I'm up with the lark. You know me! I'm fine.'

'What's going on there? Sounds like you're having a party.'

The noise of a breakfasting ward, combined with the helicopter, was reaching a crescendo. Chris would have to terminate this call quickly to protect her alibi.

'Ha! No, that's the radio. Nothing's wrong?'

'Does something have to be wrong for a daughter to call her mother?'

'No, it's lovely to hear your voice, it's just…'

'Anyway, following your weird text, I wondered whether you'd fancy a video call?'

'Err… when exactly?'

'Now? Dan's taken the boys to the cinema to see some crappy superhero movie so I've got a free evening.'

'Sorry, can't. I'm busy. Busy… working.'

'On a Sunday morning?' Chloe was as sharp as ever.

'Snowed under – you know what it's like in the giddy world of proofreading. Tight deadlines, demanding clients, split infinitives…'

The trolley for collecting breakfast bowls and refilling cups of tea had arrived. It was only a matter of seconds before all cover would be blown.

'Hmmm. Are you alone there, Mum?'

'Alone? Well, apart from Aitken, of course I'm—'

'Jell-y!' trilled Bob from Bed 6.

There was a pregnant pause in the conversation.

'Um, yes, all alone,' Chris stuttered.

'Oh, God, I'm so sorry, Mum. You should have said. I mean, don't let me disturb you if you're… Oh God… Bye, Mum.'

And with that the call ended. I could phone her back, thought Chris. I could explain it to Chloe, but perhaps not yet. Give it a few weeks. Then we'll laugh – she hoped.

Chris was staring mournfully at her phone and pondering whether she could fashion a makeshift rope out of knotted sheets, climb down from her second-floor window and hijack that helicopter, when Nurse Mary appeared at her bedside looking uncharacteristically distracted.

'You haven't seen a watch, have you, Christine?' she asked.

'A watch? No. What sort of watch?'

'Small, silver. Simple thing.'

Chris closed her eyes and could picture the watch immediately.

Circular, Roman numerals, chain strap. 'Not like you to lose things, Mary. First your pen, now your watch.'

'And a thermometer. I think I'm going mad – must be stress. I can get another thermometer from stores, and the pen, well, it's just a pen…'

'But the watch?'

'My sister's.' Nurse Mary's lip trembled ever so slightly before she gathered herself and gave another broad grin. 'Probably left it at home, like an idiot.'

Chris mirrored Mary's grin as best she could. 'Check the bed pans. I've twice nearly dropped my phone in mine!'

'Bed pans? Never thought of that!' Mary chuckled as she continued her circuit of the ward.

Chris opened her laptop, opened a new file entitled 'Mary's Watch' and added it to the 'Baxter Ward' folder, alongside some initial desk research she'd conducted that morning on the north Kent ice cream van population. Keeping written records might seem obsessive, but Chris knew more than anyone the power of words and had lately taken to cataloguing everything, no matter how irrelevant.

One of the more useful papers she'd proofread, a couple of years ago now, was 'Mind Palaces as a Student Learning Strategy'. This had detailed the Roman Room method of memory-enhancement, whereby data was assigned to particular objects or, perhaps, to pieces of furniture in mentally mapped rooms of a house. Working on the paper had coincided with a particular nasty spell of gastro-enteritis and so, in between frequent visits to the bathroom, Chris had welcomed the distraction of creating her own memory palace. In fact she had two, one based upon her childhood home and one based upon her house in Cliffstaple. And it had worked – she'd never forgotten a significant birthday since and now only left the house without her door keys a couple of times a month; a vast improvement.

Of course, for maximum efficiency, a mind palace needed regular maintenance and Chris was far too lazy to commit to that sort of time and effort. Besides, she persuaded herself, it was comforting not to remember *everything* – always good to leave a generous percentage of life's experiences in the fog of forgetfulness, awaiting the occasional, unexpected joy of rediscovery.

After lunch (veggie curry again, naturally), Physio Melanie appeared at Chris's bedside.

'Hi, Christine, this number you gave me for Grayson…'

Chris put on her best picture-of-innocence face. 'Yes?'

'It's the number for the Nice 'n' Spicy Kebab Shop.' Melanie paused and looked Chris straight in the eyes. 'In Wolverhampton.'

Her bluff had been called. 'Ah, must have got it wrong. Hang on a sec.'

Chris turned on her phone and, holding it away from Melanie's gaze, scrolled through the numbers. She settled on Next-Door Nick in her contacts and read out the number to Melanie, who wrote it on her notepad.

'Sorry about that – bit confused. Must be the morphine.'

Nurse Mary Semenyo chose that precise moment to pass Chris's bed in her scouring of the ward's bedpans for her missing watch. 'Morphine? You're only on paracetamol now, Christine!'

Chris waited until Melanie and Mary had left the ward, then ducked her head under the covers to make a life-saving phone call. Thank God, Next-Door Nick answered immediately.

'Hi, Nick, it's Chris—'

'Chris! How are you? I was just thinking—'

'No time to talk, Nick. I need a huge favour. If someone called Melanie Cooper from Kent Coast Hospital calls…'

'Yes?'

'Your name's Grayson.'

'Grayson? As in…?'

'Yes. And you live with me. OK?'

'I suppose so. Can you tell me—'

'Can't explain. No time. See you soon… um… Grayson.'

Chris felt terrible for dragging Next-Door Nick into her web of deceit, but, then again, what were neighbours for?

Three

Slowly, so slowly, Sunday morphed into Monday – Freedom Day. Chris had breakfasted and strip-washed by half past seven and was sitting upright in her chair, laptop open, waiting for the medical experts to give her the once-over, sign the forms and release her from this purgatory. She waited. And she waited. And she waited.

Unable to concentrate on anything constructive, Chris spent two hours looking at new bicycles on her laptop and then constructed a spreadsheet, ready for data entry, in her quest to eliminate every ice cream van in Kent until she'd tracked down the elusive and dastardly Mr Softee.

Finally, when she'd almost given up hope, a familiar jingle approached from the corridor. Mr Spatchcock bounced round the corner accompanied by no fewer than five fawning student medics.

'How is our Olympic cyclist today?' Mr Spatchcock beamed for the benefit of his adoring audience.

'Somewhere between mildly frustrated and psychotic, thank you for asking.' Chris beamed in return.

'Well, Rome wasn't built in a day and neither are hips healed! Up onto the bed and on your side, please.'

Mr Spatchcock pulled up Chris's hospital gown with a flourish, like a magician revealing a sawn-in-half assistant. Chris needed lightning reflexes to protect what little modesty and dignity she had left.

Mr Spatchcock turned to the prettiest of his entourage. 'Amanda, if you would do the honours and remove Ms Heron's dressing?'

Amanda blushed and with beautifully manicured fingernails

started to gently tease at the tape holding the dressing in place.

'Be more assertive, Amanda!' Mr Spatchcock brushed across Amanda – so closely that she instinctively recoiled – and ripped the tape from Chris's flesh.

Chris bit her lip, not wanting to give him the satisfaction of an agonised squeal.

'See?' Mr Spatchcock turned triumphantly. 'That's healing up beautifully. A fine bit of stitching too. In a few weeks that swelling will go down and it'll be as good as new. In fact better than new – that titanium hip will outlive the patient.'

'Does that mean I can go home today?' Chris asked hopefully, rearranging her gown.

'Don't see why not. As soon as the pharmacy has worked its magic, we can wish you bon voyage.' And with that, Mr Spatchcock pirouetted on his raised heels and jingled out of the ward.

Chris briefly considered adding him to her Revenge List (currently headed by Mr Softee), but, to be fair, he had fixed her broken body so that gave him something of a free pass, even if he was a bit of an arse.

Chris had come in with nothing but her cycling gear, and her Lycra leggings had been unceremoniously cut from her body, but somehow Nurse Mary had found some replacement clothes: a white cheesecloth shirt and a pair of gaily striped elasticated trousers so voluminous that Chris suspected they'd previously belonged to a circus elephant.

The clock crept far past lunchtime and deep into the afternoon. Still Chris waited.

'The pharmacy's always slow,' chirped Ray.

'And they close at five,' said Poor Baby, looking up from his video call.

'If they don't get to you today, you'll have to stay with us another night,' agreed Ray.

'Jell-y!' added Bob helpfully.

'Will I buggery!' said Chris, mounting her crutches and

heading for the nurses station to explain to the charming young man there that if her drugs were not forthcoming, she would not be held accountable for her actions. As Chris was about to launch into full rant, Nurse Mary Semenyo appeared, checking in for her shift. Chris noted that her wrist was still watch-less.

Nurse Mary had contacts, a friend in the pharmacy. 'Give me twenty minutes,' she said and headed for the lifts.

Mary's automatic helpfulness sparked a feeling of guilt in Chris. She'd been so self-absorbed about her own release that she hadn't given any time to consider Mary's own sense of loss, namely a thermometer, pen and wristwatch. She closed her eyes and conjured up one of her mind palaces. In her internal map, she'd stored observations about Baxter Ward in a Welsh dresser in the corner of her kitchen. Her real-life kitchen didn't actually have a Welsh dresser, but this was just a memory technique and she could furnish her rooms however she wanted and more tastefully than in real life. There, on a top shelf, printed on an imaginary tin of baked beans, was the information:

No idea about the thermometer. Well, who would notice a thermometer in a hospital?

But here was Mary doing the rounds with her burgundy pen in the top left pocket of her tunic… and then it was gone. And here was Mary wearing her watch; she hadn't left it at home, it was on her left wrist – silver, round face – and then… it wasn't. And there was a spot on the ward where both the pen and the watch existed and then ceased to exist…

Chris opened her eyes, drew a deep, satisfied breath and took the short shuffle across to Ray's bed.

'Afternoon, Ray.'

'Be sorry to see you go, Chris. Lover-ly to have a woman's presence on the ward. And if you don't mind me sayin', a classy lady too.'

'Thanks, Ray. Coming from such a discerning gentleman, that's quite a compliment. I was wondering… about your career in *logistics*.'

'What d'ya need to know?'

'Whether you still keep your hand in from time to time?'

'Ooh no, fully retired, me. 'Ealth's not up to workin',' said Ray, nestling back into his pillow.

'OK, let me be more direct. You know Nurse Mary's been looking for a missing thermometer, pen and watch?'

'Sure, Chris, the 'ole ward's been talkin' about it.'

'You've nicked them!'

Ray levered himself up onto his pillows and manufactured his finest outraged expression. 'Nicked?'

'Nicked, stolen, half inched, pickpocketed, logistically redirected.'

'You're accusing me of being a tea-leaf?'

'And unless said items magically reappear in the next thirty seconds, I'm going to ensure that someone's undiagnosed bowel condition gets a whole lot worse.'

A broad, toothy grin spread across Ray's face and he dipped his hand between his mattress and the bed frame, re-emerging with a thermometer, pen and wristwatch.

'Well done! Just seein' if I've still got the knack. One last dip for old time's sake before I snuff it. I was going to give 'em back, honest. She's a good girl, that Mary.'

'Shall I take them, so that your sleight-of-hand skills can remain unrevealed?'

'Yeah, I fink that would be for the best,' said Ray as he handed over his ill-gotten gains.

When Nurse Mary returned from the pharmacy five minutes later, Chris exchanged a thermometer, a burgundy ballpoint pen and a ladies silver wristwatch for a bundle of dressings, anticoagulants and painkillers.

Nurse Mary was visibly moved. 'But… but… where did you find them?'

'Do I look like a grass?' Chris said.

Over Nurse Mary's shoulder, Chris could see Ray giving her a double thumbs-up. Nurse Mary's cute, thought Chris. She'll figure it out and take special precautions around Bed 2 from now on.

Mary gave Chris a spontaneous hug. 'Thanks, Christine. I owe you.'

'No, you don't. You don't owe any of us anything.'

With beautiful, coordinated timing, Scott, the porter, arrived with a wheelchair, a shower stool and a raised loo seat, Chris's parting gifts from Kent Coast Hospital. She made a farewell tour of the other beds, wishing her fellow patients goodbye in much the same way that people wave off new friends they've met on holiday but have no intention of ever seeing again. Poor Baby seemed almost pleasant at last and Thomas even smiled and gave a weak little wave, which made Chris well up and curse herself for her previous wicked thoughts.

As Scott pushed her through the exit doors into the glare of the evening sunlight, Chris felt the blessed warmth of freedom. And there was Next-Door Nick standing proudly next to his car – his tiny Fiat 500. How the hell was she going to get into that?

Four

Give Chris a work deadline and her fridge would never be so clean, her cupboards so well arranged, her spice rack so alphabetised. Restrict her to the confines of her house and the great outdoors had never seemed more alluring. But the road to recovery was long and cobbled. Still, on her return from hospital, Chris remained true to the list she'd shared with Ray. Aitken was lavished with attention and cat treats, and every Monday morning, without fail, she emailed North Kent Police requesting an update on their investigation into the hit-and-run. Her first email received a generic reply: *Thank you for your email. Your enquiry is important to us and we will respond shortly.* Of course, they never did, and after that even generic responses were seemingly too much effort, but Chris was determined to keep the pressure on.

If asked to described her main pastime during her recovery from surgery, Chris would cite 'hobbling'. Hobbling from the sofa to the loo, to the kettle, then back to the sofa; hobbling down the garden to whistle for Aitken when he was being a dirty stop-out; hobbling round the corner to the chemist's on Cliffstaple High Street for drugs and, most importantly, human interaction. Being pretty much housebound, she was also an easy target for daytime TV and the endless varieties of home-improvement programmes. Chris had come to the depressing conclusion that, in the future, the world would be magnolia and overpopulated by kitchen islands.

Chris's database of local ice cream vans boasted three entries, two of which passed her on the high street, and one of which had the audacity to stop directly outside her front door one sunny Saturday morning. None of them were the elusive Mr Softee, but Father Freezee, Nice 'n' Icy and the rather boringly named Cliffstaple Ices all had their own row on her spreadsheet, which detailed 'Time/Date of Sighting', 'Place of Sighting', 'Number Plate' and 'Livery Description'. With improved mobility, the search would be much more comprehensive.

These weeks were also a voyage of discovery as she realised how many straightforward, everyday tasks one took for granted when fully mobile. She wrote her Top 50 list of 'Things That Are Bloody Annoying When You're on Crutches' when she really should have been doing the final proofread of 'Whither Compost? The Role of Micro-organisms in the Decay Process'. Top of the list was 'drying between the toes'. It was no joke, having moist toe junctions, although her obsession with them had been yet another thing that had driven a wedge between her and ex-husband Simon (the subject of a much, much longer list). She overcame the toe challenge by jamming a hairdryer, nozzle upright, against the base of the washstand with one foot and waving her other foot over it in a circular motion, then switching feet. Necessity was the mother of invention.

Her weekly video calls with Chloe had continued to run as usual, from 10 a.m. every Wednesday (UK time). She always carefully prepared the ground to conceal her temporary disability. All crutches were removed from her laptop camera's field of vision and she adjusted the levels carefully; she was usually balanced on cushions, like the Princess and the Pea, so had to ensure that the laptop was similarly raised to avoid any giveaway 'up nasal cavity' shots. She even managed to avoid wincing when Aitken leapt onto her lap mid-call. She didn't like lying to her daughter, so she carefully embroidered the truth. In their conversations she mentioned that she had 'popped to the shops' and 'run down the road', which were not lies as such, just creative use of language. If their conversation ever veered into tricky territory, she defaulted to 'How are the twins?' as a diversionary question.

Three weeks into Chris's recovery, her deception was unmasked when one Friday afternoon there came a knock on the door. Chris's incapacitation had turned her into an online shopping junkie, but that same incapacity meant that she rarely made it to the door before the driver had dumped the parcel on the doorstep and hot-footed it back to their van, *Fast and Furious*-style. Three weeks of practice, however, and her improved crutches skills had shaved her personal best from kitchen table to front door to sub ten seconds. She hurtled down the hall and flung open the door, shouting 'Gotcha!' – only to find her ex-husband standing there.

Simon looked from left crutch to right crutch to left again. 'What the hell have you done to yourself, Chris?'

'I'm not that bad, am I?' she shot back, deciding to bluff her way out of this. 'Nothing that a haircut and some lippy couldn't sort.'

'I'm talking about your crutch.'

'That'd be a first!'

'I'll rephrase that. Crutches – plural.'

Chris feigned surprise. 'Oh, these? Just a little accident. Had a bit of a fall.'

As ever, Chris had thought very carefully about her choice of words, sensitive to the fact that age dictated how the act of falling over was described. Young children had 'a bit of a tumble', teenagers 'fell arse over tit' and adults had a 'fall', but at a certain age this became a 'nasty fall', at which point you might as well give up on life.

'Do you want to come in? Kettle's just boiled,' she said, hoping the answer would be 'no'.

'Yeah, why not?' Simon stepped over the threshold.

Chris could think of a thousand reasons why not. Although she got on OK with Simon, and thirty years was too long even for Chris to maintain hostilities, that didn't really stretch to having him in her home, her sanctuary. Usually when they met up it was on neutral territory, so she could leave when her boredom meter buzzed – her record was seventeen minutes.

Simon followed Chris down the hall to the kitchen-diner, his shoes slapping on the tiled floor. Always a fine judge of character, Aitken shot past his legs and rattled out through the cat flap. Simon's head swivelled to take in his surroundings and he made those little muttering noises that used to drive her crazy during their brief marriage.

'I like what you've done to the old place,' he observed.

'I haven't done anything to it.'

'I know. I was being sarcastic.'

This had originally been their marital home. A modest three-bedroom Victorian terrace with many original features. Unfortunately, the original features included the plumbing and electrics. The postal address was 15 Sea View, Cliffstaple, but you'd have had to stand on a stepladder on top of the roof to catch a glimpse of any waves.

Cliffstaple itself was a fair-sized seaside town on the north Kent coast, within easy reach of Becketon, a student-friendly cathedral city. They'd moved there from London in the first year of their marriage because Simon wanted a safe place to raise a family. 'Safe' was not necessarily a compliment in Chris's eyes. Her first impression was that Cliffstaple was the sort of town that would feature in a Sunday supplement article: 'Top 10 Places to Curl Up and Die', but over the years she had grown to love it. It had enough quirkiness to offset the claustrophobic small-town feel and was friendly enough so that when a passer-by said hello you didn't immediately cover your pockets. When she and Simon had agreed to go their separate ways, just six years later, Chris got the house and custody of Chloe as part of their amicable divorce settlement. That was certainly amicable as far as Chris was concerned. And Simon got to breed at will, which seemed like a fair exchange.

'Nice to see you haven't lost that rapier wit, Simon. What can I get you – tea, coffee or strychnine?'

'Whatever's easiest,' said Simon, plonking himself at the kitchen table.

Handling a kettle of boiling water whilst balancing on crutches meant that neither option was 'easy', though it reminded Chris of Simon's infuriating lack of decisiveness (thirty-seventh on another list). She threw a spoonful of extra-mellow instant coffee that she had won in a charity tombola three years ago into a mug and made a grapefruit and mint camomile infusion for herself. The infusion tasted foul, but she knew the citrus-infused steam would offend Simon.

'So, to what do I owe the honour of this visit?'

Chris sat down opposite Simon and noted his eyes tracking to the tea-bag still sitting in her 'Proofreaders ♥ Colons' mug. She could tell he was fighting the urge to react, to extract the bag himself and dispose of it tidily in the food-waste caddy.

He refused to take the bait and, instead, took a gulp of coffee and nodded as though it was brewed from freshly roasted beans that had recently passed through the digestive tract of a civet.

'Chloe asked me to pop round.'

'Oh?'

'She's worried about you. Said you were acting "weird". Well, weirder than usual.'

Damn! Chloe never missed a trick. 'Really?'

'Apparently you kept asking after the twins.'

'And showing interest in my grandchildren is "weird" now, is it?'

'It is when it's six times within a forty minute Zoom conversation. So, what's the story?'

Chris gave Simon a full rundown of Chris's Adventures Through the NHS. To his credit, he was genuinely sympathetic and caring.

'You should have told me, Chris. I'd have helped.'

He didn't even laugh at the irony of her bone-crunching encounter with Mr Softee, though that was probably more down to his non-existent sense of humour. Chris gave him a flash of her scar and he sucked in his breath with an appropriate amount of awe and horror. She promised to tell Chloe the whole truth in their next video call and, in return, Simon got out the stepladder, changed the lightbulb in the sitting room that had failed on her first evening back from hospital, and kicked the hall radiator to shift a gurgling airlock. They parted with an awkward, platonic hug on the doorstep.

Halfway down the front path, Simon paused and turned round.

'By the way, Chris, that coffee…'

'What about it?'

'Tasted like shit!' Simon chuckled and looked as though he might hurdle the front gate in triumph until he realised that, for a man in his late fifties, simply opening it was the safer option.

Now that her secret was out, Chris felt a sense of liberation. Clearing the air was an important step on the road to recovery. This time when Next-Door Nick sent his once-a-week *How's the patient? Do you need any errands run? X* text, Chris responded with *Can you give me a lift to the uni tomorrow?*

Sure, why?

You'll think I'm daft.

I take that as a given, Chris.

I want to see Grayson.

Grayson was a secret shared only with Chloe and Next-Door Nick. Chloe, because mother and daughter were supposed to share everything, and Nick because she had let it slip one evening after two large glasses of Rioja.

Five

Re-engaging with Nick's Fiat 500 was also a test, a measure of how far Chris had progressed since her release from hospital. With her two extra cushions (Physio Melanie's orders), Chris had to bend her neck to the right to fit in and even then she was resting her left ear on the inside roof of the car.

'Where to, m'lady?' asked Nick, easing away from the kerb.

Chris directed them up the hill and along the road towards Becketon, taking a couple of small detours to avoid the worst of the traffic-calming bumps, which, even at Nick's gentle pace, sent painful jolts through Chris's hip and neck. After fifteen minutes, some four miles outside of Becketon, Chris instructed Nick to take a left turn that was almost hidden by the overgrown shrubbery fringing the main road. This took them onto an unmarked single track that led to the rear of the university campus.

'Park here,' directed Chris, pointing to a small car park on the left beside a large orange-brick house.

'Do you need a chaperone?' asked Nick.

'I'll only be five minutes.'

Chris released the seatbelt, eased herself sideways out of the car, taking her crutches from the rear seat, and swung herself across the tarmac for thirty metres until she was standing at the side of the house.

She gazed up at the upstairs window, where Grayson, as ever, stood looking out.

'Morning, Grayson. Sorry I haven't visited for a while. As you can see, I've been somewhat indisposed.'

*

Grayson was a dummy.

Perhaps 'Grayson was a mannequin' would technically be more accurate. Chris had first met him twelve months previously, while following the cycle path that connected Cliffstaple and Becketon. The first time she passed the house, she caught a peripheral glimpse of someone watching her from an upstairs window. When she repeated her journey the following week, he was there again, so she slowed to get a better look. That's when she realised that the figure was actually a shop mannequin, dressed smart-casual in a black suit and white T-shirt and with a mop of dark hair.

The third time, she stopped, dismounted and took a couple of photos. There was something about his solitary, ever-staring presence that was almost poetic – Pre-Raphaelite, she fancied. She called him Grayson – an appropriately artistic name. A sign in a downstairs window read 'University of North Kent: Scene-of-Crime Reconstruction'. Apparently, the house was a practical classroom for forensic science students, which made Grayson's presence even more intriguing. What did he represent? Was he a witness to a terrible crime? A plainclothes detective intent on solving the case? The murderer himself, plotting his escape? Or perhaps he was the ghost of a victim, staring forlornly out of a window for all eternity.

From this juncture, Grayson's house became a regular stopping point on her cycle trips. She'd talk to him, tell him how her week had been and ask after his – it turned out that they had similar social lives. Occasionally, Chris shared her issues. Grayson's advice was always silent but wise. Today was not quite the same, something of an anti-climax after the weeks of anticipating the reunion. Nick watching from the car park was like having a peeping Tom at her bedroom window. Still, it was good to see Grayson again, if only for a flying visit, and he would now become a cycling objective, spurring her return to fitness, giving her impetus to get a new bike and find the confidence to get back in the saddle.

'How was Grayson?' Nick asked as she settled herself back into the car seat.

'Do you think I'm crazy, visiting a dress-shop dummy?'

'Not at all. It's an affectation – quite charming really.'

'Thank you.'

'After all, people talk to pets, don't they?' Nick turned right onto the main road back towards Cliffstaple.

'I do that too. Aitken's quite the conversationalist.'

'And they shout at the TV.'

'Ditto, if hurling obscenities at your laptop when it freezes counts?'

'And King Charles talks to plants.'

'You're right – I'm not that crazy.'

Chris had once spent a two-week coach tour of South Africa with a young couple who were accompanied everywhere by their giant teddy bear named Neville. That was the benchmark of weirdness as far as Chris was concerned. Occasionally talking to Grayson the mannequin was not even in the same ballpark.

'Mind you,' said Nick, 'if Grayson starts talking back, then you're in trouble.'

'Van!' shouted Chris as a non-sequitur, causing Nick to instinctively slam on his brakes.

'What? Where?'

'Just took that left at the traffic lights. Ice cream van.'

'Oh, right. I've got some Magnums in the freezer at home if you're desperate.'

'Follow him! It could be the one. It could be Mr Softee.'

'I don't think that's a good idea. You need to get back and recuperate.'

Chris turned to face Nick and narrowed her eyes. 'Follow… that… van.'

*

Any traffic cameras covering the roads between Becketon and Cliffstaple would have recorded what was possibly the slowest car chase since OJ Simpson was pursued by Los Angeles' finest. Despite Chris's urgings, Nick barely got out of third gear. At every turning he dutifully dropped down through the gears, one at a time, and followed the mirror-signal-manoeuvre routine so obediently that Chris dug her nails into her car seat in frustration. Fortunately, their prey was blissfully unaware of the hot pursuit and rarely exceeded twenty-five miles an hour.

'Speed up, you're losing him!'

'This is a residential road, Chris. Twenty-miles-an-hour limit.'

'Sod the limit. Look, he's taken the next right.'

'And we've got to mind your hip. What would your physio say?'

'Nothing compared to what I'll say if you don't step on it!'

After five minutes of lukewarm pursuit, the ice cream van pulled to a stop opposite a playground and was immediately engulfed by a swarm of overheated parents and overfed children. On Chris's direction, Nick parked thirty metres behind.

'Lenny's Lollies,' he announced. 'Happy?'

Chris noted the registration number and livery details in preparation for loading them onto her database. 'OK, we can head for home.'

Nick paused before restarting the engine. 'Don't you think you're becoming a bit, well, obsessed?'

'It's a hobby. Chloe's always telling me to get a hobby and now I have.'

'Stamp collecting's a hobby, painting's a hobby, collecting commemorative plates of Elvis Presley is a hobby. Pursuing and cataloguing ice cream vans isn't a hobby.'

'Can be. People train-spot, collect aeroplane numbers, even go to traction-engine rallies. Ice cream vans are colourful, tuneful and there's a wide variety.'

Nick sighed the sigh of a man who could sense this conversation was not going well. 'You're going to run out of ice cream vans to spot pretty quickly.'

'Lenny's Lollies is number four. My research indicates that there are three hundred and fifteen ice cream vans in Kent and I aim to eliminate them all until I find—'

'Mr Softee. Yeah, I know, Chris. Just let the police do their job, then we'll all be happier.'

Chris set her jaw as firmly as the constricting pressure of the car roof would allow. 'Take me home, please, Nick.'

Six

Fulfilling Chris's promise to Grayson required a significant purchase. Two doors past the chemist's on the high street was an independent bicycle shop, punningly named Spokesmen. Chris would often pause there and press her face up against the glass like a kid at a toy shop. This time she pushed the door and entered the shrine.

At the sound of the door chime, a young lad appeared from the back of the shop, wiping oil from his hands. 'Young lad' in Chris's definition was any man under the age of twenty-five, one who was far too young to suffer a 'nasty' fall.

He noticed the crutches immediately and grinned cheerily. 'Morning! I'm Gus. How can I help?'

Chris looked around at the kaleidoscopic display of road bikes, trail bikes, mountain bikes, hybrid bikes. Serious bicycles for serious riders.

'Do you stock' – she leant in and whispered in a tone of voice that might be used for requesting haemorrhoid cream in a busy chemist's – 'electric bikes?'

She was half expecting to be frogmarched out of the shop and thrown into the gutter in disgrace, but instead Gus shrugged. 'A couple. We tend to order them in specially. Cycling injury?'

'Yeah, broken hip. Me and this van had a disagreement,' said Chris, moving into cycling bravado mode. She very nearly added '*Capisce?*' but stopped herself just in time.

Gus looked impressed. 'Nasty. I misjudged a downhill bend off-road last summer. Went arse over tit and broke my collarbone. I feel your pain.'

Chris felt honoured to be so readily accepted into the Honourable Society of Injured Cyclists. 'What's the availability like?'

'It's about a three-week lead time unless you're looking for something specialised.'

'No, nothing too kinky.'

Gus appeared a shade alarmed.

'I've drawn up a list of requirements,' Chris said, handing over an A4 sheet of paper with fourteen numbered bullet points, her list of specifications. 'Most important is that it must have a low step-through.' She nodded at her crutches. 'To make it easy for me to get my leg over. *Capisce?*' Damn.

Gus blushed noticeably. Chris wondered whether one could be added to the sex offenders register for having inflicted gratuitous innuendo on a cycle-shop employee. Gus took Chris's list and phone number and said he'd get back to her later in the day with some recommendations, doubtless grateful to see the back of her hobbling out of the shop. Chris imagined him tearing up her honorary membership of the Cycling Injuries Society as she exited.

She had decided to make the move from a manual to an electric bicycle while in her hospital bed. Physio Melanie had said that 'in time' a return to cycling would be a good idea. 'Swimming first,' she said, 'then cycling.' In truth, hip replacement or not, it was an inevitable progression. Chris's cycling speed had been getting steadily slower, and before her fateful meeting with Mr Softee she had already been overtaken by a man towing his child in a carrier, followed swiftly by an Albert Einstein lookalike on a folding bike. Even so, the transition from manual to electric felt as momentous as it must have felt for Bob Dylan.

Within the month, she was admiring her new baby. Gus had been true to his word and recommended a beauty. Not cheap, but seventeen hundred pounds of gorgeousness. Aluminium alloy frame, twenty-one gears, a thousand-watt motor, disc brakes – perfection on two wheels. She'd opted for a black and bright orange frame and red-trim wheels, partly out of vanity and partly out of the desire to be as visible to hostile traffic as possible. Another upgrade was a wide, cushioned saddle rather than the buttock-cleaving razor-blade version that came as standard. Emblazoned across the frame in white lettering was 'RamRod', a disturbingly macho name for a low-step-through electric bicycle. Chris decided to call him Rod for short.

Chris's love for her new toy came with equal amounts of paranoia. It would be a few more weeks until she was fit enough to take it out on the road, and leaving it chained up outside at the mercy of the weather and passing bicycle thieves had already caused one sleepless night. Her solution was to have Rod proudly standing in her sitting room as an objet d'art to be admired, stroked and polished at every opportunity. She seriously considered leaving her new bicycle there as a permanent feature to be appreciated by guests until she remembered that she seldom invited anyone round – all Chris had to offer visitors was tombola coffee and a raised toilet seat. Aitken was not impressed with the competition for her affections and sulked for a full week until she upgraded his food to a branded pâté that looked good enough to spread on toast.

On a calendar on her fridge she ticked off the days until she could take the bike out for a spin. She drew a red circle around Friday 9 August, exactly four months after her operation, and wrote 'GRAYSON!' underneath.

*

The appointed day was sunny with a gentle, cooling breeze, perfect cycling weather. Chris changed into her cycling shorts with an unfeasible number of pockets, slipped on her reflective yellow jacket, strapped on her pristine new cycle helmet and completed the look with her designer Polaroid cycling sunglasses with interchangeable lenses. As she wheeled her bicycle towards the front door, she caught sight of herself in the mirror and did the unthinkable – she pulled out her phone and took a selfie.

Outside, Next-Door Nick was loading his recycling bin. 'Have fun!' he called. 'Be sure to let me know what ward you end up in this time!'

As she set off, Chris flicked the ride computer into eco mode and flicked her middle finger in response to Nick, which, in taking one hand off the handlebars, caused a precarious wobble that nearly wiped out a child on a scooter.

This was not strictly her maiden trip. Over the previous week Chris had cycled up and down Sea View during quiet times to get a feel for her new bike and to appreciate the dynamic differences between it and her old (and now crumpled and consigned to landfill) manual model. Rod was much heavier, so Chris had to sit still in the saddle rather than throw her weight around, stand on the pedals or lean into corners as before. Her introduction to disc brakes nearly met with disaster at the first use. Gone was the slow deceleration of rubber blocks on wheel rims; now the brakes caused such an abrupt stop that Chris's groin hit the handlebars, catapulting her ride computer into the gutter and nearly down a storm drain. She quickly realised that caution would need to be exercised for quite some time until she got the hang of her shiny new dream machine.

Chris mind-mapped her route for the day. She could have picked an easier option, such as the promenade along the seafront or the straight road with excellent visibility that dissected the sheep-populated salt marshes, but, after four long and painful months, she really needed to test herself, so she set off towards Becketon.

Just a few hundred yards on Cliffstaple High Street, then Chris cut down an alley onto a traffic-free path that ran behind some new housing. Onto a main road, Southlands Street, but only briefly, and then a right through a narrow entrance onto a farm track. Corn was growing to her right and a yellow field of rape was being harvested to her left. Then up over the bridge that crossed the motorway, hearing the traffic scream beneath. A Lycra-clad biker sped past her, head down, knees pumping, sweat spraying from his brow. Chris smiled gently to herself in the knowledge that the Hill of Death awaited him.

The Hill of Death was Chris's main motivation for going electric – the dreaded challenge on every visit to Grayson's house. This cycle path followed the route of a long-closed steam-train track, and a hundred and fifty years ago there had been a tunnel through this foothill of the North Downs. That tunnel had long been sealed and its location forgotten, obliging intrepid cyclists and ramblers to take the attritional route over the top. The track started gently enough but gradually grew steeper and then, as the lactic acid screamed in your muscles and the peak was apparently in sight, the Hill of Death merely chortled and, round a bend, added a further six hundred metres of incline. Chris had seen even fit young men and women get off at the halfway point and wheel their cycles, pretending that they preferred to walk.

Lycra Man had sixty metres on her by the time she hit the first incline. Chris was ready. She switched down through the gears, from eight to seven to six to five to four. As she hit the second incline, Chris switched up from eco mode to normal. Lycra Man was just forty metres ahead now, standing upright on his pedals, swaying slightly. At the third incline, Chris engaged high mode and felt the surge of battery power through the gears. Twenty-five, fifteen, ten, five and then she surged past Lycra Man, offering him a cheery wave as she did so. I may be cheating, she thought, but for a brief moment I can dream that I am young and athletic again rather than a sixty-year-old woman with a titanium hip and a penchant for neat vodka.

There was a short descent and then a long rail-straight stretch that ran slightly uphill to the Winding Pool. The Winding Pool was a pond where, in olden days, the steam train took on water. It marked a handy halfway point in Chris's route and it was where she would usually stop to take a breather after the trial of the climb. Her hip was aching, but to stop now would invite it to seize up, so she cycled on. Lycra Man sped past her again and disappeared into the distance, but that mattered not. Chris had made her point and Rod had passed his crucial test.

From here the path passed through a narrow wooded section. There were a couple of walkers, so Chris slowed in anticipation and rang her bell to alert them to her presence. They stepped aside and she passed, shouting 'Thank you!' At the road crossing, Chris proceeded cautiously and, as it turned out, sensibly, because a black SUV with smoked-glass windows cruised by like a hearse in a hurry. She saluted it, doing her best for motorist–cyclist relations, and then accelerated again as the path took her through a farm and alongside orchards where scruffy Portakabins housed the seasonal fruit pickers. Another small climb, achievable in normal mode, and there was the second waypoint, the rear entrance to All Saints, a sweet village church. A young couple were sitting on the bench outside, rucksack nestled between them, sharing a roll-up cigarette. He was tall and athletic, she was pretty with a shock of red hair peeping out from under her cap. Chris and the couple exchanged fraternal nods as she passed by.

A long, gentle descent and the path entered the university grounds. A squirrel dashed out from the verge and then stopped mid-path as though playing chicken. He was grey, of course, but there was a flash of red in his tail as if in tribute to the native squirrels his kind had usurped. Chris was in two minds whether to brake or to swerve and she felt the bicycle flinch nervously under her as she struggled to maintain control. Mr Squirrel gave a last contemptuous look and then bolted into a hedge. Regaining her balance, Chris let out a breath and her most extreme curse. If she were to end up back in that hospital ward, adding 'unseated by a squirrel' to 'collided with an ice cream van' in her medical records, the humiliation would be unbearable.

Playing fields stretched out on either side of the path and then came a cluster of student residences, currently empty due to the summer break. And there, up ahead on the right, was Chris's destination. The large, detached house next to the small car park Nick had parked in just a few weeks previously. A stylish period house in orange brick with white sash windows. The sort of house you'd be happy to call home.

Chris stopped pedalling, cruised past the front of the house and swung round to look up at the upstairs window where Grayson was always standing, gazing out. Except that today, for the first time ever, he wasn't.

Seven

During the past year Grayson had become such a reliable presence in Chris's life that she'd never once considered he might move on, or, to be more accurate, be moved on. Her first thought was to check each window to see whether Grayson had simply been repositioned to give him a different view of the surrounding countryside. Nope. Nothing. Nada. Time to accept the breakdown of yet another relationship, Chris thought. She even got chucked by a mannequin.

But as she passed by the front door, some instinct told her to take a closer look.

She pressed her nose up against the left-hand window. Everything inside was dark, in contrast to the bright sunlight, and she needed to give her eyes a minute to adjust. A half-pulled blue gingham curtain obscured her view of the right-hand side of the room, but it looked like a typical, if unadorned, domestic kitchen. It reminded her of a show home on a purpose-built estate. There was everything you'd expect to find – tile-effect lino flooring, a table and chairs, a red four-slot toaster, a basic microwave with a dial timer, and a cheap white plastic kettle – but nothing extra, no personal touch. The only thing betraying the house's real purpose as a practical classroom was a ring binder by the sink and a rack holding three test tubes next to the toaster.

Not much of interest and Chris was about to leave when she caught sight of a shape below the kitchen table. Ah, there was Grayson! Sleeping on the job, eh? The soles of his feet were facing Chris and the rest of his torso was lost in the shadows. Some prankster student had, apparently, taken him from his rightful place at the window and dumped him unceremoniously on the floor. It was hardly befitting of his status as north Kent's premier plastic agony uncle.

Chris shook her head sadly, bemoaning the lack of respect of the youth of today. She remounted Rod, treated herself to high battery assistance and turned for home. But as she left the university grounds, something about the scene began gnawing at the back of her mind. Suddenly, Mr Squirrel (identifiable by that red flash on his tail) shot across her path again, determined for Round Two. Chris squeezed on the brakes too firmly, Rod's back end lurched to the right and Chris's left hip came perilously close to being impaled on the handlebar.

Shit! That was close. Too close. She clambered off and bent over, taking deep breaths to calm her frazzled nerves.

'Concentrate, Chris, you idiot. Concentrate,' she muttered to herself. And then, as though having an epiphany, shouted 'SHOES!'

That's what had been nagging away at her mind – the figure under the table had been wearing old shoes. The leather soles were badly scuffed and the heels had been worn away unevenly so that they had a camber on the outer edges. Of course, Chris had never seen Grayson's feet, only his upper half, but his outfit was always immaculate. In her imagination he wore only the finest designer footwear, certainly not shabby brogues.

Even so, this was hardly a smoking gun. The sensible action would have been to carefully continue cycling home, run a bath, make a huge mug of builder's tea and finish that packet of fig rolls. Unfortunately, Chris had had enough of being sensible. Once you'd crossed the Rubicon of your sixtieth birthday, she'd decided, you had permission to be un-sensible for the rest of your life.

I'll just take a quick look, she said to herself. For reassurance and to admonish Grayson for his poorly maintained footwear.

Back at the forensics house, she leant Rod against the side wall and tried the front door. Unsurprisingly, it was locked, which only increased her urge to get inside and Discover the Truth. What now? She couldn't imagine that the university would grant access to some random, curious stranger with a mannequin fetish, but… She racked her brains for a cover story.

What if… what if she pretended she was a rich mature student from overseas who was prepared to pay huge course fees to the university with the finest forensic science facilities?

She took her phone out. Hmm, twenty-two per cent battery life. Not great, but Chris's reluctance to upgrade her phone left her at the mercy of its built-in obsolescence and a battery that needed recharging three times a day. She googled the university's site and pressed the telephone icon. It rang three times before a recorded voice answered: 'Thank you for calling the University of North Kent, the South-East's gateway to world-class education. For Admissions, press 1; for Accommodation, press 2; for Recruitment, press…'

Chris had almost given up hope when finally a human voice came on the line.

'Hi, University of North Kent, how can I help you?'

It was time for Chris to demonstrate her linguistic skills and unleash her O-Level (grade D) Spanish.

'Hola! Soy Carmen. Um… Llama por el departamento forensics… por favor.'

The receptionist sounded confused. 'Your name's Carmen Llama?'

'No, o oui, I mean si. Forensics?'

'Forensic Science? I'll put you through to their offices.'

Chris glanced at her phone. The battery had ticked down to nineteen per cent.

After another wait, a female voice said, 'Life Sciences.'

Chris decided to prematurely retire Carmen Llama. 'Hi, can I speak to someone in Forensics? It's about accessing the Crime Reconstruction House.'

'I'm afraid there's no one available in that department.'

'No one?'

'It's the summer break. Professor Jasper popped in earlier to pick up his post, but I wouldn't expect to see him again until next month.'

'Is there anyone else in authority there?'

'Dr Karamak, the deputy head of department, is at a conference in Barcelona until next week. You could try phoning back then. Otherwise I suggest you look at our website.' The voice was beginning to sound terse.

'I just want to stick my head round the door. I won't be any trouble, I promise. You must have a key. Hello? Hello?' The line had gone dead.

Chris squatted down to look through the letterbox. This gave a narrow field of vision but at a lower viewpoint than the window. If my hip locks now, she thought, I could be stuck here like a constipated sumo wrestler.

She switched on her phone's flashlight to help illuminate the interior. She was becoming increasingly certain that the prone figure wasn't Grayson. The build looked... different somehow. She tried to redirect the phone light to reveal more of the figure, the upper torso that was hidden. The light flickered back and forth and then... What was that dark patch on the floor? That wasn't shadow, was it? Was it... blood?

Chris experienced a wave of fear and disorientation. She felt vulnerable standing out in the open, so she retreated from the front door to the far side of the house where she had parked Rod.

What to do? Call the police?

She could hear Chloe's voice telling her to ride away, to go home, not to get involved. 'Think sensibly,' Chris said out loud to herself. 'You're letting your imagination run riot again, aren't you? A dead body? In leafy north Kent? In a forensics house?'

What if the body was just Grayson? Sure, that would be embarrassing, but, at worst... could she be arrested for wasting police time? Ye gods! How would she explain to Chloe that her mother was currently doing a stretch in a high-security prison? Who would feed Aitken his Finest-brand salmon-style pâté?

Perhaps now *was* the time for that bath-and-fig-roll combo and forgetting that today had ever happened. But she knew she couldn't. Pre-accident Chris could have happily left the mystery unsolved like an unscratched itch, but her glimpse of her own mortality had changed her. Now she needed certainty. She craved answers. She had to know.

She took her phone back out of her shorts pocket. The battery life glowed red on seventeen per cent. There was a compromise option. She would report it to the non-emergency police number, pass the buck and clear her conscience in one fell swoop.

Chris was two digits into dialling 9-1-1 before she realised that was the US emergency number, hot-wired into her brain from countless movies. What would have happened if she'd entered that last digit? Would a Dodge Charger have materialised, lights flashing, screeching to a halt in a cloud of burnt rubber before two cops leapt out, rolling across the bonnet and whipping out their guns as they screamed, 'Freeze, melon farmer!'

She had no choice now but to use precious juice and google it. There… 101… of course!

'North Kent Police, how can I help you?'

A simple enough question, which sent Chris into an incoherent burble.

'I need to report a suspicious incident. I mean, it's probably nothing, so no need to call out Starsky and Hutch, hah! It's just this guy I was visiting, well, he now seems to be a different guy and he's lying on the floor.'

'Name, please,' said the impressively unfazed police operator.

'Grayson.'

'Is that Mrs, Miss or Ms Grayson?'

'No, that's his name not mine.'

'Can I have *your* name and address, please?'

'Um, sorry, yes. Christine Heron, 15 Sea View, Cliffstaple BK4 3BL.'

'Is that the address you're calling from, Christine?'

'No, I don't know how to describe where I am. It's the house by the cycle path near the University of North Kent's campus, by the sports fields, next to a car park. There's a psychotic squirrel nearby. Does that help?'

'One moment, please.'

Chris could hear the operator typing furiously.

'And you were phoning about a gentleman called Grayson?'

'Well… yes, I suppose… You see, that's not really his name.'

'It's an alias?'

Chris was regretting the way this conversation was spiralling out of control.

'Grayson's not real. He's a dummy. You know, like in a clothes shop.' She changed tack. 'You see, he was missing, so I looked for him and saw him on the floor.'

'Have you spoken to your doctor recently, Christine?'

'Sorry?'

'Are you on any medication?'

'Listen, I'm not insane. I'm a proofreader!'

'I see.'

'Dummies don't bleed, do they? Or wear shabby shoes? That's why I'm calling. I'm reporting a possible fatality.'

There was a long pause. Chris had the feeling she'd been put on speaker and an entire room of non-emergency operators had gathered round to listen.

'Are you aware of the purpose of this service?' The call handler's tone of voice had shifted. 'You may think this is funny, but you could be blocking a call reporting a serious incident.'

'This is a serious incident. Possibly.'

'That someone who is not real, who you've made up a name for, may or may not be dead?'

'Yes. I mean no. I'm not explaining it well. Sorry, let me start again from the beginning.'

And with that, Chris's phone battery bleeped a warning and expired.

She cursed herself. Why was she, a professional with years of experience, so bad at formal phone conversations? Proofreading was so much easier – you planned, took your time, corrected the mistakes and sent it back only when you were ready. She leant back against the wall and howled with frustration.

A young couple appeared on the cycle path and looked over at her with alarm. Chris did a double-take. Young. Athletic. Red hair. Pretty. They'd been outside the church earlier, sharing a roll-up cigarette.

'Cramp!' she shouted, pointing at her leg.

The man whispered something to his companion and they hurried away, no doubt eager to distance themselves from the crazy woman.

What to do? The trouble was she had now broken cover – North Kent Police had her details, she was on record, she could no longer pretend that none of this had happened. Her phone bleeped again, as though desperately trying to raise itself from the dead. She pulled up the camera app, thrust her hands through the letterbox and fired off two quick shots. As she did so, her peripheral vision noticed a black SUV gliding silently into the car park. Chris couldn't be sure it was the same car that had passed her earlier, at the road crossing, but she wasn't keen to find out.

In her panic, she let go of the letterbox flap, which sprang shut, separating her from her phone and sending it clattering across the kitchen floor. She stared forlornly through the letterbox to see her phone nestling neatly between the legs of the as yet unidentified prone figure. Of all possible outcomes, this was the worst. If that was a dead body and not a mannequin, then she'd just left a piece of key evidence at the scene. She couldn't simply ride away now.

Eight

Becketon was just three miles away, a short downhill ride, and Becketon had a police station, an increasingly rare thing. That was the answer, Chris decided. She would report this in person. Correct any confusion that her phone call might have caused and act first before anyone found her phone nestling against a corpse's groin.

As nimbly as she could, Chris vaulted onto Rod's saddle, cranked the motor setting up to high and, head down, sped off as fast as her newly installed hip permitted.

Three miles downhill. It should have taken Chris twelve minutes maximum – if she'd known where she was going. The combination of poor signage, a rotten sense of direction and a mislaid smartphone meant that it was forty minutes before she rolled up at the generic 1960s office block, distinguishable only by the large sign that read 'North Kent Constabulary' and the half a dozen police cars parked outside.

She leant Rod against the wall and secured the integral lock, hopeful that outside a police station was as safe a place for a bicycle as any. She took a deep breath and marched to the front door, ready to make her report. It was firmly shut.

Having led a relatively blameless and crime-free life up until this day, Chris had never had cause to actually visit a police station. Her mental image had been formed from British movies of the 1940s and childhood memories of *Dixon of Dock Green*. She was not so naive as to imagine the front desk would be manned by a rosy-faced copper with a mug of steaming tea, filling out a ledger with reports of missing dogs or sorting through the lost property, but she had assumed that she'd actually be able to enter the building.

She pressed the intercom at the side of the door.

After a few seconds a distorted voice answered. 'What do you want?'

Apparently customer service didn't rank highly in North Kent Constabulary's training programme and, from their lack of progress tracking down Mr Softee, Chris was not too surprised.

'I want to speak to a police officer.' In view of her previous chaotic conversations, she'd decided that the direct approach was best.

'What's it concerning?' came the crackling, disembodied reply.

Chris had vowed to not, under any circumstances, mention Grayson. 'I saw some activity at an address that I think is worthy of further investigation.'

The voice didn't seem impressed. 'You're reporting a crime?'

'Possibly.'

The voice paused. 'Possibly? In that case, phone 101. Goodbye.'

'Hello? Hello?'

The voice had gone. Chris pressed the intercom again.

'I think this is more serious than 101. If I could just speak to an officer? Please?'

'In that case you'd better dial 999, hadn't you?' crackled the reply.

'I can't dial 999 cos I've just lost my phone and it's practically dead anyway.'

'It's what?'

Chris leant over so that her lips were almost caressing the metal grill. 'It's dead!'

There was a buzz and the door clicked open. As Chris walked through, she could see a policeman behind a desk shielded by a wall of protective glass. The officer pushed a hidden button on his desk and his voice boomed from three speakers positioned strategically around the room. 'Helmet and glasses off!' He jabbed his finger in Chris's direction.

Apologising, she complied.

'Step into Pod 1!'

The last stage before being allowed access to the inner sanctum was to step into a tube which closed with a sound reminiscent of the doors of the Starship *Enterprise*. Logic dictated that she was only being scanned for concealed weapons, but the time between the outer door closing and the inner door opening was long enough for Chris's imagination to picture her body being blasted into orbit.

Once through, she was permitted to approach to within two metres of the hatch. Like the Wizard of Oz, the figure behind the authoritarian voice was less than impressive. Police Constable Thackery ZB2515 was slightly built, about forty, with thinning grey-blonde hair and a moustache which belonged on a seventies porn star.

He took down Chris's details and pointed to a door on her left.

'Wait in there. Someone will be in to take your statement in due course.'

PC Thackery then redirected his attention to a poorly concealed Stephen King novel.

The interview room was as sparse and unwelcoming as an off-motorway hotel for sales reps. It was windowless with a double strip of fluorescent lights that flickered almost imperceptibly. A camera positioned where the wall and ceiling met blinked a red light in harmony. The nicotine-coloured walls were sporadically papered with faded posters warning of dangers now seemingly consigned to history. 'Be Aware of Pickpockets!' warned one; 'Rabies Means Death!' warned another, with a helpful illustration of a salivating, fanged hound in case of any misunderstanding. A large yellow poster boasted that 'Bicycle Thieves Operate in this Area!', which made Chris paranoid about the safety of Rod parked outside. She gently peeled back the corner of the poster to reveal a crack in the plaster so cavernous that it could have been a gateway to another dimension. Being deep in thought about this possibility, she didn't hear the door open behind her.

'We've got a cupboard full of 'em in the office if you're that keen.'

The speaker was a police sergeant, judging by the stripes on his arm. He was physically huge, well over six feet tall, with close-cropped red hair and a gut that spilled out of his unbuttoned jacket and forced his trousers to hang precariously on his hips.

'Sorry!' she stuttered. 'Just admiring your crack – in the wall, that is.'

A police constable emerged from the blindside of his colleague. He too was vast – average height but with the build of someone who had spent far too many hours in the gym, pumping iron and mainlining protein supplements. He had a shaved head and Reggie Kray spectacles and his arms hung by his sides in an arc, so Chris doubted he could actually clap his hands should the need for applause arise. 'We'd better get you some filler an' all then!' he said, revealing a comically shrill voice for one so muscle-bound.

The sergeant pointed to a chair. 'It's Miss Heron, I understand?'

Chris nodded.

'Please take a seat. I'm Sergeant Spurgeon and my colleague is Police Constable Atherton.'

As they sat, Chris noticed for the first time a third officer, previously hidden by the vast bulk of her colleagues. She was a young, pretty, dark-skinned woman with her hair styled in neat cornrows. Her slim figure perfectly fitted and complemented her uniform, in contrast to the stitch-straining build of her colleagues. She didn't join her fellow officers at the table but sat on a chair by the door, a notebook primly perched upon her knees.

'Would you like a cup of tea or coffee, Miss Heron?' asked Sgt Spurgeon, accentuating the 'Miss'.

The frenzied cycling and high drama of the day meant Chris was parched. 'Thanks, tea would be great. White, no sugar.'

Sgt Spurgeon turned to his female colleague. 'You heard Miss Heron. Tea, no sugar.'

The female officer stood and glared defiantly at the back of the sergeant's head.

Without turning to face her, he added, 'Is there a problem, SC Jah-mah?'

PC Atherton glanced at his senior officer and stifled a giggle.

The policewoman was unmoved. 'Drinks machine needs money, doesn't it, sir?'

Chris felt the need to intervene. 'Look, I'm not fussed. Really, water's fine.'

Sgt Spurgeon sighed dramatically, took a pound coin from his pocket and flicked it back over his shoulder with his thumb.

SC Jama didn't rise to the bait but deftly plucked the coin out of the air. 'And my name is pronounced "Jama", sir.' She gave Chris a quick wink and disappeared out of the room.

'So, Miss Heron,' said the sergeant, opening his notebook with a flourish, 'I understand from PC Thackery that you wish to report a death.'

'My phone. I said my phone had died.'

'We're a police station, not a phone repair shop, Miss Heron,' the sergeant countered, causing another snigger from his colleague.

'Look, I'll start from the beginning, shall I?'

Over the next twenty minutes, Chris gave an account of the day's events – clearly, carefully, thoroughly and sanely. After the first couple of minutes, SC Jama returned with a flimsy plastic cup full of something that tasted like a lukewarm combo of tea, coffee and Bovril, but Chris thanked her profusely to compensate for the rudeness of her colleagues.

When Chris reached the conclusion, Sgt Spurgeon yawned and leant back in his chair, revealing an obscene expanse of pale pink midriff. 'That's it?' he asked, unimpressed.

'I thought it might be important,' Chris said defensively.

'Did you?'

'I've got photos.'

'Well, why didn't you say?' squeaked PC Atherton.

'But my phone's in the forensics house. As I said, I dropped it through the letterbox, but when you retrieve it and charge it up—'

Sgt Spurgeon stood and his colleague followed suit. 'Thank you. We'll make a note of your report.'

'What about my phone?' asked Chris.

'I'm sure PC Thackery will be simply delighted to register it as lost property. On second thoughts, why don't you phone the university?'

'How can I if my phone's—'

'Thank you for doing your civic duty. You can leave this with us now. Jah-mah, would you escort Miss Heron to the exit?' Sgt Spurgeon made it abundantly clear that the interview was at an end.

Chris was taken back out to Reception, directed to a pod and fired out of the police station. Thankfully, Rod the bike was still there, safely locked and unmolested. As she was in the area, Chris headed to her favourite cafe, Pete's Pantry, which served decent croissants and coffee strong enough to overpaint the beefy tea taste that still coated the inside of her mouth.

Nine

SC Zeta Jama picked up a half-empty coffee carton that someone had left, Leaning Tower of Pisa-like, on the keyboard and placed it carefully in the waste bin at her feet. This floor of North Kent Constabulary resembled an overflowing skip behind a dodgy takeaway more than a hub of investigative expertise. Other officers sat hunched in front of their computers, rendered practically invisible by the piles of empty pizza boxes, drink cans, coffee cartons and non-recyclable food packaging. This is the problem with cop-movie clichés, thought Zeta. In the end, real life imitates the art. She sighed, stretched her fingers and logged into the computer.

'You don't mind writing this up, do you, Jah-mah?' asked Sgt Spurgeon rhetorically from the desk opposite.

'Ja-ma, sir. As it's spelt,' said Zeta for the third time that day.

'Good practice, writing up statements,' trilled PC Atherton, perched on the end desk of three, concentrating on his game of Candy Crush.

'But you haven't told me the recommended course of action. I need to mention our response to Ms Heron's statement.'

Sgt Spurgeon picked up a ring doughnut from a box on the windowsill, sniffed it, wrinkled his nose and returned it. 'Course of action, Jah-mah? We'll file it with the rest of the fruit loops!'

Zeta kept her face fixed firmly on the screen. 'I disagree, Sarge.'

Those three words hung heavily over the room. Zeta heard a couple of the other officers stop typing in anticipation of the reaction.

'Oh, do you, *Special* Constable Jah-mah?'

'I think there may be something in her statement. I think we'd be irresponsible if we didn't follow it up.'

Zeta pictured how Ms Heron had given her account, the way she'd closed her eyes for a minute as though retrieving memories from a storage locker. In her limited experience, Zeta Jama had seen enough to doubt the value of eyewitness statements. People didn't observe the world around them; they strolled through their lives, heads buried in their phones or engaged in conversations apparently about nothing. Worst of all were potential eye witnesses who wanted to be helpful. They were the ones who'd embroider or completely invent evidence in their eagerness to tell the police what they thought they wanted to hear. Ms Heron wasn't like that. Her statement had been ordered, her manner composed.

The office was still staring at Zeta.

'Sorry, Sarge, that came out wrong. I wasn't suggesting that *you're* being irresponsible.'

'Apology accepted,' said Sgt Spurgeon, and the office breathed a collective sigh of relief and returned to its work.

'So you don't think it's worth even having a quick look, then – leave no stone unturned?' Zeta was not prepared to concede just yet.

'And waste valuable police time?' chirped PC Atherton as he rocked his phone back and forth, negotiating a tricky corner on a road-race simulation game.

'I always learn so much from seeing the sergeant in action,' replied Zeta artfully.

Sgt Spurgeon stood and puffed out his chest. 'Tell you what, Jah-mah, I've got to have a word with the DI anyway. Let me see what he says.' And he marched out of the room towards the lifts.

Zeta started typing up Ms Heron's statement. She occasionally referred to the notes she'd made in her battered, leather-bound notebook, but for the most part she was happy to rely on her own memory, which never let her down. By challenging Sgt Spurgeon, Zeta wondered if she'd come close to signing her own resignation letter. She had plenty of paid work to keep her busy, but, somehow, being kicked out of a voluntary job would be more humiliating. It would also be a betrayal of her father's legacy.

Within twenty minutes, Sgt Spurgeon was marching back into the office.

'Constable, put your phone away. Jah-mah, grab your gear. We're going to the university.'

Zeta resisted the temptation to punch the air. 'The DI agreed?'

'Not at first. He made me wait until he'd made a couple of calls. Apparently our colleagues in Traffic know Miss Heron only too well. They've been plagued by her weekly emails. Me and the DI agreed that she's obviously given to bouts of hysteria.'

Zeta bit her tongue so hard she could actually taste blood – she was sure that no male witness would ever be described as 'hysterical'.

'But I talked the DI round.' Sgt Spurgeon was in full flow. 'Told him it would be good for us to show our faces in the community, leave no stone unturned.'

Zeta bit her tongue again, winching at the pain.

'Come on,' cried Sgt Spurgeon to Zeta and PC Atherton. 'To the squad car!'

Ten

Three cups of Pete's Pantry's finest Colombian blend were needed to restore Chris's spirits, and a honey-soaked slice of baklava provided a complementary sugar-rush. Pete's cat, a large ginger tom named Cooking Fat, nuzzled Chris's leg, presumably flouting all manner of food hygiene regulations. She scratched the cat's ear, which reminded her that she hadn't left any lunch down for Aitken – she hadn't expected to be out for so long. She gulped down the bitter dregs of her final coffee, paid the bill and unlocked Rod from the handily placed cycle rack outside.

Sgt Spurgeon had been right about one thing, thought Chris. She had performed her civic duty and could now get on with her life. The first priority was to get her phone back, so it would be worth cycling back via the university grounds on the off-chance that someone had retrieved it in the meantime.

As Chris approached the forensics house, she could see there was a hubbub of activity. A police car was parked untidily in the empty car park, across the disabled parking bays, and the door to the house hung wide open. In the middle of the path, SC Jama was talking to a middle-aged woman dressed in a kaftan with a necklace of purple feathers and three large green feathers as a hair ornament. Chris's first thought was that she looked like a rejected *Sesame Street* character. To squeeze by, she slowed, dismounted and wheeled Rod past. She couldn't help but overhear the women's conversation, largely because she was actively eavesdropping.

The witness being interviewed was apparently the course administrator who Chris had spoken to earlier, the holder of the precious key that granted entry to the forensics house and, within it, Chris's phone.

'So, Mrs Douglas, you're sure that no one else has access to this property?' said SC Jama.

'Absolutely. Apart from the heads of department, I have the only key and I never let it out of my sight.'

'And you haven't noticed any suspicious activity?'

Mrs Douglas paused for thought. 'Well, there was a phone call this morning.'

'Yes?'

'Very strange woman. Mad as a hatter. Reception said she called herself Carmen Llama. She may be worth investigating…'

Chris moved swiftly out of earshot. As she looked through the open front door of the house, she was presented with a tableau. Sitting erect at the dining table was Grayson, his plastic hands placed tidily on the table top. Next to Grayson sat Sgt Spurgeon, chomping obscenely on a bacon sandwich whilst his colleague, PC Atherton, was perched on the counter next to the sink, playing a game on his phone.

The sergeant looked up and grinned widely, displaying bacon rind lodged in his discoloured teeth. 'Well, if it isn't Ms Heron. How good of you to join us. Do come in. I'd offer you something to eat, but, as you can see, I've only brought enough for one.'

Chris paused at the threshold. 'Isn't this a potential crime scene? I mean, contamination of evidence and all that?'

There was a familiar high-pitched giggle from the constable on the work surface. ''Sonly a crime scene if you've got a crime, innit?'

'And as you can clearly see, all is well,' his sergeant continued. 'You look surprised to see us, Ms Heron?'

'To be honest, you didn't seem very impressed at the station.' She tried to be tactful.

'I said I'd report it to the DI, so that's what I did. He suggested we drop by to follow it up.' Sgt Spurgeon picked up Grayson's hand and used it to wave at Chris. 'And here we are. And look' – he nodded towards the toaster – 'there's your phone. SC Jah-mah has even put it on charge for you.'

'But this wasn't what I saw,' Chris protested.

'And if you've finished interviewing the witness, Jah-mah, we can lock up and get back to the station.'

Chris glanced round to see that SC Jama had entered the kitchen behind her.

'Gray… the mannequin was on the floor, down there,' Chris said, pointing, 'not sat up at the table like this. Someone's been in here.'

'Students will have their fun,' said the sergeant, wiping his mouth on his sleeve.

'But the blood? I'm sure there was blood.'

The sergeant opened the fridge and extracted a small glass bottle. 'Ketchup!' he roared. He unscrewed the bottle and dolloped red goo over what remained of his sandwich. As he pushed the last piece of bread, tomato ketchup and cured pig into his mouth, he looked Chris straight in the eye. 'Nom, nom, nom.'

Chris averted her eyes in disgust and, for the first time in their relationship, glimpsed Grayson's feet. He was wearing sensible shoes. Black, lace-up, rubber-soled, but, crucially, new. Not scuffed or worn down at the heel but as though they'd come straight from the shop.

'His feet!' Chris shouted excitedly. 'Just look at his feet!' She suddenly remembered the photos. 'They're different and I can prove it. Look!' She grabbed her phone from the counter, tore the charging lead out, unlocked it and handed it to Sgt Spurgeon.

Sgt Spurgeon's pudgy fingers scrolled through the screen. He paused. 'Well, well, well. This changes everything. PC Atherton, come and have a look at this new evidence.'

The constable leapt off the counter and waddled over to his colleague.

'You too, Jah-mah. I do believe that Ms Heron has cracked this case wide open. I'd better send these photographs straight to the station to be logged as key evidence.'

Slowly and theatrically the sergeant turned the screen towards

Chris. Rather than through-the-letterbox shots of a prone, lifeless body, there was one of her open mouth contorted in a gurn and another, out of focus, which seemed to be a close-up of her left nostril. She had left her camera in selfie mode.

Sgt Spurgeon and PC Atherton laughed uproariously at Chris's humiliation, but SC Jama stayed mercifully quiet.

'And there was a car. A huge black SUV with blacked-out windows.' As she spoke, Chris knew that this sounded like a last, desperate throw of the dice.

'And where was this car?' asked Sgt Spurgeon.

'Um, in the car park,' Chris answered meekly.

'A car parked in a car park. Well, I never. PC Atherton, unless Ms Heron has got any more compelling evidence to submit, I suggest we declare this case closed. Jah-mah, if you can finish typing up that statement, I'll put my name to it, OK? You can lock up and return the key, can't you?'

Sgt Spurgeon rose and patted Grayson on the head. PC Atherton followed suit and ushered Chris out of the house.

Chris rode back home in a state of cheek-burning shame. She willed Mr Squirrel to appear and throw himself under her wheels to put her out of her misery, but evidently even he didn't think she was worth the effort.

Eleven

A morning bath was a wondrous thing. Piping hot, steaming and frothed up with avocado and camomile bubbles, or was it kumquat and lavender? No matter. Agatha Christie had apparently done her best work in the bath… and Cleopatra… and Archimedes. It cleansed the body, soothed the muscles and cleared the mind.

By the time Chris had cycled home, found Aitken, apologised to him, fed him, cuddled him and heated up some soup, she hadn't had the energy to get undressed, let alone run a bath. She fell asleep on the sofa, tray perched on her lap, only to be woken in the early hours by some overexcited guy trying to sell her a discounted diver's watch on the Shopping Channel. Her leg muscles screamed abuse at her foolishness and she had to literally crawl upstairs to her bedroom.

Now that she was immersed in a layer of fragrant suds, she became a child again. Each bubble was a glass-domed building in a city of tiny people living on the shores of a vast lake whose waves caused the buildings to gently undulate. Her bent legs were two mountains rising from the lake and the suds that clung there were the homes of the rich and powerful who could afford a dome with panoramic views. Since the accident, there was a new addition to her city – her scar was now a landing strip that ran for eight inches from the top of her right thigh. Chris named it Spatchcock International Airport.

Aitken had already paid his usual visit, walking up the edge of the bath like an Olympic gymnast on the balance beam, but evidently not a medal-winning one. He started to wobble precariously, so Chris flicked some foam in his direction (thereby destroying at least two dozen of her city's houses like some thoughtless god) to suggest that this was not the most sensible strategy for a cat that wished to remain dry.

At 09:28 Chris leant out of the bath and opened her laptop, which was sitting on the lid of the loo. It was probably foolish to jeopardise eight hundred pounds' worth of electronic hardware by siting it so close to three hundred litres of hot, soapy water, but she was awaiting a video call from Chloe and the bath was just too good to abandon. She adjusted the laptop's position so only her head and the top of her shoulders were visible to the camera. Her final act was to manoeuvre the hot tap with her toes to unleash another cascade of steaming hot water, obliterating another several hundred dwellings at a stroke. A god can be cruel like that.

At nine thirty precisely, Chris logged in and by the miracle of technology she was instantly connected to her daughter on the other side of the globe.

Chloe grinned broadly. 'Are you in the bath, Mum?' she chuckled.

'Yep, but I'm not too sure I'll be able to get out again. It was challenging enough when I was able-bodied.'

'Shall I text Next-Door Nick and ask him to pop round and help?'

'He'll have to bring his block and tackle.'

'I thought you weren't interested in his tackle, Mum.'

Mother and daughter dissolved into snorts of laughter. Thirty seconds of conversation with Chloe was enough to quell the stress of the previous twenty-four hours.

'How are the twins?' This was now Chris's obligatory opening line and had become an in-joke.

'Boys, come and say hi to your feeble, accident-prone Granny.' Chloe cheekily poked out her tongue and then the screen was filled with the faces of two boisterous nine-year-old identical twins, Mason and Jason – Chris's gorgeous grandkids.

'Hiya, Chris, how ya doin'?' they shouted in unison.

To them, she was 'Chris', not 'Gran', 'Granny', 'Nana' or 'Nanny', and she loved them for that. Physically, Chris was comfortably old enough for grandmother status, but mentally she remained a teenager. Age crept up on you like a ninja assassin, was Chris's view on life, ambushing you with a glance in the mirror or an unflattering photo.

After a couple of minutes' chat, she could sense the boys were getting restless, no doubt having been dragged away from empire building or turbo racing or monster obliterating on their games console.

'Go on, off you bugger, boys,' she said, and they disappeared from the screen to be replaced by their mother.

'They're beautiful, Chlo. Going to be real heartbreakers.'

Chloe nodded. 'Yeah, all children are beautiful from ten thousand miles away, but all things considered, I think we did all right. Anyway, enough gushing, what are your plans for Christmas?'

'Christmas? Bleedin' Christmas? It's August, for Gawd's sake, Chlo. The sun is shining, the sky is blue and the midges are biting. Let me enjoy what's left of the summer I missed without fast-forwarding to bleak mid-winter.'

'Well, we were wondering—' Chloe tried to interrupt, but Chris was in full flow.

'If it's like last year, I'll be invited for Christmas Eve neighbourhood sherry and nibbles at Next-Door Nick's. Then on the day itself it'll be me, Aitken, turkey slices in gravy for him, premium mince pies for me and that bottle of Grey Goose vodka I've been saving.' Chris had now moved into turbo rant mode. 'I'll swear at all the inane TV Christmas specials recorded in July and fall asleep on the sofa during the Bond film. This year, I may not bother to wear clothes. You?'

'Thank you,' said Chloe. 'If you've finished? Dan and I were chatting last night and we wondered if you'd spend Christmas with us this year.'

'In Melbourne?'

'Preferably – it is where we live. We're planning a big bash, to make up for all the shit people have had – including you. Dan's folks are staying over – you've not seen them since the wedding.'

Chris gulped, took a deep breath and frowned, forgetting that this was a video call.

'Is something wrong?' Chloe asked. 'I thought you'd be excited – it's been three years since you saw the boys.'

'I just did.'

'In the flesh, I mean. But if it's such a terrible idea…'

Chris had to think fast. 'No, it's just that the old proofreading is a bit hand-to-mouth and I had to cut down on my workload after the accident so…'

'I thought of that. Air miles! Dan's got loads saved up – enough to subsidise you for a round trip.'

'And then there's Aitken. I couldn't bear to put him in a cattery. Those places are like a feline Guantanamo Bay.'

Chloe was not so easily dissuaded. 'I'm sure Next-Door Nick would happily cat-sit for a couple of weeks. I'll ask him, if you like.'

'No, I'll look into it. Can I have a think about arrangements and stuff?'

'I guess I need to call in reinforcements then. Dan!' Chloe shouted. 'Come over here and sweet-talk your mother-in-law. She's being stubborn again.'

A mop of blond hair appeared on screen just as Aitken strode confidently back into the bathroom.

'Hi, Ma-in-Law,' Dan drawled. 'So nice to see you looking…'

Aitken made a bee-line for the toilet seat, preparing to leap up and dislodge the laptop.

Crying 'No, Aitken, no!' Chris instinctively leapt up to shoo him away, inadvertently giving her son-in-law a full-frontal display. In a panic, she slapped the lid of the laptop down just as Dan finished his sentence with '… so well.'

'What is wrong with me, Aitken?' Chris asked.

For most people, the prospect of spending Christmas in

Australia with their nearest and dearest would have been the stuff of dreams – it had to be the number one reason why people humiliated themselves on daytime TV quiz shows. For Chris, her immediate reaction was one of dread – and that could make her seem a truly terrible and uncaring mother and grandmother. Which she wasn't. She loved her daughter and her grandsons intensely, and she was rather fond of her son-in-law too, for all his white-teethed, square-jawed, chipper Australianness. It was just that the idea of being imprisoned with them and comparative strangers (Dan's family) over the holiday period and so far from home was, well, daunting.

Chris had the excuse of being a lifelong sufferer of Only Child Syndrome. She didn't bemoan her lack of brothers or sisters. On the contrary, Chris was thankful – it had made her independent, resilient and, yes, a wee bit selfish. Outsiders might have assumed that Chris was lonely, but if you liked your own company, you were never lonely. She missed her parents, but they lived in her heart and in her head and she still asked their advice on occasion. And she did have friends, good friends, she reminded herself. It was just that she didn't need to see them that often. Being on your own gave a girl space to think, space to know yourself. 'And of course,' Chris told Aitken, 'you're never alone with a tabby.'

She leant out of the bath and rummaged through her heap of clothes for her phone. Her behaviour warranted a phone call rather than a text.

'Chlo, darling! We got cut off. You know what it's like with this bloody broadband. Nothing works in this country anymore.'

'I now have to deal with a traumatised husband,' said Chloe seriously.

'Oh. Did he see…?'

'Everything. To think it's come to this.'

'Come to what, Chlo?'

'My mother, the cougar. You could have at least waited until I was out of the room before you made your move.'

'You're joking, aren't you? It wasn't like that, you see—'

'How could you? Exposing yourself to your own son-in-law.'

'It was a complete accident. Aitken was about to knock the laptop over and I was trying—'

'And Dan needs to know just one thing.'

'What?'

'Does he need to send you a dick pic in response?'

Chloe burst into laughter and Chris could hear Dan in the background shouting, 'I've got the camera ready. Do you want it in portrait or landscape?'

'Very good!' Chris said. 'You nearly had me there.'

'*Nearly?*' snorted her daughter. 'I got you hook, line and sinker. Anyway, I didn't mean to ambush you with the invitation. Have a think about it and let us know. We'd so love to have you here.'

'I promise. Sorry if I sounded less than grateful, it's just that since the accident I've become a bit of a shut-in. It's taking me time to venture out into the big wide world again.'

'I didn't realise, Mum.'

'I'm fine, Chloe. I'm fine. Look, give my love to Dan and the boys again and I'll give you a call in a couple of days.'

'See you soon, Mum.' And, as usual, Chloe blew a loud, rasping kiss down the phone to end the call.

Chris decided that she'd better get out of the bath before she pruned up completely. She dried herself, counting the array of new bruises accumulated during yesterday's bike ride – one on each calf, a large one on her shoulder and a whopper on her good hip, where she could actually make out the outline of the handlebar. Fortunately, her flexibility had improved and she could now reach her toes to dry them manually, mouthing the words to 'This Little Piggy' as she did so. She took her time so she could interrogate herself about that last conversation with Chloe.

'Shut-in' sounded rather extreme, but over the last couple of years she'd found herself retreating to the security and comfort of her own four walls. Perhaps it was an age thing. But sixty was still young. According to Chloe, it was 'the new forty'. Mind you, being forty had been something of a challenge too.

Working from home meant that Chris didn't have to sit in an office, and online shopping made supermarket visits redundant. 'Outside' now seemed so loud and rushed and, well, unnecessary. Chris wiped the steam from the bathroom mirror and confronted herself. She needed to shake herself out of this malaise, she decided. Leave the house, shop locally, join a book club (without single men), volunteer at the Community Garden, meet people.

Chris had got as far as the 'little piggy who went to market' when the doorbell rang. She ignored it. She wasn't expecting any deliveries, so nothing good could be a-calling on a Saturday morning. It would either be an ex-offender selling kitchen accessories (and she'd already accumulated a drawer full of dishcloths and cheap tin openers) or God-Squad offering doorstep salvation (and she'd decided she was beyond redemption).

The bell rang again and seemed persistent, so Chris threw on her dressing gown and padded into the bedroom to look down from the front window. The unwelcome visitor was standing close to the front door and Chris could only see the back of a covered head. A hoodie on a summer's day was never good news. As stealthily as she could, Chris crept down the stairs, remembering to avoid the creaky one, third from bottom.

I could look through the spyhole, Chris thought, if I had one. 'A spyhole' was riding high at number 7 on her 'Essential Home Improvements' list, between 'a new boiler' at number 6 and 'a microchip cat flap' at number 8. As quietly as possible, Chris attached the security chain, but an urgent knocking made her take an instinctive leap back.

'Whatever it is, I've got plenty, thank you,' Chris called out in a surprisingly quaky voice.

'Plenty of what?' The voice was young, female and familiar.

'Tea towels and Jesus.'

'That is Ms Heron, isn't it?'

'Down, Sabre!' Chris shouted to an imaginary guard dog

before opening the door a couple of inches.

The figure on the doorstep shuffled nervously, then looked up, pulled down her hood and smiled. She was dressed in civvies so it took Chris a couple of seconds to place her.

'SC Jama!'

'Zeta, please.'

'Is something wrong?' Chris asked.

Her default position was to expect bad news. A police officer on your doorstep suggested it was either that ex-husband Simon had been dispatched by a mad axe-murderer or that her cat had been caught crapping on someone's prize-winning lawn.

'Is Aitken all right?' she asked, choosing the most concerning of the two options.

'Aitken?'

'My cat. He loves a well-manicured garden.'

'No, Ms Heron, nothing to do with cats. Or gardens. I just wanted to speak to you… unofficially. You see, I'm not actually here.'

'Virtually or philosophically?'

'Professionally. I'm off duty.'

'I see.'

'Can I come in?' asked Zeta. 'Don't wanna have to arrest myself for loitering with intent.'

'Oh, yes. Sorry. Hang on, just a mo…' Chris closed the door and spent at least forty-five seconds fumbling to release the security chain.

Zeta stepped over the threshold and nodded in the direction of the chain. 'Very sensible. We've been having a drive to get all elderly residents to use a security chain.' She noticed Chris's horrified expression. 'I didn't mean that *you* are elderly. I meant… Oh shit, not a good start, eh?'

Chris chuckled. 'Would you care to follow me into the kitchen? That is, if my geriatric legs will carry me that far.'

'Ta. Nice house you have here, Ms Heron. Lots of… features.'

Chris gestured for Zeta to take a seat at the table, the same seat taken by Simon on his previous visit. 'You've piqued my interest, Zeta Jama. What could possibly be the reason for your non-professional, hoodie-clad presence?' Before Zeta could reply, Chris held up her hand. 'What can I get you to drink?'

'Oh, whatever's easy, ta.'

Chris was tempted to dig out the tombola instant coffee as revenge for the tea/Bovril cocktail served at the police station, but she understood that was not Zeta's fault, so instead she made two cups of builder's tea, white, no sugar.

Zeta blew on the mug and took a sip, giving the sort of contented sigh that always magically accompanied tea. 'It's about your statement, Ms Heron.'

It was what she'd feared. 'Look, first, call me Chris, and, second, I'm really, really sorry about all that. I had the best intentions and didn't mean to waste police time. Perhaps I let my imagination run away with me a little…' In panic, her mouth had switched to auto-pilot. 'You see, I had this accident a few months back—'

'I know,' said Zeta.

'So that's probably made me a bit paranoid. That's a figure of speech, of course. Ha, ha – I don't mean that I have any psychiatric issues, well, not diagnosable ones…' Chris paused as Zeta's response filtered into her brain. 'How do you know about my accident?'

'You submitted an accident report.'

'And you read it?' Chris was part incredulous and part impressed.

'Of course. I'm very thorough.'

'Not thorough enough to catch the bastard who hit me though?' Chris muttered into her mug of tea.

'Not my department, I'm afraid. I can check with the RTC officer, if you'd like an update,' said Zeta calmly.

'Is there any point?'

'Probably not. No witnesses, no CCTV and you're not dead – which is a good thing of course, Chris, but pushes it down the priority list. Anyway, back to the matter in hand…'

Chris took a large gulp of tea, which, as it was still hot, meant she had to open her mouth like a basking shark to drag in cooling air. 'So why are you here? I've said that I'm sorry.'

Zeta put her mug down and looked Chris squarely in the eyes. 'I'm here because I believe you.'

This was unexpected and required three more sips of tea to process. 'I'm confused,' Chris admitted. 'Sergeant Spurgeon and PC... Squeaky Muscles...'

'Atherton,' corrected Zeta with a hint of a smile.

'That's it. Atherton. They were quite clear that there was no blood, no body, no crime. They'd investigated the scene and concluded that, at most, it was a student prank.'

'That's very true, but you're overlooking one important thing.'

'What's that?'

'Sgt Spurgeon and PC Atherton are arses.'

Chris pondered this as though it were a deep philosophical observation. 'I had noticed, but it doesn't mean they're wrong. Please shred my statement and, in return, I'll promise to stop seeing dead people.'

'But I believe you saw what you said you did.'

'Why?'

There was a rattle and Aitken entered the kitchen via the cat flap. He headed straight to Zeta and rubbed himself against her legs. Zeta put her hand down and scratched Aitken's head and playfully tugged at his ear, which sent him into spasms of joy.

'First, because you are, in my view, a credible witness.'

'Really?'

'I may have only been doing this for a year, but credible witnesses are rare, whereas we get overrun by... um... *incredible* ones. What technique do you use?'

'Sorry?'

'Memory technique. Witnesses never have that kind of attention to detail.'

'Ah, Roman Rooms. I only dabble though. And you?'

'I don't need a technique – things stick naturally,' said Zeta, which could have sounded arrogant but somehow didn't.

'And the second reason?' asked Chris.

'The course administrator's statement.'

That familiar feeling of dread re-entered the room and took a seat at the table next to Chris. She looked deeper into her tea mug in case the finger of suspicion was about to be directed at the mysterious Carmen Llama. She tried to say a neutral-sounding 'Uh-uh?' but as her mouth was full of tea she only succeeded in spitting half of it back into the mug.

'Mrs Douglas is a good administrator. Organised, precise—'

'Feathery,' Chris added unhelpfully.

'And she confirms that the mannequin had been moved from its usual position.'

'But that could have happened any time in the last month or so,' Chris said, sliding the biscuit tin across the table to Zeta. 'Because of the accident I haven't been a regular visitor.'

Zeta took a shortbread finger from the tin and used it to emphasise her point. 'Mrs Douglas visits the house every Wednesday out of term time to check security in case of squatters. She is positive that the mannequin was at the window then.'

'So Grayson—'

'Who?' asked Zeta quickly, her mind adding the name to her infallible mental notebook.

'Er, the mannequin was moved during the last forty-eight hours?'

'Precisely,' said Zeta, helping herself to another shortbread finger.

'But that proves nothing. Anyone could have moved him. Although it pains me to say it, Zeta, Sergeant Spurgeon's right, it's just some student high spirits.'

'Maybe… or maybe not.' Zeta took yet another shortbread finger from the tin. 'There are two things that don't fit that theory. One' – she thrust the shortbread in her right hand towards Chris's face – 'it's summer. No students.'

'There are bound to be a few around.'

'And two' – Zeta emphasised her point in biscuit form by jabbing her left hand forward – 'there were no signs of forced entry and only three people have keys to the forensics house. Mrs Douglas, who has her key, Dr Karamak—'

'Who is at a conference in Barcelona,' Chris blurted out.

Zeta looked surprised at this display of insider knowledge and nodded her agreement.

'And the head of department, Professor Jasper. I've left messages on Jasper's and Karamak's phones to give me a call, but I've heard nothing yet.'

Chris gathered up the biscuit tin and restored it to its rightful position in the kitchen cupboard before her reserves were further depleted. 'This all seems rather tenuous. Forget about it – Lord knows, I'm trying to.'

Zeta paused in thought for a while. 'I can't,' she said.

'Why not?' Chris's exasperation had crept into her voice. '"There's nothing to see here. Move along." Isn't that what your lot usually say?'

'My lot?' Zeta's eyes flared momentarily.

'Police. Case closed, according to Sergeant Spurgeon. And you're not here, officially. In fact, why are you here?'

'In case you can remember any more details. Anything – it doesn't matter how insignificant.'

'What's your real interest?' Chris asked.

Zeta merely shrugged in response.

Chris stood and a twinge in her hip made her grimace in pain. 'I made a statement. My humiliation is a matter of public record. Why should I add to it?'

Zeta stood up as well, picked up the mugs and placed them next to the sink. 'Sorry to have disturbed you, Ms Heron. You and Sergeant Spurgeon may well be right, it's probably something of nothing. Thanks for the tea and biscuits. I'll leave you to get dressed.'

Chris realised that she was still in her dressing gown and, in her rush, had put on odd slippers, a black moccasin on her right foot and a novelty Christmas reindeer on the left.

Zeta paused at the front door and handed Chris a business card. 'If there's anything you think of, please get in touch. There's just something that doesn't smell right and when I get a sniff, I'm like a dog with a bone. Or should that be Sabre with a bone?'

Zeta smiled broadly and Chris felt herself instinctively smiling in response, her outrage dissipating. She even gave Zeta a half-wave as she closed the door.

*

Two hours later, Chris was hard at work in her office, aka the kitchen table. She reckoned that another two hours of solid concentration would crack the first read-through of 'Relativity vs Presentism – The Battle for Supremacy', but it was turgid stuff. Academic papers were her least favourite work – impenetrable, self-congratulatory and barely literate. She checked a couple of definitions online and, before she knew it, had plunged down a YouTube wormhole in which various Americans fell into various swimming pools. Chris pondered whether these people had a camera continuously monitoring every moment of their waking days on the off-chance that they might do something catastrophically amusing. She slammed the lid of her laptop shut in self-loathing and switched on the kettle for her fifth mug of tea of the day.

Through the kitchen window the smell of burning charcoal wafted from next door's garden and the screams of overexcited children reminded Chris that it was a Saturday. That was the thing with being self-employed and working from home, there was no such thing as a weekend. On the downside, you missed out on that Friday afternoon high, the feeling of freedom and the need to rush to the pub, but in return you lost the sickening Sunday evening back-to-the-office-tomorrow anxiety. Work at the weekend and you could operate in a different time zone to the rest of the population.

She didn't dare to open her laptop again in case she got lured down the dual paths of domestic calamity and presentism (and she still hadn't figured out what the hell that was), so she went old-school, grabbed a pen and pad from the drawer and headed up a fresh page with:

Pledges for the Future
1. Explore new cycle routes

Despite having a network of beautiful routes on her doorstep, she tended to restrict herself to three or four regulars. She needed to expand her portfolio, she decided, and put her weird obsession with Grayson behind her.

2. Start a blog about new cycle routes

'I could get a helmet cam,' she said to Aitken, who wasn't remotely interested. 'Film each journey and post it online. After all, everyone loves a blog about someone else's hobby, don't they?'

She put a large question mark next to number 2.

Aitken yawned and headed for one of his many beds dotted around the house. 'Sorry I'm so boring,' said Chris. 'Not like your new best mate Zeta, eh?'

She was still puzzled by the police officer's impromptu and unofficial visit. It seemed reckless behaviour for such an apparently clever and ambitious young woman. But that wasn't her problem, Chris decided, and moved on to the next point on her list.

3. Start saying 'yes'

That could be the most positive change – embrace the opportunity, do those things she thought she'd hate because… well, you never knew…

As if by magic her phone pinged. It was a text from Next-Door Nick. *Having BBQ with friends. Join us? X*

Chris automatically typed in response: *Sorry, busy working, thanks for invite.* She was about to press 'send' when she remembered her last pledge. She erased her text and typed: *Thanks. Better get some clothes on then!* and pressed 'send'.

If she was going to make a habit of saying 'yes' she would have to have a long hard think about Chloe's Christmas invitation too. Being a normal, social human being was going to take so much effort.

Twelve

In Chris's opinion, Sundays were usually best fast-forwarded. It wasn't that they weren't enjoyable in their own way, it was just that they were rarely dramatic and generally indistinguishable.

She was still feeling a little delicate when she woke, the combination of daytime drinking, charcoal inhalation and over-excitable children having pushed her to the limit. On reflection, it had been a good afternoon with good people, but it did mean that the superpower battle between 'Relativity and Presentism' was still unresolved and unproofed. There was only one solution: a mug of tea and a double-bacon sandwich (tomato ketchup and English mustard, naturally) at her second-favourite cafe. Wavecrest Cafe might have been less than a hundred metres from her front door, but Chris could work there without the distraction of a needy tabby, and their broadband was more reliable. Also, she did not trust herself enough to have a whole packet of bacon in the house.

The academic paper remained pretty impenetrable, but after an hour and a half, three mugs of tea, two bacon sandwiches and a chocolate brownie, Chris reckoned she'd broken the back of it. As a treat she strolled down to the seafront, found a secluded spot on the less populated part of the beach, pulled up the copy of *Brighton Rock* on her laptop and spent a blissful couple of hours with her back to a groyne, shaded from the warm August sunshine, marvelling at Pinkie's precocious psychopathy.

Life was good, Chris decided. So good that she was happy to walk the long way home along the beach where the crowds of young families gathered. Of all the seasons, she preferred winter. Then, the beach was empty except for dog walkers and intrepid open-sea swimmers. Today there was a mass of day-trippers and long-weekenders, all being led at arm's length by a flimsy plastic pint glass of lukewarm lager or a flimsy cardboard carton of lukewarm coffee. Chris tried not to begrudge their presence. After all, they were just having fun and enjoying visiting the town that she was lucky enough to call her home all year round.

Feeling the sun on her face and having the rest of the day at her mercy filled Chris with a certain joie de vivre. She had something approaching a skip in her step and she smiled at complete strangers in a way that was, apparently, quite alarming. Opposite this part of the seafront was a graffiti-festooned concrete skate park. Chris stopped and watched the activity. Young children prowled the perimeter on scooters, in awe of their elders, who plunged and jumped and spun on skateboards and BMX bikes. She envied their fearlessness as they risked colliding at high speed with the unforgiving concrete walls. One teenager attempted a trick which caused him to part company with his skateboard and crash heavily to the ground. Chris looked away in anticipation of his injury, but he merely got up, dusted himself down and laughed in recognition of his youthful immortality.

As Chris turned to leave, a couple of frenzied scooter-pushers darted in front of her, causing her to wobble and her heart to leap. Technically, she should have been walking with a stick for added balance and security, but her vanity had made that decision for her. The object of the scooter-pushers' excitement was in the car park alongside the skate park. A yellow and blue ice cream van. Chris felt an instant surge of anxiety, but rather than 'Mr Softee', the livery depicted a medieval knight in armour alongside the name 'Sir Lickalot'. Chris mentally added 'Van Number 5 – Sir Lickalot' to her list.

The trauma nightmares were no longer such a regular occurrence, but the accident still loomed large. Nick was right, she realised; she had become obsessed. Perhaps desensitisation therapy was the answer, which, in this case, would require actually buying an ice cream from an ice cream van.

She joined the queue, which consisted of three hassled-looking men fulfilling their fatherly duty. The one in front of her was chanting his order to himself like a mantra so he didn't forget it before reaching the hatch. Chris had no problem with an orderly queue, in fact, as a Briton, she positively relished them. However, after five minutes she had only moved up from fourth place to third and, distressingly, was still at the back. This seemed distinctly unfair, as the Law of the Queue should surely have ensured that you were never the last person after you'd queued for more than two minutes. The wait did, on a positive note, give her more time to study the van.

It seemed to be the same size and shape as the one that had knocked her off her bike, but, to tell the truth, Chris couldn't tell one generic car model from another, let alone a multi-purpose commercial vehicle that could have been built anytime in the last thirty years. On one side of the service hatch there was a lively depiction of the helmeted Sir Lickalot and on the other side, rather confusingly, a dragon. No doubt the brave Sir Lickalot would use the ice cream he was brandishing in place of a lance to quench the fiery breath of his foe. The mixed imagery was further confused by a St George's flag that carried the boast 'The finest Italian Ice Cream and Gelato'. The artwork seemed fresh – newer than the van itself, which, no doubt, some ice cream van aficionados would have described as a classic.

'What can I get you, love?'

Chris was shaken from her musing by the realisation that she'd reached the front of the queue. She pretended to study the menu of ice cream varieties whilst checking out the owner of the voice. He was heavyset, could have been any age between forty and sixty-five, had a gold front tooth and smelt of stale tobacco.

'Just an ice cream, please. You know, the normal type.'

'One super-deluxe Whippy-Whip coming right up!'

He half turned to operate the ice cream maker and Chris

studied his arms. They were covered with tattoos that had faded into a mahogany suntan. She couldn't see his hands but wondered whether his knuckles were similarly tattooed, perhaps with 'C-H-O-C' on the right hand and 'I-C-E-S' on the left.

Ice Cream Van Man caught Chris staring and grinned. The sunlight reflected off his gold tooth and she looked away in embarrassment. And that was when she noticed his wing mirror, crudely held fast by gaffer tape. A new paint job and a broken wing mirror? The evidence seemed to fall into place. Chris had to know.

She returned Ice Cream Van Man's smile in what she hoped was a charming manner. 'So, have you been Sir Lickalot for long?'

'You what?' he said, putting a snow-white ice cream cone in a holder on the counter.

'Your name – on the van. Have you always been Sir Lickalot?'

'Well, me mates call me Kevin, but if you want me to be Sir Lickalot, I'll see what I can do, eh? Sprinkles?'

'No, my name is… Oh.' Just in time, Chris realised that Kevin was referring to a jar containing assorted e-numbers that he was offering to cascade over her super-deluxe Whippy-Whip. 'No, thanks.'

'Sauce?' Kevin asked provocatively, holding a plastic squeezy bottle. Chris shook her head. He leant closer. 'Tell you what, love, I should be done 'ere by eight. Why don't you come back then and I'll show you my Magnum?'

Chris was sorely tempted to tell Kevin that she doubted he was packing anything more impressive than a Mini Milk, but she pursued her line of inquiry. 'What happened to your wing mirror, Kevin?'

'Oh, some kids ripped it off. Pissed off that I don't stock poppers or cider. What's with all the questions? That's £2.50. Please.'

Chris swiped her card against the reader. 'Only asking, Kevin. Or should I call you… Mr Softee?'

'Listen, love, come back at eight and you can call me whatever you like, but for now I've a queue building up.'

Chris went for broke. 'Play me your chime.'

'My chime?'

'Play me your chime and I'll go.'

A crowd of people had gathered round the van, part queue, part onlookers. Chris sensed a few camera phones pointed in her direction.

A male voice behind her shouted, 'Get a move on, will you? If I don't get back to the kids with two Whippy-Whips, an exotic Solero and a Strawberry Split, my missus will have my balls on toast!'

Kevin was no longer smiling. 'I've met your sort before. Now clear off or I'll call them police over.'

Chris stood her ground. 'Fair enough. Play the chime just once. But if it's "Greensleeves", then I think the police will be interested. Very interested.'

The crowd were getting more animated. Someone tried to start up a chorus of 'Come on Karen' to the tune of 'Come on Eileen', but this was quickly subsumed by the collective chant of 'Play the chime'.

'Sod the chime, just give me a Strawberry Split, two double Whippy-Whips and an exotic Solero!'

The man behind Chris pushed her to one side and she staggered to her left, overbalancing. She reached out, needing to grab onto something to keep her upright, and seized hold of the wing mirror, which detached in her hand. She looked down at the mirror, which neatly reflected her shocked expression.

'Officer! Officer!' Kevin squealed. 'She's ripped off me bleedin' mirror. She's trying to wreck Sir Lickalot.'

'Gosh,' Chris stammered, 'really sorry, complete accident... it just...'

'She's a bloody hooligan!' Kevin insisted.

'It's just held on with sticky tape. I didn't mean to...'

Chris felt a hand on her shoulder.

'I am arresting you on suspicion of causing criminal damage. You do not have to say anything—'

She swivelled round to face the arresting officer, SC Zeta Jama.

The next few minutes passed in a surreal daze. PC Atherton ambled over from where he had been chatting up two bikini-clad girls to assist his colleague in making the arrest. Chris was escorted to a police car while the crowd's response – a mixture of cheers, boos, laughter and applause – swirled around her head. From the rear seat of the police car, she looked back at Sir Lickalot. Kevin gave a cheery wave and her departure was accompanied by the van's chime. *Ding, ding-ding, dah-ding...* Not 'Greensleeves' but 'Home on the Range'. Bugger.

Well, Chris had after all resolved to make her life more interesting and to not drift towards old age on a diet of soap operas and easy listening. Now she'd gone and done it. 'Getting arrested' might not have been one of the items on her bucket list, but it was an impressive departure from her life thus far. Perhaps, she concluded, she should just sit back and absorb the experience.

Within ten minutes the squad car had pulled up at the police station Chris had visited just two days previously. This time, she was fast-tracked through the pods and PC Thackery put down his Stephen King novel just long enough to book her in.

A new police constable appeared, a jovial-looking man in his late fifties.

'Got a present for me, Zeta?' he asked.

'Thanks, Barry. Can I introduce Chris? She's paying us a short visit. Make her comfortable, will you?' Zeta replied.

'Will do. The penthouse suite has just become available. Would you like to come this way, please?' And Barry escorted Chris to the second in a line of three cells. As he shut the door, he gave her a reassuring wink. 'I'll bring you some tea and biscuits.'

Chris suspected that this was a level of service not afforded to the majority of the cell block's residents.

*

After four hours in the cell, the novelty had worn thin. There were phases, just as when dealing with grief, Chris decided, and she'd now reached the Fifth Stage of Incarceration, namely grim acceptance. The first hour had been OK. She'd toured the cell, reading the messages left by a previous inmate. She'd been divested of her shoes, phone, laptop and dignity when she arrived so preferred not to imagine how someone had managed to smuggle in a felt-tip pen.

Her predecessor's graffito read 'Im inocent'. Chris was grateful that she didn't have a pen as the urge to correct the spelling and punctuation – a deep-seated compulsion – would have been irresistible. She imagined the life stories of previous cell-dwellers and their impressive list of felonies. She even attempted a press-up, as seen in countless prison movies, until she remembered that she was still running in her new hip. The highlight of her stay was the arrival of a cup of tea/Bovril accompanied by a couple of custard creams, apparently from Barry's personal stash.

'Will I be here much longer?' Chris asked him. 'I've got a demanding cat that needs feeding.'

'PC Atherton wants to make you sweat a while,' Barry replied. 'He reckons he was on a promise with those girls until you picked a fight with Sir Lickalot. Hope it's OK, but I've taken the liberty of putting your phone on charge. It was looking low.'

Barry's small touches of human kindness restored Chris's rapidly descending spirits.

Deprived of a watch, a phone or any form of external stimuli, time took on a different dimension. Chris paced the cell, mentally calculating its dimensions in square metres and then its volume before that act of mental arithmetic proved to be beyond her mathematical capabilities. She even considered rattling her cup across the cell bars to attract attention, but her cell had no bars and her cup was disposable and plastic. In fact, it was to be a further three mind- and buttock-numbing hours before a key turned in the lock, heralding her release.

The interview suite differed from the room she had visited two days ago by virtue of being slightly smarter, having no posters on the walls and there being a voice recorder on the table. Sitting at the far side of the table was PC Atherton and her new-found nemesis, Sgt Spurgeon. Zeta again took a chair on the far side of the room.

'Don't I get a phone call?' Chris asked.

'Sure. Be my guest.' The sergeant took a phone out of his pocket and slid it across the table. 'Who are you going to call?'

He had a point – who would she call? She didn't have a solicitor – well, except for Ripp and Savage, and, whilst they were fearsome divorce lawyers, this wasn't their bag. Simon? Certainly not. And, despite her pledge that she would never conceal things from her daughter again, this was one exception to that rule. Which left Aitken. He was a clever moggy but hadn't quite figured out how to use the phone – yet. Besides, she had a sneaky suspicion that Aitken's loyalty only extended as far as a full food bowl and a comfy duvet.

Sgt Spurgeon interrupted her mental ranking. 'We're not charging you, Ms Heron – assuming you'll accept a police caution – so it'd be something of a wasted call.'

Chris should have just nodded meekly, but her wounded pride had other ideas. 'I should hope not. Surely it's Kevin Whatsisname, aka Mr Softee, that you should be charging – for dangerous driving and fleeing the scene of an accident.'

'You should count yourself fortunate that Mr Kevin Allsop has agreed not to press charges.'

'He's not Mr Softee, Ms Heron,' added Zeta from the far side of the room.

'He really is Sir Lickalot,' piped up PC Atherton.

'Indeed,' continued Sgt Spurgeon. 'Mr Allsop has been trading under licence as Sir Lickalot, purveyor of ice creams and chilled refreshments to the good people of Cliffstaple, for the past fifteen years. He is a citizen of good standing and the provider of an essential service to the community.'

Chris was on the verge of challenging the description of ice cream selling as an essential community service but tried instead to focus on the matter at hand. 'But the wing mirror. That's evidence.'

'Mr Allsop lodged a report of criminal damage five weeks ago.

Alas, the perpetrators have yet to be apprehended. Unfortunately, youth crime is on the rise in the area, but it's difficult to catch the little bas… rapscallions.'

Chris accepted defeat. 'I see. Does that mean I am free to go?'

Before she could stand, the door swung open with a bang and a man strode in. Chris's immediate impression was of his seniority as Spurgeon and Atherton instinctively bowed their heads. The new arrival was tall, slim and (she hated herself for thinking this) disarmingly good-looking. He was wearing an immaculately tailored blue suit, and a flash of the lining suggested it was a Paul Smith design – not cheap.

He gave Chris a broad smile, displaying near-perfect teeth, and offered his hand. 'Ms Heron? I'm delighted to finally meet you. I'm Detective Inspector Dunn.'

'Detective Inspector?' Chris was somewhat stunned. 'Why is a detective inspector interested in little ole me?'

DI Dunn laughed charmingly, those near-perfect teeth glinting in the fluorescent light. 'Because you're practically a celebrity, Ms Heron. I wanted to meet the person who has been taking up so much of our already over-stretched resources.'

'Yeah, sorry about that – bit of a misunderstanding.'

'Indeed. I'd appreciate it if in future you'd leave these matters in the hands of my skilled colleagues in Road Traffic Division and refrain from conducting a one-woman vigilante mission. After all, this is north Kent, not the Bronx, eh?'

This provoked an obsequious chortle from Sgt Spurgeon and an equally obsequious high-pitched titter from PC Atherton.

'I'll remember that,' Chris said, anxiously eyeing the exit door.

'Very good,' DI Dunn said cheerily.

As Chris stood, he vigorously shook her hand and, in doing so, pulled her closer to him. He lowered his voice. 'I advise you to change your cycling route too. I wouldn't want to hear you've been troubling those good folks at the university again.' And with that he breezed out of the room.

All that was left was the return of Chris's possessions, then she was escorted, via the pod, back out of the door of North Kent Police Station.

It was getting dark and she felt shattered, physically and emotionally. At that moment a bus trundled along, heading in the right direction. Her favourite seat was available – top deck, front right, directly above the driver – so perhaps all was well in the world after all.

She looked at her phone, resplendent with its fully charged battery – four texts, five missed calls. She glanced at the oldest of the texts. It was from Next-Door Nick and simply said: *You OK, need any help? Nick x* She assumed he was referring to her likely hangover as a result of the barbecue. There were two missed calls from Simon, but she was not going to give him the benefit of responding. She suspected he'd heard about Chloe's Christmas invitation and was digging for more information.

The glow of the phone screen was giving her a headache – there was nothing that couldn't wait until she got back home and had a large glass of wine in front of her. She turned her phone off, put it back in her pocket and closed her eyes. A group of teenagers behind her were chatting and laughing and playing music on their phones. Chris fancied she could hear the tinny strains of 'Home on the Range', but that had to be her imagination running riot on what had turned out to be A Long Day's Journey Into Night.

She must have briefly drifted off to sleep, for when she opened her eyes, the bus was pulling away from her home stop on the high street. This only added another couple of hundred metres to her journey home but it significantly added to her current feeling of self-loathing. As she reached her front door she paused, key in hand. There was a light visible through the stained-glass panelling.

Chris was sure that she hadn't left a light on that morning. It had been a brilliantly sunny day, and 'fitting timer switches' was languishing at number 37 on that 'Essential Home Improvements' list. She routinely cursed characters in films who blundered into houses despite broken locks and disabled lighting and then were surprised by a killer clown hiding behind the sofa. She weighed up the risk of a lurking homicidal circus performer versus the embarrassment of seeking help, and let herself in.

There were two hushed voices coming from her kitchen, so she gently placed her bag and laptop on the side table, picked up a now unused crutch from the umbrella stand by the front door and advanced stealthily along the hallway. She launched herself through the kitchen doorway with a battle cry, 'Banzai!', spinning the crutch above her head like a set of nunchucks, to find Simon and Next-Door Nick sitting at her kitchen table, polishing off the last of her shortbread fingers.

'Ah, you're back,' said Simon, showing keen powers of observation.

'What the fricking-frick are you two doing here?' ('Frick' had been Chris's swear-word of choice ever since she'd been shamed by a seven-year-old Chloe telling her teacher that 'Mum uses the F-word all the time.')

'I popped round to feed Aitken,' said Next-Door Nick, looking nervously at the raised crutch, 'and I bumped into Simon outside, so we thought we'd wait for you together. Didn't you get my text?'

Chris lowered the crutch slowly. 'I don't remember asking you to feed my cat today, Nick.'

'Not explicitly, Chris. No, you didn't. But I thought you'd be late and I couldn't get hold of you on the phone and...'

'I've been... busy. Haven't had the chance to catch up with admin. OK, you're excused, Nick, but this doesn't explain *your* presence, Simon.'

Nick took the opportunity to make a rapid escape. Chris felt guilty as she knew he meant well, but she was just not in the mood for conversation tonight. A disturbing thought crossed her mind.

'Shit! It's not Chloe is it, Simon? Is Chloe all right?'

'Chloe's fine. Chloe's rational. Chloe's sensible. Chloe's sane. I'm afraid I can't say the same for her mother.'

'What do you mean?'

Simon slowly and methodically took a laptop out of the bag at his side, opened the lid, pressed a few keys and turned the screen to face her. 'You're famous,' he said with a sad smile.

On the screen was a confusing image of a boisterous crowd. As the camera operator got the hang of the zoom function, the image closed in on a furious-looking woman next to an ice cream van. As the crowd chanted 'Play the chime!', the woman lurched and ripped off the van's wing mirror. The crowd cheered and the film ended.

Chris slammed the laptop lid shut.

'But how?'

'Local news. It was the funny bit at the end of *North Kent Today*, just after a waterskiing Weimaraner.'

Chris embraced denial. 'Yeah, well, local news. Nobody watches local news. It'll be forgotten by tomorrow.'

'Social media are calling you "Cornetto Karen".'

'Who's Karen?'

'God, Chris! You really are a Neanderthal when it comes to social media, aren't you? It's an insult – for a woman who's unduly stroppy.'

'I see. It's a sort of joke, is it?'

'You've gone viral, you're trending, you've even become a meme.'

It took a while for this to filter through to Chris's brain. She didn't really do social media – well, just Facebook, and that was only to check that ex-schoolfriends and colleagues had an even emptier life than she did.

'What do you mean, Simon – a meme?'

Simon reopened the laptop, clicked his mouse button and turned the screen back to face her. It was a crude adaptation of Edvard Munch's masterpiece but with Chris's face, in contorted mouth-gaping pose, superimposed on the main figure's head. A speech bubble read 'Play the chime!' The artwork had been retitled *The (Ice) Scream*.

Chris closed the laptop again and handed it back to Simon, shrugging in an unconvincing manner. 'So? I wasn't charged, no harm done. You know what people are like nowadays – no attention span. They'll have already moved on to the next shiny thing.'

'I hope you're right, Chris,' said Simon, rising and putting the laptop back in his man-bag. 'I wouldn't want this to damage your reputation.'

'Reputation?' Chris snorted. 'I'm a sixty-year-old divorced woman with a crumbling semi-detached house, a titanium hip and a narcissistic cat. What makes you think I've got a reputation to damage?'

Having shooed Simon out of the house, out of *her* house, Chris parked herself on the sofa with Aitken on her chest, a bottle of white Rioja by her left hand and some brain-dead reality programme on the TV. At times like this, it was better not to think. Having an interesting life was not all that it was cracked up to be.

Thirteen

Chris never set an alarm. Her bladder usually woke her at 07:30 sharp, and in the summer months the dawn sunlight sneaking through the curtains prompted Aitken to triple-jump onto her prone body and paw at her face a good half-hour earlier. Today was different. Her sleep was so deep, it overrode both her bladder and a tabby hungry for his breakfast. She was only woken by the urgent ringing of her phone.

Chris prised one eye open. It was a video call from Chloe and she couldn't ignore that.

'Still in bed, Mum? I thought it'd be nine o'clock there or have I got my time difference muddled up again?'

'Nine? Oh yes, shit, overslept.'

'That's not like you.'

'Morning after the night before, I guess.'

'Just the night before? I'm worried about you.'

'Worried? No, I'm perfectly fine. Keeping busy, that's all.'

'Keeping busy? That's good to hear, Mum, or should I call you "Cornetto Karen"?'

There was a pause in the conversation – either a dramatic pause or just a chance for sleep-infused Chris to recompute.

'He told you? The slimy bastard.'

'Who?'

'Who do you think? Your father. Bet he couldn't wait to tell you about your wayward mother's latest misadventure.'

'Dad's said nothing. Perhaps he respects you more than you give him credit.'

'It was just a misunderstanding. Just a silly local story. It's all put to bed now.'

'No such thing as a local story. It's all about the algorithms nowadays – it came up on my newsfeed.'

'In Australia?'

'Stupid news travels fast, I guess.'

Chris hadn't even considered that information was no longer containable. Society had changed so drastically since she was Chloe's age. Time passed in the blink of an eye, but the world had shifted; the old, comfortable ways had gone.

'Sorry, Chlo. It's all put to bed now – honestly. Embarrassing, I suppose, but that's the extent of it.'

'There's a pattern though.'

'What do you mean?'

'Secret accidents, naked video calls – no, it's not funny, Dan – and now criminal behaviour. I know we joke, Mum, but that's not normal, is it? I'm worried it's getting out of control.'

'Getting out of control? It's getting interesting! Would you rather I spent my days knitting dog blankets, watching property porn on TV and complaining about the price of a farmhouse loaf in the Co-op?'

'You need a break, Mum. Come over early to Oz if you want. I'll take some unpaid leave. You need to get out of there, get a fresh perspective.'

'You'll be asking me to emigrate next, Chlo.'

'It's a thought, Mum.'

It was a thought, maybe, but not a serious one. Chris couldn't leave her home. No way. It was her house, her town, her country, even, for all its hair-tearing annoyingness. She was surprisingly patriotic when push came to shove. It was her, it was who she was, and at times it was all she had.

She'd allowed herself to get sidetracked. She needed to get back to the plan – to work on her fitness, concentrate on her business and make the most of every opportunity. She recalled Physio Melanie's fitness programme. 'Cycling's good,' she'd said, 'but swimming's better.'

A frugal breakfast, then Chris headed to Cliffstaple Municipal Swimming Pool. Monday mornings were quiet at the pool, even during the school holidays, so she felt assured of a bit more privacy, away from gawping and inquisitive eyes. Also, entry was half price for the over-sixties and, though Chris felt like a fraud as she was still bringing in a decent income, she was determined to take any advantage that ageing offered.

She assessed her scar in the changing room's full-length mirror. It was fading slightly, but she was still self-conscious about displaying it in public. Perhaps, given time, it would become a badge of honour, a symbol of a battle won. She'd chosen her most utilitarian swimsuit – an all-in-one black sports number with, ironically, a red go-faster stripe down the side. When it came to swimming, Chris rated herself as reassuringly slow. With her strange hybrid of breaststroke and doggy-paddle, she could just about do two lengths as long as she finished in the shallow end so she could cheat and put her feet on the pool floor.

Of course, this pool was nothing like the ones of her youth, where she'd tried and failed to learn to swim properly. Here the lanes were segregated and the direction of swim strictly determined. An attendant prowled the edge on the lookout for any deviance from the rules, ready to dive in to rescue anyone overcome by chlorine fumes. A sign indicated that no running, diving, bombing or ball sports were allowed, let alone any petting. Sadly, Chris had few opportunities for petting, heavy, waterlogged or otherwise.

She had managed five lengths, not consecutively of course, when she became aware of another swimmer in the adjacent lane carving through the water at great speed. Her rival passed in a blur, but Chris could see she was lithe and athletic and, from the dexterity of her tumble-turn, a proper swimmer. She must have covered twenty lengths to Chris's last two. As Chris clung to the side in the shallow end to catch her breath, her fellow swimmer drew up in the adjacent lane, levered herself up onto the side, her shoulder muscles rippling as she did so, and removed her cap and googles.

'Chris! Fancy seeing you here,' said Zeta.

Chris tried to follow suit and lever herself up but quickly realised that she didn't have the upper-body strength and instead had to conduct the waddle of shame to the pool ladder.

'What are you going to arrest me for this time? Careless swimming?'

'Certainly not for speeding,' Zeta retorted, smiling.

Chris didn't return her smile. 'Doesn't this constitute police harassment or are you going to pretend that this is just an amazing coincidence?'

'For a start, I'm off duty, and secondly, I swim here whenever I get the chance. It's a coincidence we're in adjacent lanes this morning, but not a remarkable one.'

'I don't remember seeing you here before and you're pretty distinctive – you're ten times as quick as the rest of the Monday morning crew.'

Zeta stood, displaying an annoyingly perfect body, broad shoulders, proportionate breasts and a washboard stomach. She wandered over to a bench, picked up a towel and draped it over her shoulders. 'Frequency illusion,' she said.

'Frequency illusion?'

'When something becomes significant to you, you start to take notice of it. For example, when we decide we like an actor, they suddenly seem to crop up in everything we watch. Very problematic when it comes to eyewitness statements.'

'Oh great,' said Chris, walking past her towards the changing rooms, 'so you're a shrink as well as a cop. Are you going to section me as well?'

Zeta followed. 'I'm only a special, a voluntary police officer. Look, I didn't want to arrest you, but it was either me or PC Atherton and I knew I could… um… facilitate a better outcome.'

By this time the two women had reached the empty changing

room. Chris dragged her stuff from the locker but now had to choose whether to change in front of Zeta or bashfully slope off to one of the changing booths. Zeta apparently faced no such problem and had stripped naked to vigorously towel herself dry. Embarrassed, Chris looked away, but not before noting that, out of swimsuit, Zeta's body looked even more formidable. She couldn't possibly display her cellulited, scarred nakedness in front of such a Venus. Using a towel to conceal her modesty whilst putting her knickers on was a task which was tricky before the accident but was damned near impossible now. Zeta noted Chris's struggle so she turned her back and faced the wall.

'Can I buy you lunch?' Zeta asked when Chris was fastening her multi-pocketed cycling shorts.

Chris bent to try to put on her left trainer and nearly tumbled into the lockers in the process. 'Lunch?'

Zeta laughed. 'Whoops! That sounded like a chat-up line, didn't it? I mean, to say sorry and explain myself.'

'There's nothing to explain. I committed a crime and you arrested me. You were doing your job, even if it was in a voluntary capacity. Let's forget about it. Believe me, *I'm* trying to.'

'I did you a favour, you know,' said Zeta, now fully dressed in T-shirt and jeans.

'A favour? I spent four hours locked in a cell, I'm trending in Melbourne and my daughter thinks I'm having a breakdown. In future, can you keep your favours to yourself?'

'I stopped him from pressing charges. Mr Kevin Allsop, aka Sir Lickalot, wanted us to throw the book at you.'

'Really? And pray tell, how did you manage to get him to be so benevolent? Did you order a lifetime's supply of Whippy-Whips?'

'Kevin's ex-forces. Ex-special forces, if you believe him.'

'And you don't?'

'If you're proper special forces, you don't tell everyone. The ones that do are just bullshitters. So I played on that. Told him you were suffering from post-traumatic stress disorder on account of your accident. Now Kevin sees you as a kindred spirit – a casualty of war.'

'Thanks, I think,' said Chris, wondering whether a diagnosis of PTSD would get her an additional discount at the municipal pool. 'You still owe me, though, so I'll accept your offer of lunch. There's that new open-air place opposite the harbour. We can grab a quick bite to eat there.'

Chris's acceptance of Zeta's offer was twenty per cent down to having being won over by her charm and seventy per cent due to a growling hunger. That breakfast had been way too frugal. The outstanding ten per cent could be allocated to sheer curiosity.

They found a quiet table at the back of Harbourside Eats. The name of the place annoyed Chris, but it was convenient and now was not the time to dwell on petty principles about restaurant names. Another plus was that the breeze off the sea cut through the increasing humidity of the day.

'These are tourist prices,' said Chris, looking at the menu. 'Are you sure you can afford this?'

'I do have a job – good money too. I'm not a pretend police officer full-time,' said Zeta, scanning the menu in under three seconds.

Chris's tepid vegetarianism took another beating and she ordered the Dirty Burger (medium rare) as a reward for having expended at least a hundred and fifty calories during that morning's swim. Zeta ordered a superfood salad, virtue-signalling with food, Chris suspected. Zeta was so puritanical that she didn't even try to steal any of Chris's chips.

The 'quick bite' ended up taking nearly two hours. Chris had lots of questions and Zeta proved to be a cooperative interviewee. In real life (when she was not arresting innocent members of the public), Zeta was a techie advising small businesses on website builds and search engine optimisation, whatever that was. Chris recalled that her professional-looking business card read 'Zeta Jama – Online Marketing Solutions'.

'I specialise in law firms,' said Zeta, toying with some sort of sprout that appeared to have no gastronomic quality whatsoever and could easily have been dropped onto her plate by a passing seagull.

'Why law firms?' asked Chris, using her index finger to mop up a globule of barbecue sauce spillage from her lap.

'They're very old-fashioned. Still deal with paper documents and real signatures – the digital world's a mystery to them. And they're rich, so I can price-gouge them.'

'Don't they just pass on those costs to their clients – the little people?'

'Hadn't thought of that,' said Zeta, chasing a cherry tomato around her bowl. 'I'm going to have to stop fraternising with you, Chris. I don't need any more ethical dilemmas.'

'You can't separate your work from your social conscience,' said Chris.

They small-talked for half an hour about local restaurants, local characters and the Cliffstaple 'vibe'. Then Chris felt the time was ripe for her killer question.

'So, you're a special, a voluntary police officer. All that arresting stuff, and abuse, and putting up with crap from Spurgeon and Atherton is for no money, right?'

'Right.'

'Why do it?'

'To make a difference. To learn new skills and meet interesting people. To serve my community.'

'Bollocks! If you don't start telling me the truth, I'll force-feed you this rosemary-infused French-fry and it'll go straight to your arse.'

Zeta leant back and gave Chris that disarming smile. 'It's a bit of a cliché.'

'I've got time. Your only competition is a seriously dull academic paper with a flexible deadline.'

'I come from a long line of police officers – my father, my uncle and apparently their father too. That's the problem with family tradition – you're proud of it, but it can feel like an obligation.'

'Is he still in the force?'

'Oh, this was back in Somalia. I came here with my mum when I was two.'

'Tradition's a bugger, isn't it? Zeta, I'm sure your dad's proud of you, whatever you do.'

Zeta gave a half-nod and Chris thought she detected a slight watery sheen to her eyes, but Zeta recovered quickly.

'So that's why you want to join the police? And being a special is just a stepping stone?'

'Yes and no. It'd be a drop in income compared to what I'm currently raking in, but there is that matter of family pride. You're right, tradition is a killer. To tell you the truth, I'm still fifty-fifty in my head about applying.'

'You're certainly good enough. The way you swooped in and nabbed that ice cream van terrorist was impressive. I'd have thought North Kent Constabulary would be eager to recruit you, particularly considering the standard of their current officers.'

'But that's it. They *are*. Or at least DI Dunn is – he's always urging me to put in my application.'

Chris finished her last chip and immediately regretted her lack of self-control on the food front. 'What's stopping you then? Sounds like you're a shoo-in.'

Zeta pushed her plate away and took a long pause. 'And that's the problem.'

'I don't follow you.'

'I'm an immigrant.'

'So you said.'

'I'm black.'

'I have noticed.'

'I'm female.'

'That too.' The image of Zeta's lithe, naked body briefly flitted into Chris's mind.

'And I'm gay.'

Chris tried to delete her mental image of Zeta's lithe, naked body. Her life was chaotic enough without adding a belated change of sexual orientation to her in-tray of issues. 'Um, congratulations. But if DI Dunn's chasing you to apply, then these aren't really barriers, are they?'

Zeta paused again, as if preparing a mental run-up. 'I want to be sure that if I'm recruited, if I'm successful in my career, it's purely because of my ability, not because I fill some sort of quota – Dunn's politically correct tick-box.'

'You don't want to be seen as a PC PC?' said Chris mischievously.

Zeta grinned genuinely, the corners of her eyes crinkling in response. 'PC PC? That's brilliant. I'm gonna use that. I guess if I had a disability too, I'd have the full set.'

'I've got a titanium hip I can lend you.'

'Thanks, Chris, but I'll pass on that one – for the time being at least. Wouldn't want to give the likely lads at the station more ammo.'

Chris waved at the waiter and ordered a double espresso for her and a green tea for Zeta. 'Are there any issues at the station?'

Zeta lowered her voice as though she suspected the elderly couple at the next table ploughing their way through fish, chips and mushy peas were actually undercover informants. 'No, but that's part of it. I expect my fair share of banter and teasing, but everyone at the station's so damned nice and… well, careful. I walk into the office and it's like the conversation suddenly changes. My colleagues pause for that extra second before they say anything, as though they're terrified of getting it wrong, of inadvertently causing offence.'

'Causing offence doesn't seem to bother Sergeant Spurgeon, "SPC Jah-mah".'

'Ah, you spotted that. I think his deliberate mispronouncing of my name is just a pathetic power play.' Zeta leant back to allow the waiter to place her tea in front of her. 'It's sad, but I'm not sure it's a symptom of anything worse. As a special, I'm already a second-class citizen in their eyes.'

'So that's how you prove that you're worthy of your colleagues' unconditional respect – by bumping up your arrest-rate stats?'

'I need a case. A high-profile one so that if I join up there won't be any whispers about quota-filling. Everyone will know that I've earned it one hundred per cent.'

'Best of luck with that round here. Someone parks on a double-yellow line or gets overcharged for a pint of whelks and it's headlines in the *Cliffstaple Gazette and Shopper*. You need to stick to a bigger place like Becketon if you want the spree killings and gun-running that'll make your name. Well, rather you than me.' Chris attracted the waiter's attention and made the international sign of the bill.

'Oh, I don't know about that. The way you've been interrogating me for the last hour suggests you missed your vocation in life,' Zeta said.

'Nah, happy with my proofreading. Flexible hours, varied work and the only abusive drunk I have to deal with is me when I've been at the vodka!' The waiter arrived with the bill and Chris slapped her card wallet on the table. 'I'll pay for my share. That Dirty Burger wasn't cheap.'

'No, I'm paying – it was my invitation.' Zeta waved her phone at the payment terminal. 'Besides, you're forgetting the Mystery of the Forensics House – cases don't come much more intriguing than that!'

'I am forgetting the forensics house. I have already purged it from my memory and I suggest you do the same.'

'I'm going to take one last look tomorrow. See if there's anything that Spurgeon and Atherton missed.'

'Off duty?'

'I'll call it thoroughness. I'm so keen to make sure that all procedures are fully documented. Resources in the force are so stretched, they're grateful for any additional help, particularly if it's unpaid.'

'Why the rush?' Chris asked. 'Just wait till you're back on duty.'

'Mrs Douglas goes in every Wednesday. I have to check out the scene before she contaminates it.'

Chris gulped down the last of what was, to the credit of Harbourside Eats, a decent double espresso. 'You're mad, Zeta. Obsessed. Thank you for lunch, I'd better be heading back to the comparative sanity of Homeworking Land.'

As Chris rose from the table, Zeta placed a restraining hand on her arm. 'Come with me, Chris. Tomorrow at ten. I'll call Mrs Douglas to get the key.'

'I've told you, I'm over it, no longer interested. Me and…' Chris nearly said, 'Me and Grayson are finished,' but stopped herself just in time. 'Anyway, I'm busy tomorrow.'

Zeta took a new ten-pound note out of her backpack and pinned it to the table with her empty teacup. 'That's a shame. I need your eyes.'

'A super-sleuth, ambitious wannabe police officer like you needs the help of a self-employed proofreader?' Chris retorted, letting some tetchiness surface. 'Is that what all this buddy-buddy stuff was really about?'

'You're familiar with the scene. You might be able to tell if something's out of place. After all, you did spot that the dummy had been moved.'

'Anyway, I've been warned off.'

'Warned off? By who?'

Chris realised that DI Dunn's sotto voce must have been very sotto.

'DI Dunn. He told me to steer clear of the uni, and as a newly reformed ex-con, I can recognise a veiled threat when I hear one.'

Zeta released her grip on Chris's arm. 'That's strange. I thought him turning up at the end of your interview was rather OTT.'

Chris stood and flung her backpack over her shoulder, causing the loose strap to swipe her painfully across the eye. 'So if you're serious about a career with North Kent Constabulary, I suggest you do the same. Thanks again for lunch, Zeta. Maybe our paths will coincidentally cross again sometime.' And she left the restaurant with a determined stride, which in reality was probably more of a flounce.

*

Chris threw herself into her work that afternoon. She admired Zeta's determination to negotiate the greasy pole of career progression but couldn't shake the feeling that she was being used in some way. Perhaps, in life, she was just collateral damage. Ms Expendable. At least Aitken loved her – as far as she could tell.

In terms of output, self-loathing was a productive frame of mind. Chris finished and invoiced 'Relativity and Presentism', hoping that the subject would never cross the threshold of her in-box again. She sent out half a dozen emails to potential clients, tidied up her online business profile and tentatively opened an email from the University of North Kent. Ironically, they were looking for someone to proofread a couple of their prospectuses in time for the new term. It seemed a more interesting project than most, so Chris quickly dashed out a quote and attached her Terms and Conditions – it was a line of business that could provide a lucrative and regular income.

At exactly half past six there was a sequence of ring-knock-ring at the front door which Chris recognised as the call-sign of her ex-husband. Although she wasn't in the mood for his brand of guilt-tripping, if she didn't answer the door he'd probably report her as a missing person. He was scribbling a note and preparing to post it through the letterbox when Chris swung the door open.

'What do you want, Simon?'

'Lovely to see you, Simon. So thoughtful of you to call round. Do come in and I'll pop the kettle on,' he mimicked patronisingly, and took half a step towards the doorway.

'Hold it right there, buster! Where do you think you're going?'

'Umm, inside? Inside the house?'

'Inside *my* house? And have you steal more of my shortbread fingers and undrinkable coffee? Not a chance. State your business and bugger off.'

'I just want a chat. I called round this morning, but you were out.'

'I'd gone swimming. You should try it sometime; work off that beer gut you're developing.'

'I don't do swimming, not any more. You should know that, Chris. Ever since… well, you know.'

In the early years of their marriage, Simon had been a keen visitor to Cliffstaple Municipal Pool and it used to give Chris a couple of hours of blessed peace to send him off, trunks and towel in hand, whilst she stayed behind and looked after Chloe. Then one time, when she was feeling either vindictive or mischievous, she used a black marker pen to block out the first letter of his Speedo swimming trunks. Simon had never fully forgiven her.

'Do you really want me to talk here, on the doorstep, where the entire neighbourhood can overhear our private business?' Simon continued.

'Don't mind me,' said Next-Door Nick from the other side of the low wall that separated their front paths. 'I love a bit of gossip.'

Chris ushered Simon in, sat him at the kitchen table and plonked a novelty mouse-shaped egg-timer in front of him. She set the timer to five minutes. 'Go!'

'Have you made a decision, Chris, about going to Chloe's for Christmas?'

'How do you know about that?'

'Chloe tells me everything. We have a father–daughter relationship which is founded on trust, honesty and mutual respect.'

Chris detected the personal slight intended.

'I haven't decided. Are you and Whatshername going, then?' Chris hadn't even considered that Chloe might have extended the invitation to her father.

'Whatshername is called Jan. We've been together for twenty-eight years. That's twenty-eight years of reading her signature on every Christmas card we send.'

Chris had nothing against Simon's wife, but she had nothing for her either. Jan was the kind of woman who called her female friends 'hon', and referred to 'sleeps till Christmas' and 'going on holibobs'. Chris had never seen inside Jan and Simon's house, but she was certain that they'd have wooden letters spelling 'H-O-M-E' on their mantelpiece and 'L-O-V-E' in the master bedroom.

'Ah yes, Jan, that's it. Is she well?'

Simon nodded.

'And the rest of the brood?' Chris was trying to filibuster Simon and use up all the remaining minutes with inane small talk.

Simon sighed deeply. 'We're all fine, and, no, we're not going to Chloe's for Christmas. Jan's arranging a big family gathering for her side of the family and the kids. She reckons there'll be about sixteen of us this year. We may need two turkeys!'

'That sounds lovely,' said Chris, visibly shuddering. 'Two minutes remaining.'

'You should accept Chloe's invitation. Phone her today, start making preparations, be sensible. All this stuff you've been getting into lately, it's not appropriate for a woman of your age. You're not a teenager anymore, Chris. You know what my Jan says about you?'

'I'm sure you're about to tell me.'

'That you're going through a midlife crisis and if you just slow down and lead a quieter life, you'll be much happier and less angry with everything. And you know what? She's right, so I—'

'Time's up!' Chris shouted and pulled Simon from his chair.

'But the mouse hasn't... um... dinged.'

Chris adjusted the timer so it hit zero. 'It has now. Good evening. Don't come again!' And she shepherded Simon out of the front door.

Thankfully there was still some white Rioja in the fridge, so Chris poured herself a large glass. She selected Zeta's business card from the pin board by the fridge.

I'm in. See you at 10. Chris, she texted.

*

Zeta's phone buzzed and vibrated, almost tipping itself off her coffee table. She opened the text and smiled. The 'chance encounter' at the swimming pool had worked. Chris was on board. Zeta felt a tiny sliver of regret that she'd engaged in, well, not exactly deception, more like omission of the full facts. She could have told Chris that she'd spotted her Cliffstaple Municipal Pool membership card pinned by the fridge and correctly deduced that Monday mornings were the most likely time to bump into her. She could have told her that, but this was not the time. Something about this whole affair at the forensics house was not sitting easily in Zeta's mind and Christine Heron was just the woman to help unlock the truth.

Fourteen

Chris hadn't slept well the previous night. The weather broke and a huge storm crackled and strobed directly above her head. It kept her awake, worrying about the missing roof tiles and leaky guttering. She'd been meaning to get them looked at in the spring (number 2 on the 'Essential Home Improvements' list) but had procrastinated yet again. In her mind, at any moment a tsunami of rainwater would break down the bedroom door and wash her and Aitken out through the window. When she did finally drift off, she dreamt that she was in a cavernous auditorium and due to give a talk on 'Thermodynamic Engineering – The Easy Way', but she'd forgotten her notes and didn't know anything about the subject. The audience stood up and left in disgust and the auditorium was empty except for Simon. He was sitting in the front row with two huge roast turkeys on his lap, tearing off meaty chunks with his bare hands and shovelling them into his mouth so the juices flowed like a river over his chin.

When Chris woke, relieved to return to the real world, she replayed the previous evening in her head. She had put her most mournful iPod playlist on and finished the bottle of white Rioja and half of another one. At some stage she had thought it was a good idea to load Twitter onto her phone and then spent two hours despairing at humanity – that was one rabbit hole she didn't want to go down ever again. Thankfully, Cornetto Karen no longer seemed to be trending, her mayfly lifespan mercifully short, so she deleted the app to avoid any future drunken revisits.

Her first action was to see if it was possible to retract the text she'd sent Zeta the previous evening. As she feared, it was too late –

Zeta had replied with a thumbs-up emoji. She should text her, feign illness, say that her hip was playing up, or that she'd got swimmer's elbow. Or maybe she should simply tell Zeta the truth – that she wasn't cut out for adventuring.

Her fingers hovered over the keys and then she remembered Jan's words, so thoughtfully conveyed by Simon. Hell! Why should she 'live quietly' or 'slow down'; or 'be less angry'?

'I'm not going to be good,' Chris told Aitken. 'I'm not going to play nice and I'm not going to just wither away. When I snuff it, I don't want Chloe to be scrabbling around for bland anecdotes to pad out the eulogy at my generic thirty-five-minute funeral.'

The last thing her father had ever said to her was, 'Don't die before you've lived.' Chris could still hear the regret in his voice. 'Today's for you, Dad,' she said, launching herself out of bed.

*

Chris was on a roll. Aitken had been given a double-breakfast of his poshest food and an extra cuddle. He didn't watch the local news or use social media, so he judged Chris for who she was, and that was a good person – mainly. He wriggled out through the cat flap and went off to tell this truth to the neighbourhood. Chris looked in the mirror and assessed her battle-readiness:

Special undershorts with the reinforced gusset? Check.

Multi-pocketed cycling shorts? Check.

£10 emergency cash? Check.

Fully charged phone? Check.

Puncture-repair kit (that she didn't have a clue how to use but would panic about if she left home without it)? Check.

Set of Allen keys (see above)? Check.

She momentarily considered that there had to be someone out there called 'Alan Key' and wondered whether his childhood had been made miserable by teasing. She had enough trouble with the surname Heron, particularly given her long, thin legs, but perhaps in the end teasing did make you stronger – or it destroyed you.

'I am ready,' said Chris to her reflection. 'I am a soldier prepared for war, prepared for whatever faces me beyond my front door.'

It was a gorgeous morning. The storm had blown away the mugginess, the air was fresh, the sun warm and the light crisp and bright. Chris followed the same route to Grayson's house (as she still called it, but not with the same affection) that she'd cycled just four days previously, but so much had happened since, it felt like four years. The path was busy that morning as dog walkers, joggers and ramblers jostled for position. She rang her bell twice and shouted 'Morning!' as they stepped aside to let her pass.

They were just finishing the harvest on that field of rape and she was tempted to stop and watch the giant threshing machine in action, but the clock on Rod's ride computer read 09:45 and she couldn't be late. She hated lateness. Perhaps disturbed by the thresher, a swarm of midges rose and Chris rode through the cloud, swallowing a good half-dozen. Did that count as consuming meat, she wondered, and did it therefore hammer another nail into the coffin of her vegetarianism? How did Buddhists deal with such dilemmas of conscience? She had toyed with Buddhism a few years before, but the more she'd looked into it, the more complicated the path to enlightenment seemed. Perhaps she could give it another shot in the autumn – she looked good in orange, after all.

Chris's internal monologue had eaten up the best part of fifteen minutes. Ahead now appeared the forensics house and outside stood Zeta with a bicycle by one side and Mrs Douglas, the key holder, by the other. They'd spotted her. Too late to turn back now.

As Chris inelegantly drew to a halt, Zeta said, 'Ah, here she is!' as though she'd been patiently awaiting a late arrival. Chris glanced down at the computer clock. It read 10:02. Damn.

'Chris, have you met Mrs Douglas, the faculty administrator?'

Mrs Douglas was resplendent in feathers yet again, with three large white specimens acting as a hair display. She was wearing a jacket that featured a stylised illustration of a howling wolf before a full moon. To some this would have smacked of cultural appropriation, but on Mrs Douglas it was perfect.

Chris smiled and just gave a nodded greeting, hiding her voice in case Mrs Douglas was still on the lookout for Carmen Llama.

Mrs Douglas smiled in return and then the shock of recognition crossed her face. She pointed at Chris and gleefully shouted, 'Cornetto Karen!'

'She prefers "Chris", though,' said Zeta. 'Thanks for opening up for us, Mrs—'

'Oh, please. Rene.'

'OK, thanks, Rene. We'll only be half an hour or so. I'll drop the keys back when we've finished.'

'I may as well stay,' said Rene. 'It's a lovely morning and that office gets so stuffy. I'll sit here and enjoy the sunshine.'

'In that case, do you mind keeping an eye on our bikes?'

Zeta leant her bicycle against the wall of the house. It was a stripped-down racing bike, no frills, no accessories, lean and built for speed just like its owner. Chris parked her comparatively cumbersome bike alongside.

'Oh, I nearly forgot,' piped up Rene. 'Dr Karamak's back in this morning and said that you'd left a message. She's happy to pop by if there's anything you still need to ask?'

'The deputy head of department? That'd be great.'

Zeta took the key from Rene and opened the front door. Inside was a familiar scene, unchanged from their previous visit. 'I suggest we start upstairs,' she whispered.

The house was impressive and well maintained and Chris was rather envious. A four- or five-bedroom detached property that could be a couple of hundred years old, easily pre-dating the university itself. Perhaps it had been a farmhouse once?

Inside, it had that strange aura of a house that was not a home. It was furnished but not lived in. Lovely but not loved.

At the top of the stairs Zeta turned left and Chris followed her into a large double bedroom. Grayson's room. There was everything you'd expect to find in a bedroom: a bed with a plain pink duvet, a large wardrobe, a mirror-topped dressing table, two bedside cabinets and a chair, but no possessions, no half-read novels, no unwashed coffee mugs, no pile of dirty laundry heaped on the carpet. Zeta was straight to work, taking half a dozen photos with her phone. Then she started examining the bed, patting down the duvet and lifting the mattress.

'Can you check the cabinets, Chris?'

'Shouldn't we have plastic gloves and those little paper slippers?' Chris asked, recalling TV forensics dramas.

'Yes, if we were SOCO, but we're not. Today we're a web designer and a proofreader having a nose round. If we find anything, it's for info only.'

Chris did as she was told and examined the bedside cabinets. The furniture was of a cheap flat-pack type and not even well constructed – put there for show rather than practical use. The drawers were unused and empty except for a well-thumbed copy of *Fifty Shades of Grey* and a Gideon's Bible, both of which, Chris assumed, had been left there as a joke. Chris held open the Bible and shook the pages, but nothing fell out, not even the Word of God.

She wandered over and stared out of the window, Grayson's window, overlooking the cycle path and the small car park to the right. Rene hove into view, feathers fluttering in the breeze, talking to herself or on a hands-free phone, Chris couldn't tell which. She opened the window and leant out far enough to see that Rene was, in fact, talking to two people. Chris could only make out the tops of their heads, but she was sure she'd seen them before – she'd put money on them being that attractive young couple from outside the church. She ducked back inside before she either attracted their attention or tumbled head first out of the window.

'Sorry, Chris…' said Zeta in a monotone voice.

Chris turned to see a shiny metal barrel pointed in her direction. Zeta was standing next to the open wardrobe, arm outstretched, holding a small pistol.

'… but you know too much.'

Chris flinched as Zeta pulled the trigger. The barrel parted and a weighted piece of cloth unfurled bearing the word 'BANG!' Zeta gave a schoolgirl giggle.

'For frick's sake, Zeta!'

'Great, isn't it?' Zeta grinned. 'It was in the bottom of the wardrobe.'

'Do not ever, and I mean ever,' said Chris, unamused, 'pull a scare prank on a sixty-year-old woman who has given birth. I nearly wet my cycling shorts.'

Zeta was unapologetic. 'Right, next room,' she said, tossing the toy gun back into the wardrobe.

The room next door was another bedroom. It was smaller and made out as a child's room with a cot and two teddy bears propped up on the windowsill. Chris smiled at the cot, remembering the lengthy struggles Simon had had when trying to construct Chloe's. Spectator Chris hadn't helped matters by suggesting that Chloe would have passed puberty by the time it was finished. In the end, Simon drove to a furniture shop and bought a readymade cot instead. Here, Chris was reminded of that weird feeling, the sudden realisation that you were now responsible for another human being and that you'd sacrifice everything for her.

This bedroom was too sparsely furnished to be realistic. There was no mobile hanging over the cot, no murals of jungle animals on the walls, no box overflowing with toys from over-zealous grandparents, and, in the context of this house's purpose, Chris found it upsetting. She left Zeta to discover that the wardrobe and chest of drawers were, apparently, empty.

The third room was a bathroom, also clearly unused. There were no spatters of toothpaste on the mirror or calcium deposits on the shower head. It was surgically clean. Even the toilet seat was down. Chris opened the bathroom cabinet to discover three packages in Christmas wrapping. She carefully eased the Sellotape from the ends of each to reveal a pack of tampons, a pack of condoms and a pack of laxatives, all still in their cellophane wrapping – presumably unclaimed Secret Santa gifts. On Zeta's instruction, she even lifted the top of the cistern to see whether a Colt 45 or a bag of uncut heroin had been hidden within, but all it contained was water, a ballcock and a blue flush-freshener.

'We're wasting our time here,' Chris hissed, but Zeta just shook her head.

The next room did show signs of occupancy. It was a changing room with a shower that had obviously been used recently, the floor of the cubicle being damp. On the shelf was a bottle of Musk Ox shower gel, in case anyone wanted to smell like a half-ton herbivore. There were five lockers, four of which were open. The sum total of booty recovered was a ballpoint pen, a tennis shoe (left foot) and a copy of *Forensics Today* magazine. The fifth locker was unlocked and housed an untidy clutter of boxes containing plastic gowns, gloves and slip-on protective overshoes. There were two cylinders of cotton buds and a brown Jiffy bag that contained half a dozen outer sleeves for pills of some kind. Chris took one out, but it was not a brand she recognised: Priaman. All that was left to investigate was a black plastic dustbin. She lifted the lid and found a tangle of twine, small white flags and masking tape. Chris couldn't figure out their purpose and, judging by the shrug of her shoulders, neither could Zeta.

The fifth room was sealed by a plain door with a Yale lock. Locked, of course. Zeta rapped gently on the door, 'Hello, is anyone in there?', and she and Chris pressed their ears to it to detect any movement within. There was none, so they moved on.

The final room on the top floor had been decked out as a lounge/sitting room. There was a sofa that looked like it might self-combust at any moment, two armchairs with worn backs and frayed arms, and a TV that was so old it was almost as deep as it was wide. Wanting to look suitably thorough in front of Zeta, Chris checked down the sides of the sofa and made 37p profit in the process. She offered a 20p piece to Zeta as her share, but she didn't seem impressed. The only other thing of note was a coffee table on which stood a photo frame which still had the original display photo of a clean-cut, pearly-teethed couple in matching knitwear.

'There's nothing here, even if I knew what we're looking for,' Chris said. 'Not even any cobwebs, fluff balls or silverfish.'

Zeta shrugged. 'Let's check out the rooms downstairs.'

There was a small, smart lavatory built into the space under the stairs, but, apart from the kitchen, most of the ground floor had been converted into a lecture room. A large table was surrounded by a dozen chairs, with a projector in the centre directed towards a pull-down screen at the far end. Two large flatscreen televisions were mounted on the wall and on the windowsill there were four remote controls of increasing complexity. Chris picked one up and pressed a few buttons randomly, but, thankfully, nothing buzzed into life or exploded.

Zeta took on the cabinets that lined the wall opposite the windows and ferreted through the contents, which seemed to be mainly pads of paper and boxes of pens. Chris concentrated on the glass-fronted bookcase, which looked far more interesting. There were the expected dry academic tomes of the type that provided at least fifty per cent of her proofreading income, but there were others that looked more accessible. She picked up one titled *Blood Spatter Analysis for Dummies* and wondered whether you could do evening classes in forensic science just for the hell of it. She was just reaching for another book, *An Easy Guide to Blunt-Force Trauma*, when Zeta signalled that she had finished so it was time to move on.

There was another door at the far end of the room, almost hidden behind the pull-down screen. On closer inspection, this appeared more solid than the other internal doors and had a combination lock. Chris and Zeta both tried punching in four random numbers in the forlorn hope of happening upon the correct code. The door remained locked.

As they walked back into the kitchen, Rene's head appeared round the frame of the front door. 'Are you going to be much longer? Only I really should be getting back to the office.'

'Do you have the code to the door through there?' asked Zeta.

'Ooh no,' said Rene. 'Never been in there. You'll have to ask one of the professors.'

'What about the door upstairs with the Yale lock?' asked Chris.

'Never had a key to that one – went missing years ago, apparently. I'm happy – one less room to keep an eye on.'

'We just need five more minutes then, Rene,' said Zeta.

'Okey-dokey,' said Rene, but she remained watching from the doorway.

'I presume you searched the kitchen on your previous visit?' Chris whispered to Zeta.

'Worth another check.'

A cursory glance suggested that the folder on the work surface just contained health and safety forms for completion by students. The toaster was functional but not as forensically clean as the rest of the kitchen, judging by the fullness of its crumb tray. The kitchen cabinets held a meagre collection of utensils, pots, pans and crockery. The fridge was empty except for that bottle of tomato ketchup and a freshener in the shape of a snowman.

Chris was getting bored of this sterile version of *Through the Keyhole*, when Zeta called her over. She was on her knees in front of another cabinet.

'What do you think, Chris?'

Chris looked inside. 'I think it's empty.'

'Good. What else?'

'That I'm suffering from kitchen shame? My cabinets have never been that clean. Even the mice reported me to the council.'

'And?' Zeta sniffed twice and pointed at her nose.

Chris stuck her head in and recoiled at the smell – the smell of Cliffstaple Municipal Swimming Pool. 'Chlorine!'

Zeta nodded. 'Strong, isn't it?' She called out, 'Rene? How often are these cabinets cleaned?'

'On the last day of term. The students clean the entire house as their final task, then they crack open the beers, get drunk, cop off with each other and have casual sex behind the cricket pavilion.'

Rene paused, as if recalling her own past. 'Lucky blighters.'

'So that would be what, mid-June?' Chris asked.

'That's right.' Rene nodded vigorously.

Zeta lowered her voice. 'Pretty strong smell if it was two months ago, don't you think, Chris?'

They stood.

'Thank you, Rene,' said Zeta. 'I think we're nearly done here.'

'I'll see if Dr Karamak can pop over now.' Rene took out her phone and moved to the far side of the path to make a call.

'Oh well,' sighed Zeta, 'it was worth a try.'

'Cheer up. You never know, there may be a gang of gun-runners setting up shop in Becketon as we speak!'

The smell of chlorine persisted, even in the centre of the kitchen.

Chris gave Grayson a comforting pat on the shoulder. 'Cheerio, Grayson. I feel this is "farewell" rather than "laters".'

Zeta was staring at Chris and Grayson through narrowed eyes.

'We go back a long way,' Chris explained.

'No, it's not that. Do you have a photo of… um… Grayson?'

'You want to see my selfie again?'

'No, from the first time you saw him.'

Chris pulled her phone out of the zipped side pocket of her shorts and trawled through the photo gallery, ninety-five per cent of which were photos of Aitken in various cute poses, and, further back, some of Waterman, pre-disappearance. After a couple of minutes, Chris found what she was looking for: a photo of the house from March the previous year with Grayson framed in the upstairs window.

'Zoom in,' instructed Zeta. 'See?'

The penny dropped. 'Different jacket.'

'And I'm positive he wasn't wearing it on our previous visit,' said Zeta

Chris couldn't believe that she hadn't noticed. She had been so obsessed with the state of Grayson's shoes that she hadn't considered whether the rest of his clothing was consistent. Previously he'd been wearing a dark suit. Now he had a tweed jacket draped over his shoulders. The jacket appeared to be good quality but rather dated, with brown leather patches on the elbows. One of the buttons, the third one down, was mismatched, a mottled reddish brown rather than the dark brown of its companions. Chris had a couple of shirts like that and a tin full of spare buttons, but none were ever the right size or colour. She patted down the pockets, but they seemed to be empty. She pushed her hand deep into one of the outside pockets. There was something loose there. She draw her hand out, her fingertips covered in a fine blue powder.

'Oh God!' she gasped. 'I hope this isn't some kind of nerve agent.'

'We'd be dead by now if it was,' said Zeta reassuringly.

'Perhaps it's drugs – you know, cocaine?'

'Who'd want blue cocaine?'

'I can think of a few politicians.'

Rene reappeared in the doorway. 'Rene, do you recognise this jacket?'

She shook her head. 'Maybe. It looks kind of familiar, but the students are always abandoning clothing here. They probably dressed the dummy in it rather than make the effort to throw it away.'

'Do you mind if we borrow it?' asked Zeta.

'You can have it. If no one's claimed it by now, I'd be giving it to a charity shop anyway.'

'Thanks.' Zeta folded the jacket carefully and stored it in her rucksack.

'But no one's been in here since last Friday?' Chris checked.

Rene paused and shook her head again. 'No, no one at all.'

A tall woman with annoyingly well-defined cheekbones, bobbed fair hair and Yoko Ono glasses appeared behind Rene. 'I'm hoping that one of you is Zeta Jama? So sorry to be so elusive. I'm Dr Karamak.'

Zeta offered her hand and Dr Karamak shook it, smiling broadly. The doctor looked at Chris slightly quizzically as if in recognition and then smiled and shook her hand too. With her free hand Dr Karamak grasped Chris's elbow so that, momentarily, she had to struggle to break free.

'Only a couple of questions, Doctor, just routine,' said Zeta, and the two of them walked to the far side of the path, just out of earshot.

That left Chris and Rene standing like two wallflowers at the school disco. 'Love your jacket,' Chris said, and that successfully broke the ice.

*

First rule, thought Zeta: always break up potential witnesses. Chris was providing a valuable service in occupying Rene Douglas.

'So how can I help North Kent Constabulary today?' purred Dr Karamak.

'How was the conference, Professor?'

Dr Karamak gave a little chuckle. 'You flatter me – I'm not a professor – well, not yet. All we girls can do is keep at it, eh, Constable Jama? The conference was excellent, thank you for asking, but you're not here for a review, I'm guessing?'

'Just double-checking a couple of things. Mrs Douglas said that only she, you and Professor Jasper have keys to this property?'

'That's right. Rene is the oil that keeps our department running. She holds all the faculty's keys, our spare car keys and even a copy of Professor Jasper's house key, as he's rather forgetful at times.'

Zeta wrote in her black leather notebook, even though she had consigned this information to memory. Making notes was just for the sake of appearance.

'I haven't heard back from the professor. Have you spoken to him recently?'

Dr Karamak laughed and Zeta noticed she had pointed canines that only improved her smile. Wabi-sabi – perfection in the imperfection.

'Out of term time? I joined the faculty two years ago and I probably know him as well now as I did then. He's a man of mystery but with a first-class academic reputation.'

'You don't socialise?'

'Not outside of the university. I invited him to dinner to meet my husband, but the professor kept making excuses so in the end I didn't push it. I'm sure Rene will be delighted to help you track him down if you think it's important. Can I help you any further, Constable Jama? I'm snowed under just now, preparing for the new term.'

'Just one last question. It's about the locked room…' started Zeta.

*

Ten minutes later, Zeta and Chris were mounting their bikes. Rene Douglas and Dr Karamak had disappeared together in the direction of the main university building.

'So are you going to tell me about your little tête-à-tête with Dr Cheekbones?'

'Over elevenses,' smiled Zeta, 'and it's your turn to buy. Where to?'

'Three-Michelin-starred Pete's Pantry.'

'I know it well! You get going, Chris. I'll catch you up.'

'Catch me up?' Chris said, switching the battery mode to high. 'In your dreams, Zeta Jama! Come on, Rod, let's make 'em eat dust!'

Fifteen

Despite Chris's head start, Zeta caught up with her at the level crossing, which had closed to let the 10:56 to Victoria through.

'So how was the good doctor?' Chris asked as they stood side by side, straddling their bicycles and waiting for the barrier to rise.

'Utterly charming.'

'Hmm. I never trust anyone with a power handshake. Did you ask about the mysterious locked rooms?'

'Of course. They've never bothered with the one upstairs, plenty of space anyway, and the combination-lock room is where they keep all the serious chemicals. They don't want anyone to break in and see if they can get high by snorting hydrogen peroxide. Only the doctor and Professor Jasper have the code and it has an alarm that sends a text message whenever the door's opened so she can be certain it's secure.'

'But she didn't give you a sneak peek?'

'Not without a warrant.'

'Ooh, that sounds suspicious,' said Chris. 'Got something to hide, has she?'

'I don't think so,' replied Zeta. 'She was very apologetic but said it was university rules, health and safety and all that jazz.'

Chris was about to ask a follow-up question, but the barrier rose and Zeta sped ahead whilst Chris was still checking what gear she was in.

As it was only just after eleven, there were still plenty of free tables at Pete's Pantry. It was way too early to consider lunch, although eating at strange times seemed to Chris to be a by-product of getting old. A couple of years ago, on a biking holiday in Ireland, she had witnessed a group of elderly ladies lunching at half past eleven in a tea shop. They hoovered their way through a mountain of shepherd's pie, mashed potato and colcannon. Mash, mash and mash. That day Chris vowed that she would never, ever lunch before one o'clock.

She was going to take a vacant table near the window when Zeta manoeuvred her towards a table at the rear, where a solitary diner was taking receipt of Pete's Mega Gutbuster All-Day Breakfast. She was about to protest, when Chris recognised the gourmand as Barry, the custody officer and benevolent donator of custard creams.

'It's Barry, isn't it? Good to see you again. If you'll excuse us, Zeta and I need to—'

'We can talk in front of Barry,' Zeta interjected. 'He's my confidant, my rock, and totally trustworthy. Everyone needs a Barry in their life. That's why I invited him to join us.'

'And very generous of you it is, Ms Heron,' said Barry, dipping a corner of fried bread into his egg yolk.

'There's no way I'd have survived the past year without his wisdom and guidance. No one can game the system like Barry here,' said Zeta, taking a seat opposite.

'You're too kind.' Barry gulped from a mug of tea.

Chris ordered a rooibos tea for Zeta, a cappuccino for herself and a low-fat blueberry muffin that she reckoned they could share.

'So was Dr Karamak any help?' she asked.

'Used to love Caramac,' Barry muttered to himself, shovelling baked beans onto a triangle of toast.

'As much as she could be. She's been at the European Forensic Science Conference in Barcelona since last Thursday, attending seminars on' – Zeta pulled out a tatty black leather-bound notebook from her inside pocket – 'Advancements in Testing for Bodily Fluid Traces.'

'Someone's taking the piss,' Chris commented, and Barry grinned and made the *Badum-tish!* gesture with his fork, which caused a button mushroom to fly off the end, neatly bisecting the gap between Chris and Zeta's heads.

Zeta didn't even flinch at the flying fungi. 'She confirmed Mrs Douglas's statement that only the two of them and Professor Jasper have a key. As far as she could tell, nothing was missing from the house and the chemical storage room was secure.'

'So that leaves Professor Jasper. No word, I presume?'

'No, and Dr Karamak wasn't too surprised. She described him as "old-school" and a "bit of a loner". He's known to go off-grid at times, never responds to his emails and has an ancient mobile phone that he never answers. Always turns up again two days before the start of the new term. Sounds like he's an eccentric academic cliché – brilliant but scatty.'

Their drinks and accompanying muffin were delivered with a flourish by Pete himself.

'If he's that old-school, perhaps you should write him a letter,' Chris suggested, blowing at the froth on her cappuccino.

'Can't get his home address.'

'Not even from the charming deputy head of department? She must know where her boss lives.'

'Dr Karamak referred me to Mrs Douglas, who said that "giving out personal information would contravene the Data Protection Act" and she didn't want to be arrested for a trivial offence.'

Chris used a knife to divide the muffin into quarters. 'On that, I sympathise.'

She noticed Barry staring at the muffin lustfully, so she offered him the plate and he took a piece. She looked away as Barry used the muffin to mop up the dregs of egg yolk from his plate.

'So where does that leave us? Good old Directory Enquiries?'

'Tried that – ex-directory.' Zeta picked up the plate and offered Barry her share of the muffin. 'Barry? In exchange for this scrummy low-fat blueberry muffin, could you find the home address of a Professor Adrian Jasper? He should be pretty local. There's a tin of Family Assorted Biscuits in it for you as well.'

'No problem,' Barry said, taking his muffin consumption statistic up to seventy-five per cent. 'Who's searching for him?'

'I think PC Atherton has a professional interest.' Zeta noticed Chris's raised eyebrow but gave her a reassuring nod.

'OK. For you, Zeta, my love, anything!' said Barry, preparing to rise. 'I'll get on it straight away.'

'While you're on the case...' Zeta delved into her backpack and retrieved the jacket. She unfolded a paper napkin and gently shook the upturned jacket, collecting the contents of the pocket.

'Blue nose-candy? Is that what they mean by designer drugs nowadays?' observed Barry.

'You two should form a comedy double-act,' said Zeta dryly. 'I need this IDed. Can you get it analysed, Barry?'

'Analysed? What do you think this is, *CSI: Kent*? Phone numbers and addresses I can get; car registrations traced – usually; CCTV checked – possibly. But surreptitious chemical forensics? Not a chance.' He patted Zeta on the shoulder. 'Sorry, Zeta, love, but some things are beyond my reach. Thanks for brunch, Ms Heron.' And Barry departed the cafe.

'Looks like Professor Jasper's our last lead then,' said Zeta, flattening the corners of the napkin and placing it in the front pocket of her jeans. 'It's a shame Barry can't help.'

'Is that legit? Getting Barry to access official records?' Chris asked.

'Not strictly, but Barry has a special power.'

'Which is?'

'Invisibility.'

Chris conjured up the image of Barry and the Mega Gutbuster Breakfast. She was not sure she'd ever seen anyone less invisible. 'Explain?'

'Barry's eighteen months off retirement, strictly confined to office duties. To the likes of Spurgeon and Atherton he's irrelevant, handy to have around but no longer a proper copper. But our Barry's a shrewd one. He knows his way around the computer systems and has pretty much everyone at the station's usernames and passwords.'

'How come?'

'People give him their details – willingly – just in case they forget them. After all, dear harmless old Barry's always around the office to help.'

'Not exactly secure then?'

'All use of the IT system is traced back to the user's terminal, but if you log in using someone else's details…'

'Very sneaky.'

Zeta nodded. 'I never use it for anything serious. It's just that, being a special, my security clearance is limited. Barry helps out and I remunerate him with saturated fats. It's a win-win arrangement.'

'And by confiding in me, you've made me an accomplice?'

'I promise not to snitch on you.' Zeta laughed.

'Why don't you run that blue powder past your new BFF Dr Karamak? It's probably something she's got a tub of in that locked room.'

Zeta paused for thought. 'Could do, as a last resort, I suppose. Let's see if we can track down the Nutty Professor first. Do you mind taking custody of the jacket? I've got to run some errands and I don't want to lug it round with me all day.'

'No problem.'

Chris squeezed the jacket into her backpack. It looked like something Next-Door Nick would wear. Perhaps she could give it to him as a thank-you gift for all his cat-sitting.

Her phone buzzed. It was an email from the university in response to her quote – better still, it was an email with attachments. The day was not a total loss as this job would keep her in vodka and cat food for another month.

*

Outside the cafe, Zeta mounted her bike and turned left, weaving through the traffic towards the city centre. Chris turned right and headed for home. For safety's sake, Chris tried to avoid the main roads as much as possible, but at the same time she didn't want to pass by the forensics house again, so she continued up the hill for a further four hundred metres and took an alternative off-road route. This was a less picturesque and consequently less used path that passed by the rear of the university playing fields, where they bordered a new housing estate.

Chris switched mentally and physically into cruise mode – back by one, grab lunch, then get cracking on those prospectuses. If all went well she could treat herself by ordering a pizza delivery that evening – Vegetarian Hot, thin crust, extra chilli.

She was halfway past the rugby pitch when she heard someone closing in on her. It was pathetic, as she was well aware, but she hated being overtaken – a terrible competitive side to her she'd had since she was a child. She once lost her temper with Simon over a disputed game of Kerplunk! Judiciously used, those plastic needles could be quite a weapon.

She switched Rod's battery mode to high and accelerated. Still her pursuer continued to close the distance. Chris didn't dare look back but could hear the sound of the tyres on the loose dirt surface getting nearer and nearer. Just as the track re-joined the main cycle path, a cyclist swept past her and swung round to block her route.

Panting deeply, Zeta leant over the handlebars. 'Why… did… you… accelerate?' she gasped between breaths.

'Oh for Frick's sake, Zeta! I thought I was being bike-jacked! What is it now?'

'Barry texted…'

'Good for him. I'm going home to work. Paid work for paying clients. Remember that?'

'He's got an address for Professor Jasper. It's in Bartham, could be there in half an hour.'

'Fine. Have fun. Don't forget to write.' Chris remounted the saddle and prepare to set off.

'Oh, Chris, we've come this far. You can't step down now.'

'Why do you need my help, Zeta? You're a trained police officer, I'm a grandmother with a bionic hip.'

'We're a good team – you're the Dr Watson to my Sherlock Holmes.'

'The trusty but slow-witted sidekick? Thanks for that. Could've been worse, I suppose. I could be the Hooch to your Turner.' But that eighties movie reference was lost on someone of Zeta's tender years.

Chris's instincts screamed at her to continue home, proof those prospectuses, take the money, eat the pizza. Then again, an extra hour and a half wouldn't make that much difference, Rod still had three bars of battery life and this exercise was really strengthening her leg muscles – they felt much more robust. Physio Melanie would be proud of her.

There was also, according to one of the more interesting economics extracts that Chris had proofed earlier in the year, the matter of her own sunk costs fallacy. This theory accounted for why people continued to throw good after bad, whether in investments, gambling or relationships. Once you'd invested a significant amount of money, time, energy or emotion into a project, you felt compelled to follow it to its conclusion, even if that was the least wise decision. At least, Chris thought that was the gist of it. Economics had never been a strong point. This theory also endorsed that decision she had made nearly thirty years ago to bail out after only seven years of marriage, before she became irredeemably committed to a bad decision. If ever there was a sunk cost, it was Simon.

'And we're assuming that if Professor Jasper's at home, we can finally put this all to bed?'

'If we were American, we'd say we'll "achieve closure".' Zeta used her siren smile to lure Chris onto the rocks of collusion yet again.

Chris was familiar with the off-road path to Bartham Village, it having been one of her favourite pre-crash routes. They headed down towards Becketon's ancient city wall and then swung right, past a playground, to a path that hugged the river to its left. Now, in late summer, the river was more of a shallow stream, crystal clear and fringed by reeds. The occasional punt drifted by, ferrying sightseers and scattering coots and mallards, but otherwise it was a gently gurgling companion.

The path here was wide and well maintained. The overnight storm had settled the dusty surface and the two women could comfortably cycle side by side. The conversation soon turned to family, but Zeta seemed reluctant to share any more about her past and Chris was not one to pry. To show a spirit of openness, Chris chose to test the water by asking for Zeta's judgement regarding her Chloe and Christmas issue. Reassuringly, Zeta didn't automatically brand her as a Sociopathic Mother From Hell.

'You've got to do what feels right. Your daughter will understand.'

'Thanks. I'm sure she will. I'm not confident about the rest of polite society though.'

'Screw polite society.'

'You sound like my dad.'

'So, what about your folks?' Zeta chirped. 'Do you come from a long line of grammar Nazis?'

'No, I'm the first. My mum was a dinner lady and my dad was big in sewage, so, unlike you, I never felt the urge to carry on the family tradition, thankless child that I am.'

'Good people though?'

'Yes, very. Loving, caring and just a bit mad. They taught me everything I know.'

A mile or so later, as they stopped to let a pair of designer-buggy-pushing mothers pass, Zeta quizzed Chris again.

'So, Chloe's dad…?'

'Simon. We've been happily divorced for nearly thirty years.'

'And you never remarried?'

'Never found anyone brave enough or desperate enough.'

'Really? I'd have thought you'd be quite a catch for some lucky guy.'

'Quite a catch', 'cast a net', 'plenty more fish in the sea' – what was it with relationships and seafood? Chris glanced to her right and saw a smile play across Zeta's lips.

'I think our Barry's quite smitten with you.'

'I think I'll pass on our Barry, thank you. I've got Aitken – he's the man in my life.'

'Not forgetting Grayson,' said Zeta slyly.

Chris pursed her lips and accelerated – that girl didn't miss a thing.

The path passed a small weir and then abruptly ended at a road where a sign proudly displayed the crest of Bartham Village, a crowned trout leaping over an oak tree. Chris made a mental note to research this surreal image at a future date.

Zeta checked the map on her phone and led the way across a railway junction to a row of handsome redbrick cottages.

'Number 2, Railway Cottages – here we are.' Zeta marched up to the door and pressed the bell for what seemed to be a length of time bordering on rudeness. They waited for a minute and then she followed up with a sharp rapping of the door knocker.

Out of the corner of her eye, Chris noticed a net curtain twitching in the window of Number 1, Railway Cottages.

'Have a peek in the window,' suggested Zeta.

From an external viewpoint, the sitting room fulfilled every stereotype of an eccentric academic's abode. It was cluttered yet somehow orderly too. The walls were lined with bookshelves, which seemed to hold serious tomes – not a paperback in sight. There was an old, slightly shabby sofa with an African-print throw and a side table with a beautiful antique brass reading lamp. Most significantly there was no sign of a television and no sign of recent occupation.

'Let's try the back of the house,' suggested Zeta.

Chris started to mutter about trespassing laws, but Zeta had already gone, slipping down the side of Number 3 into a communal alley that ran behind the cottages. The garden of Number 2 was accessed by an unlocked gate. It was tidy but uninteresting. Slabs of stone were dotted with empty terracotta tubs and a dog rose had climbed the fence into next-door. The rear of the house gave a view of the kitchen and, through French doors, an adjacent dining room. The kitchen door had a cat flap, but the ivy growing across it suggested it was some years since it had been used. Perhaps Professor Jasper's cat had also left home one day, never to return. The kitchen itself seemed clean, orderly and dated. The only nod to modernity was a microwave oven in prime position on the table. The dining room was also lined with bookcases. Chris caught the titles of a couple of the academic textbooks she had noted at the forensics house.

'All seems to be in order. No signs of a break-in,' she said to Zeta.

'Perhaps I should scoot back to the uni and see if I can prise the professor's spare house key away from Rene.'

'Zeta, if Rene wouldn't cough up Professor Jasper's address, she's hardly likely to hand over his keys. I'm no expert, but this looks like the house of someone who is happily on holiday. He's probably gambling his department's budget away in Vegas or enjoying the exotic fleshpots of Skegness.'

Zeta just harrumphed in response.

As they returned to the front of the house, a reception party awaited them: an elderly lady and a young couple with a baby. The man, lean but with a muscular frame, stepped forward.

'Can I help you?' he said, raising himself onto his toes and thrusting his chest forward. His display of machismo was unconvincing and distinctly unthreatening – like an adolescent stag.

'Yeah, thanks. We're looking for Professor Jasper?' Zeta pulled out a warrant card. 'Are you neighbours?'

The man visibly sighed with relief and deflated.

'Yes,' said the woman with the baby. 'Steve and me live at Number 3, and Grace is Number 1.'

'Adrian isn't in any trouble, is he?' asked Grace, her voice quavering. 'He's such a lovely man, so helpful.'

'No, no trouble at all, Grace. We just want to ask him a couple of questions about his work at the university.' Zeta gave her a calming smile.

Grace beamed in response. 'Oh, he's such a clever man, isn't he? So hard-working too.'

'Have any of you seen him, recently?' Zeta asked.

Steve shook his head. 'Nah, but that's not unusual. The prof keeps himself to himself.' He lowered his voice to escape Grace's hearing. 'He's a grumpy old sod, so we have as little to do with him as possible, don't we, Becks?'

'Oh, come on, Steve,' said his partner. 'He's batty, but harmless. Perfect neighbour in a lot of ways. I saw him late last week. I was taking little Sophie to the park and he was on his way out.'

'Can you be precise about when last week?' asked Zeta.

'It was Thursday or Friday. We went to the park both mornings cos the weather was so lovely.'

'You don't remember what he was wearing?' Chris asked.

'Nah, sorry. I was concentrating on Sophie.'

Chris took the tweed jacket out of her backpack and showed it to the three neighbours. 'Could he have been wearing this?'

Becks shook her head. 'Maybe. Looks like the kind of thing he'd wear.'

'But sometimes we don't see him for weeks, if he's writing one of his books or summat,' added Steve.

Zeta thanked all the neighbours profusely and handed them each a business card. 'When you see him, could you ask the professor to give me a call?'

Chris waved at Sophie and was surprised to get a smile and a gurgle in response.

They mounted their bikes and set off towards Becketon. About halfway back along the riverside path, Chris's hip started to ache. Bugger! As usual, she'd rushed back into things and overdone it. If something had gone wrong and she had to go back into that hospital, into that ward… She couldn't bear to pursue that thought.

Zeta noticed her companion's distress and they pulled over to a bench nestling beneath a weeping willow. They watched a group of swans glide by, the cygnets now nearly full grown and looking like stroppy teenagers on an enforced family outing. After five minutes of gentle massaging and stretching, the pain was subsiding and, with it, Chris's panic. Zeta was writing some notes in her black notebook.

'That's a bit retro – a proper notebook.'

Zeta looked embarrassed. 'It's more secure. You can't hack hard copy.'

'You could lose it though.'

'I won't,' said Zeta. 'How's the hip?'

'Better.'

'Let's give it another five minutes. It's a good opportunity to recap where we are so far.'

'Where we are so far? If this was an Olympic swimming race, Zeta, we'd still be in the changing rooms adjusting our gussets.'

'Well, we've got a possible dead body...'

'That's probably a mannequin.'

'A missing professor...'

'Who's probably on holiday.'

'A suspiciously clean cupboard – and the same smell under the table...'

'In a forensics house full of cleaning equipment.'

'And a mysterious blue powder...'

'That'll forever remain mysterious unless we can find a way of analysing it. Humphrey Bogart would say that it doesn't add up to a hill of beans.'

'Is that your next-door neighbour?' asked Zeta and Chris shook her head, realising that all her cultural references were sadly dated.

Zeta sighed and carefully put her notebook back into an inside pocket. 'I guess you and Humphrey are right. Not much to go on. I just wish we could find Professor Jasper. I'm sure he's the key to all this. I better get back to work too – I've got an ambulance-chasing lawyer who's worried about his lowly ranking on Google Search. *Ker-ching!*'

*

By the time Chris reached home, there was just one bar of battery life left. Zeta accompanied her all the way to her front door. She said it was en route to her flat anyway, but, as Zeta hadn't revealed where she lived, Chris couldn't verify that. Next-Door Nick was in his usual position, on his front path manoeuvring his bins.

'Afternoon, Chris,' he said. 'Nice day for a ride. It's recycling this week – I've already put your blue bin out.'

Chris introduced Zeta as her new swimming buddy and she handed him her business card in the unlikely event that he needed a website built. Nick returned the favour in the equally unlikely event that Zeta needed any sociology exam papers marking.

Once Nick had disappeared back indoors, Zeta said (rather too loudly for Chris's comfort), 'Ooh, I see our Barry's got competition.'

'Not in a million years,' Chris replied.

'Why? He looks kind. Educated. Good with bins.'

'You know that saying about not crapping on your own doorstep?'

Zeta crinkled her nose. 'Ooh, he doesn't, does he?' She then produced another of her trademark winning smiles and cycled away.

Aitken was waiting for Chris indoors, along with her bath and her laptop. She interacted with them in that order. Whilst submerged beneath the suds (Tamarind and Peach Blossom – for rejuvenation, apparently), Chris pondered on today's outcome. In many ways she was pleased that this little escapade had come to a dead end. It had been a mini-adventure and, crucially, had got her out of the house and involved with human society again.

When Zeta had been listing the 'evidence', Chris had been tempted to make a suggestion about how to identify the blue powder, but now she was glad she hadn't. Zeta didn't need any further encouragement and Chris had to remind herself that she was still, essentially, a stranger.

It was eight o'clock before she finally sat down to work, a microwaved vegetable lasagne at her left hand, a glass of Rioja at her right. She refrained from switching on her laptop until Aitken had performed his perfunctory catwalk across the keyboard and then, bored, had gone out on a nocturnal mouse-hunt.

Chris had proofread many academic prospectuses before and found them comparatively straightforward. By the time they reached her they'd been past several pairs of educated eyes and the vast majority of typos and punctuation errors had been purged. These files from the University of North Kent seemed to be no exception; they were professionally produced and her input would be the last stage before they went to print. With the help of some strong black coffee and a student-in-a-panic work ethic, they'd be ready by the next morning.

The files were in copy layout, complete with flattering photos of the university and student campus. In this world the sun was always shining, the floors were spotless and the living was easy. Students with fresh complexions and eager eyes gazed at raised test tubes, gathered round computer screens or challenged each other in friendly pen-chewing debate. Chris's own university experience of anxiety-fuelling deadlines, exam terror, disappointing sex and raging hangovers was not reflected in these pages.

She was three hours into the work and onto the second document when a photo snagged her attention. Two impossibly photogenic students in white coats had been caught in mid-pose, apparently listening to the wise words of their male tutor. It was a generic photo, like a thousand others, but what held Chris's attention was the tutor's jacket – brown Harris tweed with leather elbow patches. The caption under the photo read: 'Never a dull day in forensics, according to Professor Jasper!'

Chris zoomed in on the picture. Professor Jasper was a serious-looking man in his mid-fifties: slim, average height, grey hair, tortoiseshell glasses. Characteristics shared by about a third of the UK's population of middle-aged males. She concentrated on the jacket and there, halfway down the front, was a red-coloured pixel.

Chris cleared the kitchen table, took the jacket out of her

backpack and laid it flat. On closer examination, the odd red button was not Bakelite like the others but cold, a reddish-brown stone with two small holes drilled into it for the thread. The red button's position corresponded with the photo in the prospectus. There could be no doubt that this was Professor Jasper's jacket.

She held the jacket upside-down and shook it vigorously. A pen lid that had evaded her earlier search fell out, accompanied by a light dusting of the remaining blue powder. She found an empty envelope in her odd-and-sods drawer and corralled the powder into it. As this jacket could now constitute a piece of vital evidence, Chris decided she'd better treat it with more respect, so she attempted to uncrumple it. There was something in one of the pockets, a pocket in the lining that she hadn't spotted before. It was a piece of card; an empty tablet sleeve with 'Priaman' branding.

It wasn't difficult to place this packaging – it was identical to the ones in the changing-room locker in the forensics house. Strangely, Google drew a blank on the brand, but there was familiarity in the small-print listing of ingredients on the back: Sildenafil citrate. Chris had proofed a paper on that a few months before – it was used in the treatment of erectile dysfunction. Was that the answer to the blue powder mystery? Did the professor seem a likely user? Well, he was the right age, she supposed. A powder though – Viagra in soluble form?

Who might help her? She couldn't very well text Simon or Next-Door Nick to ask them what they knew about erectile dysfunction, could she? Not without explaining why she needed to know, and that was a can of flaccid worms she didn't want to open.

Instead, she texted Zeta: *I've found something. Speak tomorrow.*

Then she texted Chloe: *Cycled lots today. Hip's good – hope you all are too. Love Mum xxxx*

And then she knuckled down to finish the prospectuses. She tapped the photo of Professor Jasper with her finger. 'Zeta's right, Professor. You're the key, aren't you?'

Sixteen

Chris had half expected to find Zeta camped on her doorstep the next morning in response to the previous night's text, but there was no sign of her. There was a slightly cryptic text from Chloe to say that she was going on a business trip so might be out of contact for a few days, but that was all. Chris gave the prospectuses a quick reread and, happy that she'd spotted three errors that made her input worthwhile, sent them back to the university accompanied by an invoice.

Stocks of semi-skimmed and cat food were getting perilously low, so she ventured out to the local Co-op, which gave her an excuse to drop by Cliffstaple Pharmacy en route. It was a small independent pharmacy, of the type that was rapidly being swallowed up by the retail giants. She browsed the shelves, pretending to be fascinated by the range of hair dye, until the shop was empty of other customers. The girl behind the counter was in her early twenties and could easily have been the twin of Gus from Spokesmen cycle shop a few doors further down the high street. She wore a name badge that read: 'I'm Poppy, ask me about hay fever remedies'. Chris was tempted to take that option rather than the one she had planned.

'Excuse me, but is the pharmacist about?'

'Have you got a prescription?'

'No, just a question – for the pharmacist.'

Poppy was young, and Chris was old – well, older. How could she broach such a delicate matter with her?

'Maybe I can help?' Poppy seemed justly affronted that her customer had immediately sought more senior advice.

Chris handed Poppy the Priaman cardboard sleeve. 'Is this a brand you recognise?' she asked in a hushed in-the-chemist tone.

Poppy looked at the sleeve, turning it over in her hand. 'Nah, but we have these.' She reached behind her and put a pack of Viagra on the counter. 'How many packets do you need?'

Chris opened the packet to confirm that the tablets matched the blue colour of the powder from the jacket pocket. 'I don't need to buy any…' There was a *Ding!* from the shop door behind her, indicating that she was no longer alone in the pharmacy. 'You wouldn't know if it comes in… powder… um… soluble form?'

'You mean, like, to drink? I shouldn't think so. MR PHILLIPS!' Poppy shouted. 'A CUSTOMER WANTS TO KNOW IF WE DO SOLUBLE ERECTILE DYSFUNCTION MEDICATION.'

Chris looked over her shoulder at the very elderly couple who had just entered the shop and gave them an embarrassed smile. The woman was distracted, fumbling in a tartan trolley for her purse, but her husband winked and gave Chris a discreet thumbs-up.

The pharmacist popped his head round the door of the adjacent room, where he was busy preparing prescriptions. 'In soluble form? Heavens! Why would anyone want that? That could be dangerous.' Mr Phillips looked at Chris as though she had just placed an order for five kilos of arsenic and asked for 'extra-strength'.

'I don't want it; it was just a hypothetical question. I… I… better be going.'

Poppy pushed the tablets forward. 'That's £34, please.'

'£34? But I don't want to buy them.'

'We can't resell them, not now you've handled them. £34, please, *madam*.' Poppy was surprisingly assertive.

Chris could feel herself getting flushed, like a seventeen-year-old Chris buying condoms for the first time, so she swiped her bank card on the reader and hurried out of the pharmacy. £34? Thirty-four fricking pounds?

She returned home, via the Co-op, with provisions for her and Aitken. As ever, she passed Next-Door Nick, who was heading in the opposite direction, towards the high street.

He smiled, nodded at her laden arms, and said, 'Morning, Chris – big night planned, I see.'

It was only when Chris reached the kitchen table that she realised she'd been carrying a litre of skimmed milk, cat food, vanilla ice cream, a cheap bottle of Sauvignon Blanc and, clearly visible, the four-pack of erectile dysfunction tablets.

There was still no response from Zeta, so she broke her golden rule and sent a follow-up text. *Did you get my text about Prof Jasper? Do we need to meet?*

After ten minutes a reply pinged through. It said simply: *Stand down. I'm on the case.*

Stand down? How dare she!

Within twenty-four hours, Chris had about-turned from reluctant investigator to vigilante. She paced the kitchen, ranting to herself. All Zeta's talk about a 'partnership' and 'Holmes and Watson' was just manipulation, wasn't it? So she could use her and then take all the glory for herself. Well, Chris would show her – she would figure out the Blue Powder Mystery and track down Professor Jasper *and* take any evidence straight to DI Dunn. Zeta wasn't the only one who could play hardball.

Chris's strategy was sketchy and her chance of success was, according to some quick calculations she made on the 'Things To Do' fridge magnet, at best fifteen per cent. However, she had no pending work in her in-box and the opportunity to cross another chore off a perpetually expanding list, so she put down some lunch for Aitken, grabbed the crutches from the umbrella stand by the front door and headed for the bus stop.

It was glorious cycling weather, but Chris didn't fancy her chances of riding the ten miles to Kent Coast Hospital with two crutches balanced across the handlebars, and she had scrapped her car two years previously when it failed its MOT. There was a bus due in five minutes, which would take her to Becketon bus station, and from there it was only another mile or so to the hospital.

There were few advantages in being seemingly disabled, but accessing public transport was one of them. As soon as the bus arrived (only six minutes late), Chris was ushered to the front of the queue. Once on board, an elderly man insisted on giving up his priority seat on her behalf. She could have protested and explained that she no longer needed the crutches, but it seemed simpler to affect a limp and ease herself into the recently vacated seat. In all honesty, she would have preferred her favoured spot on the top deck, but now she had to maintain this pretence for the entire journey.

When she arrived at the hospital it was pre-visiting time, that strange lunchtime lull. Her first thought was to call at the Outpatients reception, return the crutches and ask for information, but that would have raised too many questions and could have killed her mission at birth. Besides, those crutches were like a magic amulet. Nobody stopped a woman on crutches. She would recommend them for any aspiring bank robber – make your getaway on crutches and people would do one of two things: either offer to assist and open doors or look away in awkward embarrassment.

She didn't want to hang around for too long, partly for fear of attracting attention but mainly because of her hospital phobia. That familiar smell of despair and disinfectant was starting to make her feel nauseous. She took the lift to the fourth floor and followed the signage to Baxter Ward. There were four bays, each with six beds, and, affecting a hobble, she performed a circuit of the ward. It was lunchtime and everyone was so busy receiving lunch, eating lunch or complaining about lunch that she could scan the ward unnoticed. There was no sign of her quarry, though, and her creeping sense of anxiety was telling her not to spend a moment longer there than necessary.

There was just one nurse on Baxter Ward reception, busy fielding phone calls, entering records on the computer and eating a boxed pasta salad. It took a couple of minutes to get her attention.

'Hi, I'm looking for Mary. Mary Semenyo?'

'Visiting time's not till three o'clock,' said the reception nurse, whose name badge read 'Philadelphia Baker'.

'She's not a patient, Philadelphia, she's a nurse, on this ward. Well, she was in April.'

'Ah, before my time then. Sorry, I can't help.'

'Perhaps one of your colleagues might know?'

But Philadelphia had turned to face her screen again, indicating that this conversation was over.

It had been a long shot to start with. Four months was a long time in hospital shift patterns. Nurses regularly moved wards, hospitals and health authorities. A nurse of Mary's skill and bedside manner would be in high demand and there were the inducements offered by the private sector too. She could be anywhere and she was the only nurse Chris had got to know well enough during her stay to trust with her task.

She returned to the ground floor in a lift made claustrophobic by two wheelchair-bound patients, a coughing child and an inattentive parent. She fixed her stare firmly at the illuminated floor numbers. She just needed to drop her crutches back at Reception, then she could get the hell out of there.

She was halfway across the vast floorspace between the lifts and Reception, swinging quickly on the crutches, when a voice behind her exclaimed, 'Oh no, Christine! What have you done to yourself this time?'

Chris didn't have to turn round to know that Lady Luck had delivered Nurse Mary Semenyo.

'Mary! Just the person I was looking for.'

Mary nodded at the crutches. 'I'm not in Trauma anymore. Got me an upgrade to Urology.'

'Congratulations, I guess. But look...' Chris held both crutches in her right hand and danced a little jig, hoping that she wouldn't go arse over tit on the slippery lino flooring. 'I'm cured!'

Mary gave a spontaneous roar of laughter. 'Careful now. Don't want to be hauling your ass back upstairs. Good to see you again, Christine, but now a girl's gotta eat.'

'Can I buy you lunch?' Chris was quickly learning that 'lunch' seemed to be the common currency in investigation. 'I want to pick your brains about something.'

'Yes, but I'm buying. I want to thank you for retrieving my possessions from that low-down thief,' said Mary, proudly displaying the watch on her wrist.

'Ray? I hope you went easy on him. I don't think he was long for this world.'

'He was discharged the day after you. Hairline fracture of the tibia. No big deal.'

'But what about his dodgy ticker and undiagnosed bowel condition?'

Mary laughed loudly. 'Not that I should betray patient confidences, but his heart was fine and we can't have someone bed-blocking because they're a bit constipated.'

Chris felt mildly embarrassed that she'd swallowed Ray's patter. Fortunately, attached to the hospital was a coffee shop franchise, which meant they could eat a half-decent sandwich and not have to endure the environs of the hospital itself. They made small talk. Chris told Mary about the stages of her recovery and made her howl with laughter over the naked Zoom incident. Mary talked about life in Urology and the stresses of a career in the NHS.

As she was finishing the last mouthful of her tuna baguette, Mary said, 'You didn't come all the way over here on the off-chance of seeing me just to say thank you, did you, Christine?'

'You helped me with my release. You spoke to a friend in the pharmacy.'

'Did I? Well, Des is a good lad like that.'

'Could you ask Des another favour?' Chris took the envelope out of her pocket and slid it across the table. 'Would he analyse that?'

Mary took a peep inside the envelope and rapidly passed it back across the table. 'What are you doing, woman?' she hissed. 'Trying to deal? What do you think I am?'

'It's nothing illegal. At least, I don't think it is. I think it's

Sildenafil citrate – over-the-counter treatment for erectile dysfunction.'

'Honey, if you're that desperate, you can buy it. There's a pharmacy by A&E. What on earth made you think that a random nurse who looked after you in hospital would be prepared to risk her job on some fool-ass mission? I'm grateful that you got my watch back, but gratitude only goes so far.'

'I can't tell you why. Someone could be hurt – they may be in danger.' Chris was already regretting this whole escapade. If only she hadn't lost her temper due to Zeta's evasiveness.

'Anyway, Des is a dispensing pharmacist. He's not sat there with beakers and test tubes and Bunsen burners like some mad scientist. Go away, Chris, and take your blue powder with you. If it's a police case, then speak to them, not me – I can call security right now, if you like.' Mary stood, pushing the table back so vigorously that it nearly toppled over.

'I'm working for the police,' Chris lied, panicking. 'Here, give this person a call if you don't believe me.' She took Zeta's business card from her wallet and held it out for inspection.

Mary took the card and looked at it with a puzzled expression. She sat back down and bowed her head. After a few seconds her shoulders started heaving and she made strange snorting noises.

Chris wondered if she'd somehow distressed Mary, that she'd misjudged this situation so badly. Then she realised that Mary was laughing.

'Zeta? Bloody Zeta Jama? I should've have known that she was behind this. And to think I fell for it too – what a wind-up. That girl! Only Zeta would have the balls to send someone else to do her dirty work.' Mary wiped tears from her eyes.

'You know Zeta?'

'Know her? She's a friend – or at least I thought she was. I haven't seen her since she bailed out on a date three months ago. Not that I took it personally – she's like that, is Zeta. Her unpredictability is legendary. And now she sends you to me on an errand?'

'She didn't send me. I don't "run errands" for her,' Chris said, offended. 'Actually, she doesn't know that I'm here.'

'You expect me to believe that this is a coincidence, Christine?'

'That's what it is. Mind you, my life seems to be a series of unlikely coincidences at the moment.'

'Give me your number,' Mary said.

Chris handed over her own business card and Mary pocketed it.

'Now, when you next see Zeta, you tell that girl she owes me an apology and a pizza – pepperoni, stuffed crust.' Mary glanced left and right and picked up the envelope containing the blue powder. 'Make sure you stay safe, OK? That Zeta's got a nose for trouble.'

Mary headed off, leaving Chris sitting at the table feeling bewildered. She wasn't sure what outcome she'd expected, but it wasn't this. She considered texting Zeta, but the ball was in Zeta's court and when this blue powder malarkey turned out to be something of nothing she'd thank Chris for not having wasted her time.

*

The bus back to Cliffstaple passed by the university, and before she knew it, Chris had rung the bell, stepped off the bus and was heading back up the path towards the forensics house. Zeta seemed happy to move on, convinced that they'd found everything it was possible to find, but those two locked rooms nagged at Chris. This was the day that Rene checked the house and, if she was lucky, Chris might catch her.

As she approached, Chris saw a familiar figure. Grayson was back in his rightful position, gazing out of the upstairs window. Even better, Rene was standing outside the front door of the forensics house, her back to Chris. Chris couldn't tell if Rene was about to go in or if she was too late and she'd just locked up.

Rene wasn't alone. She was in conversation with the Attractive Couple, the pair Chris had seen outside the church and again when she and Zeta were searching the house. They were both in their twenties, the man tall, well over six foot, and powerfully built, with fairish hair cropped on the sides and longer on top. The woman was about Chris's height and had a matching haircut to her partner, but her hair was a vibrant red. On closer inspection, they were even more striking. Chris would have described their clothing as 'steampunk chic' if she'd known what that meant.

Spotting Chris, the man leant forward and whispered in Rene's ear. She turned with a start.

'Cornet… Cornet… Chris! Nice to see you again!' Rene stammered.

'Hi Rene. I was just passing.' Which was sort of true.

'This is Mia and Stan. They're second-, soon to be third-year students in BSc Forensic Science. This is Chris.' Besides her name, Rene didn't explain who Chris was or how she knew her, perhaps because she hadn't quite figured that out.

'Nice to meet you, Chris,' said Mia, with the familiar twang of an Australian accent. 'We'd better get to work. We're opening up again, so Old Frank will probably be waiting on the doorstep for his daily half of Guinness.' She and Stan nodded politely and walked off in the direction of the main road to Becketon.

Rene watched them go with the expression of a proud mother hen watching her brood make their way into the world. 'Such a lovely couple, those two.'

'I don't suppose you've heard from Professor Jasper, have you?' Chris asked.

'No. Why do you ask? You don't think anything bad's happened to him, do you?' There was a slight quiver in her voice, as if the thought had just occurred to her.

'No, no. I was just wondering, that's all.' Chris tried to quell the fears she had inadvertently raised. 'I notice you've put Gra… the dummy back in the window. You didn't happen to find the key to the locked door, did you?'

'No. No key,' said Rene rather shortly. 'Perhaps I'll call in a locksmith – if I get any free time.'

Chris sensed something in Rene's body language which suggested she was uneasy in her presence.

'I won't keep you then, Rene. Must get back. I've a demanding cat to feed.'

Seventeen

Back at home, Aitken was curled up asleep on Chris's laptop, which put paid to any thoughts of work that afternoon, so she wheeled Rod out from the newly constructed bivouac in the garden. No need to change into full cycling gear as she was just planning a short jaunt along the seafront.

Down at the usually tranquil harbour there was a relative frenzy of activity. People were unloading metal barriers from a flat-bed truck and erecting signage and a temporary stage. The fishing boats gently rocking in the ebbing tide were being festooned with Union Jacks.

Chris had completely forgotten that Cliffstaple's Festival of Fish was starting the next day – a four-day bacchanalian orgy of excessive drinking, eating and community spiritedness. There would be the usual heady mix of artisan food stalls, beer tents, musical acts, rib-crushing overcrowding and sporadic outbreaks of mindless violence. People would be flocking from all parts of the county to cheer on the oyster-shell hurling or partake in the whelks-down-trousers contest. She hated it. It was the time of year when she and other sensible members of the town locked themselves indoors and waited for the tidal wave of revelry to pass. She didn't need to cram excess into four days when she had the rest of her life to work with.

By the fish market they were erecting a banner that read: 'How Quickly Can You Get Your Winkle Out?' It didn't bode well. The activity reminded Chris of a Bruegel painting that she'd been given in jigsaw form: everyone there was purposeful. There was something fascinating about work – when other people are doing it – so she perched on a mooring bollard and watched the parade rehearsal.

First up was the Sea Scouts Marching Band. They were hopelessly uncoordinated and the young lad at the back was so delighted to have guardianship of a pair of huge cymbals that he was determined to crash them on whim, regardless of any musical notation. The conductor was at breaking point – in his head he was Sir Simon Rattle, but his anguished expression suggested a premonition of his impending public humiliation. Chris applauded the band loudly as it passed and even gave them a whoop of support. Nobody wanted to see a halfway decent marching band, but a terrible one? That was entertainment!

Next came a teacher leading her infant class, who had made papier-mâché fish. There were crabs and cod and flounders in an array of nature-defying colours. One pink monstrosity at the back of the group looked worryingly phallic and Chris suspected it would get the biggest cheer come the day of the parade. She had a flashback to her own childhood – a day trip with her parents to Brighton beach. She was skipping along the promenade in between her mum and dad, holding their hands. Around her wrist was a string connected to a balloon in the shape of a bright red fish which bobbed and nodded on the breeze. She had loved that balloon.

A cacophony shook her out of her sentimental reverie and announced a group of Japanese drummers. One shouldn't judge by appearances, but Chris suspected the nearest this lot had been to Japan was the Flying Samurai Sushi Bar in Becketon. They had doubled down by wearing silk dressing gowns and homemade *hachimaki* headbands, which Chris was sure would cause no offence whatsoever to any bemused Japanese visitors. A drummer peeled off from the back and headed towards her. It took a couple of seconds for her to recognise Next-Door Nick.

'Nick! I didn't realise you were into percussion.'

'It keeps me off the streets and they're a great bunch. You should try it – it's fun and we're always looking for people who can bash the hell out of an inanimate object.'

'Thank you for the vote of confidence, but I look terrible in printed silk.'

'Anyway, I'm glad I caught you,' said Nick. 'I wanted to apologise for yesterday.'

'Apologise? What for?'

'For commenting on your shopping. Stupid joke. It's none of my business what you do, or rather who you—'

'My shopping?' Chris laughed. 'That was research. I'm proofing a paper written by the British Foundation for Men's Sexual Health.' The lie tripped off her tongue rather too easily and she hoped that Nick wouldn't be tempted to check whether the foundation actually existed.

'Oh, I see. What's the paper called?'

Chris hadn't expected a follow-up question. 'Um, "Hard Times".'

Nick gave a laugh that seemed to be a mixture of embarrassment and relief. Relief?

'But if you're in the market for engorging medication,' Chris added, 'I'll sell you that pack for £20. That's nearly half-price tumescence!'

'No, thanks,' said Nick, smiling ruefully. 'Don't have use for that sort of thing – chance'd be a fine thing.' He adjusted the drum straps and returned to his band.

'In that silk kimono?' Chris shouted after him. 'You'll be fighting the women off with your drumsticks.'

Nick waved and the drumming beat restarted, synchronising the band's progression past the harbour.

The sound of jingling bells heralded the last arrival in this parade, a group of morris dancers, bedecked in green and red feathers that would have been the envy of Rene Douglas. The morris men (and women) pranced and danced and slapped sticks with each other. The fool, in a top hat, was waving a bladder-on-a-stick, which he used to unhumorously 'bop' the heads of the dancers and the guys unloading the barriers. The fool was Simon.

Chris laughed so loudly that the dancers stopped and stared in her direction. Simon, visibly furious that she had interrupted their flow, strode over.

'I never thought I'd see the day,' Chris wheezed.

'What – that I'd have friends and engage in social activities and contribute to my community?' Simon raised the bladder as if to give Chris a 'bop'.

She grabbed the stick and wrestled it from him. 'Listen, mate,' she whispered, 'if that thing hits me, my foot's going to make contact with your bladder – and I'm not talking about the one on the stick.'

Simon stepped back. 'There's no need to be so aggressive, Chris. It's all a bit of fun, isn't it, Jan?' He was joined by his wife, in a similar costume, who put a protective arm around his waist. 'Perhaps if you took part in things rather than sniping from the sidelines you might find that you actually enjoyed it.'

'He's right, Chris, hon. And we raise lots of money for charity too,' added Jan, making Chris bristle.

Jan pulled Simon back towards the rest of the waiting morris dancers.

'Simon!' Chris shouted, waving her arm. 'Don't forget your bladder.'

*

It was just gone five by the time Chris got home – a bit early for wine o'clock, particularly mid-week. There was no sign of Aitken, so she put down food for him. He'd turn up when he was good and ready.

Having no impending work deadlines, it was a good opportunity to update her website and add the University of North Kent to her list of contented clients. That took about ten minutes, and then she was off down another internet wormhole, reading conspiracy theories about big pharma and wondering why billionaires would be so bothered about secretly implanting microchips in everyone. She decided that if she had an implanted tracking device that could tell her what she'd just gone upstairs for, she'd welcome the help.

At about seven there was a noise at the kitchen door. Aitken returning for a late dinner.

'About bloody time, you dirty stop-out,' Chris said, without looking up from the screen.

Ten seconds later, the sound was repeated and Chris turned to see a face staring in through the window. She screamed, knocking the laptop and coffee mug to the floor.

'Zeta, for f… frick's sake! You scared the shit out of me.'

She opened the kitchen door. 'What are you doing creeping into my back garden? In fact, how did you get into my back garden?'

Zeta skulked in, lowering her hood.

'Over the wall.' Zeta picked the laptop and pieces of shattered coffee mug from the floor. 'You know, you really should take better security measures, get some wall spikes or security lighting. Give the crime-prevention team at the station a call.'

'Yeah, I'll do that. Ask them to advise on how to stop a serving police officer from breaking into my property, shall I? I've got a perfectly serviceable front door, you know.'

'Didn't want to risk it. Got this weird feeling I'm being watched.'

'Would a cup of coffee in one of my few remaining mugs help quell your irrational paranoia?' Chris asked, putting the kettle on.

'There's stuff going on behind the scenes, I can sense it,' said Zeta, taking a seat.

'What do you mean?'

'DI Dunn's specifically asked me to cover the Festival of Fish from tomorrow. Crowd control.'

'So? He rates you. You told me that he has you lined up for a permanent role. And besides, after six pints of scrumpy and a kipper-in-a-bun, that crowd can get pretty lairy.'

Zeta was becoming more animated. 'But what if he just wants to keep an eye on me – check I'm not following up on the forensics house?'

'Then just say no thanks. You're voluntary, remember? You're too busy, you've got search engines to optimise or whatever. I'm sure you've done more hours than your monthly allocation already.'

Chris judged that this level of agitation could only be quelled by opening a fresh pack of ginger nuts.

'It's not easy to refuse – you don't understand,' said Zeta, looking lustfully at the biscuits.

Chris was beginning to suspect that Zeta's health-freak stuff with mung beans and herbal infusions was just for show. Behind closed doors, her diet was probably as crap as everyone else's.

'Is that why you've infiltrated my back garden – for free counselling? A phone call or a text would have been quite acceptable.' She placed two mugs of her finest instant coffee on the table.

Zeta shook her head. 'I needed to speak to you in person. I told you to stand down.'

Chris's first thought was that Rene Douglas had reported her. It had been stupid to drop in on the forensics house again. 'So? What makes you think I haven't?'

'Mary phoned me.'

'Who?' Chris asked, playing dumb.

'Don't play dumb,' said Zeta. 'Mary Semenyo.'

'Ah.'

'Yes, ah. She told me you ambushed her at the hospital.'

'"Ambushed" is a bit extreme. I just asked if she could help analyse the blue powder from Jasper's jacket. *You* weren't doing anything about it.'

'I said I was on the case.'

'And look what I've found.' Chris slid the Priaman packaging across the table. 'It was inside Jasper's jacket.'

Zeta examined the cardboard sleeve. 'Proves nothing,' she said disdainfully, sliding it back across the table.

'Well, it implies that our professor isn't as shy and retiring as his neighbours suggested. Perhaps we should go and speak to them again.'

'Chris, weren't you listening? I told you to stand down. I'm on the case. Am I not making myself clear?'

Now Chris knew she couldn't mention that she'd spoken to Rene. 'How am I supposed to know what to do? When I want to forget the whole thing you wind me up with talk of conspiracies and secrets, and then when I'm wound up, you tell me to stand down. I don't know whether I'm coming or going and I don't know who to trust. I'm not even sure I trust you, Zeta.'

'Of course you can trust me. I'm committed to finding out what Professor Jasper's up to and uncovering the truth. That's all I care about.'

'But why, Zeta, and at what cost? Just so you can win brownie points with DI Dunn? You've got to do better than that. I don't understand what's driving you. Either you tell me the truth or get out of my kitchen.'

Zeta was visibly shaken by Chris's tirade. She took a drink of coffee and collected her thoughts. 'OK,' she said, 'but this is between you and me only. You're not to tell a soul. Promise?'

Chris nodded.

'I told you that my dad was a police officer?'

'Yes, in Somalia.'

'He was a high-ranking officer, a district commander, and he took it on himself to uncover and confront institutionalised corruption.'

'A noble cause.'

Zeta nodded sadly. 'But his actions did not make him popular with some very powerful people. Somebody informed on him, so he had to act quickly and get my mother and me smuggled out of the country to safety. But' – she paused and took another sip of coffee – 'he disappeared. Or rather, he was disappeared.' Her eyes watered once more.

'I'm so, so sorry, Zeta. But why keep it a secret?'

'It makes me weak. I can't let people see that weakness. People exploit weaknesses.'

Instinctively, Chris hugged her. 'It makes you one of the strongest people I've ever met.'

Zeta sunk her head into Chris's chest, like Chloe used to when she was young. 'I'm sorry, Chris, if I've used you. I didn't mean to, honestly. Sometimes I get tunnel-vision. I can't right what happened to my father, but if I can honour his memory somehow…'

To Chris, it now made sense. She still wasn't convinced about the path they were on, but she was beginning to understand why they were travelling.

'So what next?' she asked. 'Without Professor Jasper we've got nothing, and even if we track him down he may refuse to talk to you.'

'True.'

'Is it worth trying the forensics house again?'

Zeta shook her head. 'We've already been there twice. Any more could be provocative, particularly considering DI Dunn's warning.'

'We've hit a dead end?'

'Not yet. I've asked Barry if he can track Jasper's phone. He wasn't happy, said that it's not as straightforward as my usual requests.'

Chris could sense another task looming. 'So where do I come in?'

'Now that I've been assigned to the festival, it's tricky for me to follow up. I'm avoiding sending emails and texts – anything that could provide a trail and get us into trouble. So I was hoping you could liaise with Barry.'

'I'm not sure my powers of persuasion exceed yours, Zeta.'

'Barry likes you. I'm sure you can sweet-talk him.'

Chris felt that her chances of sweet-talking anyone seemed slim. 'Perhaps I could offer him a fig roll.'

Zeta looked startled. 'You don't need to go that far, Chris. It's important that, as women, we keep our self-respect.'

'It's only a biscuit, Zeta. Well, a sort of cakey-biscuit.'

'Oh.' Zeta looked relieved.

There was a pregnant pause.

'What did you think I meant by "offer Barry a fig roll"?'

'Nothing. Well, I saw this Channel 4 programme, *Senior Swingers*, about what older people get up to when they're...' Zeta's voice trailed off and dinner-seeking Aitken arrived as a welcome distraction.

'I'll buy Barry lunch. Is that safe?'

'Perfect, Chris.' Zeta rose from the table and pulled up her hood. 'And if you learn anything, you know where to find me. Remember, radio silence – no calls, no texts from now on.'

And then she was gone, slipping out of the kitchen door and disappearing into the twilight.

A plan was forming in Chris's mind. A plan that didn't strictly adhere to Zeta's 'stand down' instructions but wasn't direct intervention either. Besides, all being well, Zeta need never know.

Her first instinct was to phone Chloe for a comfort-giving natter, but she remembered that her daughter was away at the moment and doubted that the boys would be too keen on being woken by an early-morning phone call from their mad English granny.

Eighteen

Sometimes Chris had good ideas, sometimes she had bad ideas. Sometimes, her good ideas turned out to be bad ideas – she wasn't sure if this was going to be one of those.

Post-breakfast, her first stop was the Pit of Despair. The Pit of Despair was actually Chloe's old bedroom. When Chloe first left home, Chris had done what most parents did – she kept it as Chloe had left it, even down to the posters of Slipknot on the wall and the My Little Pony pillowcases (she had been somewhat neglectful when it came to updating her daughter's bed linen). Perhaps Chloe would need to move back in sometime or pay an extended visit, in which case her old room would be ready and waiting for her.

Over the years it had morphed into a de facto storeroom. Many families had garages that had never housed a car or loft space filled with forgotten possessions. Chris had her Pit of Despair. Chloe's bed was still in there – somewhere – but had become buried beneath stuff. Stuff such as filing cabinets crammed with receipts; cardboard boxes filled with books that Chris would never get round to reading; bin bags of clothes set aside for charity donation; obsolete technology that she couldn't bring herself to throw away. Rather than tackle the Pit, it was easier just to throw another box into the room and close the door. Once that door was closed, the problem no longer existed.

In the far corner of the Pit, under a leaning tower of never-played board games, was an easel, the legacy of an impulse purchase. Twenty minutes of rooting around in the bottom of the wardrobe uncovered a battered tin of dried-out watercolour paints, a jam-jar of matted brushes and an empty sketchbook. Chris now had the props for her cover story. Her good idea was that she would spend the morning observing the forensics house from a distance. And what could be more unassuming than an amateur artist capturing the beauty of the Kent countryside?

She tipped the sketchbook, brushes and paint into her backpack along with her water bottle. She added an old white shirt of Simon's that she used for decorating and a beret she had bought from a jumble sale but had never worn. The beret was bit of a cliché, but she decided that if you were going undercover, perversely, it was best to go big and bold.

The easel proved to be a greater challenge. It folded flat but was still a substantial piece of wood and quite heavy. Chris tried, unsuccessfully, to tie it to Rod's frame, so in the end she fashioned two leather belts into a rudimentary shoulder harness. It didn't feel very secure, but she'd be avoiding busy roads on the way so hopefully would avoid ending up in Baxter Ward again.

She did make it to her destination. Not without incident or peril, as the easel kept slipping from her shoulder and playing chicken with Rod's rear wheel. Thankfully, once she'd made it as far as the Hill of Death, she could balance the easel across the handlebars without the danger of catching any oncoming traffic.

She set up her pitch about thirty metres from the front of the forensics house. Far enough to be unobtrusive but near enough to keep an eye on the front door by occasionally turning her head to the left. Chris's subject for artistic study was an unremarkable hedge-lined field. In the foreground was a rusty agricultural rotavator hitched to a shiny red tractor. Not exactly *The Fighting Temeraire*, but then again, Chris was no JMW Turner.

She set the sketchbook on the easel, moistened the paints and brushes, put on the artist's smock and adjusted the beret to a jaunty angle. After thirty minutes' painting, she made a discovery. She couldn't paint. At school, she'd achieved an O-Level in art, but that was forty-four years ago and apparently painting was not like riding a bike – you could forget how to do it. The once pristine sketchbook was now covered in poorly executed blotches and daubs.

The other thing Chris came to realise about al fresco painting was that everyone thought they had a right to observe the creative process in action. That morning there was one particular old guy, a rambler with patches on his rucksack that bragged about all the areas of outstanding beauty he'd visited but not really appreciated. Rather than pass by making tutting noises like everybody else, this one thought his constructive criticism would improve Chris's day.

'Watch the way the light moves,' he suggested. 'Paint what you can see, not what you think you can see.' And then, 'Be bolder with your colour palette.'

'Frick off!' Chris suggested. And he did.

She was so distracted by the critical rambler that she nearly missed that the front door of the forensics house had been opened. Had someone just entered or was someone about to leave?

Rene appeared in the doorway. Not a huge surprise, perhaps, although yesterday was her regular day for her checking routine. Today's feathers made her look like an exotic bird conducting a mating display. Chris half expected her to start a strutting, head-bobbing ritual dance.

Rene looked left and right, so Chris ducked down to hide behind her easel. After a minute, Rene moved away from the door and, through a gap in the wooden frame of her easel, Chris could see she was not alone. Rene was followed out of the house by two figures she recognised. Mia and Stan. They closed the door behind them and disappeared from Chris's sight towards the campus.

Now that the coast was clear, Chris approached the forensics house, hugging the hedgerow for maximum cover. She had been specifically instructed to stand down, but this opportunity might not arise again. Zeta seemed to think that this location was not particularly significant, but Chris had to be sure.

As expected, the front door was locked, so she scurried around to the rear of the house, but the back door was firmly locked as well. Counting from right to left, Chris identified the window on the top floor that corresponded to the locked room. From her low-down viewpoint, the curtains appeared to be open, but there was no way to look inside. Or was there?

In the car park to Chris's right was a huge green recycling bin on wheels. It took most of her strength and a good ten minutes to manoeuvre it across the grass and alongside the rear of the house. Perhaps the sight of a woman in an oversized man's white shirt and a beret shoulder-charging an industrial waste bin was just too bizarre to warrant attention as nobody seemed to give her a second glance.

She clambered inelegantly up onto the bin, but she was still way too low down – the window was at least two metres above her head. Now she came up with her second good idea of the morning. She went back to her pitch and disassembled the easel. Then she used a thick rubber band to attach her phone to the end. She remounted the bin, pressed 'video record' on her phone and, standing on tiptoes with her right arm aloft, she could just, *just*, raise the camera to the level of the upstairs window. It was shaky, but if she could hold this pose for ten seconds...

'Can I help you?'

A male voice startled her and she took half a step backwards, overbalancing and tumbling from the bin towards the ground. Two strong arms, very strong arms, caught her and huge hands encircled her waist. Chris was lowered slowly and safely to the ground.

She gazed up into the face of her rescuer. Stan. Mia stood alongside him, looking distinctly unimpressed.

'What are you doing? You could have killed yourself.' Stan's accent was East European.

'*Dziękuję!*' Chris said, taking a punt with the only Polish word she knew.

'Good guess,' said Stan, 'but that doesn't answer my question.'

'I'm landscape painting. I was just seeing if I could capture another vista.'

'Of the inside of a house? Are you spying on us?' asked Mia.

'Spying?'

'You keep accidentally bumping into us.'

'Do I?'

'What are you – campus security?'

Stan picked up Chris's phone and handed it back to her. It now had a large crack across the screen. 'Or maybe a voyeur?'

'No, actually I… I…' Chris couldn't think of any more lies, so she adjusted her beret and decided to revert to the truth and to hell with the consequences. 'I'm looking for Professor Jasper, so I was trying to see inside that room in case he's… well… hiding there.'

Mia looked shocked. 'Hiding? Why would he be hiding? Is he in trouble?'

'I hope not. I don't know… There's just a lot of things that don't add up.'

'Or perhaps we're keeping him prisoner?' laughed Stan.

'I didn't say that. I'm sorry, but when I saw you both leaving the house earlier…'

'We were—' started Mia.

'… picking up some research that Mia had left there,' interrupted Stan.

Mia reached into her shoulder bag and extracted a USB stick. 'That's right. It's for my dissertation, "Toxic Shock – A Cultural Appreciation of Poisoning".'

'So we can assure you that the professor isn't "in da house".' Stan smiled.

'Can I ask you a few questions about Professor Jasper?' Chris asked.

'I'm not sure how much help we can be,' said Mia.

Stan nodded his agreement. 'But if you don't mind walking and talking, we've got to get to work. We manage the bar at The Mechanical Avocado in Becketon.'

As Chris was heading to Becketon to meet Barry for lunch anyway, this was the perfect opportunity to get an alternative view on their missing person. She parcelled up her painting gear but decided that the easel could stay behind, buried in a patch of weeds behind the forensics house. Chris persuaded herself that this wasn't fly-tipping as the wooden easel would decompose – eventually – or perhaps the surrounding vegetation would rise up and reclaim it. She rammed the easel into the grasses, which glinted, perhaps from the sunlight catching that morning's dew or, more likely, from a discarded energy drink can. She was tempted to investigate further but Mia was impatient to leave.

On first impression, Mia and Stan were a captivating couple, the sort with whom, if she were a young student again, Chris would want to hang out. Stan was originally from Krakow and Mia was from just outside of Melbourne, a coincidence that wasn't lost on Chris.

'So what do you want to know?' asked Mia.

'Do you know Professor Jasper well?'

'As well as anyone can know their lecturer after two years,' replied Stan.

'And do you like him?'

Stan was about to answer, but Mia interrupted. 'His nickname's Professor Marmite. Dr Karamak's popular with pretty much everyone, but Jasper divides opinion.'

'Apparently, Dr Karamak described him as "old-school".'

'That's a bit harsh,' said Stan. 'I'd call his approach "classic".'

'Let's face it,' said Mia, 'this isn't exactly the top forensics course in the country, and the facilities aren't the most advanced, but it's friendly and student-focused.'

'And cheaper than the rest,' added Stan.

Chris wasn't sure if this intelligence on Professor Jasper was of any value, and it was using all of her mental agility to walk, talk and file this information in a new part of her memory palace. It took her a couple of minutes to realise that Mia was still talking.

'And he's been very helpful with our dissertations.'

'What's your dissertation about, Mia? Toxic shock? I like the title,' said Chris, refocusing her attention.

'How methods of homicidal poisoning reflect the culture of the times.'

'What is it with women's obsession with poison?' joked Stan. He received a sharp but friendly punch in the ribs in response.

'Victorian and Edwardian times were the golden age of poisoning. You had proper toxins – you know, strychnine, arsenic, antimony – the ones where your humble investigator had a chance. Nasty, but with a certain honour. Now it's radioactive materials and nerve agents. Poisoning's become less fun.'

'Fun?' Chris was getting attuned to their gallows humour.

'Well, if it'd been *Novichok on the Orient Express*, it'd have wiped out the lot of them, Poirot included.'

'So do you have a specialism, Stan?'

'Stan's a firestarter,' said Mia proudly.

'My dissertation's called "Feel the Burn: The Myth of Spontaneous Human Combustion".'

'Catchy,' said Chris. 'So, I can't combust spontaneously? That's reassuring.'

'Nah, there's always a source of ignition. What I'm writing about is how, in forensic science, it's easy for people to draw completely the wrong conclusion if they only have partial evidence.' Chris thought Stan looked at her rather pointedly.

They had reached a crossroads.

'We go right here,' said Mia. 'Nice to meet you. If you ever fancy popping into The Avocado, Stan mixes a wicked chilli margarita.'

'And between five and seven it's happy hour – two for one,' said Stan, reading Chris's mind.

She waved goodbye to the pair, content that she had closed off one small avenue of investigation. She crossed the forensic house room off the list of Professor Jasper's possible hiding places, and her head began to fill with thoughts of an early evening chilli margarita. For now, she headed towards Pete's Pantry, stopping by Tesco Express en route to make an essential purchase.

*

Chris had never seen anyone so delighted at being given a packet of fig rolls as PC Barry Conway. He turned it over in his hands and studied the ingredients like an antiques expert examining the hallmark on a priceless heirloom.

'Very kind of you, Ms Heron. My favourite brand, too. Not all of them can get the fig properly gooey.' Barry placed the packet in front of him on the table in Pete's Pantry.

'I pride myself on my knowledge of fig rolls, Barry,' Chris said, taking a drink of tea.

Barry was thoughtful, examining the contents of his sausage sandwich. 'Zeta's a good one, you know. Smart too, really smart. Sure, she's driven and impulsive, but her heart's in the right place. I should know. I've been in this game for forty years, so I can spot the good from the bad.'

'She thinks highly of you. Reckons you're taken for granted by everyone else at the station though.'

'Nah, that's where she's wrong. I've engineered my position, been years in the making. Look at me – a cushy, warm spot behind a desk where I can see out my remaining months. I've seen too many movies about what happens to cops when they're on the verge of retirement to risk putting myself in the line of fire. "Just one last patrol", that's what they always say, then *Bam! Bam! Bam!* If keeping safe until I draw my gold-plated pension means being ignored and patronised, then that's a small price to pay.'

'And that's why Zeta shouldn't have asked you to trace Professor Jasper's phone. What if you're caught? If she really believes there's something to investigate, perhaps we'd better go through the proper channels. Maybe I can get one of his neighbours to file a missing persons report.'

Barry finished his sandwich and took a couple of sheets of paper from an inside pocket. 'Too late,' he said, unfolding the sheets. 'I used Atherton's login to request the info.'

Chris instinctively looked over her shoulder to check that they were not attracting attention, then moved her chair to Barry's side of the table.

'Jasper's got an old phone, so the digital forensics guys couldn't get precise GPS data. It pinged off masts a couple of times before going dead.' Barry unfolded the sheets of paper, which were printed sections of maps. 'The first time was here.' He pointed to a red circle untidily drawn on the map in biro. '10:32 on Friday 16 August. It could be anywhere within the circle.'

'Well, that's easy – that's mainly the university grounds. We know from Rene Douglas that Professor Jasper popped in to pick up his post, so that tallies. I was there about an hour later. I must have just missed him.'

'Perhaps that was fortunate for you, if he's a bad 'un,' said Barry, opening the packet of fig rolls surreptitiously. 'Then we pick him up again here, at 12:08 on the same day.' This time the map was of Bottisham, a large town about ten miles from both Cliffstaple and Becketon.

Not a natural navigator, Chris had to turn the map round to get her bearings. The red circle covered the old town, including the market square and the quayside development by the creek.

'Do we know if Jasper has a car?' asked Barry. 'If we're lucky, he could have been clocked by a camera.'

'I don't know. I can ask Zeta, but in an hour and a half he could have cycled or taken the bus.'

'Or even jogged.'

'I don't know much about Professor Jasper, but ten miles in ninety minutes would be pretty impressive for a middle-aged academic. Is this the last contact?'

Barry swallowed a fig roll. 'Yes. After that there's nothing, so either the phone's switched off, it's run out of juice or it's been destroyed.'

'Or he's switched phones.'

Barry nodded in agreement.

Chris folded the maps and put them in her backpack. 'Thanks, Barry, this is really helpful. I'll pass the info on to Zeta. I assume you're not patrolling the Festival of Fish.'

Barry shuddered. 'Not bloody likely. Last did it five years ago.

There was a punch-up between two rival morris-dancing groups – some geezer relieved himself in another's pewter tankard and it all kicked off. Got very nasty. Why they're allowed to have sticks is beyond me.'

Barry seemed in no hurry to rush back to the police station, so Chris said her farewells and left him at Pete's Pantry to finish the last of the fig rolls. She was tempted to rush this new information straight to Zeta, but to see Zeta at the harbour and then visit Bottisham would be wasting both time and Rod's battery life. It would be easier if she performed an initial scouting mission and then debriefed Zeta later in the afternoon.

Nineteen

Of course, what Chris should have done was go home, feed Aitken and put her feet up for the rest of the day. She had only been back on the bike for a week and she knew she was overdoing it. She had always been like that. In her teens she could only afford to buy one vinyl album a month with her Saturday job wages. She would memorise the album cover and then play the record repeatedly until she was thoroughly sick of it. The album would then be banished to the back of her record collection, never to darken her turntable again. She hoped she wasn't now doing the same with Rod the e-bike.

There was a direct road between Becketon and Bottisham, but that was busy, and with a sixty-mile-an-hour speed limit was no place for a nervous cyclist. Instead, Chris plotted a route that ran parallel but wound through hedge-lined lanes and eye-wateringly expensive hamlets. Even so, it was not the most enjoyable ride as local residents, familiar with each blind bend and humpback bridge, hurtled around like rally drivers. As soon as she could, Chris took a detour via the quieter seaside road. Here, the occasional driver was more gracious and gave her a wide berth when passing. The road cut across the salt marshes where sheep and their lambs that had almost reached adulthood munched grass, blissfully unaware of their inevitable fate as an accompaniment to mint sauce.

After a couple of miles, she turned right at a picturesque Saxon church and took a track that bisected orchards and farmland. She pulled over onto a verge to let a monstrous tractor trundle by and the driver gave her an appreciative wave. From here, she cut through some woodland before re-joining the marshy borders of an estuary that centuries ago had formed the basis of medieval Bottisham's economy. The grassy mounds and the rotted remains of long-abandoned boats looked positively Dickensian. Chris half expected Magwitch to leap out of the hedgerow as she rode by.

Her hip had started aching again, but she was nearly at her destination. The path now joined a tarmac road that skirted the boatyard and Chris could see assorted masts rising like branches over the tops of the trees. Just one main obstacle left – the sewage works, sandwiched between the path and the boatyard. She felt guilty that, rather than embracing the works as part of her family's heritage, she switched Rod's mode to high and held her breath as she accelerated past the area of greatest stench. Unfortunately, in high summer, that area exceeded her lung capacity.

Half a mile later, she rolled into Bottisham's market square. It was busy with shoppers milling around the dozen or so stalls that sold everything from clothing to fruit and veg. She took the emergency £10 note from her phone cover and bought a couple of attractive-looking but disappointingly tasteless apples. She was beginning to doubt whether Professor Jasper was merely 'on holiday'. Bottisham was a nice enough place to spend an afternoon, but it was hardly St Tropez.

There was no sign of her sought-after academic and, after a couple of circuits of the marketplace, Chris cycled down the main road towards the quayside.

In her years of visiting this small area by Bottisham Creek, she had seen it transform from a grubby waterfront with nothing but a disused commercial ceramics factory and resident drug addicts into a desirable location that now boasted three antique shops, a large teashop, an art gallery and a woodworking studio. It was relatively quiet at the moment, being the kind of place that got busy at the weekends.

Three houseboats were moored alongside the towpath. That was a possibility. Might Professor Jasper own a houseboat, or have hired one? A houseboat would be a great place to hunker down and concentrate on writing a book or preparing for a new term. Chris wandered along the waterside trying to surreptitiously look in the windows of each boat, but there were no signs of present occupancy.

Of the three antique shops, only one was currently open. Nigel's Knick-Knacks and Antiques. A bald, stocky man and a pencil-thin teenager, either his son or an apprentice, were manoeuvring a bulky Victorian wardrobe as Chris entered.

''Ave a look round. Let me know if there's anything that takes your fancy.' The man (presumably the titular Nigel) gave a grin, which turned into a grimace as he took the weight of the wardrobe.

On first inspection, all of the stock looked as if it belonged in the 'knick-knack' rather than 'antique' category. There were piles of rusty tools awaiting the custom of a rusty tool enthusiast; a stack of 1980s football annuals; precarious piles of crockery; furniture fit only for set dressing for a kitchen-sink drama; classic toys that might have been collectibles had they not been battered and unboxed. As a hoarder herself, even Chris knew that this stuff should have been chucked in a skip – which was presumably where Knick-Knack Nigel had found it all in the first place.

'Are you looking for anything in particular?' said Nigel, appearing magically by her left shoulder. 'I've got some nice spoons.'

Chris pondered what it was about her demeanour that said 'needs spoons'. 'I'm good for spoons, thanks. I'm actually looking for someone.'

'Aren't we all, love? Aren't we all?' said Nigel, and he winked theatrically at Chris and then at the lad to make sure they both got the joke.

'You might have seen him last Friday. Late fifties, grey hair, glasses?'

Nigel shook his head. 'That description fits half of my customers. Seen anyone like that, Ollie?'

Ollie just shrugged.

'I could show you a photo.' Chris took her phone from her zipped shorts pocket and scrolled through her emails. She located the one from the university and clicked on the relevant pdf. Her phone seemed to physically groan with the effort of summoning up the document.

Nigel and Ollie showed interest and crowded closer to look at the screen. Chris zoomed in on the image containing Professor Jasper, just about visible despite the cracked screen.

'Why do you want to find this guy?' said Nigel abruptly. 'What are you – police? Child support?'

'Benefit fraud?' suggested Ollie.

'No, no, nothing like that, nothing nasty,' Chris said, buying time to think up a reason. 'It's because I have his jacket, the tweed one in the picture there, and I want to return it to him.'

'You want to return his jacket?' Nigel sounded incredulous. 'Why don't you just phone him rather than randomly asking complete strangers?'

'He's not answering his phone.'

'Listen, love, if a guy leaves in such a hurry that he abandons his jacket and he isn't answering your calls, you should take that as a sign that he ain't all that keen.'

'He didn't leave his trousers behind an' all, did he?' piped up Ollie, and the two men descended into mutual backslapping laughter.

'It's not like that…' Chris tried to say, but she could see that she'd lost her audience and felt herself blushing. She turned to leave.

'Hang on, love,' said Nigel. 'Just having a little joke. I'm sure you've got your reasons. If you could mail us that photo or send it to our printer we'll show it to the other traders when they open up.'

This was pushing Chris way past the boundary of her technological skill. Ollie saw her pitiful struggle, gently took her phone and within twenty seconds the printer behind the counter was chugging out a perfectly cropped A4 photo of Professor Jasper.

'If you leave us your details, we'll ask around and see if anyone remembers him.'

Chris handed over her business card and thanked Nigel and

Ollie profusely. She made a vow that next time she was in there she would buy some spoons, whether she needed them or not.

Nobody in the other open retail units showed any recognition of the professor.

'Last Friday was pretty manic, so unless he stood out in some way, I doubt he'd be remembered,' noted the manager of the tearooms.

Chris noticed a narrow, nettle-fringed footpath at the end of the quay that had to connect to the boatyard and she was tempted to continue her reconnaissance there, but it would be an hour's cycle back to Cliffstaple and she needed to catch up with Zeta at the festival.

*

The clock on Rod's ride computer read 16:54, but Chris's legs felt twenty years older by the time she wobbled into Cliffstaple harbour. Although Thursday was supposed to be a gentle set-up day to prepare for the chaos of the weekend, there was already a crowd congregating in front of a stage at the far end of the harbour.

A woman ran past dragging two reluctant children in her wake. 'Come on, Jacinta and Jasmine! We don't want to miss the opening speeches,' she said excitedly.

Chris couldn't imagine there was anything that Jacinta and Jasmine would want to do less.

Ahead, on the stage, were a photographer, a cameraman and three figures behind a microphone stand: the mayor of Becketon (complete with gold chain and silly hat), some sort of bishop in an ornate frock, and (according to the amplified introduction) the police and crime commissioner of North Kent.

Chris immediately saw Zeta, standing in uniform to the right of the crowd, facing the stage. She looked up and, with subtle non-verbal communication, advised Chris not to approach. Chris spotted the danger. Not more than twenty metres in front of her stood Sgt Spurgeon and PC Atherton. Zeta's eyes then directed Chris to look at the left of the stage, where stood the tall figure of

DI Dunn, even more dashing in his dress uniform.

Chameleon-like, Chris melded unseen with the audience. The opening speeches were far from entertaining. God only knew what poor Jacinta and Jasmine made of them. The mayor burbled about civic pride, though he kept calling Cliffstaple 'Barnstaple'; the bishop preached about Jesus being a 'fisher of men' as though a whole Festival of Fish might be enough to induce a second coming; the police and crime commissioner managed to make the instruction to 'enjoy yourselves safely' sound menacing.

After the speeches, the Sea Scouts Band took to the stage, which Chris saw as her cue to leave. As she passed a stall advertising scenic boat tours, she heard a 'Pssst!' from behind a large refuse bin, where Zeta had concealed herself. She squeezed in behind the bin to join her.

'It stinks here! Why can't we meet in a cafe like normal human beings?' Chris asked.

'Can't risk being seen together. It'd raise too many questions.'

'Not as many questions as if they catch us playing sardines behind a shitty rubbish bin.'

'Spurgeon's been watching me like a hawk all day and now I've got Dunn to look out for as well.' Zeta glanced about furtively, as if either one of her senior colleagues might pop their head round the corner of the bin to say 'How do!'

'What's DI Dunn doing here? Just how much policing does a Festival of Fish need? I've seen fewer cops at a riot.'

'It's a gathering of bigwigs. It's not what you say but who you're seen with, isn't it? I'd put money on them all being members of the same lodge.'

'Look, Zeta, much as I enjoy these congenial surroundings, can we continue this conversation in my kitchen? I've got some information.'

'So have I', said Zeta. 'My shift ends in an hour. I'll see you then.'

'An hour? Can you make it an hour and a half?'

But Zeta had already gone.

Aitken was waiting when Chris wheeled in through the gate that connected her back garden to the side alley. She didn't lock the gate behind her as it would save Zeta from any more wall-climbing. An hour was plenty of time to feed Aitken, have a shower, change into less sweaty clothes and catch up on emails. There was a thank you from the university, which was nice, and the offer of more work, which was even nicer.

Chris's phone pinged with a text from Simon that read: *R U round 2morrow eve?*

She hated text speak and hated it even more when it was done badly by a middle-aged man trying to be 'with it'. How much time did Simon save by writing *2* rather than *to*? She replied: *Thank you for your text. I politely request that you mind your own frickin' business. Yours sincerely, Chris Heron (Ms)*

Even though her arrival was expected, Chris still jumped when Zeta knocked on the kitchen window at 6:30pm precisely. She had made a percolator of decent coffee in readiness. If she couldn't do anything about the state of the house, at least it would smell good.

'How was the festival?' she asked. 'Fishy?'

'Not too bad. It's only ever locals and young families on the opening day. The next three days is when the bedlam happens.'

Zeta sat at the table and Aitken immediately leapt onto her lap, seeking attention and showing blatant favouritism.

Chris spread out the two sheets of paper on the table in front of Zeta.

'Good old Barry,' Zeta said, picking up each sheet in turn. 'He always delivers. I guess we should target this area of Bottisham, see if we can find any witnesses.'

'I've already' – Chris was about to tell Zeta that she'd performed a reconnaissance of the area that morning, but something stopped her – 'um, thought about priorities. That quayside area looks promising.' Zeta didn't need to know she'd been there today, or at the forensics house. It was not as if she had unearthed any useful information.

'Maybe. What are you doing Monday? We can have a scout around then.'

'Monday?' Monday seemed an age away to Chris. 'If we're going to find Professor Jasper, don't we need to act on this information immediately?'

Zeta shook her head. 'I can't get away while the festival's on. Too many beady eyes.'

'If you're tied up, perhaps I could—'

'No,' said Zeta, abruptly shutting her down. 'Nothing happens without my say-so. Can't have you going off-piste again.'

Chris felt like her position as Zeta's Dr Watson had been downgraded to Mrs Hudson the housekeeper.

'Talking of which' – Zeta lowered her voice, even though there were only the two of them in the kitchen, three if they included Aitken – 'I got a call from Mary. They've analysed the blue powder.'

'Already? I'm amazed. I thought it'd take weeks.'

'Could have. Luckily the answer was straightforward, one of the first things they looked for.'

'Sildenafil citrate?'

Zeta shook her head. 'Nope.'

'Blue cocaine?'

Again Zeta shook her head. 'Uh-uh.'

'I assume it's not anthrax, unless you want us to spend the last hours of our lives playing annoying guessing games. Come on, spit it out, Zeta.'

Zeta folded her arms rather smugly. 'Sucrose.'

'Sucrose? As in sweet stuff? Oh, how disappointing. Does the professor just have an addiction to Sherbet Dib Dabs? I was convinced this was a lead.'

'I think it is,' said Zeta. 'It's a base substance used in the production of tablets. So, combined with the packaging you found…'

'Oh, I'm useful now, am I?' Chris couldn't stop herself from being snippy.

'… this could mean one of two things.' Zeta ignored the

snippiness. 'Either someone is setting up their own pharmaceutical factory, bypassing expensive safety regulations and taxes, or they are simply passing off sucrose tablets as medication.'

'Fake pills?' Chris said. 'I've heard of counterfeit jeans and dodgy Rolexes, but ersatz erectile dysfunction tablets?'

'Why not? I mean, a packet of branded tablets must sell for… what…?'

'£34 for four tablets,' Chris automatically interjected.

Zeta looked impressed by her knowledge.

'So even if you were selling them half price, say £4 a tablet, that's very lucrative.'

'Almost as profitable as blue cocaine?'

Zeta nodded and sipped her coffee in thought. 'And much safer. If the police catch you with a big bag of sucrose, there's no crime. "I'm just making homemade confectionery, officers."'

Chris was beginning to catch on to Zeta's thought process. 'So that's fraud?'

'Yes,' said Zeta. 'The best way to get away with fraud is to make it low value and embarrassing. That's why the vast majority of scams go unreported. People are ashamed they got fooled.'

'If you found you'd spent £16 on dodgy erectile dysfunction tablets, you're hardly likely to go on *Watchdog* to complain.'

Zeta nodded. 'And that's presuming you realise that it's the pills that are the problem. Chris, we could be looking at the perfect crime.'

'So is this the time to call it in, to make it official?'

'Not yet. This is all just a theory, guesswork. All we've really got is some blue sucrose.'

'And a professor on the run. Though I can't think of anyone who looks less like a Mr Big.'

'We've still got no real evidence. You could pass that packaging on to Trading Standards and it would go to the bottom of a mountain of cases they're investigating. We need to keep digging, but we're getting closer, I can smell it, Chris. We're getting closer.' Zeta gently removed Aitken from her lap and stood, raising her hood. 'Don't approach me at the festival again. Too risky.'

'It would help if you told me where you live,' Chris said, but Zeta was already out through the kitchen door and gone. Sudden departures were becoming her trademark.

Chris got up to put the coffee mugs in the dishwasher and could barely make it across the kitchen as her muscles complained about the abuse she had given them over the past seven days. She had to rest, but her head was buzzing with all the possibilities. How Zeta could calmly leave further investigation until Monday was unfathomable.

As she unplugged her phone from the charger, she noticed a text from Next-Door Nick. *Ordered too much pizza. Fancy helping me out? xx*

As she was in that curious state between hyperactivity and complete exhaustion, she knew she was not fit for polite company. Beans on toast, crap TV and an early night was all she could manage.

*

She reached for her phone – 02:00, it told her. She was shattered but couldn't sleep. Even counting sheep wasn't working. The sheep were wearing tweed jackets and bleating out 'Greensleeves' – *baa, baa, ba-baa, b'baa, baa, baa-baa*. She might as well make insomnia productive, so she double-checked her work emails and cleared the spam folder. Nestled between emails that told her she had won €5 million on the Lithuanian lottery and that lonely sugar daddies were looking for a match was a mail from Knick-Knack Antiques.

Gotta bite from your photo. Nige

Now she had no chance of sleeping.

Twenty

Chris had no idea when she finally fell asleep. When she woke she was still clutching her phone. She stumbled downstairs in a stupor, fed Aitken, returned to bed with a cup of tea and promptly nodded off again. She had a vivid dream.

She was about seven or eight years old, in her childhood home, playing hide-and-seek with her parents. The hallway had so many doors – hundreds. Which one to choose? There was a huge wardrobe in there, that was all, but it made a good place to hide. This wasn't a secret passage to a magical world; it stank of damp and mothballs and she wanted to get out, she wanted her mum and dad. The door was stuck fast. There was a jacket hanging at the back of the wardrobe. No, it was a blazer, a candy-stripe blazer. And there were chimes. Someone at the door? Someone to rescue her?

She was woken by her phone ringing on the pillow beside her. The screen flashed up the name 'Dan'. Shit! Her son-in-law never phoned her. Something was obviously wrong. She fumbled to unlock the phone.

'Dan! What's wrong? Is it Chloe or the boys? What's happened?'

'Calm down, Chris,' Dan drawled. 'Everything's fine. We're all well. Chloe's indisposed at the moment, so she asked me to give you a call to check that you'll be around later today.'

'God, you scared the crap out of me, Dan. Give me a second.' She took four deep breaths to compose herself. 'Am I around later? Yeah, I've got a few chores this morning, but after that I'm pretty much free.'

'Ah, that's great, Chris. Chloe will be in touch.'

It sounded like it would be an ungodly hour in Melbourne for a call. 'You're sure things are OK?'

'Absolutely. You have a great day, d'ya hear? Boys send their love.'

It had only been four days since she'd last spoken to Chloe, but she was missing her desperately. Was she metamorphosing into a clingy mother? Perhaps she was still sleep-fuddled. That dream about the wardrobe was the sort that lingered, the sort that stopped you from thinking straight.

She decided that the best thing to do would be to respond to Nigel's email and get on the road. There was no time for a proper breakfast, so she put on her cycling gear and chucked an unopened pack of plain chocolate digestives into her backpack (the heart of any nutritious breakfast). She trawled through her laptop to find a version of the 'Missing Cat' poster that Next-Door Nick had designed for the fruitless search for Waterman. Despite her rudimentary IT skills, she managed to substitute a photo of her much-missed black and white cat with one of an earnest-looking, bespectacled university professor. At the top of the page she typed the heading 'Have You Seen This Man?' in bold black Helvetica, added her name and phone number at the bottom and printed out half a dozen copies.

Rod's battery was fully charged, but the same couldn't be said for Chris's phone. Her nocturnal browsing had taken its toll. Recharging would take an hour she hadn't got and she reckoned there was probably just enough juice for the morning as long as she didn't do anything radical like use the damned thing. She was tempted to text Zeta, to let her know what she was planning, but Zeta had been very firm about the 'no contact' rule – scarily so. Instead, she tucked her phone away in one of the many zipped pockets of her cycling shorts, wrote 'Don't forget to charge phone' on a Post-it note and stuck it on the fridge as a reminder for when she got back.

Chris regretted her choice of clothing within five minutes of setting off. The weather had turned. The warm sunshine of the past week had been replaced with thick cloud cover and a northerly wind that warned of an early shift from summer to autumn. But it was too late to turn back now and look for her thermals. There was no time to waste.

Bottisham quayside was busier than the day before but not dramatically so for a Friday. Perhaps people had been put off by the chillier weather or lured towards the Festival of Fish. A few visitors were taking a mid-morning break in the teashop, and others, mainly couples, were browsing the retail outlets, which all seemed to be open for business. Incongruously, a middle-aged man was pushing a grandfather clock in a wheelbarrow along the water's edge in a scene that seemed certain to end in comedic disaster. Chris stopped and watched for a minute, but disappointingly he made it safely to the boot of his large estate car.

She completed a circuit of the quayside to ascertain that the considerable amount of money ploughed into the redevelopment of the area did not seem to have extended to the provision of a bike rack. There was a narrow passage separating the teashop from the craft centre next door, so she slipped Rod in there and chained him to a drainpipe.

Both Nigel and Ollie were there at Nigel's Knick-Knacks and Antiques. Nigel was trying to persuade two elderly women of the merits of a pair of china bulldogs and Ollie was stacking tea chests that, if the rattling was anything to go by, contained something fragile.

When the two shoppers left empty-handed, Nigel called over to Ollie, 'Thought I had a bite then with the Royal Doulton. Been trying to offload those ugly buggers for two years.'

As there were no other prospective customers, Chris made her approach. 'Hi, Nigel. I got your email?'

Nigel wiped his right hand on the front of his filthy trousers and offered it out for a handshake. 'Yeah, Anne recognised him immediately. Said he was a bit of an intellectual. That sound like yer man?'

'Absolutely.' Chris nodded vigorously. It looked like her hunch was about to pay off.

'Champion! I'll take you over and introduce you.'

He offered Chris the crook of his arm to escort her. She wasn't sure whether this was flirtatious or old-fashioned chivalry, or whether Nigel thought she was an old dear who looked unsteady on her feet. Not wishing to offend the best lead their investigation had had to date, she complied and linked arms.

He led her diagonally across the way to a much smarter-looking emporium where the ornaments for sale epitomised good taste and disposable income. The stylish sign read: 'Anne's Tiquities – Where Old Is Beautiful'. What was it about British shopkeepers and their love of a pun? Along with Spokesmen, Cliffstaple High Street boasted a fish and chip shop named Know Your Plaice and a hairdresser's called Locks-a-Lordy. Chris wondered whether shopkeepers in other countries were quite so obsessed with wordplay.

Anne herself was impressive – clad in twinset and pearls, and as substantial as the Victorian wardrobe that Nigel and Ollie had been struggling with yesterday.

Chris held out a hand contaminated with dirt from Nigel's trousers.

Anne, to her credit, didn't flinch and shook hands firmly. Chris hoped she'd got a bottle of anti-bacterial handwash under the counter. She fumbled to open her backpack and drew out one of the handmade posters of the professor.

'I understand you've seen this man.'

Anne studied the photo. 'Ah yes, that's him. Now, what was his name? Jodhpur? Joseph?'

'Jasper?' Chris suggested, leading the witness.

'Yes!' shouted Anne with so much gusto that Nigel and Chris were forced to take a half-step backwards. 'Professor Jasper, that's it. Let's see...' She reached behind the till, pulled out a large ledger and leafed through the pages. 'If I remember correctly, he bought an Edwardian reading lamp. Lovely piece.'

Chris's heart began to sink. She had seen a lamp matching that description in Jasper's sitting room. 'When was this?'

'Easter, I think. Ah, here we are: "April 14th. Professor Adrian Jasper: Payment in full (cash)." I delivered it the following day, I seem to recall. Lovely little cottage in Bartham Village – have you tried there?'

'Yes, no luck. Have you seen him recently? A week ago, perhaps?'

Anne shook her head. 'No, dear, not since then. Nigel just asked if anyone had seen him. He didn't say it had to have been recently.'

Chris's hopes hit the basement. 'So you haven't—'

''Ere, Anne,' Nigel interjected. 'I sold you a reading lamp at the beginning of April.'

'So you did, Nigel. So you did,' said Anne, smiling broadly.

'You said it woz an "attractive reproduction". Gave me twenty quid for it.'

'Did I, Nigel? Did I?' Anne widened her eyes in feigned innocence.

''Ow much did the professor pay for it?'

Chris could see that Nigel was losing his cool.

'Oh, I can't recall. Shall we see what my ledger says? Shall we, Nigel?' Anne was like a lioness toying with a baby gazelle. 'Ah, yes, three hundred, it says here.'

Nigel had reached incandescence. 'Three 'undred quid? You sold my twenty quid lamp for three 'undred quid?'

'Guineas, Nigel, darling. Three hundred guineas. Professors never pay in pounds.' Anne delivered the coup de grâce.

There was no point in staying to watch Nigel spontaneously combust, even though that would have challenged the premise of Stan's dissertation. At least Chris hadn't dragged Zeta along on what had proved to be a wild goose chase. Anne's shop lay at the far end of the quayside development, right next to the footpath that, Chris suspected, led to the boatyard. The boatyard was just about on the margin of the red circle on Barry's map. She figured that she could explore there for an hour, return to pick up Rod from by the teashop, and still be back in plenty of time for Chloe's call.

Chris's assumption was correct. The footpath meandered for a hundred metres through vicious-looking nettles before it emerged in the heart of Bottisham boatyard. She had passed through the boatyard on previous cycle trips on a detour that avoided the stench of the sewage works, but she had never taken the time to have a proper look round. There was a mass of boats of all shapes and sizes: barges and motor launches and yachts and yawls; a little boat that, apparently, had seen service at Dunkirk; houseboats and dinghies and trawlers and cruisers. Practically every kind of craft imaginable. They were at various stages of repair (or disrepair).

There were boats that were renovation projects that would never be finished – money pits that would swallow up a lifetime's savings in materials and docking fees. Perhaps that was the point, thought Chris. They represented a dream of a perfect world and that was their value, even if their hull never hit the water again. And without the chance to dream, how sterile would people's lives be?

A large shed with a slipway running down to the creek had a couple of dungaree-clad men working on the restoration of what to Chris's inexpert eyes appeared to be a wooden lifeboat. They were shrouded in a cloud of sawdust and far too busy to be interrupted. The sign above the shed read 'Bottisham Wharf Chandlers' – appropriate, she supposed, as her hunt for the missing professor could have come straight out of a Raymond Chandler novel. The trouble was she was no Philip Marlowe and the only 'dame' she'd encountered so far was Zeta, and she didn't think even Marlowe would have dared to call Zeta that.

Overlooking the creek was a substantial crane that looked like a semi-permanent feature for lifting boats in and out of the water. Although its appearance suggested it had been safely in place for decades, it still made Chris's heart beat faster to walk beneath it. Here, the creek was deeper, even at low tide, and three houseboats were moored alongside. Their gardens and seating areas indicated that they were not for moving. An elderly lady with a Jack Russell terrier was watering her flowerpots in front of the middle houseboat, a converted barge with peeling red paint. 'Morning,' she said. 'Lovely day.' Actually, it was still overcast and the wind had a bite to it, but Chris supposed that every day was a lovely day when you lived on a houseboat with your dog. She showed her the picture of the professor, but the woman just shook her head.

The boatyard was relatively busy. People had parked their SUVs alongside their boats and were presumably somewhere in the depths of the hulls or, having been reminded of the size of the task they faced, had retreated to the Sculler's Arms to drown their sorrows. Pride of place was a magnificent 1950s gentlemen's motor launch – fifty feet of gorgeousness in dark brown wood with gleaming brass fittings. The owner was polishing the panelling of the cabin as though he was caressing the thigh of a lover, making Chris feel like a peeping Tomasina for watching.

He looked up and gave her a friendly grin. 'She's for sale, if you're interested.'

'Out of my league, I'm afraid,' said Chris, smiling in return.

Perhaps if she sold the house she could afford it? Her as skipper and Aitken as faithful cabin cat, cruising round Britain, journeying where the mood took them, seeking adventure. She dismissed the fanciful notion. There were risks in life and then there was lunacy. Still, she took a photo of the boat's details board, just in case.

Her tour of the boatyard gave Chris the impression that it was a friendly community but closed to outsiders. Everyone was welcoming and chatty and delighted to talk about the history of their crafts until Chris asked about the professor's whereabouts and then they clammed up. They were not hostile as such, but she sensed they would protect their own whatever they had done. Here, as a boat enthusiast, you were among equals, accepted – what happened outside of the yard was irrelevant.

She had made no headway in her quest, so she stopped by a tiny caravan that had been converted into a makeshift cafe. The blackboard outside listed a limited but sufficient menu of tea, coffee, bacon baps and cheese and tomato rolls. She ordered the tea, which was hot and wet, and a cheese and tomato roll as a very late breakfast. The caravan reminded her of a holiday from when she was about seven. She and her parents had crammed into a stuffy, claustrophobic caravan on a dismal, muddy campsite on the Gower coast. The constant cold drizzle was miserable and little Christine was insufferable. She hated the weather, she hated the caravan, she hated the food and she hated her parents for having taken her there. Her dad ended up driving them all back home after just four days of hell. Chris never did properly apologise to them both; she wished she had.

The woman behind the counter took the poster and studied it. 'Sorry, I know all of the regulars and I'm sure I'd remember him. He's not in any trouble, is he?'

'We hope not,' Chris replied. 'We're just a bit worried that he hasn't been in touch.' She felt guilty about adopting the persona of a concerned relative, but it was the only way to get even the minimum amount of cooperation.

'Don't worry, I'm sure he's fine. He looks like a lovely man.' The cafe owner got the attention of a young man who was standing a few feet away, smoking a roll-up and staring at his phone. 'You can't help the lady, can you, love?'

'I'll do my very best.'

Chris handed the 'Have You Seen This Man?' poster to the young man. He studied it carefully and she fancied she saw a flicker of recognition in his face, but he returned the photo. 'Really sorry. I'd help you if I could,' he said and then wandered off, head down, engrossed in his phone.

Chris reckoned she still had enough time to explore the far side of the boatyard, away from the creek. She tried to check the time on her phone, but sometime in the last hour it had given up its fight for life. This area was vast, far bigger than she had previously imagined, and the opportunities for concealment were endless. If Professor Jasper had decided to hide away here, he might never be found.

In fact, he could be running a fully functioning pharmaceuticals laboratory and distribution centre without the other users of the boatyard having a sniff as to what was going on.

The further away from the water Chris ventured, the more neglected the environment became. Boats were now joined by abandoned vehicles, an old red phone box with broken windows and even a disused train carriage. There was a rusty Land Rover that was missing all four wheels – five, if you included the spare one – and a coach adorned with psychedelic swirls and flowers that had perhaps once transported hedonists to the Greek islands via the coffee shops of Amsterdam. Chris peered through the filthy windows, but the pleasure-bus was sadly a decaying memory of a simpler, carefree existence. The boats there were beyond seaworthiness. Their paintwork had peeled away, the timbers were rotting and several were being stripped down for spare parts. Away from witnesses, Chris tentatively called out Professor Jasper's name in the vain hope that his face might appear on deck, his hand clutching a wood plane or paintbrush.

At the furthest corner of the boatyard stood a line of shipping containers. Chris counted them; there were fourteen in all, weathered and rusty. As she moved towards them a volley of barking echoed off their metal walls. A dog of unidentified breed was tied to a post next to the fourth container. He seemed determined to test the tensile strength of the rope tethering him. Chris liked dogs but was still nervous around them – the legacy of having been chased by an overly playful red setter as a child. This one was giving her good reason to be scared. 'Good boy,' she said loudly, summoning up reserve levels of bravery and hoping that the wind wouldn't carry the stench of fear that exuded from her every pore.

She turned right, away from the Hound of Bottisham Boatyard, determined to complete her circuit. Here, the ground was uneven, the recent storms having turned it into a mud-bath which had then been churned up by an off-road vehicle only to be baked into rock-hard ridges by the sunshine of the following days.

In front of the last container was a vehicle loosely draped in a tarpaulin. Nothing to see here, thought Chris. Time to head back to the quayside, pick up Rod, ride home, feed Aitken, charge the phone and await Chloe's call. She had made up her mind: she would accept their offer and go to Australia for Christmas. Aitken would have to put up with Nick as a cat-sitter – at least that would be better than solitary confinement in a cattery.

As she turned, her foot caught on the edge of a rut and she stumbled.

Oh God, no, not again!

Was it better to land on her titanium hip or head first? Which would cause the least damage?

She sprawled head first on the ground by the front wheel of the covered vehicle, arms outstretched, bare knees grazing the hard earth. She lay there winded and then slowly checked her body for serious injury. Left toes wiggle? Good. Now the right? Fine. Legs, fingers, arms, ribs? All seemed to be in working order. A lucky escape.

As she levered herself upright, she noticed something half buried in the tyre rut. She used her fingers to dig it out of the mud. It was a mobile phone, an old model. She sat with her back to the vehicle and pressed the 'on' button. The screen briefly flickered into life, suggesting a large number of missed calls, and then died. She slipped it into her backpack.

The dog had started barking again, so she figured it was best not to hang around any longer. Although the boatyard people had seemed friendly, they might not take too kindly to snooping strangers. She gripped the tarpaulin in her right hand to haul herself to her feet. As she did so, part of the tarpaulin broke free, flapping loosely, revealing... a broken wing mirror.

Frenziedly, she pulled at the rest of the tarpaulin with both hands, until the vehicle beneath was uncovered. She took a step back. She was now looking at an ice cream van. An ice cream van with a broken wing mirror. An ice cream van emblazoned with the name 'Mr Softee'.

'Got you!' Chris said out loud.

She felt a sharp pain on the back of her head and her world turned black.

Twenty-One

Zeta wished she hadn't poured cold water on Chris's enthusiasm for following up on Barry's maps of Bottisham. She'd rather have been doing that than kicking her heels at the harbour. She reread the tourist information board at the waterside – 'Cliffstaple Harbour was founded in 1847 by Sir Humphrey Fynley. It is renowned for its seafood, including cockles, whelks, oysters...' – and memorised it in an instant. Maybe it would be a question in a pub quiz one day. Quite what the Victorian founding fathers would have made of the Festival of Fish and its alcohol-infused chaos, Zeta could only guess.

'Are you joining us, Jah-mah?' Sgt Spurgeon's voice boomed out from a raised stage thirty metres away.

Zeta trotted over to stand with her colleagues for the morning briefing.

The assembled company charged with keeping law and order that day comprised, in addition to Zeta and Sgt Spurgeon, PC Atherton, James (another special), and Kyle and Kirsty, a couple of friendly community support officers. As this was day two, they didn't actually need another briefing, but Sgt Spurgeon could never resist an opportunity to give it the big I am.

'Ladies and gentlemen,' he began, 'I'm sure you all heard the wise words of the commissioner yesterday, that everyone should be allowed to enjoy this festival safely. It is our task to make sure that happens.'

'Here, here!' piped up PC Atherton in his distinctive shrill voice. He was met with a glare from his senior officer.

'I expect the crowds to be larger today,' continued the sergeant, 'so I want you all to be on the lookout for the three "P"s: perverts—'

'Crowds are great cover for pervs trying to cop a feel,' interrupted PC Atherton.

'Indeed, Constable. If I may continue?' Sgt Spurgeon looked mildly annoyed at the disruption to his flow of oratory. 'The second "P" is pickpockets. We have intelligence that there's a gang operating – young men and women, and some kids too.'

At Zeta's right shoulder, James started singing 'You've got to pick a pocket or two' under his breath. She had to concentrate hard to stop herself from laughing.

'The third "P" is pissed-up people. Disorderly behaviour nearly ruined last year's festival, and that will not be happening on my watch. Understood?'

'Yes, Sarge!' they all chorused.

'Good.' Sgt Spurgeon looked satisfied. 'Any questions?'

Kirsty, a CSO who was also a hospital administrator, put up her hand.

'Yes, Kristie?'

'It's Kirsty, Sarge. People going in the water is a problem too. I've been doing the festival for five years now and there's always someone who falls off the harbourside or kids who think it's a great idea to dive off the harbour bar.'

Sgt Spurgeon nodded. 'A good point, Kristie. Entering the water is dangerous for both themselves and their rescuers. We should deter any members of the public from doing so.'

'Plungers!' said PC Atherton excitedly. 'That's a fourth "P", Sarge.'

Sgt Spurgeon considered this point for some time, perhaps checking for any sarcastic intent. Finding none, he said, 'Very good, team. Get out there and keep an eye out for perverts, pickpockets, pissed-up people and plungers. Stay safe.'

Despite Spurgeon's dire warning, the morning had been pretty quiet. James and Zeta were doing slow circuits of the main area; she went clockwise, James anti-clockwise, so their paths crossed every fifteen minutes. The overcast weather had kept the numbers down and people seemed to be content to move from food stall to food stall like a herd of ruminating wildebeest.

Food seemed to be the main attraction at the Festival of Fish, though, ironically, fish itself was down the popularity list, behind pulled pork, Thai stir-fry and venison burgers. Visitors would sample a whelk or an oyster as part of the festival experience and then move swiftly on to the meat course. Zeta gave the hog-roast stall a wide berth. The smell of sizzling pork fat at eleven in the morning made her retch. The freshly made doughnuts stall was also troubling but for different reasons – they looked and smelled wonderful, but she couldn't be seen to be eating such junk in public. What she ate in the comfort of her home, however, was her own business.

She stopped by the stage, where a small crowd had gathered to listen to a young guy with a rhythm guitar and amp who thought he was the new Ed Sheeran. He wasn't.

It gave her the chance to collect her thoughts. She recognised that she'd been mean to Chris the previous day, and she knew why. She could see that her new friend was clever and competent – was she cleverer and more competent than Zeta herself? Chris almost certainly didn't have imposter syndrome, Zeta concluded. And was also very unlikely to morph into a control-freak monster. That was the real reason why Zeta was on duty today and why she volunteered for every task – she couldn't trust herself not to be involved.

She would tell Sgt Spurgeon that she was busy tomorrow, that there was some urgent paying work that had come in, so she and Chris could get cracking on the Jasper case. Her sergeant couldn't refuse, could he? She already did over and above the required hours. She would pop round to Chris's house at lunchtime and apologise. She wouldn't over-share again and get all maudlin talking about family. No one needed to know about that. All that stuff was just for her.

Wannabe Sheeran finished a song to cheers and whoops from the dozen or so spectators. His performance didn't seem to Zeta to be worthy of whoops, but the entertainment was free and some of the audience were on their second mojito of the morning. Emboldened by this reception, Ed launched into a second number, a pop standard that even Zeta half recognised, despite his best efforts.

A woman lurched towards her, plastic glass in hand, phone in the other. 'C'mon, dance with us!' she screeched, spraying tequila rain.

Zeta blamed the Notting Hill Carnival. Everybody wanted a selfie with a jovial dancing copper. She had no intention of ending up on someone's Facebook or Instagram page as they trawled for likes. And no power on God's earth could tempt her onto TikTok. She took out her radio, gave the woman her sweetest and most apologetic 'Sorry, urgent call' smile and escaped in the direction of the lifeboat station. She met James coming the other way.

'Can you cover for me, James?'

'No problemo, Strawbs!'

Strawbs was James's nickname for Zeta, coincidentally the same nickname she'd carried through school – Zeta 'Strawberry' Jama. Zeta quite liked being called Strawbs; it was cute. She'd certainly been called a lot, lot worse.

'Just for forty-five minutes? I've got a couple of errands to run.'

'I'll give you a call if I pick a pack of pickpockets,' said James cheerfully as he set off on his beat, whistling.

As she was in uniform, Zeta avoided the rapidly filling high street, where she could easily get sidetracked by members of the public, and used smaller residential streets and smugglers' alleys to thread her way to Chris's house. The back gate was locked and she didn't fancy climbing over the wall and returning to duty covered in brick dust. As sixty per cent of North Kent Constabulary seemed to be monitoring the festival and Sea View was deserted, she felt safe approaching the front door.

There was no answer. She knocked and rang again. Still no answer.

She tried the neighbouring house, Number 17, and Nick

opened the door. He looked terrified.

'Is there a problem, Officer?'

'Hi, Nick, sorry to bother you. We met a few days ago, remember? I'm Zeta.'

Nick visibly sighed with relief. 'Zeta – of course! Sorry, I didn't recognise you with your… um… uniform on. I'm not used to visits from the police.'

'Glad to hear it,' she said. 'Just a social visit. I'm looking for Chris?'

'Ah, I saw her leaving on that bike of hers. Honestly, the past week she's barely been off it.'

'Do you know what time this was?'

'Five past nine – the news had just started. She'll probably be back soon to give Aitken his lunch. Do you want to come in and wait?' He opened the door wide to beckon her inside.

'No, thanks. Gotta get back to work. If you see Chris, tell her I'll pop round this evening, usual time.'

For some reason, Nick gave her a salute as he closed his door.

*

In the afternoon the atmosphere at the festival became more febrile. The crowds had slowly built and the combination of daytime drinking, music and pulled pork was causing a buzz, and not a totally positive one.

For the last twenty minutes Zeta had had eyes on three lads. They weren't locals and their attitude suggested they weren't there to celebrate fish in all its wondrous forms. They had been swaggering up and down the harbourfront, beers in hand, elbows out as if inviting someone to accidentally jostle them. They spotted Zeta and disappeared behind the side of the fish market. Protocol stated that she should wait for James to appear on his circuit so they could tackle this together, but Zeta decided to take the initiative.

As she rounded the corner, she was seized and slammed into the wall. The breath was knocked out of her body. Her vision was filled by the face of one of the men, the vein on his forehead pumping, sweat collecting on his brow. Her peripheral vision picked out his two mates, excited observers, unsure whether to egg on their friend or join in. In the previous year Zeta had dealt with drunks and drug addicts and football fans, but, underneath the bravado, they'd generally been surprisingly docile when confronted by the uniform. This was different.

'Why are you following us?' snarled Alpha Lad, his pupils constricting, his breath fetid with craft lager and tobacco.

'I'm a police officer. I follow whoever I want.' Zeta gathered all her inner strength to stare back, eye to eye. She wasn't sure whether to go for the baton, the pepper spray or the radio.

One of Alpha Lad's mates noticed her indecision. 'She's not even proper filth. She's a special, a pretend pig.'

Zeta undid the clasp of her baton. 'Back off. Back off, all of you, before I'm forced to—' She hoped her voice sounded assertive rather than fearful.

'To do what?' said Alpha Lad, prodding her in the chest. 'We're just having a few beers, aren't we, lads? You can't arrest us for that.'

'Assaulting a police officer in the execution of her duty is a serious offence.' Zeta's hand gripped her baton.

'I haven't assaulted you! Lads, have you seen me assaulting anyone?'

Alpha Lad's support act chorused that they hadn't.

He gripped Zeta's baton arm. 'We're just three *English* guys having a lovely day out by the *English* seaside. Why don't you stick to harassing innocent people in your own country?'

Zeta had known it was coming, she'd heard it before, but it was still a shock. That 'Sticks and Stones' rhyme was bollocks. With her left hand, she reached for the pepper spray, whether in self-defence or anger, she wasn't too sure. Strangely, she felt she was channelling the spirit of her father, a man of whom she had no memory.

'Can I help you, gentlemen? Are you lost?' Zeta heard the voice of Sgt Spurgeon. 'I think you've had enough excitement for the day, don't you? Time to toddle off back home.'

Alpha Lad took a step back. 'We've done nothing wrong. She was giving us grief.'

'I hope she was. Do you gents need to be shown the way to the train station?'

Alpha Lad wasn't giving up the challenge lightly. 'Nah. Thanks for the offer, Officer, but I think we'll have a few more beers. Won't we, lads?'

His friends mumbled their agreement but seemed far less confident.

'Oh dear. Perhaps I haven't made myself completely clear.' The sergeant was showing admirable control. 'That wasn't negotiable. Constable!'

PC Atherton appeared around the corner of the building with a muscle-bound swagger. Alpha, Beta and Gamma Lads all clocked his physique and swiftly made a collective decision for their own self-preservation.

'PC Atherton,' said Sgt Spurgeon, 'would you be so good as to escort these gentlemen to the railway station and make sure they get on a train heading homewards. We wouldn't want them to get lost a second time, and if I was to see them round here again I'd get terribly upset.'

The three lads were shepherded away by PC Atherton, in the direction of Cliffstaple railway station.

Zeta refastened the clip of her baton and brought her breathing back under control. 'Thanks, Sarge.'

'On the contrary, I did those young lads a favour. If I hadn't appeared when I did, I fear you'd have laid all three of them out cold. Then think of all the bloody paperwork that'd create!' He gave her a wink. 'Always in pairs, SC Jah-mah. Always patrol with a colleague.'

He disappeared into the throng, the crowd parting at the sight of his substantial form. Zeta was going to have to reassess her opinion of Sgt Spurgeon. He might still be an arse, but perhaps not a total arse.

Happily, the rest of the afternoon passed relatively uneventfully.

She reunited three lost children with their parents, took photographs for four posing couples, and directed the St John Ambulance team to the stage, where a woman had slipped on an ice cube that had dislodged from her mojito glass whilst she was dancing and was consequently nursing a suspected broken ankle.

By the time Zeta had clocked off, returned to the station to change out of her uniform, had a shower, gone back to her flat and had something to eat, it was getting dark. It was time to catch up with Chris.

As she reached Sea View, she could see that a light was shining through the coloured glass of the front door of Number 15. Good news – Chris was obviously back.

She slipped quietly down the alley that separated Chris's and Nick's houses. The wall that surrounded the garden was nearly two metres high, but the brickwork was original Victorian, so it was easy to get a toehold, lever herself over the top and drop to the ground on the other side. From the garden, she could see the light was on in the kitchen, illuminating the patio outside. Something nuzzled her leg. She bent down to make a fuss of Aitken. Once she'd got herself settled, Zeta decided, she was definitely getting a cat. She admired their mercenary self-confidence and reckoned she was something of a cat-whisperer.

As she neared the window, she could see there were two figures inside. Chris was sitting with her back to the window talking to a man in his late fifties. She didn't recognise him, but the body language between the two suggested they were on friendly terms. She hoped Nick had passed on her message and that Chris wouldn't mind being interrupted. She knocked on the glass pane of the door. The man looked up in shock and Chris turned round. Except it wasn't the Chris Zeta knew; it was a younger version. They both screamed.

Twenty-Two

Think, Chris, think.

Her head throbbed, really throbbed; worse than any tequila hangover. It was so dark. Complete blackness. It was like that time she got off the last bus three stops too early in the Lake District and it was only following the white stripes that kept her on the road. When you lived in a town you never saw total darkness – that was if you could actually *see* darkness. That thought was making Chris even more dizzy.

Had she gone blind? She stood up, or tried to, but the remains of the cheese and tomato roll rose in her throat and she threw up. Wipe mouth, deep breaths, try to stand again. It was just dark, wasn't it? When you were blind you didn't lose your sight completely, did you? You could see something – light, shadows. Shit – what if she'd hit her head and done something bad to her brain and that had made her blind?

Think. Boatyard, barking dog, Mr Softee, then what? Had she tripped over? Had a stroke? Why did the back of her head hurt? Perhaps she'd had an accident and was in that fricking hospital again.

She did a quick check. She still had her cycling clothes on; she wasn't in one of those backless gowns, thank God.

It wasn't another of those fricking dreams, was it?

Wake up, Chris, wake up. WAKE UP!

It wasn't a dream. Shit.

She counted backwards from 100 in sevens. 93… 86… 79… 72… 64… No, hang on… 65… 58. That seemed all right, about as good as her mental arithmetic had ever been.

'OK,' said Chris out loud to herself, 'keep calm, take control. Brain works, body works – sort of. Let's try and figure this out.'

Her surroundings didn't smell like a hospital – of disinfectant, microwaved food and urine. It smelt metallic, of rust and damp and… something unpleasant, like a rancid salad drawer. She knelt down and tentatively patted the ground with her hand. It wasn't lino; it was filthy and she could feel the grime encrusting her fingernails. She rapped the floor with her knuckles. Ouch! Shit!

There was a faint clanging sound in response.

'Hello? Hello?' she called. 'I'm awake! Is anyone there? Can anyone hear me? I need medical assistance!' Her voice sounded echoey, not at all like a hospital ward.

Silence.

'FIRE!'

She'd read that shouting 'Fire!' was the most effective way to summon assistance, more effective than 'Help!' Not this time. Everything was quiet.

How long had she been there? Was Aitken all right? He'd be hungry by now. Why hadn't she left him lunch? Had she double-locked the front door? Unplugged the kettle?

She tried the torch on her phone. It was dead – as a proverbial dodo. She remembered that she had a mini torch on her keyring, which had been serving as a standby until she got round to having an outside security light fitted – number 3 on her 'Essential Home Improvements' list. She mustn't get sidetracked by her lists. Where was her backpack? She'd been wearing it, she knew she'd been wearing it. Had she been mugged? Would someone have mugged her for the grand total of £4.20 in cash, an organ-donor card and a set of Allen keys?

She took a deep breath, forced herself to think straight, and set out her priorities.

The first thing she needed to do was map out the area; then she would get her bearings; and then she would look for her backpack.

The space felt big. She couldn't touch the ceiling on tiptoes and she wasn't going to risk jumping, not in the dark. She started to pace out the area using the heel-to-toe method.

She recalled a story she had read as a child. Her father had bought her a copy of Edgar Allan Poe's *Tales of Mystery and Imagination* one Christmas. It had those gruesome but beautiful illustrations by Arthur Rackham. There was one story she read and read again, 'The Pit and the Pendulum', about a prisoner in a pitch-black prison cell who nearly fell into a deep pit. That story had scared the crap out of her at eleven years old, and it still did. While her friends were given Roald Dahl or CS Lewis books to read, she'd got one by a nineteenth-century American horror writer – she guessed that summed up her parents. She just hoped there were no rats in there with her. She stopped and listened. No scurrying. Good.

By her calculations, the area was two and a half metres wide with metal walls. There seemed to be floor-to-ceiling doors but no way of opening them – at least from what she could tell by feeling her way around them in the dark. She tested them but they were as solid as the walls. What was this place?

She measured the length of her prison and at her thirty-eighth step she stumbled over something. It seemed to be a rolled-up carpet. She gave it a couple of hefty kicks just to confirm. The whole place was about twelve metres long by two and a half metres wide and appeared to be made entirely of metal. Her best guess was that she was in one of the fourteen shipping containers in Bottisham boatyard.

She slumped down with her back against the wall and considered her fate. If she was to die there, then so be it. She'd hoped for a longer innings than sixty years, but she'd had some good times, met some good people, and not everyone on the planet could say that, could they? She was sorry for the people she'd let down, for the people who would miss her. For Chloe, and Mason and Jason, and, yes, Dan. And Aitken of course. Four human beings and a cat – not a very impressive total for a life.

Poor Aitken. Who would look after him? It broke her heart to think of him stuck in a pod in a rehoming centre. Perhaps Next-Door Nick would adopt him, let him keep his hard-won territory. She wished she had specified this in her will, but you didn't think about that sort of thing, did you? You presumed you'd get ample notice of your demise, untimely or otherwise. She hadn't left any instructions, any requests… Oh my God! What if they played something like 'My Heart Will Go On' at her funeral? She'd die of embarrassment.

Her self-pitying was abruptly cut short by a scraping sound as a small shutter opened, no bigger than a spyhole, and a thin shaft of sunlight entered the space.

'Hello! Hello!' Chris shouted, or at least tried to. It came out as a parched croak. 'Please help!'

She staggered over to the spyhole, but it was nearly two metres from the floor and even when she stood on tiptoes it remained tantalisingly out of reach.

'What seems to be the problem?' The voice was male, youngish, fairly well spoken.

'I'm locked in here! I can't get out.'

'I'm pleased to hear it.' His voice was strangely familiar. The accent was from around the London area, but Chris couldn't quite place it. Definitely Home Counties. 'If you could, that'd mean I'm extremely bad at my job.'

'Your job?' Chris pinched herself to check she wasn't back in one of her surreal dreams.

'Yes, my job. Can't complain – pay's competitive, flexible hours and I get to travel.'

Was her head injury causing her to hallucinate? 'Abducting and imprisoning a woman is a serious offence. It's a crime, not a job.'

'Can be both. You ever tried working in a call centre? Anyway, if this goes well, the boss says I'm in line for a promotion, maybe even a company car.'

'You hit me. You knocked me unconscious and locked me in a shipping container. How is that a career move?'

'Well, for a start,' the disembodied voice replied, 'I didn't hit you. That would be against my strongly pacifistic beliefs.'

'I've got a splitting headache that says otherwise.'

'It was my colleague that whacked you. I'm sorry about that. He's got form for that sort of thing. I'd say he's got some type of impulse control disorder, but, then again, I'm not a psychiatrist, I'm just a guy who locks people in shipping containers for a living.'

Chris knew she had to think strategically. From movies she'd learnt there were two golden rules in this sort of situation. She needed to: a) build a rapport with the hostage taker, and b) personalise it so they would see her as a real person.

'Look, I'm no threat to anyone. I don't know why I'm here. I was just going for a walk, thinking about buying a boat. I don't know anything. My name is Carmen—'

'No it isn't,' the voice replied. 'Your name's Chris. Short for Christine, I guess?'

Chris was taken aback. 'Yes, that's right. Chris. And your name is…?'

'Let me just check my *Incarcerator's Handbook* for a sec… Ah, yes, "rule number 1 – don't tell the prisoner your name".'

The gentle sarcasm was rather unnerving. 'I've got to call you something. All right then, I'll call you Walter. How d'ya feel about that, Walter?'

'OK,' said her newly named prison guard. 'Walter's quite a cool name.'

'Look, um, Walter, I'm hungry and thirsty and I want to go home.' She used her most polite tone of voice, the one she reserved for waiters and customs officers.

'Well, I can help with the first two,' said Walter, also politely.

The light from a powerful torch was directed through the spyhole to illuminate a yellow plastic bucket in the middle of the floor, which, somehow, Chris had missed in her blind mapping of the area. She examined it. Inside were an unopened bottle of water and some biscuits.

'Found those biscuits in your bag. Thought you might be hungry when you woke up.'

She opened the water and gulped down half the bottle, not considering whether she should ration it.

'You've opened the biscuits.'

'Yeah, sorry,' said Walter. 'I took a couple. Plain chocolate digestives are my fave. In case you're wondering, we're looking after the rest of the contents of your backpack for you, including your phone.'

Her hand instinctively went to the shorts pocket that usually held her phone. Still there. It took her a couple of seconds to realise that Walter was referring to the phone that she had found beside the ice cream van.

'How long are you keeping me in here, Walter?'

'Dunno. Not up to me, I'm afraid.'

'People will be looking for me.'

'That's nice.'

'I'm worried about Aitken, my cat. I haven't left any food down.'

'I'm sure someone will feed him – a neighbour probably. Cats are clever like that.'

There was a *Clunk!* over by the spyhole.

'Here,' said Walter. 'Don't say I never give you anything.'

By touch, Chris could tell that a drawer had swung open, like one of those night-safe drawers at banks for the secure transfer of packages. The fact that someone had installed a spyhole and a security drawer in a shipping container led her to deduce that she was not the first person to have been detained there. Inside the drawer was a small but powerful Maglite torch. She twisted the base and a spot of light flittered around the wall, confirming her suspicions about the nature of her prison.

'Be frugal with it,' warned Walter. 'I'm not made of batteries, you know. Gotta go now. I'll check in later to wish you good night.'

'Hang on, Walter,' Chris said urgently. 'The torch is great, but… um… I really need the loo.'

'What do you think the bucket's for?'

'I can't pee in a bucket!'

'Think of it as an en suite.' Walter laughed and the spyhole closed, extinguishing the thin ray of natural light.

'Stay calm and think rationally,' Chris muttered to herself. Things looked grim, but there were always positives. Firstly, as someone had been so thoughtful as to install a means of communication with the outside world, then hopefully there was also an air vent so she wouldn't suffocate. Secondly, she was still alive. If they were planning to kill her, they wouldn't have given her food and water or, of course, the bucket.

She checked the surroundings to see if there was anything useful in the container. If only she had charged up her phone. They hadn't found it, but an uncharged phone was good for nothing. If Walter was coming back later, that suggested she hadn't been out cold for that long. There had been daylight when the spyhole opened.

She shone the torch up the join that formed the doors at the front of the container. There was no latch, bolt or anything to indicate that they could be opened from the inside. Again, she tried her shoulder against the doors, but they were unyielding. The walls seemed solid, really solid, impenetrable.

The torch picked out a vent in the far top corner. Way out of reach but still a reassuring sight. She spent twenty minutes shouting, until her throat was raw, but she was sure it was futile and, for all his politeness, she was wary of antagonising Walter. Bottisham boatyard was a noisy place, full of hammering and sawing and revving and barking, and as she couldn't hear any of that from the inside, there was little chance of anyone outside hearing her.

She needed something to bang with. The only metallic objects in her possession were her phone (too fragile) and the torch. She sat by the doors in the dark and used the base of the torch to tap out what she hoped was Morse code for SOS. Unfortunately, she couldn't remember whether it was dot-dot-dot-dash-dash-dash-dot-dot-dot or dash-dash-dash-dot-dot-dot-dash-dash-dash. She must have tapped for at least an hour. She was scared of breaking the torch but equally scared of giving up hope.

Someone had to have noticed that she was missing. Chloe might have phoned by now and got no answer. Next-Door Nick would be wondering why Aitken was hassling him for food. Zeta would have called round, wanting to plot their course of action. Someone must have noticed. All she needed to do was bed down there and await rescue. She wished she'd told Zeta that she had already checked out the maps, so she'd put two and two together. She wished she hadn't been so proud.

The thought of curling up on the bare metal floor was distinctly unappealing, so she switched the torch back on to inspect that roll of carpet. If it wasn't too manky, perhaps it could be turned into a makeshift bed.

The carpet roll was heavy and firmly wedged against the far wall of the container. She couldn't manage to unroll it with her hands, so she stood on it, bracing her back against the wall, and pushed at it with both feet. After a couple of attempts, the carpet started to shift and then, with one last effort, it began to slowly unravel, filling the shipping container with an ominous rumbling.

Six metres in, it stopped, fully unfurled. Chris shone the torch across it and stifled a shriek. Lying across the far edge of the unrolled carpet was a body.

Twenty-Three

To Zeta's relief, Young Chris now looked wary rather than terrified. The man grabbed the nearest available weapon with which to defend the household. Unfortunately, this was a floor mop with a flexible sponge head. It looked as though he was threatening to squeegee Zeta into submission.

'Leave now,' he shouted, 'or I'll call the police.'

There were two things that Zeta had always wanted to do in her life. The first was to leap into a black taxi cab and shout 'Follow that car!' and the second was what she did now. She pulled out her warrant card, held it flat against the window and said calmly, 'I *am* the police.'

The man looked unconvinced. 'Oh yeah, that ID looks well dodgy to me. You could've bought that off eBay.'

A situation that was in danger of become a protracted discussion was thankfully rescued by Chris's neighbour, Nick, entering the kitchen from the hallway. 'She is the police,' he said and opened the kitchen door to let Zeta in. 'Chloe, Simon, this is Zeta, North Kent Constabulary's finest crimefighter.'

Zeta stepped into the kitchen and Aitken followed in her wake. 'You must be Chris's daughter. You're her spitting image.'

'Yes. Chloe,' said Chloe, offering Zeta her hand. 'And this is my dad, Simon.'

'Chris's ex-husband,' added Simon needlessly, pumping Zeta's hand vigorously as if to apologise for the misunderstanding.

'Is something wrong?' Chloe looked concerned by Zeta's presence.

'No, nothing's wrong. It's just a social call. I was looking for Chris.'

'Join the gang,' said Chloe, gesturing for Zeta to take a seat at the table.

'Really sorry if I'm disturbing a family gathering. Chris told me you live in Australia. Melbourne, isn't it?'

Chloe poured Zeta a mug of tea from a large brown teapot. 'Yes, that's right.'

'She didn't mention you were visiting.'

'She doesn't know. This is a surprise visit. She's been having such a crap time what with the accident and long rehab and then her victimisation by the police – no offence intended.'

'None taken.'

'So I thought I'd take some leave, cash in a few air miles and fly over to help lift her spirits. Gives me a chance to see the old country and my other half the opportunity to cope single-handedly with our boys.'

'How do you know Chris?' asked Simon rather pointedly.

'Zeta is Chris's swimming buddy,' explained Nick.

'And friend, I hope,' Zeta added.

'I am sorry,' said Chloe. 'I don't think Mum has mentioned you in her calls. If we'd known you were her friend, we certainly wouldn't have threatened you with household cleaning equipment.'

She looked at her father, who was still holding the mop. He rather sheepishly returned it to its bucket.

'News to me too,' said Simon. 'How long have you two been friends?'

Zeta had a theatrically long think. 'Ooh, let me see, must be seven… no eight… days.'

'That long?' Chloe smiled.

'Still, longer than most of your mother's relationships,' said Simon, which drew a scowl from his daughter.

'How did you two meet?' Chloe asked.

'I arrested her.'

'So it was you who...?'

Zeta nodded. Fortunately, she didn't feature in any of the footage of the Sir Lickalot incident, apart from a blurry shot of the back of her head as she'd helped Chris into the squad car. 'Well, strictly speaking that was the second time we met. The first time was when she reported the discovery of a dead body.'

'A dead body?' chorused Chloe and Simon in the kind of perfect harmony only exhibited by blood relatives.

'Oh, she didn't mention that to you, then?' Zeta felt she'd been indiscreet. 'Nothing major – we thought it was probably just a shop dummy.'

'Am I missing something?' asked Nick. 'I feel like I've come in halfway through a badly subtitled Icelandic arthouse movie.'

Zeta explained and hoped Chris would forgive her for any betrayal of confidences. She gave a strictly sanitised account of The Mannequin in the Forensics House Incident, accentuating the humorous aspects and insisting that Chris had only been doing her duty as a concerned citizen. This was not the time to mention The Hunt for Professor Jasper or The Mysterious Blue Powder. There was still the strong possibility that this would all fizzle out and prove to be merely a product of their fevered imaginations. The professor would return from holiday bemused by all the interest in his whereabouts and wondering where he had left his favourite tweed jacket.

'You know,' said Nick after Zeta had finished her story, 'just when I think I've figured Chris out, she pitches a curveball. But now I know that Aitken's being cared for, I'll be off. Great to see you again, Chloe. I know your mum will be thrilled by the surprise.' And he left by the front door, like any sensible person would.

Simon was fidgeting and looking at his watch.

'It's all right, Dad, I know you've got to go and rehearse. Thanks ever so much for picking me up from the airport. I'll see you tomorrow at the festival.' Chloe gave her father a hug and a kiss on his forehead.

'It's typical of your mother's unreliability. You go to all that effort and she hasn't even got the grace to show up on time,' muttered Simon as he headed out the door. 'And tell her it wouldn't kill her to respond to a text message occasionally.'

As Simon left, Chloe raised her eyebrows and smiled at Zeta. 'Fathers, eh? He means well, but you know what they say, "Can't live with them…"'

'So I've heard.' A slight twang of concern was niggling at Zeta, but she didn't want her expression to convey that to Chloe. 'I presume you've called your mum.'

'Yeah, but as Dad says, it's not unusual for her to miss calls. She's got a tendency to leave her phone on silent by mistake. Or at least that's what she tells me. Do you want another cuppa?'

'Just a quick one.' Zeta handed her mug to Chloe. 'I'm grateful that you're prepared to forgive your mother's victimiser.'

'Oops!' Chloe chuckled.

'I'm sorry about all that business with the ice cream van. In the police, sometimes we have to do what's necessary rather than what we'd like to.'

'That's OK,' said Chloe. 'Mum's got a history of courting trouble. I think she likes the notoriety. She once chained herself to the council railings to complain about sewage dumping, or was it tree felling? Come to think of it, perhaps she did it twice. She's inspirational.'

'I can believe that,' said Zeta.

'But don't tell her I said so,' said Chloe in a hushed voice, even though it was only the two of them (and Aitken) in the kitchen. 'She likes to delude herself that she's a terrible mother.'

Through the kitchen window the sun was setting. Zeta wondered whether she should make a discreet call to the station when she got home to check for any reports of accidents.

'I'd better leave you to your unpacking.' She nodded at a small suitcase that was propping open the kitchen door. 'Here's my number. Tell your inspirational mother I called round.'

'Why don't you pop round tomorrow morning to catch up with Mum then?'

'Oh no, I couldn't intrude on mother and daughter reunion time.'

'That's fine, we're not soppy like that. Mum and I have got the whole week together. Anyway, I've got a treat tomorrow afternoon – I'm going to the Festival of Fish to watch my father jiggle his bladder in public.'

'In that case, I'll probably see you there. I'm on duty to protect the public from any morris-dancing-induced hysteria.' Zeta gave Chloe a wave and, following Nick and Simon's lead, left by the front door rather than over the garden wall.

Twenty-Four

Chris didn't know how to react. She didn't know how she *should* react. Her instinct was to run away, but there was nowhere to run to. She banged her fists on the wall by the spyhole, she shouted for help, she kicked at the doors, but nothing had any effect, nobody answered.

Exhausted, she crouched in the corner, far removed from the body in case it rose like a zombie and came plodding towards her, arms outstretched. She kept her torch fixed upon the shape on the ground, too scared to turn it off and face blackness.

Slowly counting to one thousand helped her to recover some composure. Then she counted to a thousand again. She realised she hadn't actually checked that this was a dead body. There was no movement, no rise-and-fall breathing, but she should check.

She didn't need to get near enough to take a pulse to recognise that the figure really was a body and was indeed dead. It lay on its left side, its back to Chris. The head's light grey hair melded into a blackness that had spread, staining the back of the white shirt. The arms had a strange mottled colouration and the hands were fixed in a grip, perhaps vainly attempting to hold onto life.

Trying to keep her nerves in check, she went nearer, training her torch over the body's lower half, the trousers and then feet. The feet were apart as though in mid-stride. One foot was bare, revealing a light-coloured ankle sock; the other still bore a shoe with a scuffed sole and worn heel. It was the same shoe that she had seen just a week earlier beneath the kitchen table in the forensics house. There could be no doubt that this was exactly whom Chris had suspected it was. Professor Adrian Jasper. Now, sadly, an ex-professor.

She didn't need or want to turn him. She couldn't bear to gaze upon his lifeless face. And three metres was anyway as close as she could get. Released from the confines of the carpet, that rancid smell she'd detected earlier was now filling her nostrils.

Chris had never met Professor Jasper and a week ago hadn't even heard of him, but she grieved for him. She grieved for his neighbours, who would never again see him leave his house on his way to work; she grieved for Dr Karamak and Rene Douglas, who had lost a much-loved colleague; and for students past, present and future, who had, or would have had, their lives shaped by his wisdom. She grieved for Mia and Stan, who would never get to present their dissertations to their professor. She even grieved for his antique brass reading lamp, which would sit there by his sofa, unlit.

Looking at Professor Jasper's impotent form, she couldn't believe he was a Mr Big, a criminal mastermind, head of a pharmaceutical counterfeiting operation. He was surely just a guy who, like her, had been in the wrong place at the wrong time.

She put her head in her hands and, for the first time since her mother died, wept.

Crying was like an exorcism. She didn't know why she avoided it so steadfastly. It made her realise what mattered and it helped her recognise that, perhaps, she was still human after all. Then, in an instant, her grief was ambushed by fear. Walter's strange sense of humour and talks of pacifism had lulled her into a sense of security, of gentle optimism. But if they were prepared to kill a mild-mannered professor of forensic science, what was to stop them dispatching a batty cat-lady with the same callous disregard?

When her senses should have be at their most heightened, Chris became overwhelmed with tiredness, slumped in a corner and fell asleep.

*

Some time later – whether five minutes or five hours, she had no way of telling – she was woken by a metallic scraping as the spyhole opened.

'Afternoon, Chris!' called Walter cheerily.

She stayed crouched, head down, and refused to acknowledge him. A small spot of torchlight swept the room, settling on her and then on the body of Professor Jasper.

'Ah,' said Walter, 'I see you found your roommate. Sorry about that. We had such little notice of your arrival that we were unable to arrange alternative accommodation.'

Chris was no longer in the mood for Walter's banter. 'My *roommate* had a name. His name was Professor Adrian Jasper and you killed him and left him rolled up in a shitty carpet in a shipping container.' She was crimson with anger.

'Whoah! Whoah! It wasn't me – that'd definitely get me drummed out of the Pacifist's Guild. My colleague assures me it wasn't intentional. Let's call it a workplace accident.'

Colleague? Chris's mind conjured up an image of Stan's powerful physique, but she shook her head, dismissing the idea.

'Let's not call it an accident. Let's call it murder.'

'He wasn't murdered,' protested Walter.

'Well, he ain't exactly playing hopscotch.'

'I can only tell you what I was told. Perhaps he just had a thinner skull than you. The professor was a tad unlucky.'

'I'll tell you what I think happened.' She was done being cautious. 'I think you're all involved in manufacturing and distributing counterfeit erectile dysfunction drugs. Either Professor Jasper was part of the operation and there was a falling-out between him and your boss or he was an innocent bystander who saw too much and had to be disposed of. Which is it?'

There was a pause. 'What do you think this is?' said Walter. '*Scooby Doo*? That the bad guys are going to reveal their ingenious plan just because you confronted them? What'd be the point? If you're going to be freed at some stage, it'd be incriminating evidence, and if you're going to be… well, if you're going to join the professor there, it'd be a waste of time telling you. Believe me, it's better that neither of us knows what's going on. Go with the flow – that's my motto. Talking of which, Chris, must crack on. I've been asked to retrieve your phone, so if you'd be so good as to pop it in the drawer.'

'I haven't got my phone. It was in my backpack. You took my backpack, remember?'

'Nice one, Chris. Except that isn't your phone, is it? We've hacked into it and discovered that it's the late professor's. Good find, by the way. We've been looking everywhere for it.'

'I left my phone at home, charging up.' Chris was determined not to give an inch.

'So you hand out flyers with your phone number on but don't take your phone with you? I'd help you if I could but I don't think I believe you. You wouldn't be lying to Walter, would you?'

Damn. That was how he knew her name and number – she had put them on those bloody 'Have You Seen This Man?' posters. She couldn't have advertised her presence better if she'd wandered around Bottisham boatyard wearing a sandwich board that read 'Looking For Dastardly Criminals!'

'I'd help you if I could.'

That phrase. That well-spoken voice. She suddenly realised he was the young guy she'd seen earlier fiddling with his phone and smoking a roll-up by the snack caravan. What a frickin' idiot she'd been.

'You've got two choices,' Walter continued. 'Either you hand over your phone now or my colleague will conduct a body search. He's very keen to do so, so I'd recommend the former.'

Chris retrieved the phone from its hiding place in the zipped inside pocket of her shorts and dropped it into the drawer. There was a *Clang!* as the drawer was pulled to the outside.

'Thank you, Chris,' said Walter. 'And the security code?'

'Figure it out for yourselves if you're so clever.'

'Smartphones are unlocked by two methods. A typed code or a thumbprint. If you won't give us the code, my colleague will have to take your thumb instead. Snip, snip.'

She wasn't sure whether a disembodied thumb could be used to unlock a smartphone, but that was not a bluff she was willing to call. She reeled off her four-digit security code, twice.

'It's no use to you anyway,' she said. 'Battery's as flat as a steamrollered After Eight mint and the only thing of interest on it is an extensive gallery of cat photos.'

'On the contrary,' replied Walter. 'Apparently, I'm taking it on a holiday. When it's next switched on and the location finder is activated, it'll be far away from here. Just a little distraction in case anyone's looking for you. See? I told you my job offers opportunities for travel.'

Chris's heart sank. The one sliver of hope that she'd been holding onto was the thought that Zeta might be able to track her phone. All she had left now was pitiful bargaining.

'Look, Walter, or whatever your real name is, I think you're a nice guy at heart, and, as you say, this is just another job. You don't want me hurt, do you? You don't want me to... to suffer?'

'Of course not. I like you too, Chris.'

'Good. So why don't you accidentally leave the door open? I won't say anything to anyone and even if I did, what could I tell them? I don't know your name, I haven't seen your face.'

'Ooh no, I couldn't do that, Chris. The boss is a stickler for the rules. You see, my colleague broke the rules earlier this year. He decided to do a bit of freelance work on the side and the boss found out and called him in for a formal disciplinary meeting. As a result of that meeting, my colleague spent the next two weeks in hospital. It wasn't pretty, so now he's a stickler for the rules too.'

'Am I going to die here?' There, she'd said it.

'I hope not, Chris. One dead body's more than enough, don't you think? In my experience, they're much trickier to dispose of than you might imagine. The operation's wrapping up here, so I'm sure it'll only be a couple more days. I can put in a good word for you if you're worried, give you a decent reference, so to speak.'

'Thank you. I'd appreciate that, Walter.'

There was a pause and Chris was beginning to wonder whether

Walter had gone, but he'd obviously been thinking.

'Tell you what I'll do. If you let me know who else can feed… um… Aitken, isn't it? I'll text them.'

'It's Nick. He's in my contacts as "Next-Door Nick".'

'I'll sort it,' said Walter reassuringly. 'I love cats. If little Aitken had to miss his supper, I'd never forgive myself. It sounds like you've got good neighbours on Sea View.'

'The best,' Chris said, realising that she should have added Nick to the list of people she'd let down.

'I'll be off, then. Nice to have met you, Chris. Wish the circumstances were better, of course. I'll leave you in the capable hands of my colleague. Sweet dreams.'

There was a rasp of metal as the spyhole closed and the golden rays of early evening sunlight were extinguished. Already Chris could feel the temperature dipping, or perhaps it was delayed shock that was making her shiver. She retreated to the corner of the container, by the doors, as far away from Professor Jasper as possible. She ate three chocolate biscuits and took small sips of water – she wanted to put off using the yellow bucket for as long as physically possible.

She tried to sleep but couldn't. How could she? She was sharing a room with a corpse. Think positively, she urged herself. Remember what Walter said: two more days and they'd be gone and she'd be rescued. Just two more days and then she would be back home, back at Number 15, Sea View. That was a comforting thought.

Sea View? How did Walter know she lived at Sea View? Her home address wasn't on the 'Missing' flyer, and she hadn't told him. If they knew where she lived, what else did they know about her? In an instant, all threads of comfort had been torn.

Twenty-Five

After her unexpected encounter with Chloe at Chris's house, Zeta returned home to her empty flat. It was a just-about-affordable two-bedroom apartment above an estate agent's on Cliffstaple High Street. Her downstairs neighbours would have struggled to describe it as having much 'kerb appeal', and that the luxury properties being advertised directly beneath her went for seven-figure sums was an irony that hadn't escaped Zeta's notice. She used to have a flatmate to share costs and pay rent, but Helen had moved back to London four months ago and Zeta hadn't felt an urge to replace her. Besides, that spare room was handy as an office, helping keep home life and work life separate – well, almost.

Solitary living was… a bit solitary, but it was good not to have to haggle about bathroom access or argue about whose fridge-cheese was whose. She could just about manage the mortgage on her own without dipping too deeply into the small nest egg her mother had left her. Perhaps she would let out the spare bedroom when the students arrived for the new academic year.

She swiftly set about preparing supper, a homemade three-bean casserole, low in fat, high in roughage, non-existent in taste. While the casserole was simmering, filling the flat with unappealingly healthy fumes, she retrieved her laptop from her office. Paid work had to take priority – that was her rule. There was only one new work email, a request from Tony Figg & Sons, a local company with eight offices across Kent. They wanted an entire website redesign and were offering a three-year contract for ongoing service and search engine optimisation – a lucrative opportunity. She checked their Facebook page, which featured a red-faced Tony Figg, as solid as a retired prize fighter, standing in front of his double-fronted new-build house, his top-of-the-range Jaguar beside him. The page boasted: 'With Figg & Sons, your problems are now our problems. Kent's leading debt-collection and recovery solutions.'

A week ago, Zeta would have seized the chance, seeing Tony Figg as the source of the extra income required for a deposit on a better flat, one with a garden. But a lot had happened in the last seven days, and all she could think of right now was what Chris had said to her at Harbourside Eats: 'You can't separate your work from your social conscience.' She smiled to herself and muttered, 'Damn you, Chris – right again!' before deleting Tony Figg's email and slamming shut the lid of her laptop.

The three-bean casserole was three beans too many – disgusting, bland, chewy and inedible. Zeta pushed the barely touched bowl to one side and carefully took her black notebook from her inside pocket and reviewed that day's entry. This was her second most treasured possession – the only link she had to her father. The leather-bound police notebook had once been his. The first quarter of the book was dense with precise notations in her father's handwriting. Many times Zeta had tried to decipher them, but even Google Translate was no help, which led her to assume that they were written in code. The middle pages were filled with crude felt-tip drawings of houses and misshapen horses, the result of Zeta's mother having entrusted her six-year-old daughter with a precious family heirloom.

Rather than store the notebook away, Zeta had decided that the best way to honour her father's memory was to use his book to make her own notes, starting from the back. The latest section contained observations on her and Chris's investigation at the University of North Kent's forensics house. She reopened the laptop, located the folder named 'Jasper', transcribed the day's notes and scanned in the maps from Barry. The folder had files marked 'Crime Scene', 'Witness Statements', 'Forensics' and 'Conclusions'. None of this had been taken directly from the official police files – that would have been illegal. These were Zeta's own creation, a hobby or perhaps over-zealousness on her part.

She concentrated on the map of the Bottisham area. Her stomach growled. Using a footstool to reach up, she took a large book entitled *The Joy of Tofu* from the top shelf of the kitchen cabinet. The book was actually a cunningly disguised safe with a combination lock. Inside the safe was a family-sized bar of hazelnut milk chocolate. Proper food at last! She'd go for a swim first thing tomorrow to work off the calories and purge the guilt.

She spent an hour studying the map on the laptop. It was a large area and would take a full search party a week to cover properly. Zooming in on the quayside, Zeta conceded that Chris had been right; this would be the best place to start. And she had to acknowledge, for the third time that evening, that Chris was also right that they shouldn't let the trail get any colder.

She sent an email to Sgt Spurgeon at his work account. *Hi Sarge, sorry – domestic situ has cropped up, need to deal with tomorrow. Should be OK for Sunday. Zeta.* He never looked at work emails out of hours, so by the time he read it he wouldn't have much choice. He might interpret her absence as being the result of her earlier confrontation with the craft lager louts, a spot of PTSD, but she would put him straight on Sunday. It would take more than a few beered-up bozos to stop her from doing her duty.

She considered giving Chris a call, to discuss plans for the investigation, but she had stressed a 'no contact' policy and by now Chris was probably in the midst of a tearful reunion with her daughter. Instead, she spent the next hour browsing the Bottisham community chatrooms to see if there was any mention of suspicious activity over the past week. The boards were clogged with complaints about missed bin collections, tearful pleas for lost pets and gripes about traffic congestion and dodgy doorstep callers. There was nothing about mysterious professors or sub-standard erections. She looked for any mention of Priaman on the usual search engines and then, reluctantly, dipped her toes into the dark web. Nothing

– which was strange in itself. If the tablets, genuine or otherwise, had reached the open market there would have been some online footprint.

Her phone vibrated as a text arrived from an unknown number. *Phew! Mum texted Nick 'cos she's running late and wanted him to feed Aitken. See you tomorrow, Chloe.* That's good.

Zeta peeled back the inside lining of the back cover of her notebook. Hidden inside was her most treasured possession, a faded passport-sized photograph of a handsome young man. Even though she was alone in her kitchen, she looked around to check she was not being observed before she gently pressed her lips to the edge of the picture. 'What would you do, Dad?' she asked the photo. 'Take the easy option, toe the line, climb the greasy pole? Stupid question. You'd do what you had to, what was right, regardless of the consequences.'

She slapped the laptop shut again. Better get some sleep. Could be a busy day tomorrow.

Twenty-Six

The fact that she had slept at all surprised Chris. The fact that she hadn't had any disturbing dreams surprised her even more. Perhaps when you were actually living in a nightmare, bad dreams were redundant. She had no idea what the time was. It was dark and cold in her prison, but outside it could just as easily have been bright noon sunshine. She had succumbed to using the yellow bucket halfway through the night, though finding it with a gradually dimming torch and then squatting over the rim wasn't as much fun as she remembered from Girl Guide camping trips.

It was difficult to come to terms with what had happened over the previous eight days (assuming that this was Saturday morning). Reality-show contestants always, annoyingly, talked about how they'd been on a 'journey'. Chris's journey had started with a scenic cycle ride to try out her new e-bike and ended up in a shipping container with a dead body for company.

She found strange comfort in compiling a mental list, even if it was a list of 'if only's:

If only she hadn't been in such a rush to try out her new bicycle.

If only she'd chosen a shorter route.

If only she hadn't looked through the kitchen window of the forensics house.

If only Mr Squirrel hadn't caused her to turn back.

If only she hadn't gone to the police station.

If only she hadn't bumped into Zeta at the swimming baths.

If only bloody Simon hadn't taunted her into going along with Zeta's plan.

If only she wasn't so pig-headed.

If only, if only, if only.

She could probably have found at least another dozen 'if only's' to add to her list, but she was interrupted by the scrape of metal and an accompanying thin shaft of sunlight that indicated that the spyhole had opened.

She walked towards the light.

'Walter, you said I might be released soon. You said "a couple more days". Only the battery's going on this torch and—'

'Who's Walter?' The new voice was a strange mix of Irish and South African with a hint of Italian, as though someone was trying to disguise their voice but hadn't quite figured out how.

It was time to rebuild the hostage/kidnapper rapport. 'Ah, right. Walter's handed over the reins, has he? Good to meet you, new person. And your name is…?'

There was the clatter of the drawer opening.

'Eat,' said her non-loquacious captor.

Chris shone her torch into the drawer and picked out a bottle of water and a wrapped mass-produced sausage roll. Not just any sausage roll – a cheap supermarket sausage roll. She had been known to occasionally succumb to a bacon sandwich, but that at least was identifiable meat. This strange mix of finely minced miscellaneous animal parts was beyond the pale.

'Sorry, I can't eat this. You see, I'm vegetarian, so this sausage roll is definitely not… um… kosher.'

'Eat.' Her new jailer was obviously not blessed with an extensive vocabulary.

She had barely extracted her hand when the drawer was rapidly closed. It was only her lightning reactions that had saved her from losing a couple of fingers.

'Hello? Hello?'

There was no answer.

'Bring back Walter,' she muttered to herself. He might have had a rather bizarre interpretation of career opportunities, but at least he'd been capable of producing words of more than one syllable. She hoped he had kept his word about texting Nick. Even though that might prevent anyone from coming to look for her, at least it would stop them from worrying. Chris was nothing if not self-reliant. She'd got herself into this mess, and it was up to her to bear the consequences.

A thin beam of sunlight was creating a spotlight on the floor. The spyhole hadn't been shut properly. Was this accidental or a deliberate ploy to lull her into a false sense of security? Craving natural light, she upturned the yellow bucket and positioned it so she could sit and feel the warmth of sunshine on her face. It was decidedly unsanitary behaviour, but the ammonia smell of stale urine trickling across the floor was preferable to the stench emanating from the professor's end of the container.

By now her stomach was aching with hunger, so she ate the sausage roll, washing it down with gulps of water. She kept moving her face so the spot of sunlight played over each and every inch, and she held up her hands and watched the light dappling her fingertips. It was only a meagre ray, but it felt good. If she ever got out of there, Chris vowed, she would never again take for granted the simple pleasures of life. She would appreciate her health, her family, her friends, her environment and her comforts. No cat-litter tray would be too stinky to clean, no academic paper too boring to read. If she escaped this situation alive, Cynical Chris would be but a distant memory. If.

So many questions. How did she even know Professor Jasper's death was 'accidental'? Why should she assume that the same fate wasn't planned for her? Had she placed too much faith in Walter's cheery outlook? Was it Stockholm Syndrome to believe the best intentions of your captors?

Did she trust people too easily? Chris had always taken pride in being an excellent judge of character, but did the evidence back this up? Take Simon for starters. Yes, that union had produced Chloe, but seven years was hardly *Till Death Do Us Part*. And then there were the others. She'd not entered into any relationship thinking that the man in question was an arsehole, but that's what every one of them had eventually shown themselves to be. She'd been wrong about Cheeky Cockney Ray in the hospital too – he'd turned out to be Lying Pickpocket Ray.

An even worse thought entered Chris's head. Was she misguided about Zeta as well? Had all that stuff about Zeta's long-lost father been just a fabricated sob story to get her cooperation, to manipulate her?

She crawled over to the doors and recommenced her SOS tapping with the torch. If this was Saturday morning, then the boatyard (if indeed that was where she was incarcerated) would be busy with part-time enthusiasts dabbling in renovation work. If she got lucky, someone might hear her. She tapped both variations – SOS and OSO – five hundred times, which, she reckoned, was about an hour's worth of tapping.

The sun was still shining through the open spyhole. If she could try to see out, maybe she could get her bearings, maybe she'd be able to shout for help. She positioned the yellow bucket directly under the spyhole and stepped up onto it. It was not the most robust of buckets and wobbled and sagged precariously under her weight. If she were to fall and break her other hip, that would be the end of her story, right there and then. She braced her hands against the wall and put her eye to the spyhole. The view was of purple gorse bushes and the side of another rusty shipping container. She pressed her ear to the hole and could just make out faint sounds of a car engine and conversation. She looked out again and saw… an eye looking straight back at her.

In fright, she fell backwards off the bucket and landed squarely and painfully on her coccyx. She lay there on the ground winded, shocked. She'd seen that eye before.

She tried to access her memory palace in search of the eye's owner. In her mind she travelled to Bottisham quayside… no, North Kent Police Station… no, then to the university… no, to Railway

Cottages… no, to the high street, to Cliffstaple Pharmacy and Spokesmen cycle shop… no. There was something about that eye, something distinctive about that pupil, something unworldly.

She took her search further back. To Kent Coast Hospital. Scott the porter? Mr Spatchcock? To Baxter Ward… Baxter Ward. And there it was – she *had* seen that eye before. Back then, it hadn't been staring through a spyhole but through a mass of bandages. That eye belonged to the one-time incumbent of Bed 4, Baxter Ward, Kent Coast Hospital. It was Evil Eye. Chris was sure of it.

Twenty-Seven

Just twenty more lengths and she'd be done, Zeta decided. Early-morning swimming was wonderful – heart-racing, lung-busting, guilt-purging. Every tumble-turn felt like a baptism. She had nearly completed a double session, getting there for when the pool opened at 06:45, and had more than worked off the calories in the family-size bar of hazelnut chocolate she'd gorged on the previous night.

As she changed back into civvies she checked her phone. Half nine and still no message from Chris. Not that surprising, given that she'd explicitly told Chris not to contact her by phone, but, even so, she wished her friend had broken the rules. Chloe had said it would be all right to pop round. Zeta wouldn't take up much of their time; she just wanted to rid herself of the nagging feeling that something was not right.

She had barely taken her finger off the doorbell of 15, Sea View when the door was opened by Chloe. The redness of Chloe's eyes showed that she had been crying and the dark rings beneath suggested she hadn't slept.

'Hi, Zeta, I hoped you were…' Chloe said, unable to hide her disappointment.

'Your mum's not back?'

'No.' The tears welled up in Chloe's eyes. 'And I don't know what to do.' She opened the door wide and beckoned Zeta in.

'Could she have stayed over with friends?'

Chloe shook her head. 'That's what Dad said, but then he just started ranting about how unpredictable and unreliable Mum's become. I don't know if she's got anyone she'd stay with. Why doesn't she answer her phone?'

They sat in the kitchen. Aitken, a great empathiser, jumped up onto the table and rubbed his head against Chloe's face.

Zeta didn't want to cause Chloe any more anxiety than necessary, so she maintained a calm exterior. 'She's probably lost it or it's broken. Tell you what, shall I call it in to the station? At least that might put your mind at rest.'

Chloe shook her head again. 'I've already done that. I went there first thing this morning. The policeman at the front desk was really unhelpful. He said, "As it's less than twenty-four hours and she sent a text to say she'd be late, she's not really missing, is she?"'

'What was this officer's name?'

'I can't remember. I was in such a state, I wasn't taking things in. He had a dodgy moustache.'

'Ah,' said Zeta, 'that'll be PC Thackery. Between you and me, not one of North Kent Constabulary's finest. He did file a report though?'

Chloe nodded. 'Thackery, that's right. When I gave him Mum's name and details he said he'd booked her in last week for causing a disturbance and he reckoned she was going senile and perhaps that was why she'd gone missing.'

'He called her senile?' Thackery's people skills needed a lot of work.

'So I lost my temper and said he was pervy-looking and stormed out.'

Like mother, like daughter. 'Can I make us a coffee?' Zeta asked and put the kettle on without waiting for an answer.

'Sorry if I'm being a bit fraught,' said Chloe. 'Perhaps it's the jet lag catching up with me. I just don't understand why Mum would send a text to Nick and then switch her phone off.'

A *PING!* sounded in Zeta's head. 'Have you actually seen the text?'

'No. Good point. I'll give Nick a call.'

Zeta had only just finished making the coffee when Chloe

answered the door to Nick. He followed her into the kitchen dressed in a magenta silk dressing gown. Around his head he sported a white bandana inscribed with Japanese characters in black ink.

'Sorry if I've got you up, Nick,' said Chloe.

'What? Oh no, this is my costume for the festival parade. We're a Japanese drumming troupe, you see.'

'It's just that Mum didn't come home last night.'

A look of concern spread across Nick's face.

'Could we see the text Chris sent you yesterday?' Zeta asked.

'The text? Sure.' Next-Door Nick fished his phone out of his kimono pocket. 'Here it is.'

The screen read: *Soz, not back til l8. Can u feed 8kin? Chris xxxx*

Chloe gasped and put her hand over her mouth. 'That's not from Mum.'

'Are you sure?' said Nick.

'Positive. She'd never use those abbreviations – she's a proofreader! I always tease her because it takes her so long to write a text. She has to have correct grammar and punctuation.'

'It's from her number though.' Nick took back the phone and looked mournfully at the screen. 'I should've known that four kisses was too much to hope for.'

'If Chloe's positive, that's good enough for me. I've got an idea where your mum might have gone yesterday.' Zeta took the map of Bottisham out of her backpack and spread it on the table. 'Somewhere in here.'

'That's a huge area,' observed Nick.

'Chris told me she thought that the quayside looked promising. I bet that's where she went.'

'Let's get cracking, then,' said Chloe, picking up her bag.

'We'll take my car,' said Nick, rushing home for his car keys. 'Sod the parade. I'm sure my troupe won't miss one drummer.'

Zeta phoned the station. 'Barry? It's Zeta. Look, urgent favour needed. Can you get the guys to trace Christine Heron's mobile number? It's on the system.'

'I won't be able to do this by the backdoor, Zeta, love. There's no one else in the office today to provide cover. I'm going to have to send this upstairs for authorisation if you want it done quickly.'

'Do it, Barry. I take full responsibility.' Zeta knew this could be a career-ending move, but her instincts were screaming that the time for careful planning had gone.

They met Nick outside the house. Chloe snatched the car keys out of his hand. 'I'll drive if you don't mind,' she said in a non-negotiable way. Somehow, Nick squeezed his six-foot frame into the rear seats of his Fiat 500 and Zeta took the front passenger seat.

Chloe revved the engine, stamped on the accelerator and they hared off at a G-force-inducing speed. 'Gonna pick up some extra help,' she said, her hands gripping the steering wheel like a vice.

The car screeched to a halt by the fish market, where people were gathering for day three of the Festival of Fish. Chloe leapt out of the car and plunged into the crowd. Less than a minute later, she reappeared, dragging her father behind her. Simon, in full morris-dancing regalia, was protesting vociferously, but his daughter somehow shovelled him into the back seat alongside Nick.

Chloe set off again, driving fast along the winding lanes that led to Bottisham, ignoring all pleas for caution from her passengers. The Japanese drummer and the morris dancer were so tightly wedged in that Simon had to stick his right arm out of the window. He was still clutching his bladder-on-a-stick, so each time they sped round a corner, his bladder thumped on the roof of the car, causing a dull echo. Zeta prayed that they wouldn't get stopped by any traffic officers as the strange assortment of passengers would take some explaining.

In less than twenty minutes the Fiat 500 screeched into a parking bay at Bottisham quayside. Chloe and Zeta leapt out of the car, but it took two full minutes for Simon and Nick to untangle their limbs and costumes and extricate themselves. Evidently, his abduction had not put Simon in the cheeriest of moods.

'Let's split up,' Zeta suggested. 'Guys, you take the shops.

Chloe and I will check out the cafe and the houseboats.' The greater distance she could put between herself and the ninja and the morris dancer, the better. 'Ask anyone and everyone. We'll meet back at the teashop in one hour.'

She directed Chloe to question the teashop staff while she headed towards the quayside. She got a sickening feeling when looking at the deep, murky water and didn't want the same thought to enter Chloe's head.

There was no apparent sign of life on any of the three houseboats that were permanently moored there. All the curtains were open on the first boat, *Marge's Barge*, so Zeta jumped down and peered through each one. Everything inside appeared neat, tidy and undisturbed. She moved onto the second boat, *Jerome's Dream*, whose curtains were securely drawn across all the windows, leaving not even the smallest gap. She boarded and knocked on the door. There was no response. She tested the handle, was surprised to find the door unlocked, and duly opened it, shouting 'Hello!' as she did so, in the hope that, if she was challenged, her warrant card would deflect any objections. The inside was chintzy with an abundance of lace, and twee bone china figurines that seemed to be either brave or foolish decorations for a water-balanced home.

The third boat was nameless as far as she could tell and functional rather than decorative. It was a steel barge, slightly rusty but very solid, the sort of construction that challenged theories of buoyancy. Its metal shutters were closed. As Zeta stepped on board there seemed to be a slight tremor beneath her feet even though the water in the harbour was still. Rather than knock, she pressed her ear to the door. She heard movement, a faint rattling and muffled sounds of… distress? Pain? Carefully she tested the door handle and pulled. The door swung open and sunlight flooded the interior, illuminating a couple engaging in passionate, consensual and, until now, secret copulation. They were so embroiled that they didn't notice, or maybe didn't care, that they now had an audience of one. Zeta quietly closed the door and left them to it.

As she climbed back up onto the quayside, Simon ran, jingling, towards her. Thankfully Chloe had persuaded him to leave his bladder-on-a-stick in the car. 'The guy who runs that shop there,' he panted, pointing to Nigel's Knick-Knacks and Antiques, 'has got a lock-up next door, but he wouldn't let me have a look. Do you want to know what he called me when I asked?'

'I can imagine,' Zeta said.

The eponymous Nigel was less than cooperative, even when she brandished her warrant card.

'I don't care if you're bleedin' Ali Baba! No one's got the right to invade the privacy of a man's lock-up.'

Zeta exhausted all reasonable avenues, but Nigel was not a man for turning.

As she was considering alternative strategies for the breaching of the Nigel Defence, Next-Door Nick arrived, chaperoning a formidable-looking middle-aged woman. Together, the man in the silk dressing gown and the Amazonian woman in twinset and pearls looked like the result of a TV dating show gone terribly wrong.

'Zeta,' said Nick, 'this is Anne. She says she saw someone matching Chris's description yesterday.'

'Indeed,' announced Anne in a sonorous voice. 'Nigel here introduced us.'

'Is that what this is about?' exclaimed Nigel. 'You reckon I've got 'er tucked up in me lock-up? You're bleedin' mad, the lot of yers. And no, you still can't 'ave a butcher's inside.'

'What was the nature of your conversation?' said Zeta calmly, attempting to counteract Nigel's agitation.

'She was trying to return a jacket,' said Nigel.

'Fortunately, *I* was able to identify the owner,' said Anne proudly. 'It was—'

'Professor Adrian Jasper,' Zeta interrupted.

Anne looked crestfallen at having had her thunder stolen. 'Yes, that's right. *Professor* Jasper is one of my most valued customers.'

Nigel made a strange harrumphing noise.

'When was this?' Zeta asked.

'About 11:30 am. She said she'd previously visited the professor's house, so I assumed I wasn't betraying any confidences.'

'And did you see where she went afterwards?'

'No, I'm afraid not. You see, Nigel here was rather overexcited about a brass reading lamp, so I was too distracted to notice.'

Simon, Nick and Zeta headed for the Quayside Tearooms to consider their next move.

'The question is, where did Chris go next?' said Nick. 'Could she have gone back to Jasper's house?'

Zeta was doubtful. 'It's a long cycle from here. Is there anywhere around here that we haven't checked out?'

'Apart from that storage unit?' asked Nick.

'He called me a circus freak,' said Simon glumly.

Zeta was about to suggest that they move their search party to the area around Bottisham market square when Chloe burst into the teashop.

'I think I've found Mum's bike!' she shouted.

Sure enough, in the narrow gap between the teashop and the craft centre next door was a locked e-bike with 'RamRod' written on the frame.

'Mum didn't leave here, did she?' said Chloe, her voice quaking.

Zeta phoned Barry, who answered immediately. 'I need some more boots on the ground here. There's clear evidence that missing person Christine Heron is in the vicinity.' She moved out of earshot of Chloe and the others. 'And how do we go about getting a dive team?'

Twenty-Eight

Chris was scared, very scared. That was the trouble with stressful situations – you went through a range of emotions in rapid time, from Panglossian optimism to acceptance to dread. Currently, she felt like a mouse pinned under Aitken's paw, paralysed.

The spyhole was still open, so she shrank as far back into the shadows as she could, clutching her knees to her chest. Perhaps if she stayed still and perfectly quiet, Evil Eye would get bored and leave her alone, find something else to toy with.

With a scraping sound, the spyhole shut and, for once, Chris felt comfort in the pitch blackness. She tried to think positive thoughts. Like Julie Andrews in *The Sound of Music*, she listed a few of her favourite things: cats, black and white movies, cool cotton sheets on a summer night, peanut butter and cucumber sandwiches. She fondly recalled Chloe's birth – not the gynaecological hideousness of the actual event, but how she'd cradled her new baby in her arms and wondered at two dysfunctional people having created a creature of such beauty.

It would have been nice to have seen the people she loved one last time, she thought. If only to say goodbye. But there was nothing to do now but sit there in the dark and wait.

'Get a grip.'

'What?'

Had she heard a voice?

'You've gone and done it now, haven't you.'

'Who's there?' she whispered.

'Made a right cock-up of things yet again, I see.' The voice had a gentle Scottish accent reminiscent of a young Sean Connery.

'Don't come any closer,' she warned. 'I've got a black belt in hara-kiri.'

'You don't recognise me?'

It was strange. The voice sounded real but was somehow internal.

Chris stared into the blackness, trying to detect movement. She took deep breaths through her nostrils, trying to detect any new scent.

'Do I know you?' For some reason, she no longer felt alarmed.

'You should do. You've visited me, on average, once a week for the past eighteen months.'

'I'm sorry?'

'So you should be. I've had to stand there and listen to all your deepest secrets, which were, to be frank, rather dull. You expect me to sort out all your problems and you haven't even got the decency—'

'Grayson?'

'By George, she's got it!'

Chris was stunned and dumbfounded. 'You're… you're… Scottish?'

'Apparently so.'

'So this is another of those God-awful dreams I've been having?'

'Not exactly.'

She paused to think. She knew Grayson wasn't actually there having a conversation with her. He couldn't be. 'I'm hallucinating? I've gone insane?'

'Sensory deprivation. Your brain has conjured me up. Bloody inconvenient, I must say.'

'Sensory deprivation? But I've only been in this shipping container for about a day.'

'I know. Surprised me too. Guess you're not as good in your own company as you like to think.'

'So why have I conjured you up?' Chris realised she was talking out loud. Talking out loud to an inanimate shop-window mannequin who wasn't there.

'The brain's a remarkable organ. It recognises that you're hyper-stressed, in peril, and so it has summoned your old mucker Grayson to help.'

'Thanks for making the journey, Grayson, but unless you've got a phone with a signal or a fully loaded Uzi, I'm not sure what you can bring to the party.'

'Some advice.'

'Advice? Oh terrific. What?'

'You're going to die—'

She laughed scornfully. 'Oh, thanks for that. I'd figured that bit out for myself. I certainly didn't need some reject from a Primark clearance sale to rub it in.'

'If you would just let me finish. You're going to die if you do nothing. Either they'll kill you or they'll leave you in here to perish from thirst.'

'You're not really helping things here, Grayson.'

She wondered whether hundreds of locked shipping containers around the world housed the desiccated remains of foolhardy amateur detectives.

'I'm here to tell you that you will get a chance. A chance not to die. When that chance comes, do not question yourself, do not hesitate.'

'How will I know?' Chris asked. But Grayson had gone quiet. She was alone again.

Something had changed though; she was back in control. Whatever Evil Eye had got planned, she determined, she would not go gentle into that good night.

*

The security drawer rattled. Lunchtime? Chris turned on her torch, shaking it to jolt the batteries into life. In the drawer was a bottle of vodka, sealed. Not any old vodka but Grey Goose, her favourite brand. Pharmaceutical forgery must be a booming business if they could afford premium spirits.

The spyhole above her head slid open.

'Drink,' ordered Evil Eye.

'Thanks. Tempting, but I'll pass. Call me a killjoy but I have a very strict rule about not drinking neat vodka before teatime.' Maybe a bit of light humour would help their uneasy relationship.

'Drink,' repeated Evil Eye.

'Sure. Can you pop it in the freezer first? A couple of days should do it. Room-temperature vodka is wrong in so many ways.'

A memory from her honeymoon popped into her head. A vodka bar in Budapest where the shot glasses were actually made of ice. A truly happy time with Simon. It had all gone downhill after that.

'If you don't drink, I'll come in there and force it down you,' said Evil Eye.

On reflection, Chris preferred him when he was a man of fewer words.

She undid the bottle top and took a sip, accentuating an extreme reaction to the alcohol for the benefit of her viewer. 'Wow!' She added a couple of coughs and a splutter for good measure. 'Um… can I ask why you're being so generous with your booze?'

'We're moving out,' said Evil Eye. 'Drink.'

'In that case, can I be the first to wish you "Bon voyage"?' Chris toasted him with another glug from the bottle. 'Got any peanuts? Or those wasabi peas? Have you tried them? They're awesome.'

'And you're coming with us.'

This stopped Chris mid-glug. All at once a kaleidoscope of questions and theories invaded her mind. The vodka was presumably intended to incapacitate her, and Evil Eye's statement could only mean one of the following:

1) They were going to dump her somewhere remote and let her find her own way home. After all, who would give any credence to the ramblings of a vodka-infused sixty-year-old woman? By the time she had sobered up and could persuade the authorities otherwise, Evil Eye and his chums would be long gone.

All things considered, that was a GOOD outcome.

2) They were going to hold her as a hostage somewhere else. She couldn't imagine she'd raise much of a ransom, but she classified this as a MODERATE outcome.

3) They were going to kill her and dump her in the creek or a reservoir. Perhaps leave her body submerged in the marshes and make her death look like misadventure, a drunken accident. This was clearly a BAD outcome.

'Drink,' ordered Evil Eye for the fourth and, Chris suspected, final time.

She had no choice but to comply so she swigged again from the bottle. Perhaps this was the chance that Grayson had mentioned? Her captor's tactic had given her an advantage, one she had to exploit. She was better at drinking neat vodka than Evil Eye could possibly have imagined.

To make this convincing for her audience, Chris enacted the Three Stages of Pissedness. For the first quarter of the bottle, she was Affectionate Drunk: 'You know, I reckon you could have been an actor. Your voice has a lovely timbre. Have you ever done any voiceover work? Tell you what, when this is all over, you, me and Walter should go out – a couple of drinks and a curry. That'd be a laugh.'

For the next eighth she was Scared Drunk, marked by a more exaggerated slurring of speech, moderate paranoia and heightened emotions: 'I… I… think I'm gonna be ill. I don't usually drink. Are you filming me? Who are you? Tell me your name. Am I going to die? I don't want to die. Please don't let me die.'

For her last eighth of the bottle (she figured that half a bottle of vodka was enough, even for her) she role-played Batshit Crazy Drunk, where anything went: 'Come on then, I'll fight you. I'll fight the lot of you. You tell your big boss man to come in here and I'll kick twenty-seven colours of crap out of him. I've got a titanium hip, I'm the frickin' bionic woman! I'm… I'm…'

With that, Chris dropped the bottle, performed a neat pirouette

and slumped into a state of apparent unconsciousness.
 And now to wait.

Twenty-Nine

Within fifteen minutes of Zeta's call, Barry arrived in a squad car, blues and twos playing. Unfortunately, he wasn't alone. He was accompanied by Sgt Spurgeon and PC Atherton.

'What are they doing here?' Zeta hissed at Barry.

'You said you wanted back-up, Zeta. This is all that was available.'

Sgt Spurgeon stretched so that bare midriff squeezed out between his waistline and the bottom of his stab vest. 'So, Jah-mah, what's this fool's errand we've been called out on? I hear it's that nutty woman on an e-bike again. What's she done this time, cycled into the creek?'

PC Atherton sniggered obediently.

'No, Sarge. Ms Heron has been reported missing and this is the location of the last confirmed sighting.' Zeta shepherded Chloe forward. 'And this is Ms Heron's daughter.'

Sgt Spurgeon paused to take in the extent of his inappropriateness, hoisting his trousers to buy time. 'Rest assured, Miss… um.'

'It's Grant, Chloe Grant. We've just found my mum's bike and two witnesses,' said Chloe, showing no reaction to the slight about her mother's sanity.

'Rest assured, if your mother is here, we will locate her,' said Sgt Spurgeon with more confidence than was warranted.

Zeta had instinctively taken charge of operations. 'Sarge,' she said firmly, 'the evidence indicates that Ms Heron is somewhere in the vicinity. We've done an initial sweep, but we can't get access to one lock-up. The owner's a bit reluctant, but I'm sure you can persuade him.'

She led Spurgeon, Atherton and the others across to Nigel's Knick-Knacks and Antiques. A small troop of other traders and curious visitors followed them.

Seeing the group, Nigel paled, as though he had been confronted by a crowd of irate villagers armed with flaming torches and pitchforks. 'Brought the cavalry, have we?' he said, with as much courage as he could muster. 'As I told this young lady, no warrant, no access. Them's the rules.'

Ollie disappeared into the back of the shop, never to be seen again.

Sgt Spurgeon placed a large hand on Nigel's shoulder. 'You're absolutely correct, *sir*. We have no legal right to search your lock-up without a warrant.'

Nigel gave a self-satisfied smile and nodded at his audience. 'Told you.'

'Of course, we could go and get a warrant,' continued Spurgeon, 'but to make all that paperwork worth the effort we'd have to go through the entire contents of your lock-up *and* your lovely store. And some of my officers are *terribly* clumsy.'

'And we'd have to get HMRC in to look at the accounts, Sarge,' trilled PC Atherton.

Nigel sensibly accepted defeat. The crowd followed him to the grand opening of his storage locker.

As Zeta had expected, the great reveal was something of an anti-climax. The lock-up contained crates, two racks of fake designer dresses and some dust-gathering exercise equipment. A pile of boxed VCRs that had missed their market by about thirty years were stacked in a far corner next to a collection of more current games consoles. The origin of much of the content of Nigel's lock-up was undoubtedly dubious but, in the scheme of things, hardly worth the attention of North Kent Constabulary. Unfortunately (or perhaps fortunately), what the lock-up didn't contain was any sign of human inhabitation.

'Very good, sir,' said Spurgeon to Nigel after they had completed a cursory examination. 'It may be wise for you to have a bit of a declutter before our next visit, don't you think?'

'Declutter? Yes, Officer, I'll get onto it right away,' said Nigel, visibly shrunken.

He gratefully secured his lock-up again and the disappointed crowd put away their camera phones and dispersed.

'Nick and Simon, can you help the officers and double-check we haven't missed any of the other stall holders?' instructed Zeta.

'I'll take the teashop,' said Barry, predictably.

'Chloe, you and I will try and retrace your mum's movements from the time she parked her bike.'

It took her and Chloe twenty minutes to track a likely route from locking up the bike to Chris's conversation at Anne's Tiquities.

'Could Mum have fallen in the water?' Chloe asked the question Zeta had been dreading.

'It was nearly midday on a Friday. Lots of people around. It's very unlikely she could have fallen in without anyone noticing.'

This seemed to comfort Chloe more than it did Zeta in the telling.

They all reconvened at Quayside Tearooms. Spurgeon and Atherton reported that none of the other traders even remembered seeing Chris. Nick and Simon had also drawn a blank. There was nowhere that they hadn't searched. Zeta was desperately trying to think up a new plan of action when Barry took a call which, from the sound of his side of the conversation, suggested new information incoming. He ended the call with, 'Thanks, Pippa. We owe you big time.'

Everyone gathered round him in expectation. 'Well?' Zeta asked.

'That was Pippa from digital forensics. Christine Heron's phone came back on thirty minutes ago.'

'Thank God,' Chloe said under her breath.

'Digital forensics?' said Sgt Spurgeon, under his.

'So where is she, Barry?' said Zeta hurriedly, before her sergeant could question the commissioning of the phone trace.

'You're not going to like it.'

'Where?'

'Calais.'

'Calais?' came the chorus from round the table.

'Yes, Calais, France. Pippa's certain,' said Barry.

'Typical,' muttered Simon.

'She's only bloody gone on holiday,' shouted Spurgeon, rising from his chair. 'You two,' he said, pointing at Zeta and Barry, 'have got some serious questions to answer – bloody time wasters. And I thought better of you, Jah-mah. This is your "domestic situ", is it? Come on, PC Atherton. God knows what's happening at the festival in our absence, probably riots.'

'I can't believe it,' muttered Nick. 'Chris wouldn't just leave Aitken to go to France. Not without checking I could cat-sit.'

'And Mum hasn't got her passport with her. It's at home by her laptop. I was hoping she was in the process of applying for an Australian visa,' said Chloe, concern etched across her brow.

'And her text was a fake,' added Nick.

Zeta ran over to her sergeant and grabbed his arm before he left the tearooms. 'Please, Sarge, can't you see what this is?'

'A lush on a cheap booze run?' suggested Atherton sarcastically.

'No, it's a false-flag operation, a decoy. Someone else has got Chris's phone,' urged Zeta. 'And why would that someone try and make us believe that Chris is in France unless they're concerned we'll find her?'

'So she's nearby,' added Chloe.

'Someone's playing us for fools,' Simon concluded.

Spurgeon, to his credit, sat down at the table again and began slowly processing this information.

Barry had been poring over the map of Bottisham. 'Pippa mentioned something else. They found another blip off Professor Jasper's phone, as though it had been briefly switched on again. That was yesterday at 12:56, at a different location to previously. And if I align the two locations of Jasper's phone' – he showed the group the map, upon which he had drawn a Venn diagram, and carefully placed his finger on a particular spot – 'they seem to overlap *there*.'

'The boatyard!' said seven people in unison.

Thirty

Silence. Darkness. Feigning unconsciousness wasn't easy. There was an overwhelming urge to fidget, scratch her arse, sneeze. And as she didn't know whether she was being watched or not, she had to resist that urge.

Chris had been mentally singing the entire album of David Bowie's *Hunky Dory* in her head. It was her first album ever, a Christmas present from her mum and dad, and she'd memorised every lyric, every chord change. She knew the duration of each track and that the proper, original vinyl version of the album was forty-two minutes long. As she didn't have any other means of measuring time, it was a perfect solution.

She was midway through the final track, 'The Bewlay Brothers', when she heard a heavy latch being drawn back. Sunlight flooded the space, which then turned black again as the container door was closed. She opened her eyes to a slit and saw a torch beam playing over the interior.

Footsteps resonated against the metal floor. He was there. She counted the steps. One, two, three, shit! A foot thudded into her ribs. Her instinct was to scream and swear, but she played her role, moaning gently and muttering nonsense.

Seemingly satisfied, her assailant moved on, the torch beam illuminating the body of Professor Jasper.

Evil Eye was now on the far side of her. She was nearer the door, but she didn't dare turn over to see how firmly he had shut it behind him. If she made a dash for it he'd probably catch her before she got halfway. It was not worth the risk. She could make out his form at the far end of the container, silhouetted by the torchlight. He was leaning over the professor's body, checking his pockets.

'It's now or never, Chris, hen,' said Grayson's disembodied voice.

She slowly and quietly got to her feet and took a deep breath.

'Charge!'

She ran – not towards the container door but towards Evil Eye. She dropped her shoulder and slammed into the small of his back.

The surprise was total. Evil Eye tripped forwards over the professor's body as Chris rebounded backwards. As she hit the floor, she heard the satisfying *Clang!* of her captor's head striking the metal wall.

She righted herself, turned and sprinted towards the door as fast as her ribs and hip would allow. It wasn't locked but it was heavy, so heavy. She pushed against it like a rugby player in a scrum. Inch by inch it eased open until there was a gap big enough for her to squeeze through.

Outside, the sunlight was blinding and the fresh air intoxicating. She leant against the door to close it shut and tried to lock it, but the bolt was heavy and rusty and her fingers clumsy and useless. She could only get it partly into its hasp before the door shuddered as Evil Eye crashed into it from the other side. The bolt held – for now.

She turned to run, but the neat vodka hit and her legs gave way. She was on her knees in the dirt, struggling to get upright with the knowledge that Evil Eye was within minutes of escaping. Her first reaction was not fear or panic but embarrassment. This would never have happened to Young Chris. Young Chris would have still been partying after necking half a bottle of vodka. But she wasn't Young Chris. She was Old Chris – a sixty-year-old woman with a titanium hip, an e-bike and possibly a broken rib.

As she got to her feet, the Mr Softee van loomed tauntingly above her head. After her isolation, the noise and light was overwhelming her senses, amplified by the alcohol rush. She had to escape, had to find the way out.

There was barking, snarling. That dog was on the loose between her and the exit to the boatyard, and she was vividly picturing its slathering jaws and razor-sharp fangs – the embodiment of that police station rabies poster. Meanwhile, Evil Eye was rattling the door, loosening the bolt.

Hide, Chris. Hide. If they expect you to run, stop and hide.

She tried the ice cream van door – unlocked – clambered up onto the passenger seat and closed herself in with a *Clunk!* The barking and clanging noises were now muffled and the bright light muted, allowing her to gather her thoughts, reorder her brain. Good thinking, Chris. This would be the last place anyone would look. No escaped prisoner would hide directly outside the prison gates. Well, no sane prisoner. She would stay hidden there for an hour, sober up and then slip away quietly. That was a plan.

Ribs aching, she squeezed painfully between the front seats and crawled into the main body of the van. It was chaos in there. The business area of Mr Softee was a jumble of boxes and plastic sheeting, cartons of multi-coloured sugar sprinkles and catering packs of wafers. On a coat hook hung a grubby white hat atop a faded candy-stripe blazer. It looked as though it had been months since the van had last been used to actually sell ice cream.

She stumbled over a jar and it broke, spreading blood-red raspberry syrup over her hands and knees as it pooled across the floor of the van. As she attempted to wipe the gloop off, she knocked over a plastic tub of hundreds and thousands, which proceeded to coat every syrupy area of her body. A cardboard box fell off a shelf and landed on her head. Contents: 200 choco-like flakes. Everything about Mr Softee was a lie; even the chocolate was fake.

Maybe she could just bury herself beneath the boxes, interred among hundreds and thousands, immersed in raspberry syrup. There was a cupboard beneath the Whippy-Whip ice cream dispenser, possibly large enough for her to squeeze into. She opened it and dozens of small cardboard cartons tumbled out. Priaman boxes, spilling their blister packs of blue pills. She was shovelling them up by the armful, desperately looking for somewhere to hide them, when she felt a hand on her shoulder, the fingers gripping tightly into the flesh between the bone. A voice rasped in her ear, breath wet and foul-smelling.

'I think you'll be more comfortable up front with me,' said Evil Eye.

Effortlessly, excruciatingly, he dragged Chris into the front of the van and pushed her down into the passenger seat. A loose spring dug into the small of her back, adding to the pain in her ribs and hip and the dull throbbing in her head.

Evil Eye opened the driver's door and an equally evil-looking dog jumped up and sat proudly between the seats, its front paws astride the gear stick. 'Look after our passenger, Sabre,' said Evil Eye.

Sabre? Chris was tempted to make a quip, but she didn't want her last words to be some poorly thought-through stand-up comedy routine about clichéd dogs' names.

She glanced up at Evil Eye's face, seeing it naked for the first time, and immediately wished she hadn't. He was an unpleasant enough sight swathed in bandages or through a spyhole, but, bare-faced, his visage matched his charming personality. It looked like it had been moulded out of Plasticine by a hyperactive five-year-old – a misshaped collection of bumps, broken bones, scars and bruises. The legacy of his beating at the fists of his boss – his punishment for going freelance, as Walter had suggested? And was this a mystery solved? Was Evil Eye also Mr Softee? Was this the face that launched a thousand Whippy-Whips?

At the third time of asking, the engine chucked into life and, after a seven-point-turn, the van moved slowly down the line of shipping containers before turning ninety degrees left into the boatyard. For the first time Chris saw people in the distance. She surreptitiously tried the door handle, but Sabre gave a deep, throaty growl that said, 'Try that again, mate, and your throat is history.'

The van swung left again to run parallel with the shipping containers. This was towards the exit that led to the sewage works bypass that Chris had cycled down two long days ago. Evil Eye braked softly and swore to himself. Up ahead was a police car parked adjacent to the exit.

'Not a sound,' he said, and with his left hand he gripped the back of Chris's head, forcing her down into the footwell.

The engine restarted and the van moved forwards, steadily, unobtrusively. In fifteen seconds it would be past the police car and away, and then… And then… what would happen to her?

From her vantage point, head down in the footwell, all she could see were Sabre's large clawed paws, empty drinks cartons, crushed cigarette packets and… a switch.

When you have no options left in life, flick the switch.

DAH, DAH, DAH-DAH, D'DAH, DAH, DAH-DAH!

The chime rang out, deafening within the confines of the van. Within seconds, 'Greensleeves' was complemented by the shrill notes of a police siren. Chris clambered back onto her seat and dared to give a grin of triumph.

Evil Eye swung the van round in a tight turn away from the police car and accelerated back down the line of shipping containers. He took a sharp left past a thirty-foot cabin cruiser, causing the ice cream van to momentarily tip onto two wheels and sending the boxes in the back cartwheeling. Mock-chocolate flakes and empty ice cream cones rained over their heads.

There was only one exit road to the boatyard. Chris realised that he was planning to take a circuit through the busiest area in the hope that the crowd of bystanders would act as a human shield and slow down the pursuing police car.

Evil Eye accelerated again and headed towards the waterside. The owner of the snack caravan leapt out of the way and the Mr Softee van skidded round another corner and headed for the chandlers' yard. There was a group of people up ahead, but Evil Eye was not slowing; he would plough right through them if he had to. Chris could see boat enthusiasts and houseboat residents and overall-clad woodworkers, and Nick and Simon and Zeta and…

and… Chloe? And then PC Barry Conway stepped out into the path of the speeding ice cream van, hand raised, commanding it to stop. But it wasn't going to stop. It was going to hit him.

Chris threw her arm across and yanked the steering wheel hard right. The speeding van lurched, hit the edge of a mooring post and was launched into the air, twisting and turning towards the water. As they revolved, she saw a houseboat pass beneath them, its owner's mouth agape as the shadow of the van passed across her face. They cleared the houseboat by just a couple of metres and hit the water.

It wasn't a gentle impact. It was like being hit with a sledgehammer. Chris was thrown deeper into the footwell and the breath was slammed out of her body. There was a sickening crack as Evil Eye's head collided with the windscreen. The van rocked in the water, engine churning, and then started to sink, water gushing in through the gaps in the doors and the crack in the windscreen.

Sabre was barking, panicking. Chris tried the door, but she couldn't open it, the weight of the water was too great. They were sinking lower; three quarters of the van was now below the surface. Evil Eye was unconscious, an ugly bump rising on his ugly forehead. He might have been wicked, but Chris couldn't just leave him to die. She pushed his head back so it was above the rising waterline. That was the best she could do.

If she opened the window the water would cascade in, hastening the sinking, but she had no choice. She took four deep breaths and pressed the button. The window whirred down and then froze halfway – the fuse must have got waterlogged and shorted. Sabre seized his opportunity, pushing past Chris, squeezing through the gap and doggy-paddling for the surface. Chris tried to follow him but her body was jammed – she couldn't get the purchase to lever herself out but nor could she get back into the van. The window frame dug into her damaged ribs, knocking the air out of her lungs. This was it, wasn't it? This was how it was going to end. When her life finally flashed before her eyes, would it be a huge anti-climax?

Suddenly, an unseen force began dragging her out of the

window. Within seconds, she hit the surface of the water and the blessed combination of sunlight and oxygen. Zeta had her in a lifesaver's hold, hand under her chin, pulling her back to the quayside. A forest of arms reached down, grabbed her and hauled her onto dry land and safety. She coughed up a pint and a half of creek water, which had at least diluted the neat vodka. That, combined with the adrenaline of her near-death experience, restored Chris's sobriety.

She gathered her breath to thank Zeta for having saved her life, but Zeta had plunged back under the water. The van was now fully submerged, its lights only showing dimly from the depths.

They waited. A second seemed like a minute, a minute like an hour as everyone stared at the water. The police car pulled up and Spurgeon and Atherton leapt out, Atherton removing his jacket and shoes as he ran to the water's edge. As he prepared to dive in, Zeta surfaced, cradling the unconscious head of Evil Eye. Atherton swam out to help his colleague and, together, the two of them manoeuvred Evil Eye to the waiting arms lining the shore.

All Chris could do was sit shivering on the concrete of the quayside. Chloe draped her arm gently over her mother's shoulders and, for just the second time since the death of her own mother, Chris wept.

Thirty-One

Chris was back in Kent Coast Hospital. Not in the chaos of Baxter Ward but enjoying the serene, fragrant peace of a private room. The sheets were crisp, the flowers fresh and attention was just the press of a button away. She wasn't sure who had wangled it or how, but she was not one to look a gift horse in the gob. She'd been in there for observation for a couple of nights and felt well observed. Thankfully, apart from an excessive consumption of creek water, mild concussion and a couple of cracked ribs, she had been given a clean bill of health. Today would be the day she went home.

Andy Warhol said that everyone would be famous for fifteen minutes. Chris had had seventy-two hours and that was plenty for a lifetime. Someone at the boatyard had filmed the climax of the drama on their phone and, this time, it hadn't just been a local news snippet – it had gone national and viral. For someone who didn't do social media, going viral twice in a week had to be some sort of record.

Fortunately, this time the vibe was more positive. Cornetto Karen was no more. According to Twitter, Chris was either 'Bionic Gran' or the 'Rum 'n' Raisin Rambo', as both were trending. Still, a hospital was a handy place to lie low and wait for the furore to die down. TV had asked for interviews, but Chris refused all offers. She didn't want fame; she liked a life spent in anonymity. Anyway, she was not the hero here. Barry was the hero for having stepped out into the path of a speeding ice cream van, and Zeta was the hero for saving two lives in the space of three minutes.

Zeta had only been kept in overnight. Chris imagined her

friend had drunk even more creek water than her, but she was young and robust and needed less mollycoddling. She popped in to see Chris before she was discharged and they embraced. Chris hoped their friendship would be more enduring than just trauma buddies.

Thanks to Zeta, Evil Eye, aka Mr Softee (allegedly), had survived relatively unscathed. Chris was happy about that – as long as he was now placed in a secure establishment at His Majesty's Pleasure for a suitably long time. The two detailed statements she had given to the police would hopefully help achieve that outcome. Even Sabre was safe, cared for and being prepared for rehoming – that's if they could find a family brave enough to adopt him.

Chris had not been short of visitors. Chloe was at her bedside the first night until the doctors assured her that her mother's injuries were not life-threatening. Chris felt guilty for having ruined her surprise visit; she would be halfway back to Melbourne by now. Nurse Mary Semenyo popped by with a hip flask containing fifteen-year-old cask-aged rum, a better get-well-soon present than any grapes or flowers. It would be a while before she could face vodka again.

Less welcome was the consultant Mr Spatchcock. Chris was no longer his patient, but that didn't stop him from trooping in at the head of his coterie of student doctors. That was the trouble with being a celebrity – everyone wanted to be associated with you. Still, she was polite and smiled at his jokes. You never knew when you might need a tame orthopaedic surgeon.

Nice as it was in the private hospital room, Chris was eager to get home, see Aitken and do as little as possible. She might give herself a holiday – nothing exotic; two weeks sat on the sofa watching old movies and eating Maltesers sounded perfect. As always, the final hurdle was the pharmacist, who arrived in person, clutching a bag full of painkillers.

'Ms Heron?' he said. 'I'm Des. Just take two tablets twice a day until you feel you can manage the pain.'

She knew perfectly well who Des was. She wanted to give

him a big kiss and tell him how his assessment of the blue powder as sucrose had been a big step forward in enabling them to figure things out, but she had to settle for giving him a beaming smile and such effusive thanks that he looked slightly puzzled and alarmed.

As before, Next-Door Nick turned up in his trusty Fiat 500 to drive her home. This time he'd borrowed a peaked chauffeur's cap from someone. 'Your limousine is here, ma'am,' he said, opening the passenger door.

'Thanks, James,' Chris replied in her plummiest accent. 'Ooh, bugger!' Her sore ribs didn't make it the perfect means of transport, but getting in was appreciably easier with two fully functioning hips. 'I'm looking forward to a deep, hot bath and a bit of peace and quiet.'

'Ah,' said Nick cryptically.

The reason for Nick's taciturnity became apparent as soon as they pulled up at the house. Draped across the front was a banner which read 'Welcome Home, Chris – Our Hero!'

'I told the neighbours you'd hate it,' Nick said, 'but I was outvoted.'

'You know, what I've learnt over the last week is to be more tolerant and appreciate people's good intentions.'

'Have I picked up the wrong Christine Heron from the hospital?' said Nick, looking genuinely relieved. 'I'll get it taken down after you've gone inside.'

'Good man.' She gave Nick a peck on the cheek, which made him blush a deep crimson.

The house was full. Chris hadn't seen that many people in there since she and Simon had hosted their Happy Divorce party. There was a buffet and drinks and balloons and streamers. Zeta was there with Barry. There were neighbours Chris only half recognised, some that she was on nodding terms with and some she was sure she'd never seen before in her life. There was Gus from the Spokesmen bike shop, together with Poppy from Cliffstaple Pharmacy. Apparently, they were not twins but boyfriend and girlfriend – an example of that slightly freaky thing whereby two very similar-looking people fancy each other. Simon and Jan were there and that was cool, they were cool, hell, everybody was cool. Best of all, better than Chris could possibly have imagined, Chloe was also there.

'Shouldn't you be at thirty-five thousand feet watching a not-as-good-as-the-book in-flight movie?' she asked, hugging her daughter as firmly as her cracked ribs allowed.

'Your feat in single-handedly sending a rogue ice cream van to a watery grave resonated around the globe. My boss was so impressed, he's given me an extra week's leave.' Chloe grinned. 'His actual words were, "Jeez, Clo, yer mum's got massive balls."'

'Can you thank him from me,' Chris said. 'I mean for the extra leave rather than the oversized testicular reference.'

*

After an hour and a half, the assembled locusts had demolished the entire buffet except for a rice salad and some mini quiches, which, in Chris's experience, were the untouchables of party food. Thankfully, one by one, her unexpected guests made their excuses and left until the kitchen finally contained just herself, Chloe, Zeta, Barry and Next-Door Nick.

'Good,' she said, metaphorically and literally rolling up her sleeves. 'As the team's all here, let's have a debrief on the Professor Jasper situation.'

'Now, Mum?' asked Chloe. 'Give yourself a break. You've only been back a couple of hours.'

'Two days in a shipping container followed by three days in a hospital bed has given me plenty of time to figure things out. We may not get the chance to have us all round the same table again.'

'I'm game,' said Nick. 'This is just like the end of an episode of *Murder, She Wrote*.'

Chris removed the magnetic noteboard and the framed film poster for *The Spy Who Came to Dinner* from the kitchen wall, revealing a lovely expanse of bare white (with a hint of apple) emulsion. She took a pack of whiteboard pens from the kitchen-table drawer and in bold blue capital letters wrote:

1. THE VICTIM

'Chris, this is CID's case now, DI Dunn's baby. There's nothing we can do anymore. We've got to let them get on with the job,' said Zeta.

'And you trust them?'

'She's got a point there, Zeta,' noted Barry.

Underneath the heading, Chris wrote:

Name: Professor Adrian Jasper

'Date of birth?'

'I don't see how that's relevant,' said Zeta.

'Mum likes to be thorough,' said Chloe, showing an appreciation of her mother's rigour. 'She's anal like that.'

Next, Chris added:

2. CAUSE OF DEATH

'I can help there,' said Barry. 'A mate's on the autopsy team. It's still ongoing, but it's clear the prof was killed by a single blow to the top of the head.'

'The top of the head? So it was inflicted by someone tall and strong?' asked Zeta.

'Or the professor was kneeling,' suggested Barry.

'Perhaps to look in a cupboard?'

'Weapon?' Chris asked, accidentally sucking the wrong end of the marker pen and turning her tongue blue.

'A crowbar or something similar,' said Barry. 'There was some bruising consistent with being kicked, but that was post mortem.'

Chris considered confessing to being responsible for having delivered two kicks to Professor Jasper's midriff, but as she'd had no idea there was a body in the carpet it wasn't relevant and would only complicate matters. Instead, she swiftly moved on to the next heading.

3. TIME OF DEATH

'That one's a bit trickier,' said Barry. 'As he'd been stored in a warm, sealed container, my mate said it was difficult to give an accurate time of death.'

'We know he was last seen by Rene Douglas at the university at 09:45 on Friday 21 August,' said Zeta, consulting her notebook just for show as she had already committed the details to memory, 'and that the last contact from his phone was at 10:32 the same day.'

'Then nothing till the following Friday at 12:56,' added Barry.

'Which was me turning his phone on,' said Chris.

'It sounds to me like the professor was probably killed in that forty-seven minute window, then,' observed Chloe, getting into the swing of evidence analysis.

'Which neatly brings us on to…' And Chris wrote:

4. LOCATION

'If we're right about the time of death,' said Zeta, 'it confirms that it was Jasper's body that Chris saw in the forensics house.'

'And remember that fresh chlorine smell in the kitchen?'

Zeta nodded. 'Deliberately concealing trace evidence. Someone knew what they were doing.'

They had been talking for an hour and Chris had filled up a third of the kitchen wall with bullet points, question marks and arrows.

'If you're going to do this properly,' said Nick, making his first contribution to the investigation, 'you need some red string. In all the police procedural dramas I've seen, they always have a web of red string connecting the points of evidence.'

'Thanks, Nick. I'll buy some tomorrow,' Chris replied.

5. JACKET

'Oh God,' exclaimed Zeta, 'you've still got it and it's now a key piece of evidence. I can't just hand it over to DI Dunn now and say, "We were just looking after it for you."'

'Give it to me,' said Barry. 'That lot are so disorganised, I can sneak it into the pile of evidence without anyone noticing.'

Chloe fetched the jacket from the coat rack in the hall.

'You're positive that this is or rather was Professor Jasper's jacket?' asked Barry.

'Absolutely.' Chris respectfully laid the jacket on the kitchen table. 'See? The red button matches the jacket he's wearing in the prospectus photo.'

'Oh, that's sweet,' said Chloe.

'Sweet? I didn't realise you were into Harris tweed. Can't imagine there's a great demand for it in Melbourne.'

'No, Mum, I mean that red button's sweet.' Chloe held the button between her thumb and index finger to examine it closer.

'Is it?'

'Yes. It's been carved out of jasper stone – you see a lot of that in Oz. It must have been a present, a jasper button for Professor Jasper.'

The group fell silent. Whoever had bought the professor that button was no longer in his life. No relatives or close friends had come forward since the discovery of his body had been made public. In their discussion, they had been treating Professor Jasper as simply 'the victim', but this button suggested that, once, he had mattered to somebody.

Chloe carefully wrapped the jacket in clingfilm and handed it to Barry.

Zeta broke the silence. 'The powder residue and Priaman packaging found in the jacket suggest Professor Jasper was wearing it when searching the forensics house.'

'So how did it end up on Grayson?' Chris said. 'The, um, mannequin,' she added, in response to some quizzically raised eyebrows.

There was a collective shrugging of shoulders around the table, so Chris wrote a large red question mark next to the *JACKET* heading.

Everyone took a synchronised sip of coffee and stared at the kitchen wall.

'There's one thing I still don't understand,' said Chloe.

'Only one thing?' asked Nick. 'I'm completely lost. And I've seen *The Matrix*. Twice.'

'Why did Professor Jasper's killer bother to replace his body with the mannequin?'

A horrible thought occurred to Chris. 'Because they realised that somebody had seen Jasper's body lying under the table – and that someone was me!'

'Maybe the murderer was still in the forensics house when you looked through the window?' suggested Barry.

There was a pregnant pause and everyone looked around as though they were being watched at that very minute.

'I believe you're right. What's next, listmeister?' Zeta said, trying to lift the paranoid mood pervading the kitchen.

6. MOTIVE

'I'm betting that poor old Professor Jasper was in the wrong place, wrong time.'

'Agreed. I can't believe he was part of a pharmaceuticals counterfeiting gang. He had no record, a modest lifestyle, nothing to indicate any involvement with organised crime,' said Zeta.

'And Mia and Stan said he was really helpful,' Chris blurted out.

'Who?'

'Oh, just a couple of forensics students, no one important. Carry on.' But Chris could see that Zeta had made a mental note of this new information.

'The fact that the professor had pocketed the powder and the packaging suggests he knew the forensics house was being used for nefarious purposes and had taken it on himself to investigate,' continued Zeta.

'With tragic consequences.' Barry stared meaningfully at Chris. 'Rather than just reporting it and then letting the police do their job.'

Chris considered protesting that it was Zeta who had lured her deeper into the investigation, but they were already well into the second hour, the wall was filled with blue marker pen scribbles and red question marks, and the members of the Sea View Justice League were looking a tad weary.

'We are talking about organised crime though, aren't we?' she said.

'Looks like it,' said Zeta. 'I wouldn't be surprised if DI Dunn just passes it on to the NCA. He doesn't seem too enamoured about it having landed on his desk in the first place.'

'The National Crime Agency,' whispered Barry to a now even more confused-looking Nick. 'But if this alleged gang exists, they've dispersed like a will-o'-the-wisp.'

'It's as though they were always one step ahead of us. They knew when to pack up and move out,' said Chris.

Barry nodded. 'No forensics, no witnesses – apart from you, Chris. No money trail, nothing.'

'Nothing?' Chloe asked.

'CID's working on rumours. East Europeans, Glaswegians, the Mafia. Everyone's got a theory but, as yet, no hard evidence,' said Barry, starting on the unloved mini quiches.

'Which neatly brings me to suspects,' said Chris, starting a third column on the wall.

7. SUSPECTS

Walter

Evil Eye

Big Boss

'What about this Mia and Stan?' asked Zeta. 'Surely anyone connected to the forensics house must be considered a suspect.'

'No, they're clean,' Chris said confidently. 'And, first up, I'm discounting Walter, my initial captor, as he didn't seem the type.'

'Met many gangland killers?' asked Barry. 'You'd be surprised – they come in all shapes and sizes.'

'I'll take your word for that. Well, we know he took my phone and we know that my phone made it to Calais, so unless he hijacked a pedalo, he took a ferry. Surely he can be tracked down?'

'That's something CID's passed on to yours truly. I'm getting the passenger lists, but there'll be over twenty thousand names on them so, unless Walter's got previous, it'll be like looking for a biscuit crumb on Bondi beach,' said Barry. 'Meanwhile it's safe to assume that your phone now sleeps with the fishes.'

'Good excuse to get an upgrade, Mum,' said Chloe, refilling everyone's mugs.

'Lost all my photos of Stock, Aitken and Waterman though.'

'They're probably backed up on the cloud somewhere,' said Chloe. 'I'll help you look tomorrow.'

'So that brings me to suspect numero uno.' Chris changed to a green pen and drew a double circle around 'Evil Eye'.

'I think we can start using his real name now, Chris,' said Zeta. 'Last name: Pipe. First name: Dwayne.'

'Dwayne Pipe?' Nick guffawed. 'The poor bugger.'

'No wonder he turned to a life of crime,' said Chloe.

'We know that Evil... Mr Pipe has a reputation for violence. He assaulted me, imprisoned me and tried to mow down my family and friends.'

Zeta drew a deep breath. 'Mr Pipe denies those accusations.'

'Well, he would, wouldn't he?' Chris jabbed her pen aggressively at the wall.

'As yet, there are no forensics linking him to the case. No murder weapon, nothing linking him to the crime scene or the victim,' said Zeta calmly.

'He was checking in with his probation officer in Becketon at ten o'clock that Friday morning. So if we're right about the time and place of the professor's death, that means, ironically, that Chris is Pipe's alibi,' said Barry. 'Assuming that was Jasper's body you saw, the timeline rules Pipe out as the perpetrator.'

'That can't be right,' said Chris. 'The probation officer must have got the time or date wrong.'

Barry shook his head.

'He was definitely my captor though. I saw him through the spyhole.'

'You saw an eye, Chris. An eye does not constitute a positive identification.'

'I know it was him. I'd know that eye anywhere. All right, what about after I escaped? Abducting me, trying to evade arrest? You all saw that – it's even on camera, for frick's sake.'

'According to Mr Pipe's statement, he was rescuing you.'

'WHAT?' Pens and coffee were sent flying through the air. Miraculously, Chloe managed to catch the mug before it hit the floor.

'He said he was passing by the shipping container and heard someone tapping out an SOS signal,' said Zeta. 'When he went to investigate, you assaulted him by pushing him into the wall. He saw you get into the van and was concerned, given that you were, in his words, "extraordinarily drunk". He thought the best course of action was to drive you to Accident and Emergency for treatment.'

Chris laughed drily. 'You do realise that's bullshit, don't you? He was trying to evade arrest. He used an ice cream van as a lethal weapon. He tried to kill us all!'

Barry shook his head sadly. 'Mr Pipe claims he panicked. He was afraid that driving the vehicle was contrary to the conditions of his licence. He says he was preparing to stop when you grabbed the wheel, causing the accident.'

'We believe you, Chris, but, until CID finds otherwise, his account isn't inconsistent with the evidence. There are no forensics linking him to the Priaman packaging or the van itself, beyond what we all saw last Friday. He's not even the registered owner of the vehicle,' said Zeta.

'This is preposterous.' Chris leant back with her head in her hands. 'I have dreams that are less surreal than this.'

Chloe sat beside her mother and put her arm around her shoulders. 'Perhaps we should call it a night. Mum's exhausted and I'm not surprised. She's been through more in a week than most people experience in a lifetime.'

'No, we're nearly there, Chlo. Besides, Barry hasn't finished the mini quiches yet.'

'CID's pretty confident they can get Pipe for dangerous driving and, as he's on licence, it's likely he'll be sent back to prison to finish the rest of his sentence. Perhaps that'll encourage him to give more info, suggest an identity for "Big Boss" up there.'

Chris shook her head. 'No, I'm sure of two things. First, that Dwayne Pipe aka Evil Eye aka Mr Softee killed Professor Jasper and abducted me to cover his tracks, and second, that you won't get him to implicate "Big Boss". In hospital I saw the injuries he got as punishment for a previous transgression – a few more months in prison would be nothing compared to that.'

'Or, if it's not Walter or Dwayne Pipe, there's someone else, someone we haven't identified,' said Barry.

He took the pen from Chris's hand and added *Third Man* to the SUSPECTS list.

Zeta rose from the table. 'That's enough for tonight. Let's leave Chris and Chloe in peace.'

Chris felt guilty for her petulant behaviour. 'Sorry, guys. I'm so desperate for Professor Jasper to get justice. He was a good guy. He didn't deserve to end his days rolled up in a manky carpet in a shipping container.'

Barry polished off the last mini quiche. 'It's something we have to get used to in the force. Only half of all murders are solved and, if it's non-domestic, that figure's even lower. It's not like it is on TV. In real life the baddie often gets away.'

'But CID is on the case,' said Zeta. 'Keep pulling at that line and one day they might catch the fish. You've done everything you can, Chris. This isn't your battle anymore.'

Zeta, Barry and Nick got up to leave.

Nick paused in the doorway. 'I don't know if I should mention this, Chris. I mean, I didn't like to say, but...'

'What is it, Nick?'

'Those whiteboard pens...'

'Yes?'

'You do realise they're actually permanent markers?'

After they'd gone, Chris and her daughter cleared up the

kitchen in silence. As she was shovelling the untouched rice salad into the compost bin, Chloe said, 'Don't be so hard on yourself, Mum. We're all really proud of you, but Zeta's right – you should leave this to the police now.'

'Professor Jasper's murderer is going to get away with it, isn't he?'

'You don't know that. My Dan is always telling me to "expect the unexpected".'

Chris heard the cat flap rattle. 'Talk of the devil – where have you been till this hour, Aitken, you dirty stop-out?'

'Mum,' said Chloe, 'Aitken's sitting under the kitchen table.'

Chris looked down at the cat flap and saw a black and white cat with distinctive markings that made him look like he was dressed for a formal white-tie dinner. The new arrival looked up and miaowed.

'Waterman!' she screamed in delight.

Thirty-Two

Autumn. The season of mists and mellow fruitfulness, according to Keats.

This was one of those blessed days when the departed summer decided to make one last fleeting reappearance. It was an opportunity not to be missed. Chris had somewhere to be and an e-bike to get her there. Being a fair-weather cyclist, she might not take Rod out on the road again until the following spring. Cycling was wonderful, but cycling into a biting winter wind and freezing rain that somehow seeped into the reinforced gusset of her cycling pants was less life-affirming.

She turned off the main road and onto the cycle path heading towards the forensics house, where it had all begun two months previously. In keeping with her promise to her daughter, she had stepped away from the investigation into Professor Jasper's murder. In return, Zeta had continued to update her with the most salient developments in the case.

There was much they still didn't know, but it was clear that Chris and Zeta had uncovered an attempt to manufacture and distribute counterfeit erectile dysfunction medication. Their investigation seemed to have stifled (or even 'stiff-led', as Barry quipped) the operation at birth, and the organisation behind it had dispersed without trace. In criminal terms, counterfeiting was not that big a deal. If it hadn't been for a dead professor of forensic science, the case would have been subterranean on North Kent Police's list of priorities.

Ironically, the Mr Softee ice cream van had been couriering

fake Viagra, which was why it hadn't stopped after it knocked Chris off her bike. Zeta seemed to think it was particularly funny that a vehicle used for drug smuggling had 'Stop Me and Buy One' on the back. White transit vans were suspicious, as were dark SUVs, but a garish ice cream van that played 'Greensleeves'? That was the very definition of hiding in plain sight.

As for Mr Softee himself – Evil Eye, aka Dwayne Pipe – to date, nothing had come to light to forensically link him to the murder of Professor Jasper. According to Barry, he had resolutely stuck to his story, even suggesting that Chris should be arrested for assault, for causing actual bodily harm when pushing him into the container wall, and for making the van crash. About the wider operation and the identities of his associates, Evil Eye had remained resolutely tight-lipped.

Not that Chris had had the time to go criminal-hunting. The publicity surrounding her dramatic bid for freedom had, strangely, boosted business. She was not sure whether people thought that the ability to crash a speeding ice cream van demonstrated proofreading prowess, but she was grateful for the work and exploited the opportunity to raise her hourly rate by twenty per cent. Any non-work time was split evenly between domestic duties, cats and blogging.

Since the end of August, she had managed to tick off four tasks from her 'Essential Home Improvements' list. Unfortunately, she had added another nine. Aitken and Waterman had re-established their brotherly bond and Chris hoped that would spell the end of Waterman's wanderlust. Most excitingly, her blog, *Chris on a Bike – Exploring the Hidden Cycle Routes of Kent*, had garnered more than three hundred subscribers. Thanks to the helmet cam she'd got as a get-well-soon present from Chloe and Dan, it even had video clips (edited for swearing).

Mists and mellow fruitfulness? There was no mist today; the air was crystal clear and the blindingly bright sun sat so low in the sky that Chris had to, counterintuitively, dip her head and look over the top of her tinted cycling glasses to see the path ahead. The fields on either side had been harvested and were now cropped short, providing an uninterrupted view of the lushly green North Downs. As she cycled through a tunnel of trees, navigating a golden carpet of fallen leaves, she breathed in deeply, inhaling that addictive combination of damp vegetation and wood smoke, the embodiment of the season. She hadn't spotted any mellow fruitfulness yet and, to be honest, she wasn't sure she would recognise it if she did.

When she was younger, she had hated autumn. It represented decay and death. Now older and (hopefully) wiser, she understood that decay and death were inevitable, a necessary part of nature's cycle. Rebirth and spring always followed. That was it, she thought. Next year she would *definitely* become a Buddhist.

'Gangway! Cyclist coming through!'

Chris's meditative state was shattered by a mountain biker who brushed past her at speed, approaching the foothills of the Hill of Death. He swerved in front and deliberately rode through a muddy puddle, spattering her luminous yellow jacket.

New 'Karma' Chris said to herself, 'No matter. The path to the summit is slippery with wet leaves; let him have his small victory. My journey is a tranquil one. OHM!'

Old 'Stroppy' Chris said, 'Frick that!'

She turned Rod's mode to high and stood upright on the pedals to generate maximum acceleration. As she sped past the labouring mountain biker near the summit of the Hill of Death, she shouted, 'Gangway! Granny coming through!'

She didn't encounter the mountain biker again after that point. Either he had given up, chastened and humiliated, or, more likely, he'd simply gone off-road, down one of the wooded tracks.

She cruised down the hill, round a bend, past the playing fields and was back where it had all started.

There was a large crowd gathered outside the forensics house. Students past and present, the university faculty (including the chancellor herself) and assorted media were gathered round a makeshift stage that had been erected by the front door. Sgt Spurgeon and PC Atherton were being interviewed by a TV reporter. It was like a *Who's Who* of Chris's adventure over that week in August. She spotted Professor Jasper's neighbours from the Railway Cottages. Grace from Number 1 was there, chaperoned by Becks and Steve from Number 3. Baby Sophie seemed to have doubled in size in the last nine weeks. Behind them, Chris could not fail to spot the imposing figure of Anne from Anne's Tiquities, purveyor of quality antique reading lamps.

She parked RamRod in the newly installed cycle rack. There was a tap on her shoulder. It was Rene, resplendent in peacock feathers.

'Chris! I was hoping you'd be here today.'

'Wouldn't miss it for the world.'

'I hope you don't mind, but we've arranged a gift for you. It's quite bulky so may not be delivered till next week.'

'A gift? You shouldn't have.'

'It's more a memento, a thank you from the faculty for having found out what happened to Professor Jasper, but mainly a thank you from me in appreciation for your discretion.'

'My discretion?'

'You figured it out, didn't you? About Mia and Stan.'

Chris nodded. 'That they were living in the forensics house? In the locked room upstairs?'

'They were conned.' Rene tutted. 'They'd put a deposit on a flat in Becketon which didn't exist and lost everything. I couldn't let them be homeless.'

'You should have said something. They were potential witnesses.'

'I couldn't. They'd have been kicked off the course and I'd have lost my job. They didn't see anything.'

Chris looked Rene in the eye. 'Are you sure?'

'I promise you. They heard Professor Jasper arriving that fateful Friday morning and sneaked out the back door. They had no idea what happened to him after that.'

'Don't worry, their secret's safe with me.'

'They asked me to give you this.' Rene handed her a picture postcard of the Wawel Cathedral in Krakow. On the back was a handwritten message: *Thanks for everything. Glad you noticed the jacket! M&S xx*

Still staring at the postcard, Chris wandered over to the far side of the cycle path, where Zeta was standing.

'Hi, Chris. You look distracted,' said Zeta.

'I think I've just found another piece of the jigsaw. I'm just not sure where it fits.'

Barry joined them. At least she thought it was Barry.

'You're looking trim.'

Barry smoothed down the front of his tunic proudly. 'Lost two and a half stone in eight weeks. Cut down on the fry-ups and bought myself an e-bike.'

A hush descended upon the crowd and Dr Karamak, cheekbones glistening in the sunshine, took to the stage and stood before a rostrum.

'Friends, colleagues, students, Chancellor. We are here today for just two reasons. To open the new University of North Kent forensics facility and, more importantly, to honour the memory of Professor Adrian Jasper. Professor Jasper was loved by those that had the good fortune to work with him and respected by academics around the globe. He was passionately devoted to advancing forensic science, a discipline that helps keep us and our families safe. In his memory we must strive to push that science further, develop new techniques, expand and share our knowledge. This new facility will be a vital step in that journey and I thank the chancellor and the board of trustees for their support.

'In forensic science we are like the early pioneers, intrepid explorers in search of truth. With that search can come peril, as our dear friend Adrian found to his cost. And for all our application and expertise, we have to accept that even our own science has its limits. I praise the work of the North Kent Constabulary, who are represented here today, for their tireless investigation into the tragic death of Professor Jasper. It is with a heavy heart that we realise that even with the most advanced forensics and the most skilled investigators, the truth can sometimes lie beyond our grasp. We may never establish how Professor Jasper died or identify those responsible. What we can do is honour his memory and ensure that his name lives on in the minds and hearts of all those who study here.

'Therefore, I would like to invite our chancellor to declare this forensics education facility officially open.'

The chancellor, in full ceremonial robes, ascended the stage and pulled a cord to unveil a metal sign that read 'Jasper House'. The audience applauded.

'That was a nice speech,' said Barry.

Chris snorted. 'She's done all right though, hasn't she? Now *Professor* Cheekbones, head of a shiny new department.'

'I was reading about it,' said Barry. 'Best in Europe, that's the aim. They've tripled the funding and are going to double the size of the faculty, build new state-of-the-art labs and attract lots of high-paying international students.'

'And all Professor Jasper gets is a sodding nameplate.'

'To be fair, Chris, Cheekbones is not the only one to have benefited from this tragedy,' observed Zeta. 'Our Barry here retires next week – a full twelve months early, and on full whack.'

'Hey!' said Barry, looking affronted. 'And you – soon to be a proper cop, and bookies' favourite for the National Police Bravery Awards.'

'We'd vote for her,' said Sgt Spurgeon, who had wandered over to their group accompanied by PC Atherton. 'SC Jama is a credit to the force.'

Chris couldn't help herself. '"Jama"? Not "Jah-mah"? You've finally learnt how to pronounce Zeta's name?'

'SC Jama has proved herself in the field. Besides, at the rate she's going, she'll be my boss within eighteen months, so I'd better watch myself.' Spurgeon winked and he and Atherton headed off in the direction of their patrol car.

'Wow,' Chris said to Zeta. 'If you've cracked Sgt Spurgeon, you've definitely achieved acceptance.'

'He got a positive mention in dispatches, and even Atherton's been commended,' said Zeta.

'Atherton? Whatever for?'

'They traced the search for Jasper's phone records to his computer login details. Senior ranks decided that he'd shown "exceptional initiative".'

Barry smiled broadly. 'Of course, Atherton can't actually recall having instigated the search, but praise is praise.'

'So it seems, Chris, that everyone has benefited from this tragedy apart from you,' said Zeta.

A hand was laid on Chris's shoulder. She looked round and up into the gorgeous facial bone structure of Professor Karamak.

'Could I separate you from your friends for a quick word, Ms Heron?'

They moved a little way apart.

'I heard about everything you did and how you put your own life at risk to search for Professor Jasper,' the professor said. 'I'd like to personally thank you for having found my colleague.'

'I'm just sorry that I was too late.'

'We all have regrets, but life goes on, I suppose. You have insight and a thirst for discovery; have you considered studying forensic science academically?'

'Me? My background's in English. I'm a complete duffer when it comes to science.'

'I pride myself on being able to spot raw talent. I'd be happy to offer you a place on my course, maybe even with a bursary.'

'Gosh, that's an unexpected and generous offer, Doctor… Professor Karamak. Can I have a think about it?'

Professor Karamak gave a broad smile, but one that strangely wasn't echoed in her eyes. 'Of course. Take whatever time you need, but choose wisely. What I've learnt from this tragic affair is that we must seize opportunities when they arise.' She gripped Chris's shoulder rather too firmly. 'After all, you never know when it could all be ended by a stranger with a tyre iron, eh?'

And with that, Professor Karamak grasped Chris's hand in her trademark two-handed handshake, turned on her heels and strode towards the car park. Chris watched, her brain reconfiguring previous assumptions.

A black SUV rolled up. The driver's door opened and out stepped a tall figure who exchanged words with Professor Karamak and then waved at Chris. It was Detective Inspector Dunn. Karamak opened the passenger door, got in and, in a puff of dust, the car was gone.

In a daze, Chris returned to her group. 'Did you see? That was… that was… DI Dunn.'

'So?' said Barry. 'He is her husband.'

'What?' said Zeta, astounded. 'Karamak and Dunn are husband and wife?'

'Thought you knew,' said Barry. 'It's hardly a secret.'

'How would I know?' said Zeta. 'I don't ask senior officers in CID who their partners are.'

Barry merely shrugged in response.

'This all makes sense,' said Chris excitedly. 'I reckon Karamak's directly involved. She and DI Dunn are in cahoots.'

'I don't think—' Barry was not convinced.

'She's got access to the forensics house, expertise in chemistry and she's married to DI Dunn. That's how the gang were always one step ahead of us. That's how they knew all about me and where I live. Karamak is Big Boss.'

'Nobody's interested in the counterfeiting operation anymore, Chris. That's small potatoes, ancient history.' said Zeta.

'But if Karamak and Dunn were running the operation, they must be directly involved with Professor Jasper's murder.'

'There's a flaw in your theory, Chris.'

'What? That because she's married to a senior officer at North Kent Police she can't possibly be running a crime syndicate and be a party to murder? Have you been indoctrinated already?'

Zeta didn't rise to the bait. 'No. She can't be directly involved because at the time of Jasper's disappearance Professor Karamak was in Barcelona at the European Forensic Science Conference.'

There was a short silence, broken by Barry. 'And we know Dunn was at the station because Sergeant Spurgeon consulted him. Nice theory, shame about the alibi.'

'Yep,' said Zeta. 'Sorry, Chris, but as far as alibis go, being in a different country at the time of the murder is one of the best.'

'And it was checked,' said Barry. 'She's on the list of attendees.'

'Well, she could have organised it remotely – giving The Third Man the order.'

'What? Murder by Zoom?' suggested Barry.

'No, but—'

'And, as you said yourself, everything indicates that Jasper's murder was unplanned. Wrong place, wrong time. Remember?'

'There's this little thing called evidence, Chris,' said Zeta. 'And well-defined cheekbones and an assertive handshake aren't sufficient.'

Chris saw her new theory into the death of Professor Jasper collapse. 'What if we checked Karamak's phone records?'

'Good luck in getting a warrant for that. Not with her hubby upstairs,' said Barry.

'And even if we did, it wouldn't prove anything. It would just flag up that we're taking an interest,' said Zeta. 'Sorry, Chris. You may be right, but we haven't got a silver bullet. Sometimes the baddies get away.'

Chris felt tearful. 'It's not fair. Professor Jasper did nothing to deserve this, and those responsible are laughing in our faces.'

Zeta put a consoling arm around her shoulders. 'All I can promise is that I'll keep a discreet eye on Karamak and Dunn from now on – just to see if a chink in their armour appears. But for you, that's it, it's over. OK?'

'OK,' Chris said reluctantly.

Zeta gave Chris a friendly nudge. 'Come on, Miss Marple. I'll race you back to Sea View. See if I can beat you on RamRod – the loser buys lunch for the winner.'

Chris mounted her bike and switched the mode to high.

'Promise me, Chris? No more investigating?' said Zeta.

'Look at me. I'm just a batty old cat-lady with a titanium hip and an e-bike. I'm totally harmless.' Chris stepped onto the pedal, raised herself onto the saddle and set off in the direction of Cliffstaple.

As she did so, she heard Zeta mutter under her breath, 'Harmless? Sure you are, Chris. Sure you are.'

Thirty-Three

Chris had a restless night. It wasn't only because, due to the dropping temperature, both Aitken and Waterman decided that her head was the warmest place in the entire house. It wasn't just because she was upset by the revelations of the previous day, to have prime suspects who could be at least partly responsible for Professor Jasper's murder but be powerless to do anything about it. It was because she had a nagging feeling that she was still missing some things, things that would make all the pieces fit.

At three in the morning, she gave up the fight for sleep and a fair share of the bed and went downstairs to make herself a hot drink. She sat at the kitchen table, sipping on a spiced apple and hibiscus infusion, and stared at the indelible case notes written on the wall. She took a pen out of the drawer and drew a red line through 'Walter' and 'Evil Eye' on the list of suspects and drew two red question marks next to 'Third Man'. She circled 'Big Boss' and drew an arrow towards a new column headed 'Karamak'.

Nick rang on the door mid-morning. It was a welcome distraction as Chris, with just a couple of hours' sleep behind her, was struggling to maintain any level of concentration as she tried her first read-through of 'The Satanic Nurses – A History of Witchcraft in Medicine'. It also gave her another opportunity to try out her get-well-soon present from Simon and Jan: an espresso machine. Feeding her ex-husband dreadful instant coffee had reaped its reward.

As he sat at the table downing a double espresso, Nick looked at the writing-festooned wall opposite. 'Tell you what, Chris. I think I've still got some white wall and ceiling emulsion in the attic. If you like, I can paint over all that. I reckon it'll need three or four coats though – that marker pen shows through everything.'

'No way, José! My mural stays until Professor Jasper's murderer is behind bars.'

He studied the wall in silence for a couple of minutes. 'Why can't Big Boss also be the murderer?'

'Because I'm positive Karamak is Big Boss and she was registered as an attendee at an academic conference in Barcelona at the time.'

'Means nothing,' said Nick laconically, sipping his coffee.

'What?'

'Academics are always on the take. I should know – I used to be one.'

'Go on,' urged Chris.

'You get three or four of you – academics who work in the same field. When conference season comes along – foreign conferences are the best – only one of you attends and signs the others in. The presentation notes and documents are shared with the group afterwards.'

'What's the point?'

'Expenses! Flights, hotels, subsistence. If you're canny, you can double your salary.'

'Don't the conference organisers get pissed off when their venues are only a quarter full?'

'As long as they get fees and glowing reviews, why should they? It's a scam where everyone wins.'

'So Karamak may not have been in Barcelona when Professor Jasper was murdered?' said Chris.

'She'll have been signed in as an attendee, but I bet you won't find her in any photos of the event.'

'I've already googled the conference. I couldn't find anything more than the timetable of events.'

'Give me your laptop,' said Nick, and Chris slid it across the table. 'What was the name of this conference?'

'The European Forensic Science Conference.'

Nick spent five minutes tapping at the keyboard like a movie computer hacker and then turned the screen to face Chris.

'But... how?' On the screen were photos from the conference.

Nick tapped his nose. 'Academic search engine – not available to your hoi polloi.'

Chris spent forty minutes going through the photos, zooming in on some images, dismissing others. Faces of academics, mainly in their thirties and forties, talking shop, drinking wine and, doubtless, deciding who they would sneak off to bed with later that evening. At least that was Chris's experience of conferences. Then she spent a further forty minutes going through all the photos again while Nick watched patiently. Finally, she gave a disappointed sigh and sat back in her chair.

'Well?' asked Nick.

'Not a sign. And it's not as if a blonde six-foot-tall woman could easily fade into the background.'

'So that's good, isn't it? It proves that Karamak wasn't where she said she was. Her alibi's worthless.'

Chris took out her phone and sent a text to Zeta: *No photo evidence of Karamak at conference. Her alibi is compromised. Chris x.*

'You're right, this is helpful. Thanks, Nick.'

'So why do you look like someone's peed in your bubble bath?'

'It's weird. Part of me would be happy if she was in those photos, to prove that I'm wrong. Then I could let you loose with your paintbrush and forget all about this,' she said, pointing at her wall.

Nick sighed. 'I know you, Chris. You're not going to let this go, are you?'

She poured them both another coffee. 'You should have heard Karamak's speech yesterday. The police, the university, they've all given up on him already. They're all planning to *move on*. Professor Jasper's got no one – no grieving relatives, no campaigning friends. There'll be no candlelight vigils or Justice for Jasper marches.'

'What about his students? They must care.'

'About Professor Marmite? I can't see them getting out from under their duvets for him. And students come and go. Those that knew Adrian Jasper will be fewer and fewer. In a couple of years, he'll be nothing but a case study.'

To Nick's surprise and Chris's horror, tears of frustration were streaming down her face. Nick walked to her side of the table and hugged her.

'Sorry,' she sobbed, 'but I can't give up on him. I'm all he's got.'

'You can't do all this on your own, Chris. Look at your kitchen wall, for God's sake. You can't let this become an obsession.'

She wiped away her tears. 'Well, nobody else is going to do anything about it, are they?'

Thirty-Four

On the seventh floor of North Kent Police Station was a room, 701. The building's lifts only reached the sixth floor, so to find Room 701 you had to take an access staircase that led to the roof. Halfway up the staircase was a large cupboard housing the building's electrics and opposite that was Room 701. Too isolated to be of practical use as an office, it had served as an unofficial interrogation room in the dark days of the sixties and seventies and then as a smoking room until the ban came into effect. At that point, a sofa was introduced and, for a brief period, Room 701 became the break-out room where stressed officers could decompress after a tough day or have discreet one-to-one conversations with the station's welfare officer, away from the prying eyes of the rest of the office. In police banter it was known as 'the breakdown room' and officers joked that having therapy sessions within such close reach of the rooftop was tempting fate.

Having a break-out room was a luxury from a more compassionate era. Nowadays there was no time to manage issues or deal with stress. There was a job to be done and too few officers to do it. Therapy was for snowflakes. Consequently, in the last few years, Room 701 had become forgotten.

For PC Barry Conway, Room 701 had two main attractions. First, that comfy sofa was perfect for sneaking a mid-afternoon nap, and second, on a table in a corner of the room sat an antique fat-backed computer that, crucially, was still connected to the system.

He opened the door and ushered Zeta into his sanctuary.

'So this is where you've been hiding,' she said, impressed.

'The station's best-kept secret.'

Barry plugged the computer into the mains and switched it on. As it lurched into life, it groaned, wheezed and buzzed in a manner that seemed loud enough to alert the other six floors. Zeta imagined that, inside the casing, valves were starting to glow and she half expected steam to come gushing out of the vents.

'This was a stupid idea, Barry. Let's get out before anyone catches us. It was wrong of me to get you involved.'

He pressed a couple of keys and the familiar homepage of North Kent Constabulary flickered onto the screen. He pulled the sofa closer to the table. 'It was *my* stupid idea. I'm the one who told you about this room. I'm the one who figured out how to access Project Semaphore.'

'Turn the computer off and let's go. This could cost you your pension.'

'I heard on the grapevine that they're already winding down the Jasper investigation. All that will be left will be one man and his dog, and the word is that the dog's the one with the brains.'

Despite them being the only occupants of that floor, Zeta didn't dare raise her voice above a whisper. 'This is mad.'

'Remind me why we're here.'

'To break Karamak's alibi. According to her text, Chris is convinced she wasn't at that conference.'

'So that's what we're doing.'

'Barry, you said it was too risky to conduct a search of flight manifests.'

'And you said it wouldn't prove anything anyway.'

'Yesterday you weren't sticking your head above the trenches. So what's changed?' Zeta took a seat on the sofa beside Barry.

'I'm a copper,' he said. 'To see a crim get away with something as nasty as this, well, it sticks in my craw. You?'

'Ditto. Proving Karamak wasn't in Barcelona won't be conclusive. It won't place her at the crime scene, but it will pull at that thread. Perhaps it'll unnerve her, perhaps we'll find some physical evidence, perhaps it'll be enough to persuade Dwayne Pipe to talk.'

'I get it,' said Barry. 'You're employing the Wait.'

'What's that?'

'It's a chess tactic. If there's no clear path to victory, you stay solid and patient. Effect small sorties and wait for your opponent to make a mistake. That's what we're doing here.'

'I do hope I'm not interrupting anything!'

Barry and Zeta turned round with a start to see that the door of Room 701 was open and the doorway filled with the imposing frame of Sgt Spurgeon.

'Oh hi, Sarge,' stuttered Barry. 'I was just, um, giving Zeta some computer training.'

'You, PC Conway, the station Luddite, are giving computer training to a brilliant young woman who designs websites for a living?'

'Well, Sarge, it was just that—'

Zeta stepped in. There was no other choice but to confess. 'It's my fault, Sergeant. I wanted to double-check an alibi. I just asked Barry to get me onto the system. He doesn't know any more than that.'

'Bullshit,' said Sgt Spurgeon. 'If you want to be a successful police officer, Jama, you've got to be able to lie better than that. Who's alibi were you double-checking?'

'Professor Karamak's, sir.'

'But that's not our responsibility,' said Sgt Spurgeon. 'The enquiry into Professor Jasper's murder has been passed on to another team.'

'It's a stitch-up,' blurted Barry. 'They're already winding down the team. It's the funny-handshake brigade – they do whatever they want.'

Sgt Spurgeon stopped and pondered this outburst, surprised at the constable's forthrightness.

Zeta realised that there was a good chance the sergeant was a member of the funny-handshake brigade himself. But she had been balancing on this tightrope for too long; it was time to leap off. 'Sergeant, it is one hundred per cent my responsibility. I wanted to check flight manifests to disprove Professor Karamak's alibi. PC Conway has no part in this.'

Barry started to protest, but she gave him such a fierce glare that he backed down.

Sgt Spurgeon nodded slowly, looking stern. 'So, SC Jama, you thought that rather than submit your suspicions through the proper channels, you'd go rogue.'

'I thought the ends would justify the means, sir.'

'Did you, Jama?'

'You'll have my letter of resignation, my uniform and warrant card on your desk within the hour, sir.'

Sgt Spurgeon took a deep breath, which caused his entire torso to ripple menacingly. 'You know what your trouble is, Jama?'

'Sir?'

'Hoo-bris.'

'Sir?'

'You think you're the only one in this station capable of proper policing. Lesson number one, Jama: law and order *must*, I repeat, *must* prevail.'

'Sir?' said both Zeta and Barry in synchronicity.

'Come on. Shove up, you two.' Sgt Spurgeon plonked his huge posterior on the sofa beside them.

Barry paused, hands hovering over the keyboard.

'Well, PC Conway? What's the hold-up?' asked Sgt Spurgeon.

'Um, whose login details should we use?'

'Oh, I think DI Dunn's would be appropriate. Don't you agree, SC Jama?'

Thirty-Five

Next-Door Nick had gone, but Chris's embarrassment lingered. She hated showing emotion. She never showed emotion. What was the matter with her? Why had she become so sensitive and sentimental? If this was what passing sixty did to you, she was not looking forward to the coming years, spending the rest of her life as a blubbering wreck.

Aitken and Waterman had been given lunch and the sun was starting to descend, but Chris was still sitting at the table staring at the scribbles on the kitchen wall. Karamak's alibi had sprung a leak but there were still unanswered questions. She reached into her backpack and took out the postcard from Mia and Stan. She stared at the photo on the front and then turned the card over. No stamp, no postmark. She walked out into the hallway and returned with her cycling jacket, helmet and glasses. This was another job for Rod.

She headed towards Becketon – not via the cycle path past Jasper House, but straight along the main road as it was the more direct route and at least had some street lighting. It was getting dingy and Chris hated cycling in the dark, but she had lights and reflective gear and had to use them sometime. This road made her particularly nervous. Local media had labelled it 'North Kent's most dangerous road'. This was meant to act as a deterrent but, perversely, it seemed to encourage all manner of boy racers to take on the challenge of its blind corners and unexpected dips.

As Chris rode into the centre of Becketon, she gave a sigh of relief. The main shops were closing for the day and it was too early for evening diners and pub-goers, so it was eerily quiet, like the start of a zombie apocalypse movie. She turned right off the high street towards the riverside, where a building that had probably once been a warehouse was now a trendy bar and eatery: The Mechanical Avocado.

She chained Rod to a nearby lamppost. The lights were on inside the bar and the door was open and welcoming. A poster at the entrance announced that: 'Thursday Nights are Karaoke Nights at the Avo!' She couldn't think of anything worse than trying to have a quiet drink whilst a stranger murdered 'Wonderwall' at maximum volume. She thanked her lucky stars that it was a Wednesday.

At this time, when late afternoon became early evening, the Avo was practically empty. At one corner table sat an old guy nursing a half-pint of Guinness – he looked as though he'd found the only pub in Becketon that was yet to bar him. On a table at the other side sat two young students who were gazing at each other with such rapt adoration that Chris judged they'd either be soul partners for life or would have split up by Christmas. At the moment they had each other but also, most importantly, unlimited wi-fi for the price of a cup of coffee and a glass of tap water.

She sat at a table next to the bar, her eyes searching the room. She didn't see her quarry at first but then spotted a familiar shock of red hair half obscured by the real ale pump handles.

Mia didn't recognise Chris until she had approached her table, notepad in hand. 'Chris! Brilliant to see you.'

'And you, Mia. Is Stan around too?'

'Yeah, he's down in the cellar putting on a fresh barrel of Parson's Malty Appendage.'

Stan's close-cropped head appeared from below the bar and kept rising, nearly colliding with the pendulum lights above.

'Stan, look who it is,' cried Mia.

He gave a wide, genuine-looking grin, strolled over to Chris's table and greeted her, his huge hand completely enveloping hers. 'Good to see you. Here for a cocktail?'

Chris placed the postcard of Wawel Cathedral on the table.

'Thank you both for the postcard. Was it a very brief stay in Krakow or was this to throw me off the scent?'

'Throw you off the scent?' Stan looked confused. 'It was more of a holiday recommendation. It's a beautiful city – you'd love it.'

'Stan used to work for the tourist board,' explained Mia.

'And I've still got about five hundred postcards in a box under my bed that I'm trying to get rid of,' he added.

'What can we get you?' asked Mia. 'On the house, of course.'

'I'd like a chilli margarita.' Chris turned the postcard so the inscription was face up. 'And the truth.'

The margarita was magnificent. The sharp salt crystals on the glass rim hit her tongue first, followed by the warmth of the tequila and the acidic kick of the lime. And then, a few seconds later, the sweetness and fire of the chilli sent a warming wave down her throat and into her stomach. This is some drink, thought Chris, and immediately had it usurp the banana daiquiri in her Top 5 Favourite Cocktails list.

'So...' She tapped the postcard with her index finger. 'Explain.'

'Rene told us that she'd filled you in about us staying in the forensics house,' said Mia. Chris nodded. 'Professor Jasper surprised us on that Friday morning, suddenly appearing like that. We were just getting ready, finishing our breakfast, so we grabbed our stuff and nipped out the back door while he was coming in through the front. We assumed he wouldn't be there for long, so we just went for a walk and a smoke.'

'You sat outside the church. That was the first time I saw you.'

'Yep,' said Stan. 'We gave Jasper a while and then headed back. Mia had left her laptop in our room and needed to work on her dissertation.'

'But when we got back to the house, you were there, doing weird animal impressions, so we kept on walking,' added Mia.

'And headed off to work – here,' said Stan.

Chris tapped the postcard again. 'What about the jacket?'

'We're getting to that,' said Mia testily. Chris had the feeling that she wore the trousers in their relationship.

Chris realised that she had already finished her chilli margarita. She stirred the ice with her cocktail stick to encourage it to melt and hide her appreciation of this new taste sensation.

'When we got back to the house that night, Bernie was sitting at the table,' said Mia.

'Bernie?'

'It's the faculty's name for the dummy.'

'After Bernard Spilsbury, the father of forensic pathology,' explained Stan.

Chris felt that Grayson was a much more fitting name. 'Bernie' didn't suit him at all.

'Another margarita?' asked Mia.

Chris nodded rather too enthusiastically and Stan obediently headed towards the bar.

'We naturally assumed that Professor Jasper had put him there. Perhaps in prep for the new term. Some sort of practical exercise.'

'But what about—' started Chris.

'The jacket? Professor Jasper had left it in the downstairs dunny... um, toilet. So we placed it on Bernie so he would see it as soon as he walked in through the door – a bit of a joke, I suppose.'

'Obviously, we didn't know then what had happened to the professor. Doesn't seem so funny now,' interjected Stan from behind the bar.

Chris felt that another piece of the jigsaw had been slotted into place and a new chilli margarita was sitting in front of her. Stan passed a Coke to Mia.

'So when we saw you'd caught the guy, we hoped that finding Professor Jasper's jacket had helped.'

'We haven't caught the guy,' said Chris, taking a small sip this time.

'Yes, you have – we saw the video,' said Stan. 'You don't forget a somersaulting ice cream van in a hurry.'

'Dah, dah, d'dah, dah dah, eeeeeeewwww, splash!' said Mia,

rather accurately depicting Mr Softee's final moments by launching an ice cube into her Coke.

'He's not Professor Jasper's killer.'

Mia and Stan seemed shocked. They looked at each other and then back at Chris.

'I think he helped with removing the professor's body and rapidly cleaning up the kitchen afterwards, but he's got a solid alibi for time of death.'

'How solid?' asked Mia

'Very. Ironically, I provided it.'

'So if ice cream guy didn't kill Professor Jasper…' said Stan.

'Who did?' said Mia.

Chris looked around in case the other customers of The Mechanical Avocado were eavesdropping, but the young couple were engaged in a frenzied bout of tonsil tennis and the old guy had fallen asleep next to his empty glass. The events of the last few weeks had taught Chris that she was not the flawless judge of character she'd once boasted of being, but she was as sure as she could be that Mia and Stan were people she could trust.

'I'm sure Professor Karamak's involved.'

There was a pause that seemed to last a lifetime. If this had been a high-stakes poker game, Chris would have had no idea of the strength of Mia's and Stan's hands.

Mia's left eyebrow rose a centimetre. 'That figures,' she said.

'I think we all need a chilli margarita,' said Stan, heading to the bar again.

Mia and Chris said nothing for a full five minutes until Stan returned from the bar with a tray bearing three chilli margaritas and a bowl of pistachios.

'I told you I'd seen her,' said Mia accusingly at her partner.

'When?' asked Chris.

'When we were heading off to work. She nearly ran us over in that bloody monster truck she drives.'

'You didn't tell anyone?'

'No, I told Mia she must have been mistaken,' said Stan. 'That Karamak was abroad somewhere.'

'But you could swear to it, in evidence?' asked Chris excitedly.

'Nah, sorry. I thought it was her at the time, but you can't see much through those tinted windows. I couldn't be one hundred per cent sure – not under oath,' said Mia.

Three young men entered the bar, so Stan served them and Mia took the opportunity to wake the old guy and gently escort him to the exit.

'So what happened?' asked Stan on his return to the table. 'I know the academic world is competitive, but you don't arrange a killing just to get head of department, do you?'

'As far as I can make out, Professor Jasper had uncovered some evidence at the forensics house that linked it, and presumably Karamak, to a drugs counterfeiting operation,' said Chris. Giving out this much information so freely was a gamble but one that she felt she had to take. If Mia and Stan were secretly in cahoots with Karamak, she'd already said too much.

'So you think that's why Professor Jasper turned up at the house?' asked Mia.

'Exactly. And I reckon one of Karamak's heavies surprised him, hit him with something heavy enough to cause blunt force trauma. And then Karamak phoned Evil Eye…'

'Who?' chorused Mia and Stan.

'The guy driving the acrobatic ice cream van.'

'Right.' They both nodded.

'… to come over and help clean up the scene. Putting Grayson… um… Bernie in the kitchen, where Professor Jasper's body had been. Then I reckon they loaded the body into Karamak's car and hid it in a shipping container at Bottisham boatyard. Which is where I found him.'

Stan gulped down his margarita in one and wiped his mouth on his sleeve. 'So, if we hadn't disappeared when Jasper visited, if we hadn't been so keen to keep our own secret… we could have saved him?'

'I don't think Jasper's murder was planned. He was in the wrong place at the wrong time, I'm afraid.'

A tear rolled down Stan's cheek and into the corner of his mouth. It was a shocking sight on someone so strong and seemingly invincible. Mia hugged him.

'There's only one person to blame for this, and it's not either of you two,' said Chris firmly.

Mia looked up, tenderly cradling her boyfriend's head. 'Karamak always hated Jasper. It wasn't obvious; you could just tell in seminars, whenever a student cited Jasper, Karamak would bristle – she couldn't help herself. I know Jasper wasn't the easiest to like, a cantankerous old bugger at times, but underneath it all, he cared. We know he did.'

Stan blew his nose noisily into a napkin. 'In my first year, I really struggled. New course, new country – the pressure really got to me. I thought I was going to have to give up, or worse. Professor Jasper talked me round, gave me confidence. I never told him, but I think he saved my life. But when he needed me, I wasn't there. I ran away.'

The three young men finished their pints and, doubtless deciding there was a cheerier ambience in other Becketon bars, departed.

'So what are the police doing, then?' asked Mia.

'There's no hard evidence, unfortunately,' Chris sighed. 'Evil Eye's not talking. There's no forensic evidence, nothing to link anyone else to the victim or the scene of the crime. Even if we could break Karamak's alibi, it's circumstantial at best.'

'Nothing?' Mia frowned. 'There's always something, some trace evidence.'

Chris shook her head. 'Not according to my contacts. Nothing in the ice cream van, the shipping container, in Jasper's home or when they swept the forensics house and surroundings.'

Stan looked up from his napkin. 'They didn't.'

'What?'

'Search the grounds around the forensics house.'

'According to the case file they did,' said Chris. 'Zeta and Barry said they'd seen the report.'

'We'd have noticed,' said Mia. 'Scene-of-crime officers swept the house, but even that took them less than half a day. Then they packed up and buggered off. Haven't seen them since.'

'But they didn't search for evidence outside the house?' asked Chris.

'Not that we saw. Certainly not a thorough forensic search,' said Stan.

A thought had crossed Chris's mind. Was that a light at the end of the tunnel? If so, it was very, very dim – dimmer than an energy-saving lightbulb. 'Could we do one? A search, I mean?'

Mia and Stan looked at each other as if gauging who should be the first to respond.

Mia smiled. 'We'd have to be quick and discreet. It's term time, loads of people around.'

'And we'd have to get Karamak out of the way,' said Stan. 'Perhaps we could ask Rene to arrange an urgent faculty meeting.'

Mia whispered something in Stan's ear and he nodded in agreement. 'Sold! We'll see you at the forensics house, nine thirty sharp tomorrow morning. OK?'

Before Chris could answer, there was a crash from the doorway and group of a dozen young women fell into the pub. They were all clad in pink and wearing bunny ears except for one who was wearing an extra-large vibrator around her neck and a sash that read 'Bride To Be'.

'Hen party alert!' Stan stood and headed to the bar accompanied by wolf-whistles and obscene gestures from the women.

Mia just grinned and shrugged at Chris. 'It's not just hunting killers that's dangerous! See you tomorrow.'

Chris wobbled on her ride back home. She wasn't sure if that was the effect of the chilli margaritas or the excitement of the possibility, that chink of light in the search for justice. She knew she should tell Zeta, particularly after last time, but she wouldn't, not yet. After all, she'd have Mia and Stan to protect her and, in a childish way, she felt they were *her* friends and she didn't need any competition.

Thirty-Six

According to Rod's computer it was 09:26 when Jasper House hove into view – perfect timing. The Indian summer had gone, replaced by a bleak, overcast day of occasional drizzle. Chris was wearing an extra layer of thermals and in her backpack she had cobbled together an assortment of items that she thought would be useful for a forensic search. There were some tweezers from a distant time when she still plucked her eyebrows; a box of poo-bags used for emptying Aitken and Waterman's litter trays; an old magnifying glass she'd found in the Pit of Despair; and two pairs of yellow Marigolds (medium).

When she saw the house, Chris felt the buzz again and this time she couldn't blame the chilli margaritas. It was the thrill of the unknown, the risk-taking, the adventure-seeking. Sensible Chris tried to take back control, reminding her that she had a daughter, two grandsons and two cats to consider, but it was a losing battle. You only got one chance at life, and solving crimes gave her a massive high.

She wheeled Rod over to the cycle rack and was locking up when she was grabbed by the arm.

'Not there, you bloody idiot,' hissed Mia. That rack can be seen from the main uni building.'

Chris followed her to the back of Jasper House, where Stan was waiting. 'Stick the bike by the bin. No one's going to nick it while we're around.'

The large green recycling bin was sited by the rear wall, exactly where she had wheeled it a couple of months previously when she'd used it to try to peep through the upstairs window. Weeds had started to entwine themselves in the wheels and climb the sides, so perhaps, through neglect and Mother Nature, it had become immobile. She leant Rod up against the side.

'Is the coast clear?' she asked.

'I reckon we've got a couple of hours,' said Stan. 'Rene is occupying Professor Karamak with some invoice queries and accommodation issues, but we can't hang about.'

'So do we check inside or out?'

'Inside's been done – well, as much as possible. We used to live there, remember?' said Mia. 'But outdoor searches take time. We've got to grid it up, be methodical and record everything.'

Chris looked around at the grassy meadow that lay between the rear of the house and the car park. It was large, about half the size of a football pitch. 'What – all of this?' she asked.

'Not in two hours,' said Stan. 'If we assume Jasper was carried from the kitchen, out the back door and into the car park, what would be the most likely route?'

'As the crow flies?' suggested Chris.

'Carrying a body? Are you crazy?' said Mia scornfully. 'People can't walk in a straight line carrying two bags of shopping.'

'So how do we…?'

'We'll have to conduct a reconstruction. Mia, you play dead and I'll carry you. Chris, you can plot the path I take.'

Mia stood still with her arms crossed. 'If you think you're carrying me anywhere, mate, think again. I'm not your bloody cave girl.'

Stan sighed. 'Well, you can't carry me, can you?'

'I can see where this is going,' said Chris.

The field at the rear of the house was largely hidden by a hedge that formed the border between it and the cycle path. If a passer-by had stopped and chosen, on tiptoe, to peer over the hedge they would have witnessed a tall, powerfully built young man carrying an older woman to the car park whilst a younger red-haired woman stuck flags in the ground to plot their path.

To her surprise, Chris found the experience of being carried by Stan rather pleasurable. Perhaps it tapped into some, as yet well hidden, submissive gene. She had never been physically picked up by a man before. After their wedding, she had tried to persuade Simon to carry her over the threshold, but he claimed he had a bad back and sporadic sciatica and so she never asked again.

Effortlessly, Stan carried her back to the house and set her gently on the ground.

'Of course, we're assuming that they could carry Professor Jasper. A dead body's a lot heavier than you'd think,' said Mia. 'Let's go again, but this time drag Chris by the arms, Stan.'

The second journey from back door to car park was far less enjoyable.

Mia was right. The most likely path wasn't straight; it was more like a shallow crescent. Armed with the tape and white twine that Chris recalled seeing in the black plastic bin in the forensics house, they divided the path into sixty-four squares. 'It's a lot to cover in an hour and a half. It would help if we knew what we were looking for.'

'Um, evidence?' said Chris stupidly.

'It's bad practice to prejudge what we might find – brings bias into the search – but we've got to cut corners. Did they find the professor's wallet or phone, for example?' asked Stan.

'I found his phone. I don't know about anything else.'

'Think,' urged Mia. 'You were in that shipping container with him – can you remember anything?'

Chris didn't want to remember anything about her time in the shipping container. She didn't want to go back there – even in her mind.

'Think,' urged Stan.

Chris closed her eyes and forced herself to slide the rusty bolt and pull open the heavy doors. As she imagined taking her first step inside, the smell, *that smell*, filled her nostrils. She opened her eyes. 'I can't.'

'You can.' Mia squeezed her hand.

She closed her eyes again, switched on her torch. The yellow bucket was there, the empty water bottle, the carpet...

'Go on.'

Chris stepped closer to the body of Professor Jasper.

'What do you see?' whispered Mia.

'Grey hair, blood, white shirt, trousers, socks, shoe.' Chris opened her eyes and took a deep breath. 'He was only wearing one shoe.'

'Did the police recover the other one?' asked Stan.

'Sorry, I don't know. They didn't mention it.'

'Even in this thick grass, it should be pretty easy to find a shoe,' said Mia. 'Come on, clock's ticking.'

Between the three of them they were able to conduct a cursory search of the marked area in eighty minutes. Mia and Stan were on their hands and knees, using metal probes to separate the grass tufts, and their gloved hands and occasionally tweezers to extract potential evidence, which they passed to Chris to bag separately.

The result of their search amounted to five ring pulls, an empty carton of orange juice, a wrapper that had once housed a liquorice-flavoured condom, and three cigarette stubs. No shoe, no wallet, no trace of anything belonging to Professor Jasper.

'What about the cigarette stubs? You can extract DNA from them, can't you?' asked Chris in desperation.

Stan picked a stub out of its bag and disdainfully flicked it back into the long grass. 'These are ancient, at least a year old.'

'We're jiggered,' said Mia. 'But at least we gave it a shot. We better be getting back – advanced odontology begins in ten minutes. You need to make yourself scarce, Chris.'

Disappointed in the failure of their search, Chris walked back to Rod. As she approached the bin, she noticed something propped against the wall alongside. It was the easel that she had abandoned after her abortive surveillance operation, when she had been caught, figuratively and literally, by Stan and Mia. Nature had begun to reclaim this too. Grass now reached up to half its height and bindweed wound snakelike around each wooden strut. Perhaps it was still usable. She could cadge another lift from Next-Door Nick and transport it home.

As she touched the top of the easel, an amorphous memory entered her mind. She closed her eyes.

Chris was back on that sunny day in August, dumping the easel, hiding it in the foliage, *something glinting*.

Gently, she parted the grass around the base of the easel. A twig, thin and dark brown, sheltered under the wooden cross-frame. A twig? Using her tweezers, Chris gripped the 'twig' and pulled, extracting a pair of spectacles. A pair of tortoiseshell spectacles with slim brown arms and a shattered lens. A lens stained with… blood?

She heard Mia gasp as she held an evidence bag open. Mia's hands trembled slightly as Chris released her grip and they safely secured the spectacles.

'Are those Professor Jasper's?' asked Stan.

'They match the ones he was wearing in the prospectus photo,' said Chris.

'Was he wearing his glasses in the shipping container?' asked Mia.

'I don't know, he had his back to me.' Each time she was forced to recall that scene was a distressing experience.

'Police might still be able to get DNA off them if they've avoided the worst of the rain,' said Stan.

At that opportune moment, the sun broke through the dark clouds, sending a biblical shaft of sunlight to halo the trio.

Mia held the bag up to the light. 'Even better than that, Stan. See that bloodstain? I do believe that's a partial thumbprint.'

'Nearly as good as finding the murder weapon, whatever that was.'

Chris held her hand in the air to indicate they should stop talking.

'Gotta move, Chris,' said Stan, looking at his phone. 'Rene just texted. Her meeting with Professor Karamak's finishing shortly.'

'I'm an idiot – again.'

Chris fished her new phone from her pocket, scrolled down to Barry Conway in her contacts and made a call.

'Hi Barry, it's Chris. Yes, that one. Look, quick question about the murder weapon in the Jasper case.'

'Fire away.'

'Could it have been a tyre iron?'

'Metal? Cylindrical? Skull-crushingly hard? Yep, that'd fit the bill. Why are you asking?'

'Oh, just curious. Thanks, Barry.' And she ended the call before he could ask any awkward questions.

Chris had been so busy storing and arranging all the information about the case that she had nearly overlooked an obvious clue.

'Karamak isn't just "Big Boss". She didn't just give the orders. She killed Professor Jasper with her own fair hands.'

'Are you sure?' asked Mia.

'She mentioned a tyre iron to me at the opening of Jasper House. She had access to the forensics house. She caught Professor Jasper when he was searching for evidence of her drug counterfeiting operation. Means. Motive. Opportunity. And she's tall.'

'I hope you're not being heightist,' said Stan.

'It was a single, forceful blow to the top of the head.'

'You mean…?' Mia and Stan chorused.

'It was Professor Karamak in the kitchen with the tyre iron.'

Mia still looked unconvinced.

'Why would Karamak tell you that she'd used a tyre iron? Why give herself away?'

'She's a narcissist.'

'You're an expert in forensic psychology?'

'I'm a proofreader. It makes me an accidental expert in lots of subjects, and, according to a thesis I proofread last year called "'Hello Gorgeous!'" – An Examination of the Narcissistic Personality", Karamak fits the profile perfectly.'

Stan nodded his agreement.

'And what's the point of committing the perfect murder if no one can appreciate it?' continued Chris. 'She thinks she's untouchable.'

'No offence, Chris, but why reveal herself to you of all people?' asked Mia.

'I'm trying to figure that out.'

'Because you're Karamak's nemesis. You're the one who found Professor Jasper,' observed Stan.

'So that's why she offered me a place on the forensic science course. I thought it was weirdly generous of her. Keep your friends close—'

'But your enemies closer,' finished Stan.

'Shit!' said Mia loudly.

'No shit,' said Stan. 'Chris is right. It fits the evidence.'

'No, I mean "shit!" Karamak's heading in this direction.'

The term 'headless chickens' could have been invented specifically for Chris, Mia and Stan's reaction. They looked at each other, they looked around and then they looked at each other again.

'She can't catch Chris here. We can explain being here, but Chris can't.'

'You've got to hide,' hissed Mia.

Chris assessed her options. If she went round the house on either side, she would be immediately visible to anyone approaching from the university buildings. She tried the back door.

'Not into the house. Not unless you want to bump into Karamak coming in through the front door,' said Mia.

'Oh, frick!'

With a *Clunk!* Stan opened the lid of the recycling bin. He picked up Chris as though she were weightless and dropped her in.

'Keep quiet and stay there till I come and get you,' he whispered and closed the lid.

Darkness. Oh great, thought Chris, getting an overwhelming sense of déjà vu.

She didn't dare turn on her phone torch, but by the dim glow of the screen she could just about discern her surroundings. Mercifully, the bin was empty and, although hardly salubrious, was not the plague pit she had feared. The only contents were a punctured football and a discarded banana peel which was just beginning to turn.

'What are you doing here?' Professor Karamak's voice made Chris jolt.

She was just preparing her explanation for why she was sitting in an industrial recycling bin behind Jasper House wearing yellow rubber gloves and holding an antique magnifying glass, when she heard Stan's voice.

'Hi, Professor. We were conducting some fieldwork practice. Mia's hidden something and I have to find it.'

'I would have thought that third years would be too busy for games.' Professor Karamak sounded suspicious.

'You can't practise too much,' said Mia. 'That's what Professor Jasper used to tell us,' she added, a touch provocatively.

'I'm sure the late professor would tell you you've got a lecture to attend.'

'Yes, advanced orthodontics. We'll just clear up the tape first,' said Stan.

'Orthodontics? You mustn't keep Dr Worsop waiting, then. You can get one of the freshers to clean up after you both.'

Chris could hear Mia and Stan making their muttered departures but could feel Professor Karamak's presence by the bin. After a minute, she heard the sound of a key turning in a lock and the back door of Jasper House opening and closing.

Thirty-Seven

Chris decided to make the best of things while she waited, imprisoned in the bin outside Jasper House. Given that she seemed to be making a habit of this, perhaps she ought to start a new blog. A review of all the enclosed spaces she'd been trapped in. She could call it 'Chris in a Bin' or 'The Crate Escape'.

She checked her phone. Ten minutes had passed. She looked at the sides of the bin and doubted she could scramble out unaided. The disadvantage of the bin being empty was that there was nothing to climb on and she lacked the upper-body strength to raise herself up and out. Perhaps if she rocked the bin back and forth she could tip it over, but it was heavy and, anyway, an apparently self-tipping bin would be sure to attract the attention of Professor Karamak, and what then? There would be no chance of escaping on Rod undetected.

She slumped back into the corner of the bin. It was best to be patient, to stay put and wait for Stan and Mia to return and rescue her. But what if they didn't return? What if they were delayed or incapacitated? How long could she survive in a recycling bin before starving to death? What was the nutritional value of a decomposing banana skin? Stupid, Chris. Stupid!

Ten more minutes passed. The coast had to be clear by now. Chris stood and, centimetre by centimetre, raised the lid of the bin. Daylight streamed in. She looked out. The field was deserted. Next to the bin on her right she could see the top of Rod's saddle, and to her left she could see… the back door opening.

She dropped the lid back down and crouched, making herself

as small as possible, as though a woman in an empty recycling bin could possibly be invisible, should someone choose to peer inside it. She heard Professor Karamak's voice, speaking on her phone.

'Hi, darling... No, everything's fine... I've double-checked. Just those pain-in-the-arse students I told you about... Yes, the Polish giant and his Antipodean sidekick... She even had the cheek to quote Jasper at me. Can you get your mate in Immigration to check them out?'

Chris fumbled for her phone and pressed the 'record' button. She held her phone as near to the underside of the closed lid as she dared.

'You're a sweetie,' said Professor Karamak. Chris assumed she was talking to her husband, DI Dunn. 'It's a crying shame, but some students have got to fail so as to make next year's results look even more impressive by comparison, and, as they are technically Jasper's intake, the more the merrier. What's that? Yes, I'll be killing Professor Jasper's reputation posthumously – it is possible to kill someone twice, then! Hang on, darling...'

There was a pause. Chris's arm ached and her palm was slippery with sweat. If she made any sound now...

'Sorry about that,' Professor Karamak continued. 'Just another text from my batty course administrator... Yes, the one who looks like an explosion in a bird sanctuary.' She laughed uproariously. 'She's got some urgent contract query apparently... I know, contract queries! Me! I'm the head of department! First chance I get, she's out too. Can't have a state-of-the-art forensics department with Looney Tunes support staff, can I? See you later then, darling. Shall we get a take-out tonight? I could murder a vindaloo... Love you too.'

Professor Karamak ended her call by blowing three kisses down the phone.

Chris looked at her own phone. The recording timer still read '00:00'. Useless. She couldn't even manage to press 'record' properly. A surreptitious recording from inside a bin may not have been legally admissible as a confession to murder, but it would have proved that her suspicions were correct.

Professor Karamak was moving about again. Surely it was only a matter of time before she investigated the recycling bin and saw a familiar figure clutching a polythene bag containing a pair of bloody tortoiseshell spectacles – spectacles that had belonged to a murder victim. The professor's footsteps were silent on the grass, but she was muttering under her breath, something angry and unintelligible.

'What the…?'

Chris jolted as she heard Professor Karamak exclaim; only the width of the bin's plastic wall seemed to separate them. There was a clatter and the bin shook as Karamak appeared to be kicking something.

'Bloody bicycles! Three grand that cycle rack cost and they still dump them wherever they want. I'll get the groundskeeper to stick it in a skip – that'll teach them.'

Chris listened intently, trying to determine Karamak's movements, trying to track every footstep. A long-forgotten memory returned. She was seven or eight and in hospital for an operation. Already dopey with pre-med, she was lying in the operating theatre listening to the sounds, trying to anticipate the prick of the needle. The squeak of a trolley wheel; the faint hiss of gas; the clatter of surgical instruments on a tray; the anaesthetist's voice: 'Counting backwards, 10… 9… 8… 7…'

The lid of the bin swung open. Chris cowered in the corner, eyes screwed shut. In her mind she could see Professor Karamak standing there, towering above her, arm raised, hand gripping a tyre iron. She hugged herself, felt an impact on the top of her head, no pain, and then blackness.

Warm liquid trickled down the side of her brow, detoured round her eye socket, travelled down her cheek and seeped into the side of her mouth. She tentatively reached out with the tip of her tongue. Caramel latte? She fumbled for her phone and turned on the torch. By her feet, next to the banana skin, was a disposable coffee carton. The contents that hadn't been drunk or dumped over Chris's head formed a puddle reaching her toes. Professor Karamak's caramel latte.

Patience. Chris restarted *Hunky Dory* from the first track. She had only got to the second verse of 'Oh! You Pretty Things' when the lid of the bin crashed open.

'Is she OK?' she heard Mia ask.

'Think so. Looks like she's pissed herself though,' replied Stan.

'I have not pissed myself,' said Chris indignantly. 'It's coffee. Caramel latte, from the taste of it. Mind you, what I've been through, it's a frickin' miracle I haven't pissed myself.'

Stan leant over the bin and hauled Chris out. 'We got Rene to arrange another decoy, but we don't know how much time we've bought.'

'While I was in the bin I overheard Karamak on the phone. She practically confessed to killing Professor Jasper. She's got it in for you two, and Rene as well.'

'Thanks for the warning,' said Mia. 'You'd better get going.'

Chris held up the polythene bag containing the spectacles. 'What shall I do about these? Tell the police that I was strolling past Jasper House and happened to find them?'

'You were in the shipping container with Professor Jasper. Couldn't you claim you picked them up then?' suggested Stan.

'And kept them in my pocket for two months? I'd be banged up quicker than you could say "jailbird".'

'Chris is right. She's too close to the case – it'll look like contaminated evidence. Give them to me.'

Chris handed over the spectacles. Mia treated them reverentially, placing the bag inside another bag and then into her backpack. 'It makes absolute sense for a forensic science student to discover them at her place of study,' she said.

'We'll make sure they get to the proper authority,' added Stan. 'But you, Chris, must get out of here. Right now.'

'Take extra care, you two. Karamak is capable of anything,' said Chris.

'Don't worry about us,' replied Mia. 'We can look after ourselves.'

Chris unlocked Rod, took her helmet off the handlebars and switched battery mode to high. She looked back at Mia and Stan. 'Thanks, guys. For everything.'

'No. Thank you, Chris,' said Stan.

'Now, vamoose!' shouted Mia.

Chris vamoosed home as fast as her legs could pedal.

*

With her toe, Chris eased the hot tap to off. She had just finished a call with Chloe (not a video call this time), making arrangements about the coming Christmas in Melbourne. For the first time in years Chris was actually looking forward to the festive season. She lay back and examined her scar, six months old and looking magnificent, and thought about how far she had come since those long days in Baxter Ward.

She was tempted to lean out of the bath and pick up her phone to tell Zeta about that morning's excitement, but there was no rush. After all, Chris hadn't actually promised her friend that she wouldn't conduct any further investigations, had she? She manipulated the tap back on again and steam rose in response. She was content that she had done everything she could. The jigsaw was finally complete.

Thirty-Eight

Aitken, Waterman and Chris were fast asleep, deep in their respective dream worlds of mouse chasing, fence climbing and cycling. She was riding downhill, the longest, steepest hill imaginable – faster and faster. Her brakes had failed and she was ringing her bell furiously to get pedestrians to leap out of the way. *Tring! Tring! Triiing!*

Aitken pawed at Chris's face, but she would not wake up. Cat claw met eyelid and Chris rolled over. 'Too early,' she mumbled. She forced one newly scratched eyelid open and looked at the radio alarm clock on her bedside table. It read ten past seven. 'Too early.'

She wriggled her toes, searching out the warmest spot in the bed. 'Just another ten minutes.' She wanted to get back to her dream, to see the outcome. She hadn't felt fear at her out-of-control bike. Similarly, she got a thrill every time she thought back to the previous day. There had been moments of genuine terror while she was crouched in that recycling bin, waiting for the lid to fly open, waiting to be discovered, but she regretted nothing.

This had to be why people engaged in extreme sports. Cliff-diving, free-climbing or attending Black Friday sales – putting yourself in mortal danger made you feel alive. As we get older, thought Chris, we get more cautious, but the reverse should be true. After all, we have less life to lose. She was old enough to know better – and realised she did.

Tring! Tring! Triiing! This wasn't her dream; it was someone at the front door. Aitken and Waterman leapt off the bed and scratched at the bedroom door. Chris indulged in her own extreme sport – descending the stairs whilst two hungry cats wove through her legs.

Rap! Rap! Rap! The bell-ringing was replaced by urgent knocking.

'All right! Keep your wig on!' shouted Chris at her impatient caller. If it turned out to be a delivery driver for the wrong address, she would slash their tyres in revenge.

She had reached the last stair when the letterbox flicked open.

'For God's sake, get a move on, Chris,' yelled Zeta through the slot.

'Zeta, it's quarter past frickin' seven. I wouldn't get up this early unless the house was on fire and even then I'd be tempted to hit "snooze" on the alarm.'

'It's all going down!' said Zeta's disembodied voice.

Chris swung the door open. Zeta was standing there, one hand holding her bicycle, the other poised over the doorbell.

'You got me up to tell me it's going down?'

'At Jasper House. Come on, we've got to get there PDQ.'

Chris yawned. 'Give me twenty minutes. I've got to feed Aitken and Waterman and have a shower and a mug of builder's tea, in that order.'

'No time for all that. I've been ringing your doorbell for the last ten minutes. Just get some clothes on. You can have breakfast later.'

Chris threw some cat kibble into the feeding bowls, pulled on a pair of jeans and a sweatshirt she'd left in the laundry basket, grabbed her helmet and was outside with Rod in three minutes and twenty-two seconds.

'What took you so long?' said Zeta, setting off on her bicycle at speed. 'Follow me.'

By the time Chris had mounted Rod and set the mode to high, Zeta was already fifty metres ahead. Chris needed to tell her friend about yesterday's events before they reached their destination, but it was going to take all of her energy just to get within shouting distance. As they reached a turning onto the last section of Southlands Street before the cycle path resumed, she managed to draw alongside.

'I got photos from Karamak's conference—'

'I know. There's no record of her having left the country. I checked the manifests yesterday.'

'Then I followed up the postcard that—'

But Zeta had spotted a break in the rush-hour traffic and was away before Chris could complete her sentence. She managed to close the gap slightly as they hit the Hill of Death, though, despite the severe gradient, Zeta barely seemed to slow.

'And... we... searched... field...' Chris panted breathlessly.

'What's that?' asked Zeta, looking over her shoulder.

'Yesterday... found... glasses...'

'And very funky your cycling shades look. Wouldn't want to lose those.'

'No... I mean... Jasper...' Chris gasped, but Zeta had breached the brow of the hill and was accelerating away towards the university grounds.

As she neared Jasper House, she could see activity in the car park. Zeta appeared from behind a hedge and beckoned her over. Zeta was crouched in the same field that Chris had vainly tried to capture in watercolours two months previously. The tractor had gone, but the rotavator was still there, unmoved and gathering rust. Zeta parted the shrubbery so that she could look through the hedge towards the car park.

Chris propped Rod against the hedge alongside Zeta's bicycle. 'What I've been trying to tell you for the last twenty-five minutes—'

'Shhh!' Zeta held a finger to her lips and gestured Chris to follow her as she duck-walked a further fifty metres closer to Jasper House, still concealed by the foliage. Chris was dubious that either her real or bionic hip could manage such a manoeuvre, so she crawled on her hands and knees, muddying her already dirty jeans. From this new vantage point, two police cars and a van were visible in the car park. Four official-looking people stood by the vehicles, watched by a small group of early-morning joggers and dog walkers, who all seemed to be filming the event on their phones.

'Apparently there's been a tip-off. Barry heard something was going down first thing.'

'What's going on?' asked Chris.

Zeta opened her backpack and took out a small pair of binoculars, which she trained on the scene. 'It's not our lot. I reckon it's NCA and they've got a forensics team with them.'

On cue, a couple of figures clad in white overalls, masks, gloves and overshoes emerged from the doorway of Jasper House and walked across towards the car park. They were met halfway by a plainclothes officer and, although Zeta and Chris could not hear their conversation, it was apparent their search had not borne fruit.

'I reckon they must have got a warrant to search that chemicals room, the one with the combination lock which we never got to see inside,' whispered Zeta.

'I told you you were wasting everyone's time.' The familiar voice of Professor Karamak boomed out as she appeared from the far side of the police van – tall, slim, blonde-haired, recognisable at any distance.

'I haven't had the chance to update you about yesterday,' said Chris. 'I've been trying to tell you—'

'Shh, I'm trying to concentrate. Tell me later,' said Zeta, peering through her binoculars.

'This is just someone with a grudge.' Professor Karamak was talking loudly, as much for the benefit of the growing crowd of onlookers as for the investigation team. 'Someone trying to besmirch my reputation and the reputation of my department.'

The target of Professor Karamak's derision seemed to be the officer in charge. He was not to be goaded into a shouting match and his body language suggested someone who was calm and doing everything by the book. He pointed towards a black SUV parked a couple of spaces from the van. Professor Karamak threw her head back, laughed and tossed a set of car keys to a nearby uniformed police officer.

'The chief constable's coming to my house for dinner on

Saturday evening. I'm sure he'll be fascinated to hear how his own force have been harassing and persecuting one of his oldest friends.'

The uniformed officer in turn passed the car keys to a member of the forensics team.

'What are they doing now?' said Chris. Without the benefit of binoculars, she had an inferior view of proceedings.

'They're about to search Karamak's SUV.'

The forensics team opened the boot.

'Be my guest,' said Professor Karamak.

A small suitcase was removed from the car, followed by a red warning triangle. The forensics officer with his head in the back of the SUV called out to a colleague and handed him large, heavy item.

Zeta passed the binoculars to Chris, who took a couple of seconds to adjust the focus. 'A tyre iron!' she exclaimed.

'What's so exciting about a tyre iron?' asked Zeta.

Like Zeta, Professor Karamak was far from perturbed by this discovery. Indeed, she seemed positively amused. 'I'd better have that back when you've finished with it. The roads around here are in such a state that one never knows when one's going to pop a tyre.'

'Why is she so happy?' asked Chris. 'My money says that's the murder weapon.'

'I doubt it. The actual murder weapon's probably at the bottom of a reservoir somewhere.'

There seemed to be renewed activity by the forensics team. Zeta grabbed the binoculars back, yanking Chris's neck in the process.

'Agh! You could just ask.'

'They've found something else.'

Chris could just about make out the forensics officer extracting a small item, which his colleague carefully bagged up. Dr Karamak's jovial mood changed abruptly.

'What the...? They're not mine. You've just planted them!' she shouted.

'What've they found?' asked Chris.

'Looks like a pair of glasses.'

'Professor Jasper's glasses?'

'Could be. They were never recovered and Karamak's not a happy bunny.'

As bunnies go, Professor Karamak was the unhappiest in all of the warren. 'I have never seen those spectacles before in my life. That car is clean. Everything in it is clean. I should know – I cleaned it myself.'

The officer in charge was formally speaking to Professor Karamak, and then a fellow officer secured her with handcuffs. Dr Karamak started struggling, trying to shrug off the attentions of the police officers and free her hands from the cuffs.

'This is an outrage,' she shouted. 'Get me my lawyer. I'll sue the lot of you!'

It took four police officers to manhandle the professor into the back of the police squad car, cracking her head on the doorframe in the process. To add to her public humiliation, the squad car put on its lights and siren as it sped out of the car park to a destination unknown. The crowd applauded.

Chris and Zeta stood and looked over the top of the hedge. The watching ensemble of joggers and dog walkers, who had been treated to some free drama, started to disperse. Neither of the two women said a word for five minutes.

'Wow,' said Zeta, breaking the silence.

'Wow,' Chris concurred.

'When life comes at you, it comes fast.'

'Expect the unexpected.'

They collected their bicycles and wheeled them across to the car park. The forensics team were packing up the van and a couple of police officers were guarding and securing Professor Karamak's SUV in preparation for the arrival of a tow-truck.

Chris and Zeta stood in front of Jasper House, the University of North Kent's forensic science facility. The place where the adventure had started and, finally, had now ended.

'You wanted to tell me something? Something about yesterday?' asked Zeta.

Chris thought for a second or two. 'Oh, it was nothing. Well, nothing important.'

'Oh, right.'

'So, if those *are* Professor Jasper's glasses…?'

'That would be the physical evidence we're missing. Combined with the gaping holes in Karamak's alibi, I reckon that'd be enough to charge her.'

'Enough to convict?'

'If her arrest encourages Dwayne Pipe to start being a bit more cooperative, it might well be.'

'So, Zeta, we've done it.'

'The crimefighting proofreader.'

'And the most special of special constables.' Chris smiled. 'Justice for Jasper?'

'Justice for Jasper,' Zeta confirmed.

They hugged. A hug of relief, achievement and friendship. Chris felt Zeta's body stiffen and she pulled away.

'What's wrong?'

'Karamak's a professor of forensics – professional, meticulous and calculating.'

'Agreed.'

'And if it wasn't for your persistence, Chris, she'd never have been apprehended.'

'And a huge dollop of luck too.'

'So why would she leave a key piece of evidence, something that linked her to a murder victim, in the boot of her car?'

Chris paused as though deep in thought. 'I don't know – schoolgirl error, I guess.'

'Really?'

'Even the cleverest of criminals makes silly mistakes.'

Zeta nodded but looked unconvinced. Chris glanced over her friend's shoulder, up at the top-floor window of the forensics house,

Grayson's window. In place of Grayson, two people were standing there, one tall, the other shorter with red hair. Mia and Stan gave Chris a wave and then they were gone.

She turned on Rod's ride computer and stepped into the frame. 'Best get back and give the kids a proper breakfast. Perhaps we could catch up next week?'

Zeta was staring at the ground deep in thought. She just gave Chris an absent-minded wave in response.

That's one secret that stays with me, thought Chris as she set off in the direction of home. Zeta was a stickler for the rules. She couldn't possibly appreciate that for one time and one time only, the end had justified the means.

Epilogue

Sunlight filtered through the blinds, dappling an ever-changing pattern on the kitchen table. The smell of freshly percolated coffee filled the air. To Chris's mind, fresh coffee smelt better than it actually tasted, but when you had a discerning house guest you needed to make the effort.

She placed the coffee jug on the table beside a wicker basket of warm croissants.

'It's such a glorious morning. You all right if I pop out on the bike for a couple of hours?'

Her breakfast companion evidently had no opinion on the matter.

'Then, when we get back, we could sit in the garden. You could keep me company while I proofread "Using the Stanislavski Technique in Crime Scene Reconstruction". You'd like that, wouldn't you?'

Her companion seemed unimpressed by the prospect.

'And Zeta's coming over for lunch. I was going to rustle up a salade niçoise in her honour. You like Zeta, don't you?'

Her companion didn't answer. He just sat at the table in silence. That was hardly surprising, because he couldn't speak.

After all, Grayson was just a dummy.

Printed in Great Britain
by Amazon